CINDERELLA IN THE SICILIAN'S WORLD

SHARON KENDRICK

PROOF OF THEIR FORBIDDEN NIGHT

CHANTELLE SHAW

MILLS & BOON

First Published in Great Britain 2020
by Mills & Boon, an imprint of HarperCollins*Publishers*
1 London Bridge Street, London, SE1 9GF

Cinderella in the Sicilian's World © 2020 by Sharon Kendrick

Proof of Their Forbidden Night © 2020 by Chantelle Shaw

ISBN: 978-0-263-27805-7

MIX
Paper from
responsible sources
FSC™ C007454

Printed and bound in Spain
by CPI, Barcelona

CINDERELLA IN THE SICILIAN'S WORLD

SHARON KENDRICK

For my father, Donald Llewelyn Wirdnam,
one of life's truly contented people,
whose favourite toast will never be forgotten
(and neither will he).
'Here's to my wife's husband!'

PROLOGUE

SALVATORE DI LUCA stared out at the bright blue Sicilian sea and felt his heart twist with something he had spent years trying to avoid. With pain. With regret. And with a bitter awareness that he had never really loved this beautiful island as much as he should have done. But how could he love it when it was bound up with so many bitter memories of the past? A past he had tried many times to escape, sometimes with more success than others.

Because wherever he went, he always took the past with him.

On this island he had possessed nothing and had known hunger. Real hunger. His clothes had been ragged and—when he hadn't been running through the streets barefoot—his shoes second-hand. It had been a long time since he'd known hunger like that. A long time since he'd wanted for anything. These days he had everything which had once been his heart's desire. There were properties around the world in addition to his San Franciscan home—a vineyard in Tuscany, a castle in Spain, and, up until very recently, a *pied-à-*

terre in Paris. He had planes and cars and an Icelandic river in which to fish, whenever the whim took him. His property business had long been in the ascendancy and these days he channelled his profits into his charitable foundation, which reached out to children the world over. Dispossessed children. Children who had never been loved. Children just like him.

And there were women. Plenty of those. Beautiful, sophisticated, elegant women. He dated lawyers and bankers. Heiresses and scientists. He was highly sought after as a partner—his skill as a lover, his quick mind and vast personal wealth made sure of that. The only thing he couldn't provide was love, because that had been removed from his heart a long time ago and that was what inevitably proved to be the death-knell on any relationship, for women craved love even when they had been warned it was never going to be on the cards.

In theory, he should have been perfectly content. Didn't his friends—and his enemies—think he'd forged for himself the perfect life? And didn't he allow them to carry on believing that? But occasionally he became aware of an aching emptiness deep at the very core of him, rumbling away in the background, like an incipient thunderstorm on the dark horizon. Sometimes he didn't think that ache would ever leave him and sometimes he told himself it was better that way.

Because the memories which provoked that pain made him certain of what he did want, but equally important—what he didn't. And if that knowledge had turned him into someone who was perceived as cold and unfeeling, then so be it. Let people think what they wanted.

It was time to embrace his freedom and drink a toast to it.

Turning away from the blinding glare of the ocean, Salvatore lifted his hand, and summoned over the waiter who had been hovering within his eyeline for the last half-hour.

The funeral was over and the inevitable introspection which followed such an event was also over. It was time to move on.

CHAPTER ONE

'WHAT THE *HELL* do you think you're doing, Nicolina?'

The words sounded sharp. Sharp as the tip of a needle or the sting of a bee. Lina's throat tightened as she pulled the thin cotton blouse over her head and turned to meet the accusing gaze of the woman who had just entered her bedroom. Not for the first time, she wished her mother would knock before she came barging in, but she guessed that would be like wishing for the stars.

'I thought I'd go for a drive,' she said, winding a scrunchie around her thick hair, even though trying to get her black curls to obey her was a daily battle.

'Dressed like *that*?'

The word was delivered viciously and Lina wondered what had caused this reaction, because no way could her outfit have offended her mother's overdeveloped sense of decency. 'Like what?' she questioned, genuinely confused.

Her mother's look of contempt was moving from the modest shirt, down to the perfectly decent pair of handmade denim culottes, which Lina had run up on her old sewing machine only last week, from some leftover fabric she'd managed to find lying around the workshop. According to the pages of one of the on-line fashion journals, which she devoured whenever she got the chance, they could have done with being at least five inches shorter, but what would have been the point in showing too much flesh? Why make unnecessary waves and have to listen to a constant background noise of criticism, when she spent most of her time trying to block it out?

'You are supposed to be in mourning!'

Lina felt the urge to protest that the elderly man who had recently died was someone she'd never even met and whose funeral she had only attended because that was what people did in this tiny Sicilian village where she'd lived all her life. But she resisted the desire to say so because she didn't want a row. Not when she was feeling so flat and so vulnerable, for reasons she didn't dare analyse.

'The funeral is over, Mama,' she said quietly. 'And even the chief mourner has left.' For hadn't Salvatore di Luca—the billionaire godson of the recently deceased—purred away in his car that very morning, leaving Lina staring glumly as the shiny limousine retreated down the mountainside, knowing she would never see him again? And wondering why that should bother her so much.

You know why. Because whenever he looked at you he made you feel alive. Because that was his skill. His special ability. To make women melt whenever he flicked that hooded blue gaze over them.

His occasional visits to her village had been something to look forward to. Like Christmas, or birthdays. Something shining bright in the future, which she would never see again. And somehow that left her feeling like a balloon which had just been popped.

'Salvatore di Luca!' Her mother's voice broke into her thoughts as she spat out his name, with even more contempt than she had displayed towards Lina's outfit. 'In the old days he would have stayed for at least a week to pay his respects to the community. But I suppose his fame and fortune are more important than the Sicilian roots he has turned his back on in favour of his new and fancy *American* life!'

Lina didn't agree with her mother's condemnation but there was little point in arguing. Because her mother was always right, wasn't she? Early widowhood had given her the moral high ground, as well as an increasing bitterness towards the world in general as the years passed by. And with that bitterness had come a highly sophisticated ability to create a feeling of guilt in her only child. To make her feel as if she were somehow responsible for her mother's woes. And wasn't that state of affairs becoming increasingly intolerable? Picking up her helmet, Lina made a passable attempt at a smile though she met no answering smile in response. 'There's been a lot going on, Mama. I just…need a break.'

'Oh, that I were twenty-eight years old again! When I was your age I never used to complain about tiredness. I was too busy running this business almost single-handed. You are too young to be *taking a break*. When

I was your age I never stopped,' her mother mocked. 'And there's work for you here.'

Of course there was. There was always work for her here. Lina toiled from dawn to dusk in the family's small dressmaking business, running up cheap skirts and dresses which would later be sold on one of the island's many markets, with barely a word of thanks from the woman who had birthed her. But she didn't really expect any, if the truth be known. Obedience had been drummed into her for as long as she could remember—even before her father had died so young, leaving her to bear the full brunt of her mother's ire. And Lina had accepted what fate had bequeathed her because that was what village girls like her had always done. They worked hard, they obeyed their parents and behaved respectably and one day they married and produced a family of their own—and so the whole cycle was repeated.

But Lina had never married. She'd not even come close—and not because there hadn't been the opportunity. She'd caused outrage and consternation in the village by rejecting the couple of suitors who had called for her, with their wilting bunches of flowers and sly eyes, which had strayed lecherously to the over-abundant thrust of her breasts. She had decided she would prefer to be on her own than to sacrifice herself to the unimaginable prospect of sharing a bed with either of those two men. It was a black mark against her of course. For an only child, a failure to produce a clutch of grandchildren would not easily be forgiven. And although Lina didn't regret either of those two decisions, it sometimes left her with the feeling that she had somehow burnt her boats. That she would remain here for the rest of her days and that this was to be her future.

As her mother slammed her way out of the bedroom, Lina was aware that nothing had really changed in her life since yesterday's funeral, yet she was aware that something had changed inside *her*. It had been a busy time—especially for the womenfolk, who had been preparing all the food which had been consumed by the mourners. They had buried Paolo Cardinelli with all the honour and ceremony with which Sicily traditionally regarded the deceased. But now it was over and life went on and Lina had been struck by the realisation that time was stretching out in front of her like an uninspiring road. Suddenly she felt trapped by the towering walls of oppression and expectation and her mother's endless demands.

And she needed to escape.

She didn't really have a plan. Her best friend lived in a neighbouring mountain village and often they would meet for a coffee. But their friendship had taken a hit since Rosa's recent marriage and travelling solo to one of the fancier seaside resorts at the foot of the mountain wouldn't usually have been on Lina's agenda. Yet today she felt like breaking a few of her own self-imposed rules. Scrabbling at the back of the wardrobe to locate some of the money she'd stashed away from her ridiculously small wages, she found herself itching for a different experience. For something *new*.

Pausing only to stuff her swimsuit in the back of her rucksack, she wheeled out her little scooter and accelerated away from the village, the dust from the dry streets billowing up in clouds around her. Past the last straggle of houses on the edge of the village she negotiated the winding bends, and a sudden unexpected sense of freedom lifted her spirits as she sped downwards towards the coast. She could smell the sea before she saw it—a wide ribbon of cobalt glittering brightly in the afternoon sunshine and it smelt delicious.

Breathing in the salty air, she drove towards a beach famous for its natural beauty. It was the kind of place where people spent vast amounts of money to lie beneath fringed umbrellas and have iced drinks brought to them on trays. The kind of place she would usually have dismissed as being too grand and too fancy for someone like her. But today? Her heart pumped as she parked her bike close to the seafront bar. Today she felt different. She felt almost *fatalistic*.

Lina walked towards the open-air bar, acutely aware of how much she stood out from the rich tourists with their glitzy beach outfits and gold jewellery, but since she would never see any of these people again—did it really matter? She would perch on one of those tall bar stools and enjoy an icy sharp *granita* and afterwards drive off to her favourite secluded cove and have a swim. Pulling off her helmet and tucking it beneath her arm, she was shaking out her long hair as she picked her way along the sand-covered decking towards the beach bar.

And that was when she saw him.

Her knees went weak and something powerful unfurled low in her belly as she stared at the man who was sitting in the shade of the awning, effortlessly dominating the space around him, and Lina could feel the sudden racing of her heart as her gaze drank him in. Because it was him.

Him.

What were the chances?

Salvatore di Luca was perched on one of the tall bar stools, staring at his cell phone, seemingly oblivious to the fact that he was attracting the gaze of every person in the place, though surely he must have been used to it by now. Hadn't the eyes of every villager been fixed on him from the moment he'd stepped from his chauffeur-driven car onto Caltarina's dusty main street for his godfather's funeral? Hadn't women—of every age—surreptitiously patted their hair and pulled their shoulders back, as if unconsciously longing for him to gaze with admiration on their breasts?

And hadn't Lina been one of them? Struck dumb by his potent presence. By his thick dark hair and bright blue eyes.

He was still wearing the required black funeral attire—an exquisitely cut suit, as her professional eye had noted earlier, which emphasised the innate strength rippling through his muscular frame. His only concession to the powerful heat had been to remove his jacket and tie and undo the top two buttons of his shirt, but he still stood out from the carelessly dressed holidaymakers like a forbidding dark cloud which had moved dangerously close to the glare of the sun.

Lina hesitated as she glanced down at the grains of sand which were clinging to her well-worn trainers, uncertain whether to introduce herself and say something, because surely that would be the right thing to do in the circumstances. To tell him she was very sorry about his godfather. Though what if he just looked through her blankly? He certainly wouldn't have noticed her back in Caltarina—he had been too busy dealing with the attentions of the village elders who had surrounded him from the moment he'd arrived. And since he didn't come from around here, he didn't really know anyone by name. Yes, she had sometimes seen him from a distance when he had paid one of his unannounced visits, but she'd never actually spoken to him. Like her, most people in the village had simply gazed at him in wonder, as you might gaze on some bright star if it had tumbled down from the night sky.

Should she go up and offer him her condolences, or leave the poor man in peace? She almost smiled at the wildly inaccurate track of her thoughts because *poor* was the last word you'd ever use to describe a man like Salvatore di Luca. Even living in a village which sometimes felt like the land time had forgotten, none of Caltarina's inhabitants could have failed to be aware of the fortune and wealth of the powerful tycoon.

She decided it was best to slip away unnoticed, but he chose just that moment to slide the cell phone into his jacket and to lift his head. His eyes narrowed and then refocussed and he appeared to be staring. At *her*. Lina blinked, half tempted to turn around to see if there was someone else he might have recognised standing behind her. Someone as rich and as beautiful as him. But no, his gaze was definitely on her. It was piercing through her like a bright sword and Lina felt momentarily disconcerted by his arresting beauty. Because...those eyes! Those incredible blue eyes, which were rumoured to be a throwback to the days when Greek warriors had conquered the jewelled island of Sicily. Hadn't she overheard women whispering about their astonishing hue, not long after the coffin had been lowered deep into the hard, unforgiving soil? Talking about a man so avidly at such a time was perhaps a little disrespectful, but in a way Lina couldn't blame them. Because wasn't Salvatore di Luca the embodiment of everything it meant to be virile and masculine, and who wouldn't be tempted to comment on something like that?

And now...

She blinked.

Now he was beckoning her over with an imperious curl of his finger as if he wanted her to join him and Lina froze with indecision and hope.

Surely there had to be some sort of mistake. Maybe he'd got her muddled up with someone else. Maybe he didn't mean her at all. And yet she found herself praying he did. That she could go over there and join him and for one afternoon forget she was Lina Vitale, the poor dressmaker who lived in a forgotten mountain village. The woman who seemed to observe life from a distance as it swiftly passed her by...

Salvatore narrowed his eyes as he stared at the dark-haired beauty with the windswept hair, pleased to have a diversion from the disturbing cycle of his thoughts. He recognised her, of course. Even though she'd been one of a multitude of women wearing black, she had the kind of curves which nature had designed to imprint onto a man's memory, as well as the softest pair of lips he had ever seen, and naturally a man would register those facts, almost as a matter of course.

He wondered if she had followed him here. It happened. In fact, it happened a lot. He was pursued frequently and without shame, and while some men might have chosen to capitalise on the potential for such easy seduction, Salvatore wasn't one of them. Given a preference, he preferred to be the hunter—though these days, most women seemed oblivious to that simple fact.

The Sicilian woman who stood on the other side of the bar was worlds away from the type of woman he usually dated, yet, despite this, Salvatore's gaze flickered over her with interest. She certainly looked out of place in this chic bar with her commonplace outfit and a dusty motorbike helmet, which was tucked beneath her arm. But the dark curls which bounced down her back were lustrous and glossy and her denim culottes emphasised the undulating swell of her generous hips. And her breasts were luscious, their firm swell emphasising her innate femininity.

He felt an unmistakable prickle of interest. Hers was one of those old-fashioned figures he rarely encountered in his busy transatlantic life, or at home in San Francisco, where he was surrounded by wafer-thin socialites, whose main aim in life seemed to be to maintain an abnormally low body weight. He wondered whether to offer to buy her a drink. Surely it would be bad manners to ignore her—particularly as she had done him the courtesy of paying her respects to his godfather. Lifting his finger, he beckoned her over and, after a moment of hesitation he wasn't expecting, she walked slowly towards him, a faint flush of colour highlighting her sculpted cheekbones as he rose to his feet to greet her.

'Signor di Luca,' she said, when at last she reached him, her obvious nerves making her words trip over themselves. 'I didn't mean to disturb you. I... I saw you at your godfather's funeral.'

He had to bend his head to hear her properly, for her voice was soft and melodic and her faltering words rang with such genuine condolence that Salvatore felt a wave of unexpected emotion washing over him. It wasn't the first time this had happened since he'd learned that his godfather had died, but it was hard for him to get his head around, because he was a man who didn't *do* emotion. He was someone who prided himself on his detachment and had told himself repeatedly that the old man had been given a happy release from his earthly bonds.

For although he owed a deep sense of gratitude to the man whose generosity had allowed him to spread his wings and leave his native land, he had never loved him. He had never loved anyone since his mother's callous and brutal rejection.

So why had his eyes prickled with tears and his heart contracted with pain when he had been taken to view the cold and silent body of his godfather? Why had he felt as if something had ended without him quite knowing what it was?

'And I'm very sorry for your loss,' the curvy brunette was saying, biting her voluptuous bottom lip rather nervously.

'*Grazie*. He is at peace now after a long illness, and for that I give thanks.' Salvatore watched as she chewed her bottom lip again and as he found himself increasingly fixated on that dark, rosy cushion an idea occurred to him, which he was finding impossible to shift. 'You are meeting someone?' he probed softly.

She shook her head. 'No. No, I'm all alone. I came on a whim,' she answered and then shrugged rather apologetically, as if aware of having given more information than he'd asked for.

'Then you will join me for a drink?' he questioned, inclining his head towards the vacant stool next to him. 'Or perhaps you disapprove of the fact that I am sitting in the sunshine, listening to the sound of the sea at such a time, when my godfather was buried only yesterday and now lies deep beneath the soil?'

Again, she shook her head and her thick black curls shimmered in the light sea breeze. 'I make no such judgment,' she said, placing her helmet on the bar and wriggling onto the bar stool he was holding out for her. 'In the village you must have noticed people chattering even while they carried the coffin towards the cemetery. It is always like that. Life goes on,' she continued, with a quiet rush of confidence. 'Such is the way of the world.'

She sounded both old and wise as she spoke, as if she were repeating the words of her elders, and Salvatore's eyes narrowed as he tried to guess her age because that was a safer bet than focussing on her delicious bottom. Late-twenties, he thought. Possibly more.

'In many ways, my godfather's death was a blessed release,' he said, staring into dark-lashed eyes which were the colour of the old and expensive bourbon he'd first encountered when he'd arrived in America, so young and so very angry. And something in those eyes made him confide in her about the old man's final years. 'You are aware that he lay in a coma this past decade?' he questioned. 'Not seeing, not speaking and possibly not hearing anything which went on around him?'

She nodded. 'Yes, I do. One of my friends was one of the many carers you employed to look after him, Signor di Luca. We thought it was wonderful you didn't move him out of the village into some big institution in the city. Particularly as you are a stranger to these parts. And of course, everyone knows that you visited regularly, which couldn't have been easy for a man as busy as you must be.' She hesitated. 'You are very kind.'

Salvatore tensed, briefly startled by her words because this wasn't a character assessment he was used to. Unsolicited praise wasn't something which came his way very often, unless from women cooing over his prowess in bed. Yes, he was often applauded for his business acumen and ability to be ahead of the curve. And, yes, he was a significant philanthropist. But to be commended for his personal kindness? That really was a one-off. As he looked at her sweet face he felt the stir of something unrecognisable deep in his heart. Something which did not sit easily with him. Was it the realisation that, suddenly, he really *was* all alone in the world? Even though his godfather had not been sentient for over ten years, he was his last and only link with his past.

Salvatore shook his head, as if he could dislodge the dark thoughts which were stubbornly refusing to shift. He needed a distraction, he decided, and here was one sitting next to him in the shape of this local beauty. But would it be wise to pursue such a diversion? He examined his motives for wanting her to stay. He didn't want to seduce her. Hell, no. Not only was she most definitely not his type, she probably had a fistful of vengeful brothers and uncles who would demand he married her if he went within touching distance!

But the thought of spending a couple of uncomplicated hours in her company and letting her naïve chatter wash over him was suddenly appealing. Besides, wasn't there something a little *careworn* about her features? As if she had been carrying the weight of the world on her shoulders. A moment of unfamiliar compassion spiralled up inside him as he came to a rapid conclusion.

'Do you have to rush away?'

Lina narrowed her eyes, wondering if she'd heard him correctly but also wondering what had caused that intense look of pain to have crossed his face. Was he thinking about his godfather, or had it been something else? She reflected how strange life could be sometimes. When here was a man who appeared to have everything, yet for a moment back then his expression had seemed almost...*haunted*.

He was waiting for an answer to his question and she knew exactly what she should say. Thank him politely but decline. Walk away from the bar and the faint sense of edginess he exuded, while reminding herself that she and this man had nothing in common. Some bone-deep instinct warned her he could be dangerous— and who in their right mind would willingly embrace danger? But vying with that certainty was something stronger. Something which was telling her to do the very opposite. Hadn't she driven away from the village today precisely *because* she wanted to experience something different—and wasn't this her opportunity to do just that?

Up this close, his proximity was making her body react in a way which was shocking yet delicious. Her nipples had begun to tighten beneath her handmade blouse—and now a low curl of heat was pulsing somewhere deep inside her and setting her blood on fire. Was this what it was all about? she wondered as she felt her lips grow dry. Was this what all her friends chattered about—a desire which had always eluded her up until now?

'No, I don't have to rush away.'

'Then will you have a glass of wine with me?' A flicker of humour danced in the azure depths of his eyes. 'Are you old enough to drink?'

He was flattering her, she knew that. But Lina shook her head. She didn't want wine. She wanted as clear a head as possible. 'No, thank you,' she said. 'It's much too hot. I'd like a *granita*, please.'

'A *granita*,' he repeated thoughtfully. 'I haven't had one of those in years.'

He ordered two and the granitas were delivered in chunky little glasses clouded with condensation and it wasn't until after they had drunk for a moment, in silence, that the Sicilian tycoon turned to her again.

'Do you realise you have me at a complete disadvantage?' he observed slowly. 'You seem to know exactly who I am, while I have no idea what your name is.'

She took another sip before replying and the sweet-sharp taste of the lemons was icy against her lips. And wasn't it bizarre that her senses suddenly seemed *raw*, so that the *granita* tasted better than any *granita* she'd ever had, and the glittering sea had never appeared bluer than it did right now?

'It's Nicolina Vitale,' she said. 'But my friends call me Lina.'

There was a heartbeat of a pause. 'And what would you like me to call you?'

His question hung on the air—as fragile as a bubble. An innocent question which suddenly didn't feel innocent at all because the smokiness in his eyes was making her want to tremble, despite the heat of the day. Lina was a stranger to flirting, mainly because she'd never met anyone she'd wanted to flirt with, but suddenly she was finding it easy. As easy as the smile she slanted him, as if she mixed with handsome billionaires every day of the week.

'You can call me Lina,' she said huskily.

His blue eyes hardened with something she didn't recognise, but it was gone so quickly that she didn't have time to analyse it.

'So are you going to stay here for a while, Lina Vitale?' he was enquiring softly. 'Are you going to throw caution to the wind and have lunch with me?'

Lina was aware of a sudden rush of colour to her cheeks as briefly she wondered what her friend Rosa would say if she could see her now. She wouldn't be teasing her about being a cold fish, would she? And those two spurned suitors would have been forced to retract their cruel comments about her being uptight and frigid.

'Why not?' she said shyly, and gave him a breathless smile.

CHAPTER TWO

THE AFTERNOON SUN was low in the sky and people were beginning to make their way back to the sunbeds now that the fierce heat of midday had subsided. Against the ocean's glitter, Lina could see women on loungers reapplying suncream and thought how cool and composed they all looked.

Unlike her. It was hot down here on the sand and her body was reacting to it in a way which wasn't particularly attractive. Sweat was beading her forehead beneath her thick curls and her clothes were sticking to her skin. She shifted a little in her seat, still unable to believe she was having lunch with a world-famous tycoon.

She wondered if she'd outstayed her welcome. Probably. Though since she had no experience of this kind of affair, it was impossible to know. But surely someone like Salvatore di Luca must have grown bored with the conversational limitations of a village girl by now. Maybe it was time she gave him an exit route.

Pushing her plate away, she glanced up into his arresting face and, once again, her heart gave a powerful punch of pleasure. 'I guess it's time I was going.'

'You don't say that with any degree of conviction,' he observed, an unfathomable expression darkening his ruggedly handsome face. 'And you've barely touched your lunch.'

This much was true. Lina felt a rush of guilt as she stared at her plate. She was fond of her food and had been brought up never to waste anything and certainly not a meal as expensive as this. But she'd barely been able to swallow a morsel. The food had tasted like sawdust and her throat had felt tight with a tension she couldn't seem to shift. Because beneath the fierce light of Salvatore's potent charisma, she could feel her senses unfurling. As if the cautious and inexperienced Lina Vitale was blossoming into someone she didn't recognise, dazzled by the attentions of a man who was little more than a handsome stranger.

He had commandeered a shaded table which sat on the edge of the sea, where, after a little persuasion, she had removed her socks and trainers so that her bare toes could wriggle luxuriously in the sand. Then she'd sat back in her chair watching the crystal blue waters lapping against the crushed silver shore, as armies of waiters rushed over to serve them. It was the most luxurious thing which had happened in her twenty-eight years and Lina found herself savouring every moment. Terrified of doing the wrong thing, she'd watched Salvatore closely throughout the meal to make sure she didn't let herself down. But he had surprised her. He hadn't behaved remotely how she thought a billionaire *would* behave. He hadn't ordered lobster or scallops or any of the fancier items which adorned the menu. Instead, he had rolled up the sleeves of his white silk shirt and devoured his meal as hungrily as any labourer and Lina had been surprised at his very traditional choice of tomato sauce, fried aubergine and ricotta cheese.

'I didn't notice it on the menu,' she said.

'That's because it isn't. But they always make it for me when I come here.'

'Was it something your mother used to cook?' she guessed.

As far as she was aware, it was the only awkward part of the meal for his face suddenly grew cold. Cold as the ice bobbing around in her glass of sparkling water. Suddenly his voice sounded like stone. 'No,' he clipped out. 'My mother wasn't into *cooking*.'

She found herself wishing she could take the words back and attempted to lighten the mood by asking other questions, more questions about his life, and he filled in some of the gaps which village gossip had been unable to provide. He told her that he'd been a humble waiter in America when he had overheard his boss complaining how difficult it was to transfer money internationally. At the time, Salvatore had been doing a course on digital technology at night school and this one remark had inspired him to invent an amazingly simple phone app which solved just that problem. He'd made a fortune in the process.

'Just like that?' Lina asked, wide-eyed.

'Just like that,' he agreed.

'And then what did you do?'

He then went on to explain that he had diversified, buying up property and department stores and a small airplane company which chartered rich passengers between the different Caribbean islands. And when he'd made more money than any man could spend in a hundred lifetimes, he poured his funds into a charitable foundation for children, set up in his name.

But he seemed more interested in talking about *her*, though Lina couldn't quite shake off the feeling that he was regarding her with the interest one might display towards an unusual exhibit at the zoo. Maybe he saw her as some kind of relic as she chattered away about the family dressmaking business. Like some sort of curiosity.

She remembered his stand-out incredulous question.

'So you've never even been abroad?'

'I almost did once,' she replied, a little defensively. 'Last year, I was supposed to go to Florida for my cousin's wedding and I was going to spend a little time working out there, but...'

'But?' he probed.

'My mother got ill and said she'd rather I didn't go, so I didn't.'

'Let me guess—she got better straight away?'

'She did, yes. How did you know that?'

He had given a bitter laugh. 'Human nature. Otherwise known as manipulation. You don't need to be a genius to work it out.'

But now the empty coffee cups and scatter of *amaretti* crumbs on the table indicated that the meal was well and truly over and Lina was aware that she really ought to make a move.

'I'd better go,' she said again.

'You sound as if you don't want to go anywhere,' he observed, lifting his fingers in a careless gesture, which instantly had a waiter scurrying towards them with the bill. 'Is there something special you need to be back for?'

Lina couldn't help the feeling of dread which fluttered inside her stomach as she reached beneath the table to retrieve her trainers and wondered what he'd say if he knew what she was really going home to. Not the pared-down and slightly amusing version of village life with which she'd regaled him, but her mother's sour face and incessant demands. Cheap denim and cotton stacked into high piles, waiting for her to turn them into skirts and shirts and knock-off designer dresses. The endless hours alone with her whirring sewing machine and then those long and desperately lonely evenings which followed—the silence broken only by the constant chiming of the church bells. Suddenly it all seemed so empty—and more than a little bit sad. Was that what made her look into his eyes with a sudden rush of resolve, which was accompanied by an unfamiliar sense of defiance?

'Not really, no,' she said. 'I'll have to get back in time for dinner, of course.'

'Of course.' There was the merest flicker of a pause as he deposited a wad of notes on top of the bill and his blue eyes were shuttered when he glanced up at her again. He slid his wallet back into his jacket pocket. 'Well, then. What would you have been doing this afternoon if you hadn't bumped into me?'

Lina thought about it. She would have driven to her

favourite hidden cove, hoping that nobody else would be there. And, after swimming until she was cool and pleasantly tired, she would be attempting to brush the stubborn sand from her body and performing a few clumsy acrobatics as she tried to modestly remove her swimsuit from behind a towel. 'I was planning on going swimming,' she said.

He looked across at the rows of loungers which were laid in neat lines. 'Swimming?' he repeated. 'You mean here?'

Lina followed his gaze, noting that the occupants of the loungers wore bikinis which were little more than a series of flimsy triangles, which someone as curvy as her would never be able to get away with. She thought about the swimsuit she'd stuffed at the bottom of her rucksack. Imagine the reaction if she took to this exclusive beach wearing *that*! She'd probably be frogmarched straight off for committing a crime against fashion!

'No, not here,' she said quickly. 'This beach is private. Only guests of the hotel are allowed to use it.'

'Oh, don't worry about that,' he said, with the cool confidence of a man for whom no door was ever closed. 'Nobody's going to stop you from swimming.'

Not while you're with me, went the unspoken subtext but Lina still shook her head. 'No, honestly,' she said quickly, unable to keep the sudden panic from her voice. 'Forget I ever said it. I don't… I don't really want to swim here, if it's all the same with you.'

He gave her a considered look. 'Well, what about a swim at my villa, if you don't want an audience?'

Lina's throat thickened with an emotion she didn't

recognise. Just as she didn't recognise the sudden hopeful squeak of her voice. 'You mean you're staying here? In Sicily?'

He shrugged. 'Only tonight. My plane will take me back to San Francisco tomorrow.'

'I don't want to put you to any trouble.'

'It's no trouble. My car is outside.'

'So is my scooter.'

'So why don't I get my chauffeur to ride your bike for you, and I can drive you to my villa myself? You can have a swim and leave when you like.'

'Won't your chauffeur mind driving my scooter?'

'He isn't paid to *mind*,' he drawled arrogantly. 'He's paid very handsomely to do exactly what I tell him to do.'

Salvatore watched as she worried her bottom lip again, a gesture which left her mouth looking so unbelievably kissable that he wondered if it was done for precisely that effect. He was used to instant acquiescence—especially from women—but Lina Vitale kept him waiting for an answer and the novelty of that was more than a little exciting.

'Okay,' she said eventually, pushing a thick handful of hair back from her face. 'Why not?'

Why not? Salvatore frowned. She obviously didn't realise that he wasn't usually given to handing out invitations to waifs and strays and that a little gratitude might have been welcome. He pushed back his chair. He couldn't work her out. Not only that—but he still hadn't quite worked out his own motives for inviting her. Was he intending to seduce her? To peel off those over-long denim shorts and the almost puritanical cotton shirt to see what voluptuous delights lay beneath?

His mouth hardened. No. He had never been into one-night stands and even if he were he certainly wouldn't choose a woman from a tiny mountain village who would probably read too much into it. He was being kind, that was all. Hadn't she praised him for such kindness earlier?

So stop being such a cynical bastard and make the poor woman's day.

'Come on, then. Let's go,' he said abruptly, rising to his feet and causing a woman on a nearby table to completely miss her mouth as she prepared to take a drink of wine.

As Lina had suspected, Salvatore's chauffeur looked distinctly unimpressed at being presented with her helmet and told to drive her scooter. But he didn't protest. His bulky body dwarfed the small fifty cc machine, but by then Salvatore was opening the passenger door of the limousine and Lina was climbing inside. And, oh, it was gorgeous. It smelt of leather and wealth, and the powerful engine made less noise than her hairdryer as Salvatore drove along familiar roads before turning onto a hidden track on the opposite side of the mountain.

And this, Lina quickly realised, was a completely different world from the one she usually inhabited. A quietly wealthy part of the island, where rich tourists parted with huge amounts of money in order to be able to live the Sicilian dream—or rather, their version of that dream. But it was difficult to concentrate on the scenic beauty of these new surroundings. Difficult to look anywhere other than at the powerful thrust of Salvatore's thighs.

'Comfortable?' he questioned obliquely.

'Very,' she lied.

The shades he had donned made him seem even more sexy and inaccessible than before. *Because he is inaccessible,* she reminded herself fiercely. *He's a hunky billionaire who's got a whole different life on the other side of the world.* But none of those thoughts seemed to have any effect on her escalating excitement. It didn't stop her breasts from hardening, or lessen the imperceptible tension which seemed to be building between them within the confined space of the car. Soon, it had reached such a pitch that Lina felt as if she'd forgotten how to breathe normally, and as a pair of ornate iron gates swung silently open she reached into her rucksack and surreptitiously turned off her phone, determined that nobody was going to disturb this day, least of all her mother. Because this was a one-off. She knew that. She wasn't going to entertain any unrealistic expectations or try to second-guess what was about to happen, she was simply going to enjoy every second of it.

'Madonna mia!' she breathed, unguarded pleasure slipping from her lips as the gates closed behind them. 'Is this for real?'

A faint smile touched the edges of his lips. 'Do you like it?'

'Yes,' she breathed. 'Yes, I like it.' Alighting from the car, she stood in the courtyard and stared up at an imposing house, surrounded by tall palm trees which soared up into the bright blueness of the sky. Dotted around the place were antique terracotta pots containing bright flowers and in the distance she could see the dark glitter of a swimming pool.

A housekeeper appeared from within the shadowed entrance of the house—a sharp-eyed woman wearing black who failed to return her nervous smile of greeting. But Lina heaved a silent sigh of relief because at least she didn't recognise the woman as being from Caltarina. How difficult would that have been?

'Carla, could you please arrange to have coffee sent down to the pool?' Salvatore's voice was smooth and entitled, before turning to Lina. 'Come with me and I'll show you where you can change.'

Lina followed him through the grounds, telling herself she should be enjoying every aspect of this lovely garden, but it wasn't flowers or shrubs she wanted to look at, and it wasn't the exotic cacti or carefully positioned statues which were dominating her attention. She couldn't seem to tear her eyes away from Salvatore's broad shoulders where the thick black waves of his hair were curving decadently over his collar and making her wonder what it would be like to trickle her fingers through them. She stared at the fluid thrust of his hips as he walked along the path with a confident stealth which radiated power and strength.

At last they came to a vast infinity pool—its water as dark as sapphires—with panoramic views over the green and golden countryside. But even that knockout view didn't have any impact on her sudden overwhelm-

ing sense of self-consciousness at being in such an intimate situation with a man she didn't really know.

And yet she wasn't scared. On some fundamental
level she totally trusted him—and how crazy was *that*?

'You can get changed in there,' he said, pointing to
a small building which resembled a Swiss chalet. 'I'm
going up to the house to put on something cooler.'

Lina was relieved when he left, giving her time to
compose herself, her relief short-lived when she con-
sulted the full-length mirror and realised how fright-
ful she looked. Hot and bothered and… She unbuttoned
her blouse and unzipped her denim shorts and gave a
silent groan as she slithered out of panties which felt
uncomfortably…*wet.*

And you know why that is, don't you? mocked a taunting voice in her head. *You might be a virgin who has
never experienced a scintilla of desire but that doesn't
mean you can't recognise it when it comes your way.*

Digging around in her rucksack, she located her
swimsuit and pulled it on over her increasingly sticky
body, before stepping back to look at the result. Only
now the mirror revealed a much too curvy body unflat-
teringly covered in a plain navy swimsuit and Lina's
heart plummeted. What was she even *doing* here?

Slipping from the chalet, she was thankful that Salvatore hadn't returned, though she could see that a
tray of coffee had been left on one of the tables. But
she wasn't going to hang around for refreshments. She
would have a quick swim, get changed and then drive
her scooter back home. Go back to where she belonged
and forget all her foolish fantasies.

Curling her toes over the edge of the pool, she dived deep into the sapphire waters and a restorative underwater length of the deliciously cool water calmed her fractious nerves a little. Rising up to the surface, she shook her head like a wet puppy, blinking against the sunlight to see Salvatore standing on the side of the pool, and she could feel the painful tightening of her nipples because he was wearing nothing but a pair of bathing trunks.

Exasperation flooded over her. Of course he was wearing bathing trunks! Did she think he was about to go swimming in the black suit he'd worn for the funeral? *So stop staring at him,* she urged herself furiously. *Do some more swimming and then get the hell out of here, back to where you belong.*

But she couldn't.

All she seemed capable of doing was treading water and staring up at him, because he was the most beautiful thing she'd ever seen. His sculpted body gleamed olive in the bright sunshine and his dark, hair-roughened legs were planted firmly on the side of the pool as he stared right back. Lina licked her lips and tasted chlorine but barely noticed it because she couldn't seem to drag her gaze away from him. His broad chest tapered down to a pair of narrow hips and the black Lycra of his bathers was clinging with disturbingly graphic definition to…to…

Lina swallowed, feeling the sudden rise of colour to her cheeks, and swiftly she dived beneath the water again to swim another couple of lengths. But this time the water didn't cool her and when she reached the shallow end of the pool he had slipped into the water and was waiting for her, just as she'd somehow known he would be. He was standing waist-deep, with tiny droplets glittering like scattered diamonds against all that rich golden skin. She wanted him so badly it was as if every atom of her body was longing for him to touch her. Suddenly she understood the reason for all the tension which had been slowly mounting throughout lunch and in the car afterwards. And despite her complete inexperience, Lina knew there was only one thing which could happen now.

If she wanted to.

She looked into his eyes and licked her lips again.

She wanted to.

Did he somehow read her thoughts or was it the hard thrust of her nipples against her navy costume which gave the game away? Was that why his body stiffened, as if someone had just turned him into stone? Lina didn't know and she didn't care, because suddenly it was as if she were being governed by something outside her control—by a force much greater than herself. It was as if she knew exactly what was going to happen, despite her total lack of experience and the laughable inequality which existed between them.

He didn't move—not one inch—but that didn't come as a surprise to her either. She'd somehow guessed he wouldn't.

Because he doesn't really want this, she recognised with a sudden understanding which went way beyond her actual experience. *Oh, on one level he does—on the physical level, for sure. But he's reluctant to initi-*

ate anything he might later regret. He doesn't want to take responsibility for this.

But she did.

Somehow she knew she needed to.

Which was why she went right up to him and turned her wet face to his, standing on tiptoe and placing her trembling palms on his broad wet shoulders so she could support herself. But mainly so she could touch her lips to his, and kiss him.

CHAPTER THREE

SALVATORE TRIED TO do the right thing. The only thing. Which was not to respond to her in any way. Even though her fingers were digging into his shoulders and her soaking breasts were pressing against his chest. Even though his erection was so hard it felt as if he were about to explode. His throat constricted as he attempted to keep as still as possible and not react, but it was proving almost impossible because he wanted to kiss Lina Vitale more than he could remember wanting to kiss anybody.

He tried to tell himself she was not his type. In fact, she was the antithesis of his type. But that didn't help him much either, because there was something so joyously *vital* about her. Those thick-lashed bourbon eyes. The mass of wet curls, which were streaming in a heavy mass over her luscious curves. It had been the same during the car journey here, when he'd been so achingly aware of her as she'd sat beside him. How had she managed to do that? He'd barely been able to keep his eyes on the road and when they'd arrived he'd left her to swim, quickly absenting himself in order to rid himself of his erotic thoughts. Alone, in the sane and cool surroundings of his bedroom, he'd thought he'd succeeded in that mission. And then he had seen her rising out of the water like a dark and voluptuous mermaid and—wham. Instant lust had combusted, and now this.

His throat dried because something told him she had the potential to be trouble and he needed to get her out of here as quickly as possible. But then his intentions were detonated by the way she pressed herself closer so that their bodies melded together as if they'd been glued. He could feel the exquisite press of her diamond-hard nipples pushing against the wet material of her swimsuit. Still he didn't voluntarily touch her, just moved his lips so that he could whisper directly into her ear as if someone were listening. But no one was listening. He knew that. He knew it because he'd dismissed the housekeeper and chauffeur for the afternoon so that the place was now empty save for them. Had this been his unconscious agenda—to have a nearly naked Lina Vitale standing compliantly before him, and to be poised on the brink of having sex with her, despite his very real misgivings?

'We aren't going to do this,' he husked, but he could feel his body tremble as he said it and it felt like a betrayal.

'W-why not?'

'Because...' Pulling away from her ear, he forced himself to look into her eyes and he trembled again, cursing the inexplicable hunger which was heating his blood. He ground out the words with difficulty. 'Because it's pointless.'

'Pointless?'

Salvatore nodded. He'd noticed things about her when they'd been having lunch on the beach. Her trainers had been old and so had her scooter. She was poor and he wasn't stupid. Newspapers regularly highlighted his eligibility. In the race to get him to the altar—which seemed to have been ongoing since he was barely out of puberty—Lina Vitale wouldn't have made it past the starting post, so different was she from his usual choice of sexual partner. And she needed to be aware of that. He needed to destroy any foolish fantasies she might be nurturing before this went any further. He needed to tell her that any kind of shared future was a non-starter.

'I'm leaving tomorrow. And even if I weren't, nothing could ever come of this, Lina, for all kinds of reasons. We're too different, do you understand?'

'I don't care about the differences!' she burst out.

Salvatore narrowed his eyes. He wasn't used to such honesty and her fervent declaration was chipping away at his resolve. 'If you really want this—'

'I do!'

'If you're absolutely sure about it,' he continued, biting each word out with deliberate emphasis, 'then it's going to be nothing but sex. One night and nothing more. And that's why it shouldn't happen.'

'But what if…?' She hesitated before replying, like someone contemplating the wisdom of their next words, and her soft Sicilian voice was tantalisingly husky as she seemed to draw courage from somewhere deep inside her. 'What if I don't want anything but sex?'

It was the right answer and the wrong answer, all

rolled into one. It was like starting a fire and dousing it at the same time. He stroked his finger down over her forearm and felt her shiver. 'You're sure you don't have a boyfriend waiting at home?'

'Quite sure.'

'Or a pack of angry brothers?' he murmured, only half joking.

She pressed her lips together. 'I'm an only child.'

He nearly told her that he was, too, until he remembered that conversation wasn't the reason he was here.

And that was when he kissed her, pulling her into his arms so that he could devour her lips with the hard pressure of his own. He heard her gasp. He very nearly gasped himself and he tightened his grip on her because suddenly this was a kiss like no other. Powerful. Electric. His body shuddered as she thrust her tongue into his mouth in a way which was almost *primitive* but also intensely erotic, as was the brush of her soft belly against him as she circled her hips. Lacing his fingers into her wet curls, he hauled her closer, kissing her for so long that eventually he felt her knees dip, as if she were about to slide to the ground. And that was when he dragged his lips away, hearing her muffled murmur of protest as he did so.

'I want to touch you. To explore this delicious body of yours. Like this,' he husked as he cupped one swollen breast in his palm, and she shivered convulsively. 'Does that feel good?'

'Yes,' she breathed thickly.

He smiled as he peeled the sodden fabric away so that her breasts were bared and bent his lips to first one and then the other, tasting chlorine and salt as he grazed his teeth over each puckered nipple. She gasped again, her fingers curving possessively into his hair, and once again her hips moved in unspoken invitation. He felt the urgent jerk of his erection and the sudden, almost debilitating sense of lust which rushed through his body. Distractedly, he pulled his mouth away from her nipple. He wanted to do it to her here. Now. Maybe on one of those convenient loungers, or maybe in the pool itself with the cool water contrasting against their heated flesh and giving them a space-age feeling of weightlessness. But he didn't have any protection with him and that was something which needed to be addressed, and if he went off to fetch something, mightn't it shatter this incredibly erotic spell?

Placing his hands on her shoulders, he brushed his lips over hers. 'I don't think we're being watched but you can never be too careful and I'd hate to think we were providing some voyeur with a floor show,' he murmured. 'So why don't we go inside?'

Her lips trembled. 'What about…your staff?'

'The house is empty. I gave them the afternoon off.'

She looked as if she was about to ask why, and if she had—would he have told her that, on some subliminal level, maybe he had wanted the house empty in case of just this scenario? But she didn't ask. Just hauled her swimsuit back in place to cover her breasts. 'Okay,' she said.

'Let's go,' he said roughly, linking her wet fingers with his.

Lina could feel her stomach performing flip-flops as

Salvatore led her back through the gardens towards the villa. She skirted a large, spiky cacti which lined the path. Now she was out of the water she could feel her skin growing dry, but the warmth of the afternoon sun was having no impact on the goose pimples icing her skin. Her throat tightened as she contemplated what she was about to do. Was she mad? Maybe. She was mad for *him*, that was for sure. He only had to look at her, let alone touch her, and she felt undone. He had tried to talk her out of doing this and maybe that should have been a warning, but in the end—did it really matter? He had been perfectly honest about the temporary nature of this liaison, yet strangely, she didn't care. Wasn't it better that way than if he'd lulled her with lies? If he'd promised to get in touch and then not bothered, wouldn't that be even worse?

As he pushed open the door to the huge house and she followed him inside, Lina realised her conscience was clear. Because who could blame her for wanting this? Bound by a promise she'd made to her dying father, she had stayed with her mother for too long. She had lived a loveless existence for so many years, hidden away in her tiny village and feeling that life was passing her by. She'd never even felt sexual desire before, but now here was the opportunity to experience it for herself. She could find out what all the fuss was about. It wasn't against the law, was it?

Salvatore had paused in the vaulted splendour of the panelled hall and his face was shadowed as he bent to brush his mouth over hers. 'I'd love to give you a guided tour, but I don't think I could give it my full attention at the moment,' he said, the unevenness of his voice betraying an urgency he seemed to be fighting. He tilted her chin so that their eyes met. 'So why don't we just go upstairs? Unless you've changed your mind, of course?'

Lina shook her head. 'No,' she whispered shyly. 'I haven't changed my mind.'

A trace of something like darkness had crossed his features and for one awful moment Lina thought that *he* might be the one having second thoughts. But then his fingers tightened their grip on hers as they ascended a swooping staircase of unimaginable grandeur. Upstairs, a solid wooden door was opened by the impatient thrust of Salvatore's foot to reveal an ancient room. But there was no time to admire the embroidered wall-hangings or the stunning views of the Sicilian countryside as the door swung shut behind them—because Salvatore was pulling her into his arms, undisguised hunger darkening his rugged features and setting up an answering clamour deep inside her. He was stroking damp curls away from her face and his eyes were blazing as he bent to claim her mouth, in a slow and drugging kiss.

And Lina's world tilted, because it was like discovering the existence of a different dimension. She opened her mouth, her fingers kneading the silken flesh at his shoulders, and within seconds she was kissing him back with untutored fervour. For a moment he seemed content with her eagerness and inexperience, before he moved away from her, a touch of impatience darkening his voice.

'Let's get rid of this, shall we?' he ground out, tugging the damp swimsuit over her body and the natural resistance of her undulating hips. 'I want to see you naked.'

It was a masterful command and perhaps Lina should have felt shy as her costume slithered to the ground, since no man had ever seen her like this. But she didn't. She felt strong and powerful as his gaze raked over her, because who *wouldn't* feel good if a man was looking at you with that raw gleam of hunger in his eyes?

Gingerly, he removed his swim-shorts, uttering a low Sicilian curse she was surprised he knew, and Lina felt her cheeks burn as she registered the reason why such a simple manoeuvre had proved so difficult.

'Are you blushing?' he questioned teasingly as he walked towards her. 'And why might that be, Signorina Vitale?'

Lina wondered what he'd say if she told him she'd never seen a naked man before, let alone one who was so obviously aroused. But if she did that then he would guess she was a virgin and she couldn't risk that. Because she wanted this. She wanted this more than she'd ever wanted anything. She didn't want Salvatore reeling back in horror when he realised how inexperienced she truly was. She didn't want him doing the 'right thing'—which she suspected he would—by snapping at her to get dressed and then sending her back to her village. She could just imagine the ride home on her little fifty cc bike, quivering with frustration and humiliation and feeling like a woman who'd been cheated just seconds away from discovering sexual pleasure for the first time in her life.

'It was very hot out by the pool,' she said truthfully.

'And it's going to get even hotter in a minute.' He gave a low laugh of pleasure. 'Come here, *bella*.'

Without warning, he scooped his arm beneath her knees and carried her across the room before placing her beneath the embroidered canopy of the enormous bed. And with that fierce light shining from his blue eyes, Lina really *did* feel beautiful.

He began to stroke her, tracing erotic pathways over her naked skin—only he did it so slowly that it made her want to dissolve with pleasure. Lina swallowed. She was melting! She could feel the heat increasing and the inexorable building of fluttering excitement inside her. She writhed her hips impatiently but still he wasn't making contact with the place where she most wanted to be touched.

'Salvatore,' she whispered, wanting something more without really knowing what it was.

'Mmm?' he murmured, his mouth grazing against her neck so that she could feel the warm fan of his breath, which echoed the rise and fall of his powerful chest. Slipping his hand between her thighs, he parted them before hovering one finger tantalisingly over the sensitive bud of her quivering heat. 'Is this what you want?'

'Yes.' She closed her eyes tightly.

'And this?' he teased as he flicked her a touch.

'Yes!'

His laugh was soft as he began to strum her and Lina almost shot off the bed as he established a soft rhythm. Breathless anticipation captured her in a silken snare as he lured her on towards some unimaginable peak.

And suddenly she was falling. Or flying. He shattered her completely, as if he were slowly taking her apart before putting her back together again.

'Yes,' he breathed approvingly and she was aware that he was watching her spasming body with unashamed pleasure. 'I knew you would be passionate from the first time I saw you.'

She thought she must have murmured his name for he gave that satisfied laugh again before reaching out to the nearby table to grab at something—which Lina quickly realised must be a condom. She kissed his bare shoulder as he moved to lie on top of her and his mouth sought hers in a way which suddenly seemed way more intimate than before.

He said: *I want you so much, Lina.*

He said: *You feel incredible.*

And Lina was so dazzled by those words of praise that she touched her fingers to his face in wonder, because even if he didn't really mean them, couldn't she just enjoy being made to feel gorgeous by a man who had fallen into her world like a dazzling star?

And then the fairy tale began to take on a new and unwanted direction. Was it the obvious resistance he encountered as he pushed inside her which made him grow very still? Which made his face darken with something which no longer looked like passion, but a dawning recognition? He uttered another Sicilian curse, one which might have made her blush if she'd heard it anywhere else. But Lina was too concerned about what was happening to worry about profanities. Something much more serious—mainly the very real threat that this might end before it had properly begun.

'You're a virgin?' he verified.

Dumbly, she nodded.

'Why didn't you tell me?'

But Lina wasn't really interested in answering his question—her body was too busy instinctively clenching around the rigid length of him as, softly, he cursed again. But this time his words seemed to lack conviction and suddenly he was moving. Moving inside her. Thrusting up deep into her body and taking on a hard rhythm which felt relentless and incredible. That amazing feeling began to build inside her again and Lina could feel control slipping away as she poised in readiness to take another heavenly flight. Or fall. But it was too late—or too early. Or something. Because Salvatore was choking out a helpless-sounding cry as he bucked within her, sweat sheening his muscular back, so that her own desire shrivelled and died. And when he'd finished there was nothing but the sound of their ragged breathing, which seemed to echo discordantly around the vast room.

CHAPTER FOUR

AT FIRST LINA thought she was alone, mostly because it was quiet. Unbelievably quiet—save for the tweeting of some distant bird. She opened her eyes, aware of nothing other than the tangle of fine sheets and an unfamiliar aching deep in her body. She stretched luxuriously, caught in the dreamy world halfway between sleeping and waking, as fragments of memory came filtering back into her mind. And then she saw Salvatore, silhouetted against the morning sun, which was streaming in through the un-shuttered window beside which he stood. Dark and forbidding and sexy as hell.

And fully dressed.

Now the memory became a sensual stream as she remembered the way it had felt to have him deep inside her. Making her cry out with ecstasy time after time, so that he'd had to kiss her quiet until her body had recovered from that sweet, slow shudder which made everything else seem so insignificant.

Had he heard her stir? Was that why he turned to look at her? She felt her heart turn over as she remembered that time in the middle of the night, when they'd been dissolved by passion and she had felt so close to him. When she had snuggled up against his chest and he'd been stroking his fingers through her hair, and she had confided in him all her dreams that one day she might be able to break away from her mother and make something of herself.

'You're awake,' he observed.

'I am,' she said, trying to keep her voice steady. As though what had happened hadn't been a big deal. And it wasn't, she told herself fiercely. She'd lost her virginity, that was all. She'd spent her adult life wondering whether she'd ever meet anyone who could stir her to the kind of passion she'd only ever read about and now she had. That could be regarded as a positive—just so long as she didn't start having unrealistic expectations about what was going to happen next.

It was a one-night stand, she reminded herself. *It was never intended to be anything else.* And she would be crazy if she ever thought any differently about it.

She smiled. 'You look like you have places to go, things to do—so please don't let me stop you if you need to be somewhere else.'

Salvatore met her eyes, uncharacteristically unsure of how to respond to her words as a rush of conflicting feelings washed through him. He wanted to tell her, yes, he had to be somewhere else. Somewhere as far away from here—and her—as possible. But that would be tantamount to running away. It would be the action of a coward and he was no coward, even though his head was all over the place this morning. Because Lina *had* been a virgin—something he had suspected even though he'd done a brilliant job of pushing that possibility to the back of his mind. Yet despite her inexperience, she had provoked a seemingly insatiable hunger in him. At times during the night it had felt as if she had cast a spell on him, without his permission. He liked control in the bedroom—as in every other area of his life—and this unsophisticated village girl had temporarily robbed him of that control.

And he didn't like it.

He didn't like it one bit.

'Are you okay?' he questioned.

'I'm fine.'

He shook his head. 'I don't understand,' he breathed, genuinely perplexed. 'Why give me your virginity, Lina? A man you barely know.'

She sat up in bed then and the sheet slipped to her waist, so that it bared her breasts. Dark curls were tumbling in profusion over rosy-tipped nipples and Salvatore felt the betraying stir of his body.

'I didn't *give* my virginity to you,' she corrected. 'Just like you didn't *take* it from me. It's natural. It's the way of the world and it happens all the time.'

'But clearly not to you. And I fear you may have squandered it with a man like me, who was seeking nothing more than a swift liaison. A pleasant diversion at the end of a tough couple of days.' He sighed, wondering why, after that first time, he hadn't done what he *should* have done and sent her back to her little village. Driven her back in the fading light after she'd freshened up and eradicated the evocative scent of his sex from her skin. Yet she had looked at him with those wide bourbon eyes and he had felt all his resolve slipping away.

'I don't want to go. I want you to teach me,' she had whispered.

'Teach you what?' he remembered whispering back, even though the silken caress of her fingers around the hard jerk of his erection had told him exactly what form her proposed lessons should take.

'About pleasure,' she'd purred.

And he had. God forgive him, but he'd done exactly that. Maybe it had been the heady combination of innocence and appetite which had completely blown his mind. Or the fact that she'd been so eager to learn the things which pleased him. Whatever the reason, he had been suckered in—losing himself in her amazing body, over and over again—until the rose and saffron light of dawn had begun to glimmer on the horizon.

He looked across the room at her as she sat framed against the white pillows, like some fallen Madonna. Her blue-black curls were wild and a rosy flush emphasised the angled slant of her cheekbones and suddenly he wanted her all over again. 'Won't anyone notice that you've gone?' he questioned as, abruptly, he moved a little further away from the temptation of the bed. 'Won't they care that you didn't bother going home last night?'

She shook her head. 'I'm safe. I sent a text to my friend Rosa in the neighbouring village, asking her to cover for me if my mother rang up.'

'Well, you'd better go and shower. Maybe do something with your hair,' he offered critically. 'And then I'll arrange to have your scooter loaded up onto one of the trucks. I can drop you off on the outskirts of your village so you don't have to drive the whole way back.'

'No, really. There's no need. I'm perfectly capable of making my own way home.'

His eyes narrowed, as if he was unused to having his wishes overturned, and Lina managed a thin smile as she pushed aside the rumpled sheets and got out of bed. But her bravado only lasted as long as it took her to get to the bathroom, where she leaned against the door, her heart thumping as she thought: *What have I done?* She stood beneath a terrifyingly efficient shower while powerful jets of water briefly lessened the aching of her body, but nothing could eradicate the painful clench of her heart as she realised that last night hadn't been as straightforward as she had imagined. It was supposed to be about sex and only sex. So why had it felt like something more? Why, when Salvatore had kissed her and stroked and caressed her, had she felt more cherished than she'd ever done before? And it was dangerous to feel that way. She knew that. He'd spelt out word by brutal word that he wasn't looking for anything more.

Raking her fingers through her curls and scrambling into last night's clothes, she returned to the bedroom to find that a tray of coffee had magically appeared. Was his housekeeper back on the premises? she wondered awkwardly as she recalled the unmistakable look of disapproval she'd seen clouding the woman's watchful eyes when she'd arrived.

'Sit down. Have some of this before you go,' Salvatore said as he handed her a delicate cup of the inky brew.

She didn't want to sit down, but she took the coffee and it was delicious. Lina drank down the strong and reviving liquid before picking up her rucksack, and as she straightened up she knew she had to put on the performance of a lifetime.

'Right.' Her smile was bright. 'I think that's everything. It's time I was on my way.'

His eyes narrowed. 'Lina—'

'No.' She would never know where she got the nerve to cut off what sounded like words of regret, but Lina realised it was imperative she didn't slink away, acting as if she'd committed some sort of shameful crime. Because she hadn't done anything wrong. She'd had sex—amazing sex—with a man who had turned out to be a skilled and considerate lover. Surely that was something to rejoice about? He hadn't promised her the stars and she hadn't asked for them. 'You don't have to say anything, because it isn't necessary,' she continued. 'I enjoyed it. More than I ever imagined I would. I've never done anything like this before and I doubt I ever will again. So I'll just say goodbye and let you get on with your day.'

She wouldn't have been human if she hadn't enjoyed the very real sense of discomfiture which briefly darkened his features—as if her words were confusing him. As if he was the one who always called the shots and resented anyone else for daring to take on that role. But what could he say? He certainly couldn't *object* to her dignified departure, could he? She was liberating him from all responsibility and, as a result, Lina felt an unfamiliar sense of liberation herself.

'I'll see you out.'

'Honestly, there's no need. I can find my own way out.'

Some of his steeliness returned as he gritted out his next words. 'I *said*, I'll see you out.'

It felt weird to retrace her steps of the previous night and even weirder to see her little scooter sitting outside the grand villa, with the helmet hung neatly over the handle, looking so sparkly that she guessed the chauffeur must have polished it. But she guessed that was what happened when you were as rich as Salvatore... you just turned your back for a moment or two, and some underling was busy making your world look all perfect and shiny.

'Lina.'

She looked up into his rugged features and saw the sudden darkening of his eyes and for a moment she thought he was about to kiss her goodbye—as if he were offering her some kind of small consolation prize. And something told her that if she allowed him to do that, then all her newfound bravado might just crumble and disappear. Because wasn't her dignity vital at a time like this? Quickly, she took a step back and saw his brow knit together in a frown.

'What's wrong?'

'Your housekeeper is standing behind the shutters watching and she can see everything.'

'I don't care what she can see.'

She thought about the things he'd said. About her having *squandered* her virginity. Why would she want to kiss a man who had delivered such a damning assessment of their night together? Lina crammed her crash helmet down over her curls. 'Well, maybe I do.'

With a feeling close to disbelief, Salvatore watched her walk towards her bike. He'd expected her to hang around until they'd exchanged phone numbers, at least. But instead Lina Vitale was buckling up her helmet as if she couldn't wait to put as much distance between them as possible and, as a consequence, that made him reluctant to see her go, because he was a man who always liked to do the leaving.

He watched as she swung one shapely leg over her little moped and although the denim shorts could in no way be described as revealing, he knew all too well the soft and velvety flesh which lay beneath. Flesh which had been soft and full, like an overripe damson before it dropped to the ground, weighted down by all that sweet, dark juice. He told himself he should be grateful that she had accepted the limitations of their night together with such grace.

But as she twisted the hand-grip of her little scooter and the engine spluttered into life, he could feel the renewed heat of his blood. And a frustrated beat of longing washed over him as she drove away down the drive, the streaming banner of her hair shining blue-black in the bright Sicilian morning.

'You little *slut*!'

Lina bit her lip. 'Mama, please—'

'What else should I call you when you've just spent the night with Salvatore di Luca?' A truculent jaw was thrust forward. 'Are you going to deny that, Nicolina?'

'I—'

'*And* you lied to me about being with Rosa, didn't you? Or are you going to deny that, too?'

Lina stood completely still as she stared at her furious mother, her heart racing as she tried to piece together her thoughts. She'd known something was wrong from the moment she'd entered the neat little house, her body still warm and tingling with pleasure. She'd been feeling almost *proud* of herself for having walked away from Salvatore's luxury villa so coolly and calmly. For having accepted the status quo. Of course, she wouldn't have been human if there hadn't been a tiny ache in her heart as she'd driven away, because who wouldn't have wanted more? But all those hopeless longings had been forgotten the instant she'd walked in and seen her mother's angry face.

'How did you find out?' she questioned, her cheeks flushing.

'How do you think I found out? I rang Rosa. The friend you were supposedly spending the night with!'

'You *rang* her?' Lina repeated dully.

'Oh, she tried to lie.' Her mother was in her element now. 'To make up some sort of flimsy excuse about why you couldn't come to the phone. But I didn't believe a word of it, and then Sofia Bertarelli confirmed that you'd been with *him*—that you'd turned up there yesterday afternoon, as bold as brass!'

'Sofia Bertarelli?' Lina was puzzled now.

'A customer of mine, who happens to be a cousin of the billionaire's housekeeper!' Her mother spat the words out. 'Whose cousin is a customer of mine and who couldn't wait to tell me!' She clenched her hands, her bony knuckles growing white. 'I can't believe you would behave like that, Lina—like a common little slut! That you would spend the night with a man you barely know and ruin, not just your own reputation, but mine too—as if it hasn't suffered enough already! But it has confirmed one thing. Oh, yes.' A grim look of finality locked her mother's bitter features. 'You won't be leaving this village again until you have had a few lessons in morality.'

Afterwards Lina would wonder what gave her the sudden urge to stand up for herself in a way she'd never been able to do before. Had her first experience of sex liberated her in more ways than she'd thought? Was that why she was able to stare at her mother, not with fear or dread or regret, but with a growing awareness that this was all wrong? That it had been wrong for a long time and she could no longer tolerate it. 'You were checking up on me,' she said dully.

'Of course I was checking up on you—and with good reason, it seems!'

'You have no right to check up on me,' said Lina very quietly. 'I'm twenty-eight years old and I should be free to behave as I wish, just so long as it doesn't hurt anyone. And I haven't.' She lifted her chin very high. 'I haven't hurt anyone.'

But it was as though she hadn't spoken, for her mother raged on. 'You will not leave this village again until I say so! You will work hard and accept your position in life. It's time you were grateful enough to marry a decent man who truly wants you—that's if it's not already too late! But never again must you involve yourself with someone who just takes advantage of your stupidity and lack of judgement by bedding you and then discarding you!'

It was possibly the most brutal thing her mother had ever said, but in a way it spurred Lina on to do something she should have done years ago. But that didn't make it easy. It was never easy to break a pattern which had become so entrenched that you couldn't image a different way of living. 'You can't keep me here by force,' she said quietly.

'Just you try to stop me!'

'No, Mama. I don't think you realise what I'm saying.' Somehow Lina managed to speak quite calmly, even though her stomach was churning. 'I want a change. I *need* a change and I should have done it a long time ago. I've had it with slaving my fingers to the bone and getting no thanks for it. Just like I've had it with you bossing me around as if I'm a child of five, rather than a fully grown woman.' She sucked in a deep breath. 'I'm leaving, Mama. And I'm leaving right now.'

'Oh, really?' Her mother's voice ascended into a shrill shriek as she followed Lina upstairs. 'How am I expected to run the business without you to make clothes for me?'

Lina pulled out an old suitcase and started packing the clothes she'd made to take to her cousin's wedding in Florida, but which had never been used. 'You're perfectly capable of sewing them yourself. Or why not take on an apprentice? There are young girls in the village who will be glad of the opportunity.'

And just see if you can get away with treating some-one else the way you've treated me. But she didn't say that.

'And where do you think you're going to go?' demanded her mother. 'Who on this island do you think will want you?'

Lina snapped the suitcase closed, found her pristine passport and her small stack of savings, then she removed her denim shorts and blouse and wriggled into a clean dress, wishing her mother would give her a little privacy. 'I'm going away. To San Francisco.'

'To be with *him*?' Her mother gave a discordant laugh. 'You think he'll want you now he's got what he wanted?'

Lina shook her head. No. She wasn't that stupid. She didn't think there was going to be some kind of fairy-tale ending for her and Salvatore di Luca. In the intervening hours since she'd left his bed, he was unlikely to have decided she was the woman of his dreams and he couldn't live without her. But although her billionaire lover had painstakingly explained that he didn't want a relationship with her, he didn't strike her as a dishonourable man and surely he would help her. He owned a plane and was presumably in a position to help her find a job in America. For someone with his wealth and influence, that wouldn't be too big a deal, would it?

After all, it wasn't as if she wanted anything else from him.

Was it?

CHAPTER FIVE

LINA SHIVERED AS the icy look in Salvatore's eyes told her more than words ever could.

She'd known straight away that this was the last thing he wanted—last night's lover turning up on his doorstep and asking him for help. Literally, as he was about to leave. But it was too late to back out now and, besides, what else could she do?

She had been tense with nerves as she had returned to the sprawling villa, terrified he might already have left Sicily and flown back to his home in America. She had arrived in time to see his chauffeur loading smart leather suitcases into the boot of the luxury car, her relief that he was still here soon replaced by the fear that he might not want to see her again. A fear which had been confirmed when Salvatore had appeared at the door of the house and watched her get off her motorbike with suspicion darkening his bright blue eyes. Her heart had sunk as she had looked at his coldly beautiful face because there was no welcoming smile on his lips, nor any kind of greeting to acknowledge the passion they'd shared during the night. Only a cool and steady regard, tinged with a faint but unmistakable impatience. Lina felt like someone who had stepped out of line. As if this wasn't what was supposed to happen and she should have been clever enough to have realised that for herself.

'Lina,' he said carefully, his dark brows raised in arrogant query. 'Did you forget something?'

And Lina knew that if she babbled out an explanation about how a tiny earring belonging to her grandmother, or something equally sentimental, must have slipped down the side of the bed, then a smile of relief would break out on his sensual lips and someone would be instantly dispatched to find it for her. But there was no earring. Nothing had been forgotten or misplaced. She was here to throw herself on his mercy and she tried to think of a diplomatic way to lessen the impact of her request, but there was nothing to fall back on but the unvarnished truth.

'I need… I need your help,' she said.

His blue eyes became hooded. 'I'm not sure I understand.'

Lina tried not to wince at that dismissive response because the subtext to his words was: *This has nothing to do with me, so please don't bother me with your problems.*

She swallowed, twisting a tiny silver ring around her middle finger. 'I need to leave Sicily,' she whispered.

'Your holiday plans are not really my concern.'

'I'm not talking about a holiday.'

'What, then?' he questioned impatiently.

'I was hoping I might be able to ask your advice.'

'About what?'

'About finding a job.'

His powerful body stiffened, like a natural predator which had just heard the crackle of danger, but he flitted her a brief smile, as if the temporary illumination of his handsome face would take the sting out of his next words. 'I'm afraid you're talking to the wrong person,' he said. 'It's true I have a large workforce but I don't micromanage employment issues and, even if I did, I certainly don't take on casual labour on a whim. My human resources team handle that side of my life, so you would need to deal with them. Look, Lina, I don't want to be hurtful, but—'

'No! Maybe I'm not making myself clear.' Her words came tumbling out and she saw his look of surprise, as if he wasn't used to being interrupted. Come to think of it, she was pretty surprised herself—but what was it they said? Desperate times called for desperate measures and she was feeling pretty desperate right now. Didn't matter that Salvatore di Luca was a billionaire and she was a village dressmaker without any formal qualifications, because right now he represented the only hope she had. 'I can't go back home,' she explained. 'My mother has discovered that I spent the night with you and it's the talk of the village. If I stay, she'll make my life a misery.'

His voice was dismissive. 'I'm afraid that's not my problem.'

'I know that. But surely—'

'Surely since I've spent the night with you, it now follows you're my responsibility?' he snapped. 'Is that what you mean, Lina? Even though I specifically asked you whether you were sure you wanted to have sex with me. And you said yes. In fact, you instigated it, as I recall—even though you must have anticipated that you could get found out.'

Lina clenched her fists. She wanted to spill out her hurt at the way he was making her sound so predatory. To tell him he was the most arrogant man she'd ever met and she wondered how she could have fallen into bed with him. But what did she know of the ways of men? Maybe they all acted like this if a woman gave themselves so easily. Wasn't that what she'd been told all through her growing-up years—that a man would lose all respect for you if you had sex with him too quickly? She swallowed, knowing what had happened between them had felt so right—but that wasn't what mattered now. The only thing which mattered was that she had nowhere to go and she needed Salvatore di Luca on her side.

'Of course I'm not your responsibility,' she answered quietly. 'But my life will be intolerable if I remain here. Surely you can understand that. I'll be seen as a woman of loose morals. I'll be judged every time I walk down the street to buy bread. Have you forgotten what these small villages are like?'

His lip curled. 'I made my escape just as soon as I could. Why didn't you do the same?'

'Because it's different for men, and because I made a promise…' Her voice trembled. 'I made a promise to my father that I would stay and look after my mother, only I've realised it isn't doing her any favours. It's just making her more dependent on me, and it's time she stood on her own two feet. I need to get away, Salvatore—surely you could help me.'

'How?' he demanded, then narrowed his eyes as he appeared to sift through a series of possibilities. 'Do you want to carry on staying in this villa, once I've left? The rental is paid for another week.'

'No. I can't stay in Sicily.'

He gave a slightly impatient flick of his fingers. 'I have a house in Rome you could use.'

Did he really think she could take a flight to the mainland and go to the capital city of Italy, a place where she knew no one? 'That wouldn't work either.' She drew in a deep breath and prayed for courage. 'What I'm hoping is that you could take me to America with you.'

He gave a short laugh and stared at her, as if waiting for the punchline. 'Seriously?'

'All I'm asking is for somewhere temporary to stay until I can get myself settled.'

'Is that *all* you're asking?' he echoed sarcastically.

'I'll pay back any expenses I run-up, I promise you that, even if it takes me the rest of my life. I just need a break, Salvatore,' she finished, on a whisper. 'Didn't someone give you a break when you were starting out?'

Salvatore scowled as her words struck an unwanted chord. Yes, he'd had a break. His godfather had given him enough money to buy an airplane ticket to the New World and to feed himself until he found himself a job.

He knew there was nothing to stop him from telling her she wasn't his problem. From jumping in his limo and roaring away without a backward glance. Her mother might be angry but she would soon get over it—she'd have to. And if the neighbours gossiped, so what? They would only gossip until the next scandal came along. Because she *wasn't* his responsibility. They were both grown-ups. They'd had a one-night stand, that was all.

That was all.

He'd made her no false promises.

He owed her nothing.

Nothing.

But, unerringly, Nicolina Vitale had touched on a raw nerve for Salvatore *did* know how small-town gossip worked. He knew how powerful it could be. How people were quick to judge you, especially if you were a woman. If he turned his back on her now and walked away—wouldn't that be like throwing her to the lions? And wasn't there something about her fervour which made him think of the person he'd been all those years ago—so full of drive and ambition and hope? Was it that which made him hesitate?

'You've never even been abroad and I don't think you understand just how different Sicily and America are,' he argued. 'Culture shock won't come close to it. You don't even speak English.'

'Yes, I do,' she said, instantly switching to that language, admittedly with a rather pronounced Sicilian inflection.

Immediately, Salvatore did the same. 'And just how much of it do you understand?' he questioned imperiously. 'Knowing how to ask the time or get directions to the nearest railway station is one thing. But if that's your standard of fluency, you'll be completely out of your depth.'

She tilted her chin upwards. 'Would you like to test me, then?' she challenged, her voice growing more heated now. 'Do you want me to assure you that I won't make a mistake about "flower" and "flour" and that I know the difference between "angry" and "hungry"?'

Salvatore very nearly laughed and then very nearly pulled her in his arms to kiss the truculent tremble of her lips, because her defiance seemed to have kick-started a slideshow of erotic recall which was starting to heat his blood. Suddenly he could picture her dark olive curves outlined against the white sheet. He could remember how soft she'd felt as she had eagerly opened her fleshy thighs to accommodate his thrusting body. He could recall the sweet tightness as he had broken through her hymen with what had felt like the biggest erection of his life.

'Where did you learn to speak English like that?' he queried unevenly.

'I've always worked hard at my studies and we had a teacher in the village,' she explained. 'A woman from England who fell in love with a Sicilian waiter and came back to Caltarina to be with him. She made it her mission to teach all the children in her care how to speak her mother tongue. She said…' She hesitated. 'She said we never knew when it would come in useful.'

'And maybe she inspired you with more than her language skills,' he suggested silkily. 'Did she also teach you that if all else fails, you can use a man as an escape route from a situation which no longer appeals to you?'

Lina's heart was beating very loudly as his words

sank in and she stared at him in growing disbelief. 'Do you think…?' *Say it,* she urged herself, even though it made her feel sick to articulate the insulting implications of his words. She sucked in a deep breath and the air felt hot and raw against her throat. 'Do you really think I slept with you in order to get to America?'

'Who knows?' He shrugged. 'People have done a lot worse to get themselves a Green Card.'

It occurred to Lina that maybe he didn't think so highly of *himself* if he thought she'd targeted him because of that. Surely he didn't imagine that a woman would have sex with him for any other reason than because he was irresistible. But his beliefs weren't her problem. It didn't *matter* what the billionaire thought of her. What mattered was that he gave her a seat on his plane and a temporary roof over her head. Surely that wasn't too much to ask.

'So will you help me, Salvatore? Will you take me to America with you?'

The pause which followed seemed to last for ever until he glanced down at his watch with the slight desperation of the condemned prisoner counting down the seconds to his own execution. 'My jet is leaving in an hour.' His narrowed eyes were shards of unfriendly blue ice as he lifted his gaze to her face and his words were equally cold. 'You can stay on my estate for a few weeks, but no longer. Do you understand what I'm saying?'

'Perfectly,' she said, her heart racing, wondering why, suddenly, he was looking like the enemy.

'Then get in the car,' he snapped.

CHAPTER SIX

It was a day of firsts.

Lina had never been whisked to a private airfield before, or been treated almost like royalty by everyone they came into contact with. As soon as she and Salvatore stepped from the limousine, the tycoon's personal crew flocked around him like fireflies on a summer's night, though she couldn't miss their looks of surprise when they registered that *she* was to be his travelling companion.

Did she look out of place in her handmade dress and the sneakers she'd bought from the local market?

Of course she did, but she couldn't allow such things to bother her. Her position here was nothing to be ashamed of. She wasn't Salvatore's lover. Not any more. That part of their relationship was over. He'd told her very clearly that it was never intended to be anything other than a one-night stand and she told herself she was happy with that decision. She was simply hitching a ride from a man who could help her, and one day she would pay him back in full.

But nerves got the better of her as she fastened her

seat belt and she turned to the man beside her, trying not to focus on the long legs which were stretched out in front of him, or the quiet strength which was radiating from his powerful body. 'Do you think we're going to crash?' she asked as he pulled a computer from a soft leather briefcase and the plane's engines roared into life.

He frowned. 'You really think I wouldn't make a point of using the safest planes flown by the best pilots in the business?'

'Then why did the stewardess spend so much time pointing out the emergency exits and showing me how to put on my life jacket?'

He gave a flicker of a smile. 'It's a legal requirement on all flights, Lina. And I hope you're not going to come out with that type of inane comment for the entire journey. Transatlantic travel can be tedious at the best of times, but that would really stretch my patience.'

'I'm sure it would and I'll try my best to keep my *inane* comments to myself. It's just that I've never been in a plane before. I told you that.'

Salvatore stared unseeingly at the blur of figures on the screen in front of him, because that was easier than looking into her dark and smoky eyes. Yes, she had told him. She had told him lots of things but it seemed his hearing had been selective and he'd only registered the things he'd wanted to hear. His fingers hovered over his laptop; for once he was failing to be absorbed by the graphs which dominated the bright square in front of him. Lust had triumphed over reason and, as a consequence, he now found himself in a situation not of his choosing.

'Just read something to pass the time, will you?' he growled. 'Ask one of the crew to bring you some magazines.'

Expelling an impatient breath, he turned his attention back to his computer, because his plan had been to work, just as he always did when he was travelling. He never really stopped working. In interviews, he was often asked why he kept going when his fortune was already so vast, and, although he sometimes brushed the question aside, deep down he knew why. It wasn't just the adrenaline buzz you got while chasing down a tough new deal, or the flush of success when you pulled it off, sometimes against all the odds. It wasn't even the irrational dread which lingered on from his childhood—his determination never to know hunger again.

He narrowed his eyes. No. The reason was far more elemental than that. At least you knew where you were with hard cold dollars and cents. They didn't betray you, or hurt you, or lie to you. It was only people who did that. And it was the people closest to you who could tell the biggest lies of all.

An image of painted red lips and nails the colour of blood swam into his mind, accompanied by the memory of a low, taunting laugh. And Salvatore gave silent thanks for being the man he was today. A man who was psychologically self-contained and immune to the wiles of women. He sighed. If only desire could be controlled as tightly as his emotions. His gaze flickered across to Lina, transfixed by the way her raven curls tumbled down over the swell of her breasts.

Had he thought he could compartmentalise their explosive night of passion and put it firmly in the past, because to do anything else would be an act little short of insanity? Against his better judgement, he had agreed to provide her with a temporary place to stay, and keeping his distance from her was essential if he wanted to drive home the message that he was unavailable. But maybe he had misjudged her appeal or maybe he'd underestimated how powerful it felt to have his sexuality so keenly awoken after what now seemed like a long time. Because suddenly his work was forgotten. Suddenly Lina Vitale was the sole focus of his attention.

In her simple dress she looked as fresh as a blossom which had tumbled from a tree—despite the fact she'd had very little rest last night. He could personally vouch for that. Sleep had eluded them both as they had lain with their limbs tangled and, as dawn had washed the bed with warm shades of rose and gold, he had been aware of the olive sheen of her skin, only a couple of shades lighter than his own. There had seemed something indefinably erotic about that. She was the first Sicilian lover he'd ever had—probably with good reason. But reason was the last thing on his mind right now.

He felt his throat thicken as she lifted her head and her lips parted, reminding him of the way she had softly clamped them around his erection in the preceding hours. He wondered if his breath had quickened. Was that why her nipples had started to show through the cheap cotton of her dress?

With an effort, he flicked his gaze back to the screen, but no matter how many emails he tried to compose, the words just kept blurring, because all he could think about was the throb of desire which was hot and heavy at his groin. When she crossed one ankle over the other like that, it seemed like the most erotic action he'd ever witnessed. He couldn't stop thinking about his fingers travelling up her leg to linger on the cool satin of her thighs, or how good it had felt to make that first, tight thrust inside her molten heat. He had taken her over and over again and each time it had felt just as sweet as the first time. Hell, *she* had been so sweet. So openly blown away each time he'd made her come, which had been a *lot*. She had rained kisses all over his lips over and over again, as if she was thanking him. Were all virgins so touchingly grateful?

He didn't want to think about it.

He couldn't stop thinking about it.

His mouth grew dry as the tension between them mounted. It felt as if all the oxygen had been sucked from within the confines of a cabin which had never felt this small before. He was having difficulty breathing and started wondering if the captain had adjusted the pressure. He swallowed.

'So how are the first-time-flyer nerves?' he said, the conversational tone of his question belying the erratic thunder of his heart. 'Feeling a little less anxious now?'

Lina swallowed as she rested her hand on the magazine—the glossy page feeling sticky beneath her hot palm. Less anxious? Was he kidding? She might have had fears about flying, but they had been replaced by a concern about her reaction to him, and the way she couldn't seem to do a thing about it. Did he realise he was making her breasts ache just by looking at her, or that her panties had become embarrassingly damp?

But she wasn't supposed to be thinking about him like that. The brief sexual side of their relationship was a thing of the past—from now on he was nothing other than her reluctant mentor.

With an effort she dragged her mind back to his question and attempted an equally polite answer. 'A bit better, thanks. I think I'm getting used to it. It's certainly a very smooth flight and the clouds outside the window are beautiful.'

The hard glitter of his blue eyes seemed to mock her. 'Are you hungry?'

She shook her head. Was she going mad? Why did she feel as if they were having one conversation, with a whole completely different conversation going on underneath? 'No. Not really.'

'Tired, perhaps? This kind of journey is always draining. There are a couple of bedrooms at the back of the cabin and perhaps you should try to get some rest. The one on the right is quieter. Try that.'

'Good idea,' she said, unclipping her seat belt and rising to her feet. She told herself that sleep was essential. More importantly, it would get her away from Salvatore and the disturbing impact he was having on her senses. He probably wanted to get rid of her. For all she knew, he might be desperate to contact some woman in San Francisco and start arranging to see her the moment he arrived back. And if that were the case then she was going to have to deal with it. He'd made her no promises, had he? He'd offered her no future.

And she'd been okay with that. She needed to be okay with that. He was already being generous in providing her with a flight and a home.

If she started wanting anything more, she was risking heartbreak. And she couldn't allow herself to be vulnerable like that—not when she was starting a new life in a new country.

A ridiculous feeling of self-consciousness rippled over her as she picked up her handbag and made her way towards the back of the cabin, wondering if he was watching her. And the crazy thing was that she *wanted* him to watch her—to run that appreciative blue gaze over her in a way which could make her hungry body quiver with longing. But he said nothing more as she left the cabin and Lina quickly went into the bathroom, where she stood for ages holding her wrists beneath a gushing tap. But no amount of cold water was able to bring down her body temperature and eventually she washed her face, brushed out her hair and decided to try and get some rest as Salvatore had suggested. Hopelessly distracted by a head full of erotic images, she walked noiselessly along the softly carpeted corridor and pushed open the bedroom door, her heart missing a beat as she walked in.

Because there was Salvatore.

He had obviously just showered because tiny droplets of water were glittering in the thickness of his jet-dark hair and he was pulling a black T-shirt down over his rippling torso. And he was wearing jeans. Black jeans which hugged the powerful length of his legs. Lina had never seen him wearing anything so casual and he looked almost shockingly sexy. A low curl of heat began coiling itself tightly inside her, round and round and round it went, the pressure building and building with each second that passed. The spring of her nipples began to push almost painfully against the lace of her bra and she wriggled her shoulders a little. It felt as if she were dissolving with desire and she swallowed as she struggled to get the words out.

'I think… I think I may have the wrong room,' she said.

He looked right back at her and the silence which followed seemed to go on for a very long time.

'Not necessarily,' he said, at last.

Lina was no expert when it came to what men wanted, but maybe she didn't need to be. She could see a pulse flickering at his temple and the almost imperceptible tightening of his lips. His smouldering blue gaze and the unmistakable darkening of his eyes were sending out the unspoken message that he wanted her as much as she wanted him. But she had been the one to make the first move last time and since then Salvatore had made it very clear that their relationship was going to be platonic. And wasn't that the best thing? Wouldn't that help to protect herself from the way he made her feel?

She knew what she should do. Squeeze out a polite smile and excuse herself. Find the other bedroom and stay in there until all this inconvenient desire had left her. But she couldn't. And if that could be described as a weakness in her character—Lina didn't care. Because she had spent most of her life being a good girl.

Who could blame her if she was enjoying this tantalising feeling of being naughty?

Was that why she just continued to stand there, drinking in his magnificent body with a sexual hunger which was growing stronger by the minute? And suddenly she was getting the distinct feeling that they were each fighting some kind of private inner battle, waiting to see which of them would break first.

It was him.

With something which sounded like a helpless groan, he walked across the cabin towards her and pulled her into his arms, looking down into her face for one long and searching moment—as if seeking the answer she was sure he could read there, before bending his head and blotting out the world with his kiss. And Lina kissed him back. Hungrily. Fervently—dimly acknowledging how different it felt from the first time he'd kissed her. That time it had been all about newness and discovery and his inevitable reaction to her virginity. He had been careful with her, taking his time to extinguish every last bit of apprehension so that she had been bombarded with pleasure, over and over again.

But now he was kissing her in a way which was raw and heightened with untempered passion and suddenly Lina felt more like an equal than a novice. Hadn't he taught her how to enjoy pleasure last night and shown her some of the things *he* liked? So why not show him what an attentive pupil she'd been? Boldly, she slid her hand down the front of his T-shirt, and as she began to massage the hard contours of his torso through the dark material she could hear his slow expelled breath of pleasure.

'Take it off,' he urged her unevenly. 'Undress me, Lina.'

It was empowering to register that note of undisguised need in his voice. But it was nothing but lust, Lina reminded herself as she pulled the garment over his head, though he seemed reluctant to allow her trembling fingers anywhere near his jeans. Quickly, he unzipped her cotton dress and tossed it aside, though he hesitated when he saw her plain white underwear beneath. What was it about that which made his rugged face darken, as if he were having second thoughts? Lina tightened her arms around him and could feel the hard spring of his erection pressing through their clothes, and as he gave what sounded like a soft moan of surrender, everything began to happen very quickly.

Peeling off his jeans, she saw he was naked underneath and very aroused and she let out a gulp of pleasure as he took off her bra and panties and pushed her down onto the bed. Her heart slammed against her ribcage and already she was at such a pitch of excitement that she couldn't bear to wait for a second longer. Was that why she opened her thighs to give him access to the engorged little bud which he began to strum with sweet accuracy, making her cry out with pleasure, so that he had to kiss her into silence.

'Salvatore,' she moaned, against his lips.

'More?'

She ground her hips against the mattress. *'Yes.'*

His movement became more intense, the position of his fingertip uniquely provocative.

'I've been thinking about doing this ever since you left my bed this morning,' he bit out roughly.

'So have…so have…' But her sentence was destined never to be finished because an orgasm had begun to clench its way through her body and Lina cried out as she began to convulse with the first of those achingly sweet spasms.

The sound seemed to galvanise him into action but he waited until her body was no longer shuddering, before reaching for a condom and stroking it on. And then he moved on top of her and pushed deep inside her, his face dark with fierce concentration. At first, his movements were slow and considered and somehow Lina realised he was waiting for her to have another orgasm before giving into his own. That first fluttering realisation gave way to a heavy beat of expectation, which kept on growing and growing until suddenly her rainbow world was splintering all over again and he was choking out his own gratification.

Afterwards, her arms tightened around him until the sound of his breathing grew less ragged. Tentatively, her tongue flicked out to taste the salt of his skin and she could feel the hardness of one hair-roughened thigh as it lay sprawled over hers. It felt intimate. Intensely intimate—as if they were the only two people in the world. As if all that perfect physicality had forged a special bond between the two of them. As if all the barriers they had both erected around themselves had just slipped away. And somehow that made what had just happened seem perfectly acceptable. Did sex always make you feel like this? she wondered dreamily as she reached out her finger to trickle it slowly down his chest. But her innocent gesture seemed to stir him into action and, even though she could have stayed like that all day, he now seemed determined to move away from her. Suddenly he was rolling onto the other side of the bed and it was as if a giant canyon had sprung up between them.

'Is everything okay?' she asked, before wondering if that was the kind of thing you were *supposed* to say at a time like this.

Salvatore heard the soft uncertainty in her voice and guessed what she wanted. She was probably craving reassurance, keen for him to offer something tangible in terms of a relationship now that they'd been intimate again. But he couldn't do that, and what had just happened should never have happened. He felt a surge of anger, knowing he should have left well alone. He should have blocked out her intoxicating allure, which had reeled him in for all the wrong reasons. He should have sent her away to the other cabin and ignored the urgent throb at his groin which had made him lose control. Because she was wrong on so many counts. Too sweet. Too trusting. Too innocent and untried for a man with his track record of emotional coldness. He would hurt her and he had no right to hurt her, though maybe he wouldn't tell her that. Better she think of him as indifferent, rather than understanding.

Or try to change his mind.

'We need to get a couple of things straight before we

land,' he drawled. 'The sex we've just had was amazing, for sure, but it hasn't actually *changed* anything. It was just a moment of physical desire which demanded some kind of release. That's what sometimes happens between a man and a woman. Do you understand what I'm saying?'

'I think I'd have to be pretty stupid not to,' she said.

Salvatore hesitated. He was finding this much harder than he'd expected, mainly because she looked so damned beautiful lying there, her olive limbs sprawled against the sheets with indolent abandon. But he steeled himself against the sudden bewilderment which had clouded her lovely features. 'You're going to be staying in my home and that's something which has never happened before. I like my own space and the idea of a lover being around all the time fills me with dread.'

'I suppose I should thank you for your honesty,' she said.

'I am nothing if not honest, Lina.' He swung his legs over the side of the bed. 'Up until now your life has been protected—by your mother and by the constraints of a small community. But you're going to be living in a big city from now on and you need to learn how to protect yourself. I'm not your guardian and I'm not your boyfriend.' His mouth twisted as he stood up and looked down at her. 'And a naïve young woman clinging to me like a limpet has never been on my wish-list.'

'I have no intention of behaving like a limpet,' she said, with a sudden proud tilt of her chin.

That one simple movement was enough to stir the beginnings of another erection, and Salvatore nearly reached for her again, before stopping himself. Because Lina Vitale could so easily become a millstone around his neck—and that would be way too high a price to pay for the fleeting pleasures of sex.

A chill of awareness whispered over his skin.

She knew no one in San Francisco other than him.

Despite her undeniable sweetness and the lure of her lush body, from now on she needed to be off-limits.

He would provide her with a temporary home, yes. He would ensure she met some of his contacts so she could find herself a job. And once she had gained some independence he could filter her out of his life, for good. He could move her on, having taught her a very important lesson.

That she must never grow to depend on him.

CHAPTER SEVEN

'WE'RE HERE,' SAID Salvatore curtly as the car glided through noiseless electronic gates to draw up in a sheltered inner courtyard.

They had flown into San Francisco—over the iconic bridge and the wide sweep of water which it straddled—before making their way to Salvatore's home. He lived in an area called Russian Hill and Lina thought she'd never seen anywhere quite so affluent. Yet from the outside, the property was relatively unassuming, with tall gates concealing the building from prying eyes. But once those gates had closed she found herself staring up at a modern four-storey building, set in surprisingly extensive grounds, studded with brightly flowering shrubs and heavily loaded citrus trees, which reminded her of home.

'Like it?' Salvatore questioned, his eyes on her face.

She nodded, not terribly interested in his real estate, but at least it was good to have something to focus on other than the way he had been keeping his distance from her since they'd fallen onto that bed together, high up above the world, in the clouds. Sex on a plane. Nobody could deny that her world was opening up in all kinds of unexpected ways. 'It's beautiful,' she said dutifully.

The front door was opened by a sombre-faced man, wearing a formal dark suit. 'This is my butler, Henry,' said Salvatore.

His *butler*?

'It's good to have you back, Signor di Luca,' Henry said, with a pronounced English accent and the faint semblance of a smile.

'This is Nicolina Vitale, Henry. She's going to be staying here for a few weeks until she's settled in the city. I thought we could put her in one of the vacant cottages. The one furthest from the house might be best.'

'Certainly, Signor di Luca. One of your assistants telephoned earlier and the farthest cottage is already prepared,' Henry answered. 'Perhaps you would care for me to give Miss Vitale a tour around the compound?'

'If you wouldn't mind.' Salvatore pulled his phone out of his pocket and briefly scanned the screen, before shooting Lina an absent-minded look. 'Look, I need to work. Henry will answer any questions you may have and you and I will eat dinner later, as it's your first night here. Eight o'clock, on the terrace. Okay?'

'Thank you,' said Lina, watching him walk away and wondering what on earth she could find to say to the intimidating butler. But she hadn't exactly had much conversation with Salvatore over the past few hours, had she? In fact, their erotic encounter seemed to have created a great space between them. He had treated her with the same polite detachment as he had the stewardesses who had been serving them drinks and food during the transatlantic flight. And Lina had been left trying to focus on that wretched magazine—trying to blot out the aching in her breasts and the memory of him feasting hungrily on her nipples.

She followed Henry through the house and tried to drink it all in, but it wasn't easy for her to get her head around the fact that one man could own a property this big. It was all clean lines and uncluttered space which contained sleek, modern furniture. A space-age kitchen led into not one but two dining rooms, one of which was reached by a glass elevator. The basement housed a carefully lit subterranean art gallery as well as a private cinema, and outside were more seating areas amid tangles of fragrant climbing plants, and a long, cantilevered swimming pool. The highest point of all was the dining terrace, with its sweeping views all the way to Alcatraz and everything in between.

'It's gorgeous,' said Lina politely, though in truth she found it all a little overpowering. 'Have you worked for Salvatore for very long?'

'Five years,' said Henry. 'I first met Signor di Luca at a weekend house party in England when he poached me from the host, and I've been with him ever since.' He gave the hint of a smile. 'He tends to inspire loyalty among his staff.'

'Just how many staff *are* there?' questioned Lina.

'He has a full-time chef and Shirley, who helps out when Signor di Luca chooses to dine at home. And, naturally, there are cleaning staff, gardeners, drivers—the usual kind of thing.'

Lina nodded sagely, as if the concept of personal staff was something she encountered every day of the week.

'Was there anything else you wanted to know, Miss Vitale?'

'No, you've been very helpful. Thank you, Henry. And, please, I'd much rather you called me Nicolina.'

Henry nodded but gave no outward response to her request, other than indicating she should follow him, before leading the way through the grounds to a compact cottage surrounded by trees.

Once the butler had gone, Lina stared out of the window, watching the light beginning to leach from the sky and thinking how surreal this all felt. Because it *was* surreal. One moment she had been living in a village with practically nothing and the next she was staying in the grounds of a billionaire's mansion, being shown around by a butler.

She had no real place here, she realised. Only a temporary one. Just as she had no real place in Salvatore's life. He had seduced her on the plane and she'd let him. Actually, she'd felt herself powerless to do anything else. It had been like a river she'd once seen after the rains, when the water had swollen and banks had burst—flooding everything in its path. And that was what it had been like with Salvatore. That sweet tide of desire had been overwhelming and maybe she needed to think how best to defend herself from feeling that way in the future.

She unpacked her case, then enjoyed a long shower in a bathroom of unspeakable luxury, and, after she'd untangled her curls and dressed, decided to email her mother. They might have parted on bitter terms, but she needed to know that her only child had arrived safely. She switched on her old computer, the glow from the screen dominating her line of vision so that for a while Lina forgot all about Salvatore di Luca and the Californian sky outside her window.

Salvatore walked out onto the wide sweep of terrace and at first he didn't notice her. The light had almost faded from the day and he was preoccupied, as he'd been from the moment he'd arrived at the office, where the staff had seemed surprised to see him working so soon after a long flight. He couldn't blame them because usually he would have spent the afternoon relaxing. He might have swum in the pool or worked out in the gym. But not today—and he knew why. He'd been afraid of running into Lina. Afraid of reliving the way she'd made him feel during the journey from Sicily, when he had felt himself being sucked into that sensual maelstrom despite his determination to resist her. But he hadn't resisted her, had he? He'd allowed her uncomplicated Sicilian beauty to lure him into an unforgettable mile-high encounter—the memory of which he suspected would never leave him.

He'd come home just an hour ago but even a long, icy shower had failed to cool the heat in his blood, and now his attention was caught by the woman sitting on the terrace in front of him, her profile etched starkly against the fiery glow of the setting sun. She was leaning back against a bank of cushions on a low divan, her posture outwardly relaxed as she gazed out at the city view, but her shoulders were hunched with that expectant air of someone who was waiting.

Waiting for him, he thought, and that realisation filled him with an instinctive shiver of disquiet.

She must have heard him for she turned, unable to hide the quick flash of pleasure in her eyes, which she instantly tried to disguise with a look of polite interest.

'Salvatore! You're back.' She was speaking softly in Sicilian dialect, which itself was disorientating. Was that because it made him think of the past—and of a homeland from which he had been so keen to distance himself? He wanted to tell her to speak only in English, which he knew was unreasonable, yet their spoken bond only added another unsettling layer to his dealings with her. And he wondered yet again what strange sorcery she possessed which was capable of cutting through his habitual iron-hard control.

She scrambled to her feet, the skirt of her cotton dress whispering like a summer breeze, and Salvatore felt a sensation of something unfamiliar as her black curls rippled down around her shoulders. Lust, yes— there was definitely plenty of *that*, along with an instinctive appreciation for her natural beauty, but there was another flicker of apprehension, too. Don't let her get used to this, he found himself thinking. Don't let her think he wanted this kind of cloying homecoming every night.

'Yes, I'm back,' he said smoothly as he ran his finger around the collar of his shirt. 'Did you settle in okay? Did Henry give you the full guided tour?'

'Yes, he did. The tour was amazing and the cottage is lovely.'

Heaven save him from sustained small talk, he thought acidly as he lifted his hand to summon the portly figure of a woman who had silently appeared in the shadows, switching rapidly to English as he spoke to her. 'We'll eat as soon as you're ready, Shirley.'

'Very good, Signor di Luca.'

He half filled two glasses of Gavi and handed one to Lina, but he noticed that she barely tasted the drink, cupping it in her hands as if she'd forgotten she was holding it. It was probably completely unconscious, but in that moment she looked so...*fragile* as she sat there, so clearly out of her depth that Salvatore felt a sudden wave of compassion—and empathy. Because hadn't he once been exactly where she was now? Hadn't he once gazed around at the sumptuous surroundings of billionaire homes and felt as if he'd fallen onto an alien planet?

'So.' He put his glass down on one of the low tables and fixed her with an encouraging smile. 'Did you manage to amuse yourself while I was out?'

Lina nodded as she wrapped her fingers around the cold glass of wine. 'I wrote to my mother and let her know I'd arrived safely and then I started looking online to see what kind of jobs I might be able to find. Soft furnishing companies which need people to sew cushions, or drapes—that kind of thing.'

'And is that what you *want* to do?' He frowned. 'What about all those dreams you talked about?'

She shrugged. 'They don't just happen.'

'Couldn't you make them happen?'

Lina swirled her wine around in her glass. It was so easy for him to talk. What would he say if she confessed she was terrified her ambitions might wither under the brightness of the Californian sun? 'I have to have some money coming in first,' she said. 'And then I'll see. I have savings, but I'm going to be very careful about how I spend them.'

'Well, that sounds like a very sensible plan.' His voice was grave but she could see the faint upward curve of his lips. Was he inwardly laughing at her? she wondered.

But Lina pushed aside her concerns as she sat down at the table, determined to enjoy her dinner. The meal began with a creamy fish soup, which Salvatore called chowder, followed by a fillet of perfect fish, served with its own little jug of sauce. She tucked into every course with a keen appetite, putting her dessert spoon down at the end to find Salvatore studying her, with what looked like amusement sparking from his narrowed eyes. 'It's good to see a woman who enjoys her food,' he observed.

'I was hungry.'

'I could see that. Don't look so defensive. I meant it. Most women order a plate of rabbit food and then just pick at it.'

'That's why they stay so slim.'

'Don't ever think you don't have the perfect body, Lina,' he said softly. 'Because you do.'

It was like a rock being dropped into a still stretch of water—the relative calmness of the meal disrupted by the sudden violent splash of memory. Powerful and erotic memory. Silhouetted against the glittering backdrop of the city, Lina thought how unbelievably virile the tycoon looked in a shirt the colour of an oyster shell—the silky material emphasising his broad shoulders. It was weird to think they had been eating their meal so primly when just hours ago he had been deep inside her body. Yet his words were unexpected and they changed the atmosphere completely. His quiet praise made her feel almost confident. Was it that which made her ask the question she'd been longing to ask him all day?

'Do you think you'll ever go back to Sicily?'

His voice was repressive, his powerful body tense as he put his coffee cup down. 'I doubt it.'

Lina pushed her dessert plate away. Okay, so he didn't want to talk about Sicily—but they had to talk about *something*, didn't they? Otherwise every time she ran across him she was going to feel increasingly agitated.

Focus on something other than the curve of his lips and the carved contours of his face, she told herself fiercely. *Ask him something easy.*

'Where are your parents?' she asked suddenly.

Almost imperceptibly, his knuckles tightened. 'Why do you ask?'

'It's a normal question. Nobody in the village knew anything about them. Apparently your godfather never talked about them, even when he was well. I was just thinking how proud they must have been of your success.'

Salvatore stilled. Funny how a guileless statement like that had the power to tug you back towards a darkness and a past he tried to keep out of bounds. 'My parents never got to see it,' he said coolly. 'They were dead by then. They died a long time ago. Long enough for everyone to have forgotten about them.'

'I'm so sorry,' she said quietly. 'What happened to them?'

There was a pause and Salvatore felt a flicker of irritation. Didn't she realise from his tone that he didn't want to talk about it? That over the years he had built a high wall around his emotions? An impenetrable barrier, which discouraged investigation into his past—a concept easily accepted by a culture which was keen to live in the moment. But Lina Vitale was looking at him with such genuine compassion shining from her eyes that Salvatore felt some of his usual resolve melt away.

Was it because she was Sicilian and they were speaking quietly together in dialect that he found himself wanting to break the most fundamental of his self-imposed rules and talk to her on a level he never usually engaged in with other people? Or because she looked so damned lovely that he needed to distract himself from giving in to what he most wanted to do—which was to carry her off to his bedroom and ravish her over and over again, until she was shuddering out his name and biting her little white teeth into his bare skin?

And he wasn't going to do that any more. He'd demonstrated quite enough powerlessness around her. He needed to claw back some of the control which had so disturbingly left him on the plane today.

But she was still looking at him and something about her soft gaze was making him want to spill it all out.

And why not? It wasn't as if he *cared* about what had happened in the past, was it? Not any more. He had schooled himself to ensure he didn't really care much about anything, or anyone. A brief explanation might provide a welcome diversion from the rise and fall of her breath, which was making her luscious breasts move provocatively beneath her dress. And mightn't talking about it prove to himself once and for all that the past no longer had the power to hurt him?

He swallowed the last of his wine and put the glass down. 'My father was a fisherman, though not a particularly effective one,' he began, arching her a questioning look. 'You know what they say about fisherman's luck?'

She shook her head. 'Not really.'

'Getting wet and catching no fish,' he explained, with a rare flash of black humour which made her smile. 'As a consequence we had very little. We were among the poorest in one of the poorest villages on the island. The bottom of the heap, if you like. And it made my mother…discontented.'

She didn't say anything. If she had, he might have clammed up. But as her silence washed over him with purifying calm, he found himself continuing.

'A life of poverty wasn't what she had signed up for. She was a beautiful woman who had always attracted the attention of men and that made my father jealous. Jealousy is an ugly trait,' he added, his mouth twisting. 'I could hear him shouting at her at night-time, when I was trying to sleep. He used to accuse her of flirting. Of wearing clothes which were too tight and lipstick which was too red. Sometimes their rows were so loud they used to wake up the neighbours and all the local dogs would start to bark. And she used to taunt him back. She told him he couldn't even provide for his family. She said he wasn't a *real* man.' He gave a bitter laugh. 'Living with them was like watching a never-ending boxing match, with each one circling the other, waiting to make the killer blow. Like having a bomb ticking away in the corner of the room, just waiting to go off.' It hadn't felt like life, it had felt like *existence*—a claustrophobic prison from which he'd been unable to escape and which had soured his appetite for close relationships in the years which had followed.

'Go on,' she said, in a voice so soft it was barely audible.

He drew in a deep breath, surprised by the ease with which he was saying it, as if someone had sweetened a mouthful of poison and made it almost palatable. 'One day, when my father was out on his boat, a travelling salesman came by the house—a slick stranger who seduced her with the promise of silk stockings and a better life. By the time I got home from school she had already packed her things and was getting ready to drive away in his fancy car.'

He was lost in the past now; he could feel it sucking him back into a great gaping vortex of darkness. His mother had crouched down and told him she would send for him just as soon as she was settled but something inside him had known she was lying. He would never forget the kiss-shaped mark of lipstick she'd left behind on his cheek, which he had scrubbed afterwards until his skin was red raw. Or the way the salesman had looked right through him, as if he were invisible—a tedious little obstacle which had been put in their path. His father had erupted with a heartbreak which had made the young Salvatore flinch with shame. Crying big savage sobs, he had thrown himself down on his knees in front of his straying wife, his shoulders shaking as he'd begged her not to go.

But she had. She and the salesman had driven away in a cloud of dust. And Salvatore had been left with his father's grovelling display in front of the small crowd who had gathered there. Just as he'd been left with his own sense of confusion and outrage. In that moment he had recognised the humiliation that women could heap upon men, and how a man could let his obsession for a woman make him lose his mind. He had never forgotten either of those lessons. And he had been right about his mother's lie, because she had never sent for him, despite the promise she had made. 'My mother and her lover were killed in a car crash the following year,' he added grimly. 'And soon after that, my father was lost at sea.' He gave a bitter laugh. 'They called it an accident, but I never considered it one, for he lost the will to live after her desertion.'

'Oh, Salvatore.' Her voice trembled and he could hear the soft note of tenderness in her voice. 'That's... that's awful.'

He shook his head and held up his palm. 'Platitudes are not necessary, Lina,' he said, hardening his heart to the way she was looking at him, as if she wanted to cradle him in her arms and take away all those bitter memories. And *that* was why he didn't ever talk about it, he reminded himself grimly. He would not be seen as a victim. As someone to be saved, or pitied, or rescued. Because he'd managed to mastermind his own rescue and he'd done it all himself. 'I didn't tell you because I wanted your sympathy.'

There was a flicker of a pause. 'Then why did you tell me?'

'Maybe I just wanted to make it clear what has made me the man I am. To make you understand that I mean it when I say I don't want any long-term emotional commitment. Perhaps now you can understand why.'

'Because you don't trust women?'

'No.' He shook his head. 'Because I know my own limitations. I just don't have the capacity to care, Lina— or the willingness to do so. I've always been that way and that's the way I like it.'

He saw the clouding of her eyes just as his phone began to vibrate on the table and he snatched it up, glad of the interruption. He listened intently for a few moments before terminating the call and rising to his feet, his heart twisting with something inexplicable as he looked down into her big, dark eyes. 'I need to deal with this call and then I'm going to turn in for the night,' he said abruptly. 'But stay as long as you like and ring for anything you need. Shirley can get you coffee—'

'No. I mean, thank you, but no.' With a fluid movement she rose from the table. 'I'm tired too and I'd like to turn in.' She hesitated. 'I don't suppose you'd show me the way? This place is so big I'm terrified of getting lost.'

The last thing he wanted was to escort her back in the seductive light of the moon. To imagine the bed which lay within the little cottage and think how good it would feel to sink down on it with her in his arms and to lose himself in her sweetness. The spiralling tension which had tightened his groin into an exquisite ache made him want to refuse her innocent request, but wouldn't that imply that he couldn't trust himself around her?

He stayed silent as they walked through the grounds, trying to concentrate on something other than the whisper of her skirt in the light breeze and the way it swayed over her curvy buttocks. But as she stopped in front of the door, with the scent of flowers heavy and potent in the night air, and the black curls streaming over her thrusting breasts, he felt a rush of desire so powerful that he almost succumbed to it.

It would have been so easy to take her into his arms and kiss her. Too easy. Despite everything he'd said on the plane, he was beginning to realise that resisting Lina Vitale might not be as simple as he'd thought. Would it hurt to retract his words? To override his original intentions and give into the most powerful sexual attraction which had ever come his way? Surely it was insane to deny them both what they wanted, when this kind of physical chemistry was so rare.

He swallowed. Maybe, at a later date—when he was certain she could accept his boundaries and his limitations. Because if—when—he had sex with her again, it would be at a time of *his* choosing. When he was certain Lina understood that *he* was the one in the driving seat. The one with all the control. He would make himself wait, because not only would it increase his hunger, it would prove he didn't need her. Maybe the time would come when they could be friends with benefits, yes, but it could never be anything more. And in the meantime, he needed to ensure she had some kind of focus other than *him*.

He stopped outside her doorway and looked at the moonlight-dappled darkness of her hair. 'One of my charitable foundations is giving a gala ball tomorrow night,' he said. 'Why don't you come along?'

'You mean, as your guest?'

Deliberately, he downplayed it. 'Why not? You'll get a chance to meet some people. Contacts which may come in use, if you're going to start looking for a job. You might actually find something to do with your life which is a little more exciting than sewing drapes and curtains. Isn't that what you came here for?'

'Yes, yes. Of course it is. It's just that…' She hesitated as she fingered the flared fabric of her dress before lifting her gaze to his. 'I've never been to a ball before.'

'I don't imagine they're a big feature of life in Caltarina,' he said drily.

'Which means I don't have anything suitable to wear,' she continued. 'And there won't be time for me to make anything suitable.'

'No problem. I can buy you something.'

'That wasn't what I meant, Salvatore. I can't possibly let you do that. You've already been more than generous.'

'The subject isn't up for debate' he said coolly. 'I

can afford it and you can't. You can add it to the list of things you say you're going to pay back.'

'I say it because I mean it!' she clarified fiercely. 'I'll pay back every cent.'

He gave a slow smile, because in that moment she reminded him very much of himself. 'Okay. Now go and get some sleep,' he said softly. 'It's been a long day.'

He turned and walked away and Lina watched him, still trying to absorb everything that had happened. He'd told her about his childhood, which had made her heart bleed for him. Things which had made her want to wrap her arms around him and comfort him and try to take some of his pain away. She bit her lip. Her own mother might have been stupidly strict, but at least she'd *been* there for her. And Salvatore's face had looked so stern as his story had unfolded, his troubled features shadowed by the flicker of candlelight. He had obviously intended to convince her that the past no longer had the power to affect him, but Lina had detected the faint dip of vulnerability in his voice. She had seen the ravaged expression which had darkened his face when he'd described his mother driving away in the salesman's car. And she had died before they'd had an opportunity to resolve their broken relationship. Of *course* it must still hurt, no matter how hard he tried to deny it to himself. She suspected he'd buried it away so deeply that he'd never really allowed himself to grieve.

And his father had left him, too. So wrapped up in his own bitterness and heartache, he had neglected the little boy who must have been missing his mother—

and, in so doing, had managed to destroy yet another area of trust.

Stepping inside, she shut the door behind her, leaning heavily against it and closing her eyes. Had she thought he might kiss her when he'd walked her to the moonlit cottage? Yes, she had. Of course she had. And even though she was starting to realise that she couldn't just keep being *available* whenever he snapped his fingers, she couldn't deny that she wanted him.

But she couldn't afford to behave like a passive puppet around this undeniably sexy and charismatic man, because she had come to America to make something of herself.

Not to get her heart broken.

CHAPTER EIGHT

THE KNOCK ON the cottage door sounded imperious and Lina felt a ripple of apprehension as she opened it to find Salvatore standing there, his muscular physique dominating the star-sprinkled sky behind him. And despite all her intentions to do otherwise, her heart began pounding frantically beneath the fancy fabric of her new dress.

It was a little under twenty-one hours since she'd last seen him. Twenty-one hours of trying to get to know some of the staff a bit better and asking Henry if there was anything she could do to help. Answer: no. In theory, twenty-one hours to build up some immunity against the charismatic tycoon. So why hadn't it worked? All the stern talking-tos in the world didn't seem to have changed her body's instant response to him, which was as powerful as ever.

It was as if she'd been stumbling around in the dark for a long, long time and Salvatore had suddenly become her bright, hard focus. Whenever he was around her skin felt sensitive—her limbs weightless and her senses soft. It was as if the very substance of her was capable of dissolving whenever he was in the vicinity.

He flicked his gaze over her and Lina wondered if she'd imagined the brief flash of disbelief in his eyes. She doubted it. Hadn't she experienced a similar reaction when she'd stood in front of the mirror a little earlier and surveyed the image reflected back at her? She shifted her weight on her stiletto heels because she was doing everything she could to avoid getting a blister this evening. She wasn't used to wearing an evening dress, nor shoes this high, and as she waited for Salvatore's verdict on her appearance her already jangled nerves felt even more frazzled. It was exactly as she'd thought. She looked a disaster. She was going to let him down. She would turn him into a laughing stock. 'You don't like it?' she said.

There was a pause as he continued to study her with an unhurried scrutiny which was making her nipples tighten.

'You look *different*,' he concluded eventually.

It wasn't the reply she'd wanted but maybe it was the only one which was appropriate. Because she felt different. She felt… Lina shook her head, but not a single hair of her perfectly coiffed head moved, thanks to the careful ministrations of the in-store hairdresser. It was difficult to describe exactly how she felt. Disorientated might be a good place to start. She'd never been to an upmarket department store before, nor been assigned a personal shopper—but apparently this was perfectly normal when you possessed the platinum store card to which she'd been given unfettered access by Salvatore di Luca. But nothing could have prepared Lina for the lavish interior of the sumptuous San Franciscan store, nor the expensive outfits of her fellow customers, who glided over the marble floors as if they had been shopping there all their lives. Never had she felt quite so poor or provincial.

Her relief at being given guidance by the personal shopper was tempered by the realisation of how many of the dresses—which all looked remarkably similar— she was expected to try on.

After countless hours she ended up with a simple floor-length robe in cobalt-blue—which wasn't her usual style *or* colour, but which she was assured made her look *stunning*. The shopper had arranged for a make-up artist to apply unfamiliar cosmetics to Lina's face and, in the brand-new and restrictive underwear which was containing her curves beneath the dress, she felt like a sausage about to burst out of its skin. She was dressed up like a painted doll in an expensive dress so narrowly cut that she had to take ridiculously tiny steps in order to walk.

Salvatore was still looking doubtful.

'I'm not sure it suits me,' she said, thinking that the same thing certainly couldn't be said for him. With a dark dinner jacket clinging to his broad shoulders and impeccably cut trousers emphasising the length of his powerful legs, the Sicilian tycoon looked cool, handsome and impossibly inaccessible.

'You *don't* like it,' she continued when he failed to contradict her, her hands falling to her sides and brushing impatiently against the heavy material.

'I didn't say that. You look chic and sophisticated,'

he amended smoothly. 'Wasn't that supposed to be the whole idea?'

'I guess so,' she said, but suddenly Lina felt like a fool. In principle the idea had seemed so simple—in reality, less so. Buy a poor girl a fancy dress and then take her to the ball. Why hadn't either of them stopped to consider that a Cinderella-type transformation might not work in her case, since the raw material was too rough to ever be properly smoothed off at the edges?

He glanced at his watch. 'Since we're already fashionably late and the car is outside, we really ought to leave. Are you ready?'

She shook her head. 'No. I've changed my mind. I don't want to go. You go without me. You'll have a better time.'

'Falling at the first hurdle?' His blue-hued gaze was direct and mocking. 'I thought you were made of stronger stuff than that, Lina. Or have you had a sudden personality change from the woman who begged me to take her to America so she could start a whole new life? Isn't this what you wanted?'

On one level she was aware he was goading her, but somehow it worked. Because what else was she going to do, if she pulled out? Hang around the estate all evening and risk annoying Henry, or ruffling the feathers of the chef, who wasn't expecting either of them to be home this evening?

'It's true. I can't back out now.' She drew in a deep breath. 'You're right.'

'I nearly always am.'

His arrogance almost made her smile and, ignoring the matching cobalt clutch bag which the in-store dresser had insisted on foisting upon her, Lina grabbed one of the embroidered velvet bags she'd brought with her from Sicily. With its distinctive beading and flouncy tassel, it was obviously home-made and didn't partic- ularly match the severe dress she was wearing. But at least it was *hers*—she had made it herself—and right now it felt like the only authentic part of her appearance.

The waiting limousine purred them through the steep streets until they reached a luxury hotel, not far from the glittering waterfront. Soaring up into the starry sky, its floodlit pillars reminded Lina of a Grecian temple she'd once seen in a book. Outside, thick scarlet ropes kept back hordes of onlookers brandishing cell phones, and the whole scene was illuminated by the bright flash of paparazzi cameras.

She could feel herself freezing, wondering how on earth she was going to get out of the car in front of such a massive crowd of people. Her legs were so wobbly that, once again, she was paralysed by fear. She shook her head. 'I can't go in there,' she husked.

'I thought we'd already had this conversation,' he said, not bothering to hide the boredom in his tone. 'Of course you can.'

'My heels are too high.'

'They look pretty good to me.' She saw the glint of something vaguely unsettling in his eyes as he fo- cussed his gaze on her footwear. 'You can hold onto me if you're worried about your balance.'

'Salvatore, you don't understand.' Lina clutched the

handle of her little velvet bag. 'I've never been anywhere like—'

'I understand better than you think.' He cut across her words. 'Don't you think I've experienced exactly what you're going through right now, Lina? Or do you imagine I was admitted to these types of glittering affairs with open arms? That society matrons didn't feel they had to lock up their daughters whenever I put in an appearance, while their billionaire husbands nervously watched their backs in case I deposited a blade in between their shoulder blades?'

'Did they?'

'Yes, they did. They saw me as a threat.' His mouth twisted into a grim smile. 'Because I was. My hunger to succeed made me ruthless and my determination to escape the shackles of my past drove me on. I wouldn't let anything stand in my way to get what I wanted.' There was a flicker of a pause. 'Can't you try and do the same?'

Lina shook her head. 'That's easy for you to say. People don't judge you on your appearance or whether you can walk straight in a pair of shoes so high you feel as if you're on stilts. You're a man.'

'Then don't *let* yourself be judged,' he urged. 'Wasn't that one of the reasons you left Sicily? Don't forget how much you wanted to get out of there. It's not going to work for you unless you're prepared to be brave.'

It was difficult to think of bravery when he was sitting so close to her, making things more complicated than they needed to be. She thought how much simpler it would be if she hadn't had sex with him. Wouldn't that have made it easier to concentrate on what lay ahead, rather than on the tingling sensation that his hard thigh was mere millimetres away from hers?

'Maybe I should just have stayed where I was in Caltarina and ridden out the storm,' she said.

'And done what? Carried on slaving away doing something you didn't really like, for a woman who took you for granted? Squandering your youth and your beauty while the years passed you by?' Suddenly he put his hand on her forearm, but with the impersonal touch of a dentist patting a child's arm and reassuring them that it wasn't going to hurt. 'You don't have to do that any more, Lina. You have a chance to make something of yourself here. A career, most certainly, if you're prepared to work. And a husband, perhaps, in time. Isn't that what most women of your age want? Some all-American boy who can provide you with the white picket fence and roses round the door.'

Lina could tell he was trying to reassure her and supposed she should feel grateful for that, but the stupid thing was that his words *hurt*. They hurt far more than they should have done. She turned her head to stare fixedly out of the window, blinking furiously, terrified by the sudden threat of incipient tears. How dared he talk so casually about the husband she might or might not one day have, as if he didn't care about her? To paint a picture of a future which most definitely didn't include him?

Because he doesn't care.

He'd made that clear. Right from the start.

He had told her very definitely she was not what he

was looking for. That no woman could give him what he wanted other than sex. So maybe it was time she started believing him.

She drew in a deep breath. 'Okay. You're right. Let's go in. I'm ready now.'

'Take my arm.'

She hesitated. 'I'm not—'

'Take it,' he interrupted impatiently. 'Anything is preferable to spending the night in the emergency department if you're genuinely afraid of tripping over on those killer heels.'

That *did* make her smile, and she nodded. 'Okay. Thanks.'

But Salvatore could feel the nervous pressure of her fingers as they ascended the marble stairs leading into the famous Westchester Hotel, in a flurry of flashbulbs. He didn't know why she was so worried about her appearance, not when she looked so arresting. In fact, he'd barely recognised her, and not just because her hair had been intricately fashioned on top of her head, drawing his attention to her delicate profile and the graceful line of her neck. He'd found himself thinking that the style was light years away from the billowing curls which had flowed from beneath her dusty crash helmet as she had ridden away in the Sicilian sunshine. That young woman had been replaced by a sophisticated socialite with darkened lashes and provocatively gleaming lips. He'd never seen her wearing make-up before, just as he'd never seen her voluptuous body sculpted in a way which seemed to have made her exceptional curves disappear. She no longer looked like the vibrant woman he had seduced—more like an identikit version of the type of partner who usually graced his arm.

Did that make her more or less desirable? He couldn't quite decide. It certainly made her seem more...*manageable*.

He could hear the ripple of interest from the milling crowd as they entered the ballroom and every head in the place turned to look at them, though that came as no surprise. His appearance at this kind of events always excited fascination—though never more so than when he had a new woman in tow. The press were always trying to marry him off—as were the matrons who had once spent so much time trying to shield their daughters from him. Yet there hadn't been a woman on his arm for a long time. There had been speculation that his heart had been broken or that he was conducting an affair with a married woman, but neither of these were true.

The reason for his lack of a partner he put down to a growing cynicism about the way his fortune impacted on those around him, especially women. It had at first made him feel deeply uncomfortable, and then to grow exceedingly bored by the predictability of it all. He'd discovered that as his wealth grew, so his lovers had started going out of their way to accommodate him. To be understanding and undemanding. They made sure they were up to date on current affairs and knew a healthy amount about his various businesses. He'd noticed too that they became increasingly daring in the bedroom—or out of it. No matter how high-powered their working lives, at the end of the day they'd all seemed cast from the same mould. They suggested newfound erotic diversions alongside their determination to craft the perfect *mille-feuille* pastry, as if by combining all these attributes and presenting them to him in a sleek and very sophisticated package it would make them the perfect wife material.

But he wasn't looking for a wife. He never had been. To him, marriage had always seemed something to avoid. And even though some of his best friends had recently succumbed—Lucas Conway and Matteo Valenti being two cases in point—Salvatore's fixed stance on matrimony hadn't altered. He suspected that his distrust of women had been the reason why he'd been so susceptible to a brief fling with someone like Lina—a simple country girl who seemed to possess no airs or graces. That night with her had been the first time in a long time that he'd felt control slipping away, and it had disturbed him. And he had succumbed to her again during the flight from Sicily, despite his determination to resist her.

But he had clawed back that temporary loss of control, hadn't he? He hadn't kissed her after dinner last night, despite his overwhelming desire to do so. He had concluded that maybe he would wait a little longer before he made love to her again, but when he'd called for her tonight and seen her dressed up and ready to go out, his resolve had wavered, big-time.

He wanted her.

He wanted her now.

'Salvatore?'

Lina's soft Sicilian accent broke into his thoughts and Salvatore focussed his attention on the fractured light from one of the chandeliers which was painting rainbow hues over the dark coils of her hair.

'What?'

'Is that Siena Simon over there?'

He glanced across the ballroom in the direction of her gaze, where a glamorous woman in a pale dress was surrounded by an adoring group of younger men. 'Yes,' he said absently. 'What of it?'

'Gosh.' Lina felt a flare of disbelief as Salvatore confirmed that one unbelievable fact—because the world-famous American dress designer had long been a hero of hers. Everyone in Sicily went wild for SiSi clothes, though not many people could afford to buy the real thing. 'I'd love to meet her.'

Salvatore flickered her a brief smile. 'Then why don't you go up and say hello?' he suggested softly.

'I can't just walk over there and introduce myself!'

'Why not? You can do anything you set your heart on. It's called networking and it's what you have to do if you want to get on in the big city. Go on.'

His tone was weirdly encouraging but Lina's heart was in her mouth as she walked across the ballroom and hovered nervously on the edge of the circle until one of the flamboyant young men noticed her and drew her in. And that was when she was introduced to Siena Simon. Clad in a sculpted cream gown, the international designer was gracious as she extended her hand, though her gaze kept flickering to the little velvet bag which was dangling from Lina's arm. And even though Lina wasn't sure if it was a good idea, she found herself confiding that SiSi clothes were the most popular rip-offs on Sicilian market stalls, and Siena actually laughed.

'That's good to know,' she murmured, in her soft American drawl. 'And don't they say that imitation is the best form of flattery?'

After that, her confidence boosted, Lina met loads of people. To her surprise, the evening passed in a blur of chatter, champagne and a very fancy dinner—during which she was seated between an Australian entrepreneur and an actor called Sean MacCormack, who was apparently a big star on a daytime soap she'd never even heard of. At first she was so nervous she could barely get a word out and terrified that her Sicilian accent would make her difficult to understand. But both men were absolutely charming, and Sean told her she was welcome to go and watch him filming any time she wanted. When dinner ended, the band began to strike up a tune at the far end of the ballroom and Lina's heart gave a predictable punch of excitement when Salvatore returned to her side.

'Can we go now?' she asked him.

He seemed surprised. 'Are you sure? The dancing is about to start.'

'I know that.'

'So let's dance.'

'I thought you'd already said you didn't want to spend the night in the emergency department. I might stab your foot with my heel.'

'That's a risk I'm prepared to take.'

She wondered if his words were intended to be provocative and Lina was unbearably tempted to take him up on his offer, but what would be the point? He'd already kept his distance from her since their intimacy on the flight and had made it clear that was the way he wanted it to stay. And deep down she was sensible enough to know that was the right decision, even if every pore of her body was desperate to feel his fingers and lips on her again.

But dancing with him would be insane—an exquisite kind of torture to be held in his arms in public. So close and yet not close at all. Their bodies touching and tantalising, reminding her of things she was trying very hard to forget. And wasn't she getting a little tired of the conflicting messages he kept sending out to her? 'I'd rather not,' she said. 'If you wouldn't mind. My feet really are killing me.'

He looked *shocked*. There was no other word for it. As if no woman in her right mind would have turned down such an opportunity and Lina experienced a fleeting feeling of triumph of having asserted herself as they left the crowded ballroom.

But her satisfaction only lasted as long as it took to get in the waiting car, when she suddenly found herself thinking about all the balls Salvatore would go to without her and she got an odd, twisty kind of feeling in her stomach. Did all women feel this powerfully connected to the man they had given their virginity to, she wondered—as if they were joined by some invisible life force?

In the dim light of the limousine she was having to avert her gaze from the sculpted perfection of his profile and suddenly she felt a great rush of unwanted longing.

Stop it, she thought. *Just stop it.*

'So, did you find the evening helpful?'

His question broke into the silence and Lina nodded, pleased to have some respite from the muddle of her emotions. She nodded. 'Very helpful. Siena was really interested in my handbag.'

'Your handbag?'

She held the tasselled velvet bag aloft, although all you could really see was the glitter of the beads and the shimmer of the tassel. 'This. She asked where I'd got it from and I told her I'd made it myself. She wants me to call into her studio tomorrow. Says she might be able to do something for me.'

'Wow,' he said softly. 'That is some result.'

Resisting the desire to bask with pleasure beneath his obvious approval, Lina gave another brief nod. 'Possibly. But I'm not going to build my hopes up until I've spoken to her.'

'Very wise.'

'Yes.' Deliberately, she averted her gaze from him to stare fixedly out of the window as the San Franciscan night flashed past.

Salvatore observed her stiff shoulders and off-putting body language as she sat beside him and told himself he should be grateful she was sending out such an offputting subliminal message because, in theory, that should make it easier for him to resist her. But all he could think of was the growing desire which had been plaguing him with infuriating persistence all evening. He'd told himself she was still off-limits. That putting space between them for a while was necessary—for her sake mostly, so she didn't start having unrealistic expectations. And for his own sake, too—to reassure himself that he could take her, or leave her, as he did all women.

But somehow the chic sophistication of her appearance was skewing his thoughts and making him rethink his decision. Because which of them was benefiting by his unasked-for restraint? Not him, certainly—and not her either, he suspected. Suddenly he wanted to peel off that armour-plated dress and feast on the soft flesh beneath. He wanted to see her writhing helplessly in his arms just like she'd done before.

'Lina,' he said softly as she turned her head to look at him. 'Do you have any idea how much I want to kiss you?'

He heard the shuddered intake of her breath. 'I got... I got the distinct impression that was something you definitely *didn't* want,' she managed, as if the words had cost her a lot to say.

And something about her candour made him answer in kind. 'I'm fighting it,' he admitted huskily. 'And it's a battle I seem to be losing right now.'

Her lips parted in silent invitation and he saw them tremble as he reached across to trace their sensual curve with the pad of his thumb. And when he replaced his thumb with the slow brush of his mouth, he could feel the instant jerk of lust—as powerful as if he were a teenager who'd just discovered sex. It was the slowest kiss in the world and it was also the hottest. Before too long she was clawing at his shoulders and he was pushing her back against the seat, his hands all over the rich satin of her gown. He could hear her murmured little moans urging him on and he wanted to touch her bare skin. He wanted to do that so badly. But the dress was stretched tightly across her thighs and what he emphatically did *not* want was an undignified struggle.

'I have no intention of doing it in the car,' he said evenly. 'Even if you didn't happen to be wearing the world's most constricting dress.'

'I *knew* you didn't like it.'

'I don't give a damn about your dress, other than the fact it's in the way. It needs to be removed as quickly as possible and I think that could best be done in the comfort of my bedroom.' He paused. 'Unless you have a better idea?'

He could see the faint doubts which drifted across her face, like the flashes of gold from the passing streetlights. He could banish those doubts by telling her stuff she wanted to hear. Weasel words and soft enticements. Things he didn't mean. Things he could never mean. But he had never made false promises to get a woman in his bed and he never would. Either she accepted him for the man he was, or she got nothing.

She was sitting perfectly still and the intricate confection of her dark hair made her look like a cool and beautiful stranger. 'I can't think of one,' she said, in a whisper.

As the car swung in through the electric gates and security lights illuminated the grounds, Salvatore felt the heavy beat of anticipation. The house was quiet as he took Lina up to his private suite, as he had taken women there many times before, but never had he felt this hungry. He offered her a drink but when she refused he was glad, leading her straight into the bedroom, taking the small velvet bag from her hands and placing it on a nearby chair.

He bent his head, kissed her and began to undress her, sliding down the zip of the fitted dress with a little difficulty until the rich fabric concertinaed to the ground, leaving her wearing underwear which was almost certainly new. Salvatore's eyes narrowed. The delicate bra and matching thong panties undoubtedly made the most of her curves—so why had he started to ache with something which felt like nostalgia for the no-nonsense white knickers he had encountered on the plane?

Very soon she was completely naked and he removed the last of the pins from her hair. And as her black curls tumbled free, he was filled with a rush of lust so pure and so instant that he made a small growling sound beneath his breath.

'You are so beautiful,' he rasped.

'I'm… I'm not.'

'Believe me, you are.' And she was. Because now she looked like Lina again. Like the earthy Sicilian beauty who had given him her innocence. Her firm curves were outlined against his white sheets and her nipples were thrusting little points of deep rose, just begging for his lips to kiss them again. She was bending her knees and her soft fleshy thighs were parting and suddenly Salvatore found himself mesmerised by the dark triangular blur at their apex, as if he'd never seen a naked woman before.

A shimmer of resentment heated his blood as he tore off his own clothes, in between giving her one hard kiss after another, because his hands were shaking like a drunk's and he had drunk nothing stronger than water all evening. But all that resentment had melted away by the time he was straddling her on the bed, watching her awe-struck face as he made that first sweet thrust. And soon after that, he was wondering if he was ever going to be able to stop coming as he bit back a word which was rushing from the very depths of his lungs, a word which might just have been her name.

CHAPTER NINE

IT WAS THE most beautiful view she had ever seen.

From the comfort of Salvatore's king-sized bed, Lina stared out at the bright blue of the distant bay. Beneath the fine linen sheets she was completely naked and her cheeks grew warm as she remembered what Salvatore had said just before he'd left for the office at some unspeakable hour this morning, when he had observed her silently watching him from her prone position.

'That was fantastic.' His gaze had met hers in the reflection of the mirror as he knotted his silk tie.

'Yes.' Her voice had faltered and it was only afterwards that she realised how servile she must have sounded. 'Not that I've got anything to compare it with, of course, but I—'

'Believe me, Lina, it *was* amazing,' he had interrupted, almost as if having to make the admission wasn't something he particularly relished. He had glanced down at his watch with the relief of someone lost at sea who had suddenly spotted a lifeboat. 'I really have to go,' he'd said.

His goodbye kiss had been brief, almost perfunctory—

as if he couldn't wait to get away from her. As if daylight had destroyed the potent alchemy of what had taken place between them during the night, when her body had felt as if it were on fire every time he'd touched her.

A glance at her phone reminded her she had an appointment with Siena Simon, who'd told her to call by the store at noon. But it wasn't until she had got out of bed that Lina realised her predicament. Her expensive dress lay discarded on the floor—dropped at the exact spot where Salvatore had removed it from her quivering body when they'd returned from the ball. Exquisite lingerie lay scattered alongside the towering pair of shoes she'd been so eager to kick off. She was marooned in Salvatore di Luca's bedroom with nothing suitable to wear back to her little cottage and through a house which would probably be crawling with staff.

She picked up the cobalt evening dress and quickly put it down again. No way could she wear *that* in the brightness of the morning. Distractedly, she looked around, thinking maybe she could borrow something of Salvatore's, and a quick search soon produced a pair of joggers and a faded T-shirt, which carried the name of some band she'd never heard of. The outfit was way too big but at least it was anonymous and Lina rolled up the joggers before quickly gathering together her clothes and tucking them under her arm.

Quietly opening the bedroom door, she cocked her head to listen. The distant hum of the vacuum cleaner sounded a long way off and, judging herself safe, she set off along the corridor, her bare feet making no sound on the bleached wooden floor. She had almost reached the front door when a perfectly modulated English voice almost made her drop her clothes.

'Good morning, Miss Vitale.'

Composing her face into a fixed smile, Lina turned round to see Henry who was wearing a pair of striped grey trousers and what looked like a black tail-coat, and, not for the first time, thought how uncomfortably *hot* it must be if you were a butler.

'Good morning, Henry.'

'Will you be requiring breakfast? Chef has made fresh pastries and kedgeree and...'

He paused, delicately, and despite Lina's total lack of experience at handling this type of situation she somehow knew exactly what he meant.

Did the chef usually provide his boss's lovers with a sumptuous breakfast in one of the two dining rooms, or was it ever served on the terrace?

She gave a weak smile. 'I'm fine, thanks. I'll have something back at the cottage.'

'If you're sure.'

'Quite sure.' She pulled her shoulders back. 'Thank you, Henry.'

'Very good, Miss Vitale.'

Lina made her way through the gardens, where legions of staff were pruning, spraying and mowing various patches of lawn. She could see them turning to watch her as she passed and it struck her how unfair this situation was. You could count on one hand the number of times she'd spent the night with a man, yet this was the second time she'd had to endure a humiliating walk of shame next morning.

But she had nothing to be ashamed of. She might not have Salvatore's social status or wealth, but last night she'd truly felt as if they had come together as equals. He had trembled when he'd touched her. He had moaned almost helplessly as he had entered her. And when, afterwards, she had whispered her lips over his chest to cover it with tiny, tentative kisses—he had given a low rumble of a laugh and tangled his fingers in her curls and told her she was beautiful. And just like last time he'd said it, he had made her *feel* beautiful.

Back in her little cottage, she quickly showered and dressed and fished out the three handmade bags she'd brought with her from Sicily, putting them carefully in a canvas tote. Then she let herself out of the cottage and, with the aid of her cell phone, set off to walk downtown to Siena Simon's store.

She found it with pleasing ease—a large double-fronted building, situated in a pretty tree-lined street. Inside, it was vast and cleverly lit, showcasing some of the designer's iconic designs, all of them worn by impossibly tall and skinny mannequins. Scattered throughout the room on racks and glass shelves of different heights were handmade shoes and exquisite shoals of jewellery. Everything gave off a costly patina and, in her simple cotton dress, Lina felt self-conscious as a beautiful assistant sashayed towards her, a slightly bemused smile on her face—as if doubtful whether Lina was a bona-fide customer. Which, of course, she wasn't.

'May I help you?'

'I hope so. I'm looking for Siena Simon.'

The assistant's smile became even more doubtful. 'Do you have an appointment?'

'Well, I met her at a ball last night and she—'

'It's okay, Tiffany.' The drawled words were followed by the appearance of a figure at the back of the store, and suddenly there was Siena Simon dressed in her trademark cream, with a pair of gravity-defying shoes and a choker of pearls at her throat as big as gulls' eggs. 'I asked Nicolina to call by today,' she said, and then smiled. 'Good to see you again, Nicolina. Did you bring any more of your work with you?'

Rather self-consciously, Lina held up the canvas bag containing her totes. 'They're all in here.'

'Good. Why don't you come on through to my office and I'll have Allegra fix us some coffee?'

Lina nodded. 'Sure.'

The interview which followed was daunting and yet, in a funny kind of way, it was also one of the most rewarding things which had ever happened to her, and when Lina emerged just under an hour later, it was with a feeling of excitement bubbling away inside her. She'd almost dropped to the floor when Siena had informed her just how much she could charge for one of Lina's little handbags and had instantly agreed to make as many of them as possible. She had a job—of sorts. Wasn't this the first step on the road to independence?

She wondered what to do next, whether to find herself a sandwich for lunch, or try to hunt down a second-hand sewing machine. She had just decided that the latter option would be the most sensible, when she noticed a tall and powerful man who was walking purposefully along the street.

In her direction.

He was instantly recognisable on so many levels—visual, visceral and emotional. Lina's heart squeezed as her eyes feasted themselves on the blue-black gleam of his hair and the coiled strength of his muscular physique. She had been trying not to think about him all morning. Trying to concentrate on work and ambition and thoughts of the future and wondering what an independent life would look like. But now that she'd seen him, all those thoughts seemed to crumble away because that was the effect of the strange power he had over her. Lina felt her stomach dissolve as he reached her and for a moment or two it felt as if she'd forgotten how to speak.

'Salvatore.' She licked her lips like a starving cat which had just spotted food. 'This...this is a surprise.'

'I came to meet you.'

'But you didn't know where I'd be.'

'Obviously, I did, otherwise I wouldn't be here.' His blue gaze mocked her. 'You told me you were going for an interview with Siena—remember?'

Of course she remembered, she was just surprised he had—because hadn't he seemed more concerned with plunging into her body for the umpteenth time, rather than hearing about her plans for the following day? She looked at him in confusion. 'But I still don't understand why you're here.'

Salvatore wasn't quite sure about that himself—and felt a flicker of irritation that she'd been gauche enough to draw his attention to it. Because hadn't the voice of reason warned him against coming here, telling himself to leave it until the end of the day, at least. Telling himself that a few hours' grace would give him time to untangle himself from the potency of the spell she seemed to have cast over him. And then he'd thought: what the hell? He wanted to have sex with her again and as soon as possible—and judging by the smoky darkening of her eyes, she was feeling it too. 'I thought we could have lunch.'

'Lunch?'

'There's no need to make it sound as if I've made an indecent suggestion. Though I'm perfectly prepared to do that afterwards,' he murmured. 'And you're really going to need to stop blushing like that, Lina.'

'I can't help it,' she whispered. 'And I haven't got time for lunch. I have to get hold of a sewing machine.'

'You can do that later,' he said firmly. 'Just get in the car.'

At last it seemed to dawn on her that he wasn't taking no for an answer, but her stumbling reluctance was surprisingly charming, and as he lifted his hand to summon his car, he could feel lust spearing through him like a hard and relentless arrow. And just as soon as the vehicle moved away, he pulled her into his arms and started to kiss her, her squirming excitement turning him on even more.

He had intended the kiss to be hard and swift—a possessive declaration of his intention to seduce her as soon as they'd eaten. But instead it became a deep and drugging interaction which dragged him down into some dark and silken place, and maybe her hungry response had a lot to do with that. As she curled her fingers around his neck and pressed her breasts against him, his passion for her combusted. His heart was pounding as he realised they had approximately twelve minutes until they reached the restaurant. Time enough for what he wanted. He could slip his hand beneath the hem of her sundress and quickly bring her to a shuddering orgasm before unzipping himself so that she could take him in her mouth as she had done so exquisitely last night. He could tell the driver to keep circling the block until he tapped on the window. It wouldn't be the first time he had done it.

But somehow, with Lina, it didn't seem *appropriate*— and although it was the most difficult thing he'd ever had to resist, he drew away from her and tersely instructed her to smooth down her ruffled hair. As the car drew up near the Embarcadero, he found himself perplexed by his own behaviour, but reassured himself that the wait would be worth it—and a demonstration of his rigid control would not go amiss.

The restaurant was crowded and Lina's predictable delight on her first sight of the iconic bridge view was pleasing, though she seemed oblivious to the fact that people were turning their heads To look at her, despite the many society beauties who were dotted around the place. Would it have surprised her to know that her naturalness was like a breath of fresh air in the rarefied atmosphere of this famous city eatery? he wondered.

Soon they were seated at his usual table, with crisp linen, crystal and silver laid out before them, as waiters and sommeliers clustered around them. Salvatore ordered lobster and salad, a bottle of cold water and a dish of olives, before leaning back in his chair to study her.

'It sounds like your interview with Siena went well,' he observed.

'I think so.' She hesitated as she picked up her napkin and shook it out. 'She asked me lots of questions. How well I knew you. How long I was planning on staying in the city. That sort of thing.'

'I guess she wants to be sure you'll stick around if she's planning on giving you work.'

'I guess.' She hesitated. 'She seemed particularly interested in the fact that I was living with you.'

He frowned. 'But you made it clear that we're not actually living together?'

'Of course I did,' she said, and hesitated again. 'It just made me wonder…'

His gaze bored into her. 'What did it make you wonder, Lina?'

She had started pleating the edge of her napkin now, as if unable to keep her fingers still.

'If you'd ever been in a relationship with her.'

'No. I've never been in a relationship with Siena,' he said slowly. 'Would it bother you if I had?'

Abruptly, she stopped pleating and looked up. 'It's nothing to do with me who you've had a relationship with.'

'So you wouldn't mind if I brought a woman back to the house?'

'Of course I wouldn't.'

'Liar,' he said softly.

Lina stared at him, shaking out her napkin in an attempt to remove the pleats. She had been finding the whole situation daunting, even before he'd said that. The fancy restaurant with a terrifying amount of cutlery. The other diners, who were watching them while pretending not to—or, rather, watching *him*. The realisation that once again they had slept together last night and indulged in all kinds of delicious intimacies. And now he had accused her of lying. 'Excuse me?'

'It *would* bother you, Lina. It's bothering you right now just to think about it—it's written all over your face. But that's okay. It's perfectly normal to feel sexual jealousy in a situation like ours.'

She told herself to leave it. That his use of the word 'ours' was not meant to be inclusive and it certainly wasn't meant to give her hope—and bearing in mind how arrogant he could be, she was amazed that she even *wanted* to be hopeful where Salvatore di Luca was concerned. But wasn't it funny how all the reasoning in the world didn't stop you yearning for something you knew was ultimately futile, so that you came out and asked the question anyway? 'And what exactly is our…situation?'

'Difficult to define,' he said, his blue gaze splintering through her. 'I wasn't intending for us to continue to be lovers once you came to America. I thought it was better if our relationship became platonic since you were going to be living on my property, but that clearly hasn't been the case.'

Lina told herself to leave this one, too. To maybe change the subject and ask him about that woman on the far side of the restaurant who was clearly trying to catch his eye. But the newly liberated Nicolina Vitale wasn't intending to spend the rest of her life being a moral coward by avoiding subjects which had the potential to be tricky, was she? Hadn't she done that too often in the past, with her mother? Played safe to keep the peace—and look where that had got her.

Last night in bed, she had felt like Salvatore's equal—and wouldn't someone who was truly equal refuse to be a coward and ask the difficult questions, questions that previously she wouldn't dare ask, just in case she didn't like the answers? She lifted her water glass and took a sip from it. 'Why?'

He said nothing more until the waiter had placed the food in front of them and, although he gestured for her to help herself, Lina didn't move.

'I think we both know the answer to that. Because it's pretty obvious to me, at least, that I can't seem to resist you, despite all my best intentions.'

'Okay...' she said uncertainly, wondering why his words sounded more like an insult than a compliment.

'But you're worlds away from my usual kind of partner, Lina.'

Lina had been about to help herself to a portion of avocado, but now she put the serving spoon down, strangely repulsed by the sight of all that glistening green flesh. 'And what's your usual kind of partner?'

He picked out every word with forensic care. 'Women who know the score. Who understand the way I operate.' His blue eyes darkened, like sudden storm clouds appearing on a summer's day. 'And if we are to continue like this as lovers, you need to know the score too. I can offer you fidelity and generosity for as long as we're together, but commitment is a non-starter. So if you think this is going to end with a golden band gleaming on your finger, then it's over as of now.'

It took Lina a moment to realise what he meant. 'And you think all women want to marry you—is that what you're trying to say?'

'In my experience, yes.'

Lina shook her head because his poise was breathtaking, as was his cool arrogance—unless he was simply telling her the facts as he saw them. But maybe it didn't matter what motivated his words, she either agreed to his terms, or he walked. He would and could do that, she realised. Despite all the push-me, pull-me stuff he'd been doing these past few days—if he thought she was getting serious, she wouldn't see him for dust. Even if he missed the sex, it wouldn't be for long. You only had to look at the expressions of some of the women in this restaurant to know that here was a man who was universally lusted after. He would soon replace her with someone else, someone who was more his 'type'.

And Lina wasn't ready to let that happen. Not yet. She wasn't ready to turn her back on this incredible awakening, because of some kind of misguided idea that deeper emotions had to be involved. You didn't have to be in love to do what they were doing. Those kinds of beliefs belonged in storybooks, or within the repressed confines of the tiny village into which she had been born. Hadn't she come to America to shake off those old-fashioned assumptions?

'Well, I don't want to marry you,' she said, making sure she kept her voice very quiet in case someone overheard and thought he was actually *proposing* to her. 'That's not the reason I'm here. I told you back in Sicily that I had dreams and they haven't gone away. And Siena has shown me that I might be able to make those dreams a reality. I'm never going to conquer the world, I'm sensible enough to realise that, but if I can make a decent living for myself, then I'll be satisfied.'

She could see the sudden hard burn of his eyes. The sudden tightening of his lips. 'I'm glad we understand each other, Lina,' he said softly, casting a rueful glance down at the untouched food in front of them, before lifting his charged blue gaze to her. 'And since you've brought up the subject of satisfaction, let's take it one step further. It doesn't look as if either of us are going to do this meal justice—so what do you say we get out of here so that we can spend the rest of the afternoon in bed?'

Lina's heart was thumping as she stared back at him across the table. He had suggested going back to have sex as coolly as if he were calling for the bill, and part of her wanted to do that, despite the callous things he'd said. Because now she knew something about his background, didn't that make his cynicism more understandable? He'd been lied to and deserted at an impressionable age by his mother—the one person he should have been able to rely on above all others. Why *wouldn't* he develop an aversion to close relationships after an experience like that? Then he had grown spectacularly successful and perhaps been targeted as much for his wealth as his rugged beauty, though she would have desired him just as much if he'd been a poor fisherman, like his father. And wasn't there a part of her which wished he were? That he came unencumbered, without all the homes and staff and fancy aeroplanes.

But Salvatore wasn't looking for understanding or compassion. His needs were simply physical and Lina needed to cultivate a similar mindset if she wanted this to continue. And she did. Why let her own emotional vulnerability spoil her very first sexual relationship?

But even so...

He needed to understand that from now on she wouldn't be a pushover. That he couldn't just click his fingers to have Lina Vitale fall in with his plans. That he needed to respect her as well as desire her.

'Tempting,' she said. 'But I can't really afford the time right now.'

She saw his look of surprise.

'You're kidding?'

Lina shook her head. 'I told you, I have a sewing machine to buy and materials I need to order so that I can make my handbags. I promised Siena I'd have three prototypes with her as soon as possible so I need to get on with that.' Her smile was serene but maybe that was because her words were making her feel positively *empowered*. 'And since you know the city better than I do, perhaps you could take me shopping?'

CHAPTER TEN

A RED LIGHT on Salvatore's desk was flashing and the disembodied voice of his assistant echoed around the vast office.

'Miss Vitale on three, Salvatore. Are you in, or out?'

It was a question his assistant had asked him many times in the past when a woman had called, and his answer would inevitably provide some clue about the state of whatever relationship he happened to be in. During those early days of heady sex, he was usually indulgent if a lover rang him at the office, although he never encouraged it. A couple of weeks in and he was prepared to be tolerant, but by the one-month mark he was inevitably irritated if he was disturbed—because by that stage there seemed little to say to a woman which couldn't wait until later.

Yet with Lina it seemed to be different. It had been different from the start—and all the times in between. Like that surreal afternoon when she'd turned down the opportunity to go to bed with him—and had him accompanying her to bizarre fabric wholesalers, in areas of the city he hadn't even realised *existed*.

And she had been true to her word about working hard. Each day she spent working in her little cottage before emerging blinking into the light like a little animal which had been underground, her eyes tired from sewing but with a look of immense satisfaction on her face as she sewed handbag after handbag.

Her hand-crafted wares had been snapped up by Siena Simon and, after a little questioning on his part— for Lina was nothing if not modest—he'd discovered they were creating something of a buzz, not just in San Francisco, but beyond.

Salvatore had been quietly impressed with her endeavours, for there had only ever been one other woman he'd shared a living space with before Lina, and she couldn't have been more different from his idle, entitled mother.

He was just perplexed that he seemed content spending more time with her than was usual with a woman. Was it because she was living on his property that he found himself unable to keep her at his preferred emotional distance? Or because she spoke to him exclusively in Sicilian dialect—a language which nobody else in his orbit understood? Their shared tongue locked them both in a private world which sometimes felt achingly familiar, yet, at others, darkly claustrophobic. He had expected to be bored with her by now. For the allure of the simple country girl to have become tarnished by exposure to the bright lights of the city, but to his surprise—though it hadn't been a particularly welcome one—that hadn't happened.

And his thoughts were growing increasingly troubled.

Because hadn't he become faintly *obsessed* with the Sicilian dressmaker? Hadn't he found himself endlessly fascinated by the way she slowly brushed those waist-length black curls, knowing he was watching her? Her eyes would sometimes meet his with the faintest hint of mockery lurking in their bourbon depths, as if in silent acknowledgement of his vehement demand that she never wear her hair up again.

Hadn't he broken the rule of a lifetime and taken her to every damned tourist destination in town, watching almost indulgently while she cooed her way through each tour with breathless delight? And hadn't her genuine enjoyment of San Francisco's famous sights made him view his adopted city with a different, less cynical eye? Yet most of all, he relished those intimate moments when they were alone together and he could observe her soft wonder as he pleasured her. She never shut her eyes when he was inside her. That smoky bourbon gaze was always fixed unwavering on his. Sometimes the intimacy of that made him uncomfortable—sometimes not. All he knew was that her voluptuous body pleased him immensely, as did her generous nature. She never used sex as a weapon, or a bargaining tool as had happened in the past. In fact, she never asked him for anything. There had been no 'casual' references to diamonds or pearls. She hadn't even hinted that she might like to use one of his cars. For a man who was forever being tapped for money, this was a first.

But Salvatore was discovering disturbing parallels between himself and his father. Because his father had been obsessed with his wife, hadn't he? He'd let his hunger for her rule his life. And that had been his downfall. It had taken Salvatore a long time to realise why his mother had been so cruel to her husband, in a way which had impacted so negatively on all their lives. It had taken adulthood and his restless flight to America before he was able to work it out for himself, through his own relationships. Only then was he able to understand the inevitable power struggle which existed between a man and a woman, and how finely balanced it was. He'd discovered that some women despised men who loved too much and craved the ones who did not love at all. He'd had that demonstrated over and over again. His emotional indifference seemed to have inspired slavish adoration from the opposite sex. Or perhaps he was simply seen as a challenge. As a prize to be won.

Men who loved made themselves vulnerable, he realised.

And he was never going to be vulnerable again.

Wasn't it time he proved that—not just to Lina, but to himself?

'Salvatore?' His assistant's voice broke into his reverie. 'Are you still there? Do you want me to put Miss Vitale through, or shall I tell her you're in a meeting?'

Salvatore's mouth tightened. And wasn't it *insane* how disloyal it felt—to contemplate colluding with his assistant to tell a blatant untruth to Lina? She had never rung him at the office before, had she? What if she was in some kind of trouble—what if she needed his help? 'Put her through,' he gritted out.

'Salvatore?' Lina came on the line and just the way

she said his name was like having cool water sprinkled on a heated brow.

'Is something wrong?' he demanded.

'No, nothing's wrong.'

Relief gave way to desire and he could feel it coursing through his veins, but infinitely more disturbing was the sudden race of his heart in response to her soft voice. 'Then why are you calling me at the office?' he growled. 'I'm working.'

'Yes. I know that.'

He could hear the sudden insecurity which edged her words but forced himself not to react to it. Because she needed to know that this kind of behaviour was a sure-fire way to hasten the end of their relationship, and he wasn't quite ready for it to end. Not yet. 'What can I do for you, Lina?'

'I just wondered what time you would be home.'

It was the most mundane of questions and it filled Salvatore with a cold dread because it embodied the kind of cloying domesticity he had spent his life avoiding. 'You called me to ask me that?' he questioned, not bothering to hide the faint incredulity in his voice. 'I'll be home before seven, same as always. Why do you need to know?'

'It doesn't matter,' she answered hurriedly. 'I'll see you later.'

Lina replaced the telephone with nervous fingers as she tried to block out Salvatore's terse response to her question, wondering why he had gone so cold on her. Maybe she shouldn't have rung him at the office, but surely it was okay just this once—when she was preparing a surprise for him. And she *wanted* to surprise him, as well as celebrate her own good news. To give something back. Because hadn't he been incredibly generous towards her? Hadn't he taken her in against his better judgement and given her a roof over her head, thus allowing her to find her feet? Yes, she had promised to pay him back—and she would—but that was going to take time.

She began to crack eggs into the flour and to mix them together, the rhythmical movement reminding her of a thousand pasta dishes she'd made back home. But these days she felt completely different from the woman who had endured that miserable existence. At first she hadn't been able to believe that life could be like this—that every day could feel special—and she knew much of that was down to Salvatore. It had been hard to get her head around the fact that someone could make you feel funny and sexy and desirable, without even really trying.

Sometimes he would turn up at her cottage if he finished work early, looking utterly irresistible in his suit, his immaculate appearance marred only by the loosening of his tie, which had the effect of making him appear rakish. And even though she would remind him that they weren't supposed to be seeing each other until later, she would invite him in, as casually as if he were paying nothing more than a social call, just in case one of his staff happened to be passing. But the moment the door had closed behind him, she would be pushed up against the wall while he kissed her as if he were trying to suck all the breath out of her lungs and she'd be tearing at his clothes like a wild thing. Sometimes they didn't even make it as far as the bed. It was electric between them. It always had been— he'd told her that more than once. Lina could feel the sudden rush of warmth to her cheeks and wondered if every woman felt like this in the early stages of a rela- tionship. As if you'd discovered a new kind of power, but, weirdly, as if you'd lost a different kind of power in the process.

Because lately it hadn't been all roses and moonlight and she'd been plagued by doubts, which she couldn't seem to push away, no matter how hard she tried. Nag- ging doubts which lurked in the shadows of her mind, just waiting to spring on you when you least expected them. She'd started wondering if she had allowed herself to become a victim of her own self-deception.

She'd thought…

What?

That she could neatly compartmentalise her life, so none of the edges would overlap? That she could sew all day and deliver her little handbags to Siena's store, where later they would appear on the arm of a man- nequin, or on one of the tables or glass shelves, all at an eye-wateringly marked-up price? That she could do all this and try to pretend the other stuff wasn't hap- pening. The stuff which felt real but which wasn't real. Stuff which involved Salvatore. Because, somewhere along the way—during all the meals and the tourist trips and the sex-filled nights—something had changed. Her fixed ideas had shifted and altered and the subject of sex didn't seem so black and white any more. She knew all about the whole friends-with-benefits thing because Salvatore had painstakingly explained it to her. She'd thought she understood it. She had signed up for it knowing it was all he was prepared to offer and convinced herself she was okay with it. She'd thought she could handle it.

But suddenly she was having difficulty handling it because something had changed. In her, not him. Not suddenly and not overnight. It had been like the drip, drip, drip of a leaking tap which somehow managed to fill an entire bath before you realised it. At first she'd thought it was because of the sex. That the response he drew from her eager body was the reason for the erratic see-sawing of her mood. But the dreamy aftermath of yet another shuddering orgasm didn't explain away the yearning in her heart as she bit back the tender words she was longing to say to him. She wanted to run her fingers through his hair and whisper her lips across his mouth at the most inappropriate of times. She felt as if she was falling in love with him.

Her fingers dug into the pasta dough. These were just complicated feelings for a man who didn't want emotion—the trouble was that she wasn't sure how to deal with them. Because she didn't *want* to feel this way. She wanted to wake up one morning and be free of all this aching and yearning deep in her heart. Yet instinct warned her that wasn't going to happen. The same instinct which knew the relationship would eventually run out of steam, unless she had the courage to push it in a different direction.

Was it a flicker of her newfound confidence at work

which made her willing to give it a try? Her handbags were proving surprisingly popular and had been flying out of the store. It seemed that rich women were prepared to pay a lot of money to own something so obviously handmade. Siena Simon had become a big fan of her work, prompting her to talk to the features editor of one of the biggest fashion bibles in the country, which had produced an exciting result. Which was part of the reason for this meal. But only part of it. Lina felt her chest tighten with apprehension. Because she wanted to give Salvatore something which all his billions couldn't give him. She ran her fingertips over the gleaming purple flesh of the aubergine. Some heart. Some thought. Some care. Something which had been made from…not love, no, because that would freak him out. But surely it was okay to demonstrate her deep affection and her gratitude to him, by cooking him a simple meal.

Her preparation finished, she stole a quick glance in the kitchen mirror at the hair which she'd tied back so it wouldn't flop in the sauce. A smile curved her lips as she touched her fingertips to an imprisoned wave. Better unpin it before Salvatore got home…

At first he couldn't find her. In fact, he couldn't find anyone. The house was unusually silent and there was no sign of Henry, or Shirley, who often served dinner.

Salvatore flared his nostrils, like an animal finding itself in unknown territory which had begun silently sniffing the terrain for threats. There had been a faint foggy drizzle in the air tonight and the table had been set for dinner in the smaller of the two dining rooms, rather than out on the terrace. Tall lit candles flickered a golden light show across the creamy walls and the air was thick with the scent of cut roses. Almost automatically he noticed crystal glasses and a bottle of champagne chilling in a silver ice bucket and a feeling of disquiet whispered down his spine. Just then Lina came running up from the kitchen, her cheeks pink with exertion, a scarlet dress clinging to her abundant curves and her luscious curls bouncing around her shoulders. Usually, he liked her in red, but tonight his senses were on alert and he wasn't quite sure why.

'What's going on?' he questioned. 'Where is everybody?'

'It's Henry's night off and I told him we didn't need any replacement help.' She smiled. 'And I gave the chef the night off.'

He stared at her. 'You did what?'

'I didn't think you'd mind. He works very hard and seemed very pleased to have an unexpected free evening. I've cooked you something myself instead.' Her smile became a little uncertain. 'We don't need anyone else.'

'That is beside the point,' he said impatiently. 'Since when did you start taking over roles which were never supposed to be yours, Lina? Or did you think that several weeks of sharing my bed has given you carte blanche to exert your will and start dismissing my staff whenever you saw fit?'

'No! Of course I didn't.'

'Then why didn't you run it past me first?'

'Because…because it was supposed to be a surprise.'

Ever since the day when he'd arrived home from school to discover his mother ready to drive away with that slimy salesman, Salvatore had had an abiding contempt for surprises. But from the dark hurt he could see clouding her eyes, he wasn't going to tell her that, in case she switched to unwanted sympathy. The last thing he would be able to stomach would be her compassionate tears on top of everything else. 'Fine,' he said, forcing a quick smile. 'Why don't you just serve it up?'

He could see from her pinched expression that she was feeling wounded and, while that didn't make him feel particularly good, he was unwilling to repent. Because hadn't he been soft around her? Too soft, maybe. Had he been blinding himself to the truth because it had suited him to do so? Intoxicated by her vibrantly passionate nature and their unique sexual chemistry, he had ignored the very obvious signs that she was starting to care for him. He plucked the champagne bottle from the bucket and began to tear off the foil. And that was the last thing he wanted.

He had just poured out two glasses when she carried the steaming dish into the dining room and Salvatore felt his stomach heave as he detected the familiar smell. 'What's this?' he asked, even though he knew damned well what it was.

'Pasta alla Norma,' she said, just a little too brightly. 'Your favourite.'

But it didn't feel like his favourite right then. It felt as if two very different worlds had just come crashing together, leaving him disorientated by the fall-out. Ignoring the generous portion she served him, he slanted a questioning glance at the glass of champagne which he handed to her. 'Are we supposed to be celebrating something?'

She sat down opposite him and he realised he hadn't even kissed her and somehow that seemed very relevant, because this was the first time he had ever looked at her without desire. And she was the one who was killing it, he thought furiously. Destroying a perfectly good relationship with high-handed behaviour and her manipulative attempts to rein him in with an unwanted domesticity which felt like the doors of a jail clanging closed.

'It's *kind* of a celebration,' she said, with a smile.

He forced himself to go through the motions of appearing interested although his mood was so dark, all he could manage was a single word. 'Oh?'

'The good news is that my bags are selling well and the store is very pleased—more than pleased. In fact, it's as much as I can do to keep up with demand and Siena has spoken to a features editor at *Trend* magazine.'

'A features editor at *Trend* magazine?' he repeated blankly.

She nodded, and her thick black hair shimmered in the candlelight. 'It's the number one fashion bible and they want to do a piece for their accessories issue. And Siena thinks we should have a party at the end of the month, to make the most of all the publicity. Open some champagne and invite some of the city's movers and shakers, that kind of thing.'

'How is advertising your wares going to help if

you're already struggling to keep up with demand?' He took a sip of wine. 'Talk me through that one.'

'Siena thought we might be able to employ out-workers. You know, women who can't do regular hours because they have young children. It means...' She gave an almost embarrassed shrug of her shoulders. 'It means we could increase production and widen our reach.'

'And make you a household name in the process, I suppose?'

Her voice sounded defensive. 'That was never my ambition, Salvatore.'

'But it looks like it might happen anyway.' He pushed away his plate and lifted his champagne glass in a toast. 'Congratulations. I guess that means you'll be able to start looking for a place of your own very soon.'

It hurt.

Lina bit her lip. It hurt way more than it should have done, mainly because she hadn't been expecting it. It was a curve ball, as they said over here. Lina had been busy cooking a surprise meal and buying a bottle of champagne because she wanted to share her good news with him. And he just wanted her out of here.

Well, of course he did. That had been one of the conditions for letting her live here in the first place. That she would be here for a few weeks and no more. What had she expected? That wall-to-wall sex would have made him start reconsidering his initial intention that she leave, and he'd tell her she could carry on living in the cottage for as long as she liked? *In your dreams, Lina. In your dreams.*

'You've barely touched your dinner,' she observed.

'I could say the same about you.'

'I thought you liked it.' She pressed her lips together. 'You ate it on that beach in Sicily as if it were going to be your last ever meal. I can remember it as if it were yesterday.'

He shrugged, lifting his hands in a silent gesture of apology. 'I guess it's like buying a shirt when you're in a foreign country—it never looks quite the same when you wear it at home, does it?'

'No. I guess not.' Lina felt deflated as she cleared away the dishes and carried them down into the kitchen and she was standing over the sink when she sensed, rather than heard, Salvatore enter the room behind her. She could feel the sudden, subtle change in the atmosphere. The way it became charged with electricity— like the heavy, thick thrum of air you got just before a thunderstorm.

For once he didn't tease her about her opposition to dishwashers as he sometimes did if he caught her washing up coffee cups in her little cottage. Did he guess she didn't want to meet his probing gaze right then, that she was terrified he would read something of her emotional turmoil in her eyes? Did he realise how stupid she felt because somewhere along the way she had fallen for him, despite all his warnings to the contrary? Was that why he walked across the room and wrapped one hand around her waist, using the other to lift up a heavy curtain of hair so he could kiss the back of her neck, his lips brushing lightly against her skin. And wasn't it infuriating that she could feel a whisper of response shivering its way down her spine, despite the discord of the meal they hadn't shared?

'Did I mention that I have to fly to Rio de Janeiro first thing tomorrow morning?' he murmured into her hair.

'No, you didn't tell me.' She dunked a saucepan into the hot, soapy water and tried not to react to that seeking kiss. 'How long will you be gone?'

'A couple of weeks.'

'Right.' She tried to stop her breathing from become ragged even though all she could think was that they'd never been parted for that long before and, more crucially, he was only announcing it now—at the last minute. Do you think you'll be back in time for the party?' she asked calmly.

'I'll do my best.'

It was not the answer she'd wanted but it seemed it was the only one she was going to get. She closed her eyes and wondered what he would do next.

She wanted him to leave.

She wanted him to stay.

He turned her around and started to kiss her and, to her shame, she let him. No, that wasn't strictly accurate. There was no shame involved in any of this—only pleasure. She was giving as good as she got and kissing him back with a fervour which felt angry as well as hungry. And maybe those two words were easier to muddle up than she'd initially thought. It felt as if she wanted to punish him. Which she did. As if she wanted to hurt him as much as he had just hurt her. It might have been wrong but it felt so right and he laughed softly against her lips, as if he were trying to provoke her into an even more passionate response. And he was getting one, because now it was rapidly getting out of control. Her hands flew to his shoulders as he bent her back towards the table and his teeth were grazing at her breasts though the thin jersey of the red dress. Her nipples puckered into painful points as he rucked up her dress and she heard his ragged murmur of desire. She felt so wet and she could hear the rasp of his zip as roughly he freed himself, followed closely by the sound of crashing china and cutlery as he swept it off the table and it hit the kitchen floor.

But Lina didn't care and she didn't stop. She didn't think anything could have stopped her right then, she wanted him so much. He ripped off her panties, damp, tattered fabric fluttering down to join the other debris, to the accompaniment of her own slurred words of approval. She was barely aware of him tearing open a condom and putting it on before opening her thighs and positioning himself. He thrust right up to the hilt and never had he felt bigger or harder or more aroused. She came so quickly it took her by surprise—though not him—for he gave a moan of relieved satisfaction as he followed her, his jerking body taking a long time to subside afterwards.

He buried his head in her curls, which were spread like a black cloth over the table, and when she turned her head to survey the shattered glass and crockery, she could see the pasta already congealing, like tomato-covered snakes. She had wondered if he might show remorse or regret, but there were neither as he brushed his mouth over hers in a careless kiss, before slowly following the direction of her gaze.

'To hell with domesticity,' he grated. 'There's only one thing I want to see you doing in my kitchen, Lina, and it's this.'

CHAPTER ELEVEN

THE DECORATED STORE looked as if Christmas had arrived early and there was barely an inch to move. Lina hovered near the entrance, busy scanning the new arrivals who were being waved through by security guards, and trying not to look as if she was waiting for someone—which of course she was. She gave a quick glance at her watch. Where *was* he? She could see Siena walking towards her—her cream chiffon evening dress floating behind her like a cloud—and she smiled at the designer who had been so kind to her.

'What are you doing hanging around by the entrance instead of out there basking in the glow of your success?' Siena questioned.

Lina's smile didn't slip. She'd been producing it at regular intervals since the party had kicked off with a blast of Sicilian music, cascades of twinkling rainbow lights and non-stop pink champagne. No need to tell Siena that she was waiting for Salvatore and didn't have a clue what time he was getting here. That he hadn't called her since the day before yesterday, saying that the line was bad and his schedule busy. Or that there had been several long, awkward silences throughout a conversation he clearly hadn't wanted to have. Was that why they had talked about the weather, and how long the flight had taken and whether the famous Brazilian feijoada dish was as delicious as everyone said it was. Because ever since that night when they'd had sex on the kitchen table, it had felt as if there were more than just the gulf of a different country between them. And she couldn't quite shake off the dark ache of foreboding, for she suspected things were ending between them.

She looked at the designer, who was twisting a long rope of pearls around her finger. 'I was just looking out for Salvatore's car.' Lina shrugged. 'Because I'm guessing people will want to see him.'

'Oh, people always like to see Salvatore di Luca.' Siena slanted her a wide smile. 'But you're the star here tonight, Lina, and don't you ever forget that. You can be perfectly successful in your own right, with or without your billionaire lover.'

Lina wondered if that was simply a kindly intervention from the older woman, warning her not to rely on a man who was only ever going to be a temporary fixture in her life, but she nodded, even if right then she didn't really believe it. 'Thank you.'

'You are going to speak to the journalist, aren't you?' Siena continued. 'He says he's a little worried. He thinks you've been avoiding him all evening.'

'But… I've already given an interview to *Trend* magazine.'

'Yes. I realise that.' Siena twirled her pearls round

and round her forefinger. 'But the local paper has a very popular gossip column, which is bread and butter for people in the luxury-brand business. It shouldn't be too onerous. Just tell him a bit about yourself. How you got started and what you like doing in your spare time. Readers love that kind of thing.'

A sudden lump sprang up in her throat and Lina swallowed because this was the bit she was terrified about. What could she possibly say to elaborate on the basic facts of her life—that she enjoyed sewing little beads and sequins onto squashy pieces of velvet and making each one different? That she enjoyed pottering around in Salvatore's huge gardens whenever she got the chance and felt a distinct sense of achievement that she had finally managed to get the frosty Henry to warm to her a little. But her main passion was for Salvatore, and that was the trickiest part of all.

Because her feelings for him had grown in a way she'd never planned. Maybe that was why the power balance between them had shifted so radically that she now felt as if they were living in different dimensions. And it had all happened since she'd cooked him that wretched meal. Since she'd stupidly tried to take their relationship onto another level.

Nervously, she swallowed. 'Must I?'

'It's essential,' said Siena firmly. 'In fact, here's Brett Forrester now and he's heading our way. Look, why don't you take him over there, away from the music deck—go and stand over by the evening coats, where it's quieter?'

Lina's heart was racing as she watched the journalist making his way towards them. Brett Forrester was a man in his late forties with a ridiculously over-long blond fringe flapping into his eyes, which she thought might have looked better on someone two decades younger. Ditto his leather jacket and very tight jeans. Shunning the champagne, he seemed welded to a tumbler of whisky, from which he constantly sipped, and he gave Lina a critical once-over as Siena introduced them before diplomatically drifting away in her cloud of chiffon. The greetings over, he raised his arm and a woman with an enormous camera instantly appeared by his side.

'We'll get some shots of you now, and a few more when your boyfriend arrives,' he said, his voice very slightly slurred.

A flash exploded in Lina's face, and she blinked in alarm.

'I don't think—'

'Lick your lips, honey. Stop looking so scared. Camera's not going to bite you—and don't forget this is all for *your* benefit.'

Was it? Lina wondered why this whole evening was suddenly starting to feel as if she'd released a monster from a cage. She hadn't realised just how many people would be attending, or that they'd be crammed into the huge space of Siena's store like sardines in a tin. The music was too loud and the half-glass of pink champagne she'd drunk was already giving her a headache. In fact, the only friendly face she'd seen all evening had been Sean MacCormack—the soap actor she'd sat next to at the charity gala when she'd first arrived in the city, and Salvatore had insisted on buying her that designer dress, which she hadn't worn since. But she had worn it tonight because it was the only thing in her wardrobe which was halfway suitable and, despite Salvatore's preferences, she had worn her hair up—mainly to showcase some of the jewellery which the store also stocked. Which was why she currently had two waterfall diamond earrings dangling by the sides of her neck, along with a matching bracelet which flashed rainbows whenever she moved her wrist.

At least tonight's party had proved an effective distraction, barely giving her time to think, let alone brood about how bad it had been between her and Salvatore before he'd flown to Rio. Awful didn't come close to the way that night had ended. She had insisted on clearing up the mess they'd created on the kitchen floor and had insisted he help her. At first he hadn't believed she meant it—as if someone like him shouldn't have to participate in something as ordinary as housework. But she had held firm, her emotions still running high after the furious words they had shared and the highly charged sex which had followed.

'Do you think it's magically going to clean itself?' she had demanded. 'Or that one of your staff should have to deal with it in the morning? You were the one who threw everything on the floor!'

'I didn't hear you objecting at the time!' he had flared back.

He had been angry and moody and she had felt... *weird*. As if he'd used her, even though she'd enjoyed every second of it and had been an active participant.

She'd figured out that the best thing to do would have been to have taken herself off to her cottage and spent the night apart from him. To have given them both the space she'd suspected they needed to cool down.

But something had held her back from walking away from him. Maybe it was because sometimes, in the darkness of the night, she felt closer to him than at any other time. Not necessarily during sex, but afterwards, when he would lie stroking her hair, his voice lazy and reflective. As if within the enclosed space of their bedroom none of the worries and cares of the outside world existed. As if, for a few brief moments, he allowed all the barriers with which he surrounded himself to crumble to the ground.

And that was why she had allowed him to take her in his arms and kiss her again, once they'd finished scrubbing at the kitchen tiles. Because in the face of all her growing insecurity about the future, his embrace had felt comforting and safe. And that was just an illusion, she reminded herself bitterly.

And then she looked up and saw Salvatore standing on the other side of the crowded room, his eyes trained unwaveringly on her, and everything else just faded away. Lina's heart burned, as if someone had punched a red-hot fist to the middle of her chest. She'd told herself she was going to get over him and prove she didn't need him—emotionally *or* physically. But what power on earth could ever make her immune to him?

Salvatore felt a stab of awareness as his eyes connected with Lina's and a wave of something extraordinary flowed through his body like a powerful surge of electricity—an effect she had on him which no other woman had ever been able to match. Two whole weeks had passed yet it seemed he was still susceptible to her particular magic. But she could make him angry as well as filling him with desire, and he was angry now, because he didn't want to feel this way.

Not about her.

Not about anyone.

His gaze scanned over her and he realised she was wearing exactly the same outfit as the night he'd taken her to the gala ball, when he hadn't recognised her. But tonight he wasn't having any difficulty recognising her, despite the rigid gown and intricately coiled hair. Because no amount of face paint or gilding could deflect from a sensual and earthy beauty which needed no artifice. His eyes narrowed as he noticed the man beside her—some creep of a journalist he thought he recognised. And as the man moved closer, Salvatore experienced a savage jolt of something which felt like possessiveness. His throat dried. Or was it protectiveness?

He began to walk towards them and flinched as a flash went off in his face, but he carried on walking, weaving his way through the crowd and ignoring the sound of people vying for his attention and the hopeful smiles of so many women, until eventually he reached Lina. The man with the ridiculous hairstyle brightened and held out a hand, which Salvatore ignored.

'Hi! Brett Forrester of *San Fran Daily*. We've met before. At the races last year. Do you remember?'

'No, I don't,' said Salvatore repressively, but the other man failed to take the hint and leave.

'So, what do you think about your girlfriend's designs, Sal?'

Salvatore felt his fists tighten as the nickname he never used took him right back to the schoolyard. Suddenly, he had the urge to lash out, in a way he hadn't wanted to do since those circling fights when the other kids had taunted him and called his mother *puttana*. Did Lina guess at his discomfiture—was that why she put her hand on his bunched forearm, her fingers acting as the gentlest of restraints, just as the blue-white flash of a camera exploded around them?

'We don't have to stay, you know,' she said, very quietly, blinking against the bright light. 'We can leave any time you want.'

He resented her understanding tone. He wanted to tell her that he didn't *need* her kindness or her soft compassion. That he could manage perfectly well on his own. 'But this is your night, Lina,' he answered dangerously. 'Surely you want to enjoy every second of your success?'

Did the journalist sense the sudden scent of conflict in the air? Was that why he pulled out a notebook and a pencil? 'Tell me how you two met.'

Salvatore's gaze was stony. 'That is not for public consumption.

Still the journalist didn't give up. 'But you're both Sicilian, yes?'

'Listen to me,' said Salvatore in a voice of silken finality. 'The evening has obviously been an absolute triumph for Miss Vitale, though in future it might be better if you gave your subject matter a little more personal space. And that's the only quote you're going to get from me, Forrester. Understand?'

'But—'

'The *only* quote,' affirmed Salvatore grimly.

Maybe it was the ripple of danger in his voice which finally convinced the journalist to retreat, leaving Salvatore alone with Lina and the furious beat of his heart. She was looking at him nervously, as if she couldn't quite gauge his mood. And the crazy thing was, neither could he. It was as if he didn't dare open his mouth for fear of what was going to come out of it next.

'I'm glad you managed to make it,' she said, her voice edged with a kind of desperation as if she was trying to pretend nothing was happening.

What *was* happening? he wondered as a waiter came by with a tray of drinks and he took a crystal beaker of fizzy water to slake his thirst before looking around the room. 'This is some party,' he observed softly.

'I'm glad you like it.'

'I didn't say that.'

'You mean you don't?'

'I didn't say that, either.' He gave his empty glass to another waiter. 'But doing seedy interviews with journalists like Brett Forrester has never really been my scene.'

Her teeth were chewing on the gleam of her lips. 'Nor mine.'

'Neither do I enjoy the way I was ambushed by the paparazzi from the moment I arrived.'

She looked at him acidly. 'Then maybe you should have surrounded yourself with security!'

He glared at her. 'Maybe I should!'

Her voice dipped into an angry whisper. 'Why did you bother coming at all, when you're in such a filthy mood?'

'I suppose I wanted to support you.'

'Forgive me for saying so, Salvatore, but this doesn't feel remotely like support.'

He knew that. He knew it, but he couldn't seem to stop himself from the bitter words which were tumbling out from somewhere deep and dark within him. Because something bitter had begun to harden inside him. Something which was making it difficult for him to breathe. He looked around to where one of Siena's assistants was standing in front of a queue of people, tapping out frantically on her tablet—presumably compiling a wait-list.

'You've come a long way from the woman who just wanted to make a living,' he observed softly. 'You've changed, Lina.'

She was shaking her head as if she couldn't quite believe what he was saying. 'Of *course* I've changed,' she whispered. 'I had to. Didn't *you* change when you came here? Didn't you feel you had to do that, so that you'd blend in? Or do you think I would have fitted into this glitzy city if I'd just bombed around on my little bike, wearing dusty old sneakers and frumpy clothes? Maybe that's what you would have preferred me to do?' she added, into the charged silence which seemed to have enveloped them. 'To have stayed exactly the same as I was.'

He stared at the tight shiny spirals of black hair

which were coiled on top of her head. At the heavy satin gown which effectively ironed out every one of her luscious curves. At the diamonds which dazzled at her neck and her wrist, their blue-white fire almost as bright as the photographer's flash.

'Yes,' he ground out. 'That's what I would have preferred. Because you don't look like Lina any more.'

'And yet when I *did* look like Lina and behave like her—doing that very traditional thing of cooking a Sicilian meal for you as a surprise—that wasn't right either, was it?' she questioned. 'In fact, you acted as if I had committed a terrible crime.'

'Because I didn't sign up for domesticity!' he retorted. 'I didn't want some West Coast recreation of a life I left behind a long time ago!'

She stared at him for a long moment. 'Do you want to know something?' she said, at last, her voice low and trembling. 'That I had stupidly started to care for you? Yes, I admit it—even though you had warned me against doing so—I had fallen into the same trap as so many others! I cared because I liked the man you were underneath all the trappings. In fact, sometimes I found myself wishing you didn't have all that damned money, because it suits you to think women are only interested in your wealth, doesn't it? Just like I wish your mother hadn't deserted you and your father hadn't neglected you afterwards. But we can't rewrite history, Salvatore, no matter how much we'd like to. And you will never heal from the wounds of your past—because you'll never allow yourself to!'

'That's enough,' he snarled.

'No. No, it's not enough. I've listened to you often enough when you laid down all your *terms*. The least now you can do is to hear *me* out. Because no woman is ever going to be right for you, are they? There is no female on earth who could possibly fulfil your exacting and contradictory demands—because they are unachievable!'

'Too right, they are. And do you want to know why?' He stabbed his fingers into the air, in a way she'd seen him do once before. 'Because I don't want all that *stuff*! I don't want domesticity and living by the clock. And I don't want children, either—do you understand? Children who become the unwilling victims of the mess their parents make of their relationships! I'm not seeking the chains which other men strive to anchor themselves with. So why don't you do yourself a favour, Lina—and stay away from me?'

Lina's throat was so dry she could hardly breathe and the fitted dress felt as tight as a shroud. She would have run out of there—she *wanted* to run out of there—but she couldn't. Not with these stupidly high heels and a wall of people in front of her. But importantly, she knew she *shouldn't* run away, even if it were physically possible. Not with her potential future lying in front of her. Here there were potential clients and potential backers and she couldn't just storm out of there because her heart felt as if it were breaking. Siena had taken a chance on her and given her the opportunity of a lifetime and now her efforts were finally beginning to bear fruit. And this had been what she'd wanted, hadn't it? In fact, her ambition had over-vaulted itself and not only had she achieved far more than she would ever have believed possible, but Siena had told her that a lot more lay ahead.

More than that, she had learned something about herself along the way. In her eagerness to please people and keep the peace, Lina had allowed herself to ignore the way they were treating her. She had pretty much always fallen in with other people's demands. Her mother had done it and now it seemed she was in danger of letting Salvatore do it, too. He wasn't interested in what she wanted—only in his own closed and selfish agenda.

And suddenly, she could feel her nerves and her fears slipping away from her. Somehow she would get through the rest of the evening and the rest of her life, just not with Salvatore. Never again with him. Why try to cling to a man who could be so hurtful? Why chase after something he would never be prepared to give her? Because she had wanted this. Worked hard for it. Was she really going to let it slip away because she was pursuing someone who had always been beyond her reach? She owed herself more than that.

So, although her heart was beating so hard that it hurt, she tilted her chin and fixed him with a cool look. 'Look, you're clearly not enjoying yourself and I really ought to circulate. So why don't you go on ahead? It looks like I'm going to be here for some time.'

He shook his head. 'I'll wait,' he said.

'No.' Her voice was quiet, but determined. In fact, she'd never felt quite so determined in her life. 'Honestly. Just go. I really don't need you here.'

He opened his mouth as if to object, as if her sudden

poise had perplexed him. As if he were the only one in this doomed relationship who was allowed to make decisions. But what could he possibly object to, when she was giving him everything he wanted?

He'd provided her with an escape route, hadn't he? Surely now she could return the favour.

CHAPTER TWELVE

SALVATORE STARED AT the newspaper which had been placed neatly on his desk and the anger which had been smouldering inside him since he'd got out of bed that morning now threatened to combust. Splashed all over the inside pages was a feature about last night's launch party for Lina's handbags, with the usual shots of seasoned attendees presenting their best sides to the camera, their posed smiles in place. But it was the photograph of him with Lina which disturbed him most, the one with her hand on his arm, which had inspired the excruciating headline speculating on whether San Francisco's most famous bachelor had finally lost his heart to a woman from his homeland. Which made a pulse begin to flicker at his temple.

If he looked closely—which he seemed to be doing, despite his initial inclination to crush the offending journal in his fist—then he could see something in her unguarded expression which disturbed him. Which seemed to vindicate his determination to move on from her. He swallowed. For wasn't her Madonna-like face soft as she looked at him, her dark eyes full of the care she'd confessed she felt for him? He felt his heart clench with something which felt like pain, but instantly he blocked it out. Because he didn't do that kind of pain. Not any more.

Pushing the paper away, he looked up at his assistant who had appeared at the door, carrying a tiny cup of super-strong espresso, her sharp attention immediately drawn to the article in front of him.

'You've seen it?' she said. 'I thought it best to draw your attention to it. I know you never usually read that rag.'

He took the coffee from her and sipped. Delicious. 'Must have been a slow news day,' he said acidly. 'Could you bring me in the files about the orphanage in Romania, please, Maggie? As quickly as possible.'

He could tell from her slightly aggrieved expression that she was irritated by his terse response and lack of additional information, but Salvatore didn't care. He didn't want to discuss it any more. Not with anyone. The subject was closed. He disposed of the newspaper and threw himself into his work, and for several hours it proved engaging enough to allow him to forget all the domestic trivia which had been weighting him down of late. He told himself he should be celebrating what looked like the end of his liaison with Lina, and the freedom that would bring. But the crazy thing was that several times he found himself wanting to lift the phone and talk to her. He frowned. He didn't usually ring her from the office. But then, he was usually sated from a blissful night of sex, which kept him going until he saw her again at dinner time. With narrowed eyes he gazed out of his office window, but for once he failed to be dazzled by the spectacular view across the roof-tops to where blue sky met blue water.

Because there had been no sex last night, had there? Irritated by her cool assertion that she would prefer to remain at the party without him, Salvatore had indeed jumped into his waiting limousine and been driven home. But he hadn't gone straight to bed. He had sat out on the softly lit terrace, with music playing in the background, looking up at the stars. On a purely logical level he had been aware that the relationship was approaching its final meltdown stage and would soon be over. But it hadn't quite reached that stage and he hadn't stopped wanting her, just as he knew, deep down, she hadn't stopped wanting him. So why shouldn't they both capitalise on that? They had entered this arrangement sensibly, which meant there was no reason why it shouldn't end on a similar, sensible note.

He had been feeling almost nostalgic as he'd waited for her and the minutes had ticked slowly by. He might open a good bottle of champagne and they would toast her success before retiring to his bedroom and satisfying each other in a way he'd been missing ever since he'd flown to Rio. And who was to say that some kind of arrangement like that couldn't continue, once she had moved into a place of her own?

He heard the sound of the electric gates opening and a car stopping. The slam of a door, and her softly accented voice saying goodnight. His body tensed as he waited for her.

But Lina didn't come.

She must have known he was there, for the drift of the music would have reached the courtyard and she would have looked up to see the lights on.

Why didn't she come?

Slow minutes ticked by before it dawned on him that she must have gone straight to bed and his initial surprise and faint outrage was replaced by the quick stir of desire. He was tempted to go over to her cottage and let himself in, as he'd done so many times before. To steal inside and take her silently, absolving them both of the need to talk about what had happened tonight. He wanted nothing more than to lose himself in her soft body. To press his lips against her silky, cushioned flesh. He wanted to feel her tense when he was deep inside her and then to shudder with mindless pleasure. Because wasn't that the one thing which was always right between them, no matter what else was going on? But he was damned if he was going to tacitly admit he'd done something *wrong*, following her like a chastened puppy which wanted to be forgiven.

He'd wondered if she might appear this morning to share a coffee with him before he left for the office as she sometimes did, but she hadn't done that either. And that was when his anger had begun to ferment into an ugly brew. No matter what was happening between *them*—something which had always been on the cards—shouldn't she at least have shown a little gratitude that he'd turned up at the damned party and given it his seal of approval?

He left work early and rang for some iced water as soon as he got home, but Henry didn't answer his summons immediately, and when he did, he looked so unlike his usual unflappable self that Salvatore was forced to ask:

'Is something wrong?'

'It's Miss Vitale, sir. She's gone.'

'What do you mean, she's *gone*?'

But Henry shook his head, almost as if he were *upset*, and Salvatore got up immediately and went straight over to the cottage, surprised by what he found there. Because she really *had* gone. Bedlinen had obviously been laundered and neatly piled up on the mattress and every small room had been scrubbed clean. There was no trace of her. No clothes or books. No sewing machine or velvet. No beads—other than a couple of tiny droplets which were glittering on a rug and which she must have missed when she'd been vacuuming.

Confused now, Salvatore reached into his jacket pocket for his cell phone—and that was when he saw the fat-looking envelope, propped up on the mantelpiece next to a small jam jar of flowers she obviously couldn't bear to throw away. He ripped it open and withdrew a sheet of writing paper and, mystifyingly, a large wedge of dollars. It was the first time he'd ever seen her writing, he realised—and it was curving and easy to read. A bit like her, he thought with a pang, before allowing righteous anger to flood through him as he read her words.

Dear Salvatore,
It's difficult to know how to start this letter, but
I guess first of all I must thank you for bringing

me to America and giving me a home until I was able to establish myself.

It has been a roller coaster of a ride and it looks as if my dream to make something of myself has exceeded anything I could have ever thought possible.

I've moved in with Sean for the time being.

Sean? Salvatore thought, with a frown. Who the hell was Sean? His eyes scanned the letter again and he could almost hear her soft voice answering his question.

Do you remember? He's the lovely actor I sat next to when we went to the gala ball.

He's got an apartment in Haight Ashbury and says I can have a room there for as long as I need it. So that's what I'm going to do.

Please could you forward any letters from my mother?

You'll find some money in the envelope, which covers the cost of the dress and the shoes you bought me for the gala ball. Please accept it, with my thanks.

If starting this letter was difficult, I'm finding it even harder to end it. Maybe I'd just better say that I will never forget you, Salvatore, and that I wish you every happiness.
Yours, Lina.

How ironic, he thought, his body tensing. Over the years he'd received texts and cards liberally adorned with kisses, from women who meant nothing to him. And yet not a single *x* followed Lina Vitale's name.

How could something like that hurt?

How could he *let* it hurt?

His cell phone was ringing and he snatched it out of his pocket, a faint feeling of disappointment washing over him when he saw it was Maximo Diaz, even though he was a good friend from way back. He was tempted to ignore the call, but why ruffle the feathers of one of the most powerful men in Spain, and one with a notoriously tight schedule?

He clicked on the 'accept' button. 'Maximo?'

'Usually, my phone calls are accepted with a little more enthusiasm that that, my friend,' mocked the rich voice of the wealthy industrialist.

Salvatore gave a short laugh. 'Forgive me. It has been a long week. Good to hear from you, Max. What can I do for you?'

'I'm coming to San Francisco at the end of the month. I thought that maybe we could catch up. Unless you're too occupied with this woman I've seen you pictured with in the papers.'

Salvatore's mouth hardened. 'Absolutely not,' he said firmly. 'That ship has sailed and I'd love to spend a night on the town with you, like the old days.'

Why not? he thought as he terminated the call. They were both virile and eligible men.

And they were both single.

His jaw tightening, Salvatore put the phone back down on his desk.

* * *

Haight Ashbury was certainly *buzzy*.

Sean's apartment was directly above a Chinese restaurant—which offered them a discount on its delectable food. To Lina's surprise there was a beautiful tree planted on the pavement outside—along with numerous stalls selling rainbow flags and badges, and music by people she'd never heard of. It was a bit strange to get used to jostling tourists taking photos of the iconic building whenever she went outside, but Lina convinced herself it made good sense to have such a startling change of circumstance.

Because this is my new life, she told herself fiercely.

With Sean's help she pushed her bed up against the wall, creating as much space as possible for her sewing machine, her velvet and beads. Her actor flatmate's hours were long. He started early, didn't get back until late, then spent much of the evening learning his next day's lines. It certainly disabused Lina of the idea that an actor's life was one of glamour.

He'd asked her questions, of course. Or rather, he'd tried. But she had explained very firmly that she didn't want to talk about Salvatore. She didn't feel ready to and her emotions were still so volatile that she was terrified of bursting into tears.

Anyway, it was over. Salvatore hadn't bothered ringing after she'd left him that letter, or tried to get in touch. She'd told herself she hadn't been expecting him to and had tried very hard to crush her aching disappointment. What had come as a bit of a surprise—a gut-twisting shock, if she was being honest—was when, yesterday morning, Sean had shown her a picture taken of Salvatore and some darkly-handsome man, emerging from a famous San Franciscan nightclub. Lina had stared down at the photo with a feeling of growing dismay, because behind the two men it was possible to glimpse the tanned and toned legs of two gorgeous blonde women. The twist in her gut had tightened. That hadn't taken him long, had it? Less than a month and it appeared he was dating again.

She had spent a miserable night after seeing that, waking up this morning bad-tempered, with a headache and craving a sugar rush, which was why she'd gone down to the nearby bakery to buy herself some breakfast. She was just offloading her frangipane croissant onto a plate in Sean's cluttered kitchen, when she heard the sound of the doorbell.

It was probably a delivery, Lina thought as she ran down the rickety wooden staircase to answer it. Sean seemed to spend his life ordering things online, then sending them back again.

It wasn't.

Standing on the doorstep, and somehow managing to own every bit of the space around him, was Salvatore. In his immaculate suit, snowy shirt and silk tie, he looked very formal against the colourful backdrop of Haight. But then she noticed his unshaven jaw and the dark shadows beneath his tired eyes and a very instinctive spiral of jealousy made her want to slam the door in his face.

But that wouldn't be dignified. It would be tantamount to showing him she cared—and why on earth would she do that?

Instead, she injected her voice with friendly enthusiasm, as if they were old friends who'd just met again after a long absence. 'Salvatore, this is a surprise! Did you bring my mail?'

'Your mail?' he repeated blankly.

'From my mother. You remember? I said I was expecting a letter. You could have forwarded it, you know.'

'There is no mail.'

'Oh. Right. She's obviously still sulking. She has ignored every letter and email I've sent her.'

'I didn't come here to talk about your mother.'

'Oh?'

He was glowering at her now. 'Aren't you going to invite me in, Lina?'

There was a pause. 'I wasn't intending to, no.' He appeared to be waiting for an answer and so she gave him one, even though every pore of her body objected to sending him away. 'I can't see the point,' she said in a low voice. 'There's really nothing left to say, is there?'

Salvatore felt the painful punch of his heart as he looked at his soft Madonna and noted the unusually stubborn set of her chin. He thought how incredible she looked in that short cotton dress, her thick hair dangling over one shoulder, and he thought how unbelievably stupid he'd been. He felt a jolt of rage and pain which stirred somewhere deep inside him. 'Can we please go inside?' he said. 'Because I don't want to have this conversation on the doorstep.'

There was a split second of a pause when he actually thought she was going to refuse him entry, before she gave an ungracious nod. 'You'd better come in.'

'Thanks.' Quickly, he stepped inside and shut the door before she could change her mind, following her up a scratched wooden staircase and into a small, untidy kitchen. A take-away cup of coffee was cooling on the side, next to a sickly-looking croissant.

'Are you hungry?' she asked.

'No. But please don't let me stop you eating breakfast.'

'I'm not hungry either. Not any more. Look, why don't you just tell me why you're here, and then let me get on with my work?'

Salvatore had spent the whole night and all the journey here working out exactly what he planned to say, but suddenly his breath caught in his throat as a dark wave of fear washed over him. A fear like nothing he'd ever felt before, and he had only himself to blame. Because what if it was already too late? What if he'd blown it with his arrogance and his control-freakery and his inability to really let go of the past?

That was a chance he had to take. A chance all men took when they put their feelings on the line. When they met a woman they were willing to take a risk for, and when they'd behaved like a fool. But even so…this was pretty scary stuff. 'I've been a fool, Lina,' he said, and looked at her.

'You won't hear me denying it,' she said.

Had he thought that would be enough? That she'd open her arms and forgive him with the minimum of fuss? Yes. He had. But it was not enough, he could see that now. He sucked in a deep breath and tried to continue but it wasn't easy to express himself. Hell, he'd never *had* to express himself like this before. 'You made me look at the past and realise that I was in danger of ruining the rest of my life if I wasn't careful.'

'I'm pleased for you,' she said primly.

Did she want *more*? It seemed she did. 'The house feels empty without you and so does my bed. I miss your soft smile and your laugh and the way you sometimes lose your temper,' he said and then, when she didn't speak, he sucked in another breath and said the words very carefully, just to make sure there could be no mistake. 'The thing is, that I love you, Lina Vitale. I didn't want to. I didn't plan to, but I do.'

If he had been expecting laughter, or tears, or gratitude, he got none of those. Just a faintly hostile expression which radiated from the depths of her bourbon eyes.

'Did you say that to one of the women you were with last night?' she asked, in a voice he'd never heard her use before.

'What women? Oh!' He clapped the flat of his hand against his brow. 'You're talking about the women outside the nightclub?'

She gave a bitter laugh. 'You mean there are more?'

'None. None at all. They spent the night following us round the club like detectives and were as devious as a pair of foxes—we only managed to shake them off once our car had arrived. Listen to me, Lina. Hear me out—that's all I ask.' His throat felt as if someone had attacked it with a blowtorch but somehow he managed to fire the words out. 'I've spent the past few weeks telling myself I'm no good for you, that you'd be better off without me, and, yes,' he admitted, 'that I'd be better off without you.'

She was silent for a moment, then turned and stared out of the window, as if she'd rather look at a mosaic of Jimi Hendrix than at him.

'Go on,' she said, in a small voice.

'An old friend of mine flew into town yesterday and we decided to…'

'To what, Salvatore?' she quizzed, whirling round to face him as his words tailed off. 'What did you decide?'

He sighed. He'd wanted to go to the nightclub to see what effect it had on him. He'd hoped to find an easy solution to his ongoing heartache in the form of one of the women who regularly swarmed over him. He'd thought he might be able to forget about Lina and the way she made him feel. But he couldn't forget. What more, he didn't want to. The glitzy women who had tried to come onto him had meant nothing. They never had done. Only this woman had got close to him, despite him doing his level best to push her away. And that was when he'd realised how hard he'd tried to protect himself from emotional pain. That, for all his towering success, he could rightly be accused of being a coward. That with his charitable work he had attempted to help people who'd been deserted and never known love— he had just neglected to help himself in the process.

'I decided I needed to come and tell you the truth,' he bit out. 'Which is breathtakingly simple. That I love you. You and only you.'

'Salvatore,' she said, a little desperately, and now her face had become a twisting conflict of emotions, so that for a minute it looked as if she was about to cry. 'Don't say any more.'

'I have to. Listen to me, Lina. Please.' His plea was heartfelt and maybe she guessed that, for she grew silent again. 'I fell for you the first time I saw you, in a way I'd never done before. It's why I broke the rule of a lifetime and had a one-night stand. You blew me away with your freshness and sweet charm and made me feel as if you wanted me for the man I really was. But it suited me to disregard that simple fact, because you also made me feel like I was losing control, and that was the one thing I had relied on in my life, in order to survive.' He paused. 'The only thing.'

'That was why one minute you pushed me away and the next, you were pulling me back again,' she said slowly. 'Why you kept saying about how you liked me to look. That's why you liked to dictate how I wore my hair.'

'It's true I prefer it down,' he admitted.

'To be honest, so do I.'

He swallowed. 'I thought that if I could control you, then…'

'Then you would have all the power and I would never leave you the way your mother left you. You didn't want anyone to be able to hurt you like that ever again.'

His throat was tight and he could hardly breathe, because her level of understanding was devastating. It was as if she knew what he was thinking. As if she could peer deep into his soul. But whereas once that thought would have filled him with dread, now it filled him with awe.

'But I've come to realise that by playing safe,' he continued bitterly, 'I am closing myself off to the greatest potential for happiness I've ever known. Because when you weren't around I discovered how empty my life felt. And I realised that by trying to control you, I risked crushing your inner strength and that burgeoning independence which makes me love you even more. And that is why I'm asking you to forgive me, Lina. Forgive me and stay with me and let me make amends. I want to marry you, if you'll have me, so I can spend the rest of my life loving you, as you deserve to be loved.'

She didn't have to think about it for long, because Lina knew there could only be one answer to a question she hadn't dared ever believe he'd ask. She had admired him from afar and then she had loved him up close. She'd seen the darkness in his soul and had wanted to flood it with daylight. She didn't care about his money. If he told her he wanted to go and live in Caltarina in a little house like the one she'd grown up in, she would be happy with that. Then she thought about her mother living down the road and thought…well, maybe a different village.

She opened her mouth to tell him all these things, but she was so overcome with emotion that the words just wouldn't come. And perhaps he read her answer in her eyes, because his own were suspiciously bright as he pulled her into his arms and kissed her. It was a long time after that kiss had ended, and the coffee on the kitchen counter had grown completely cold, that she brushed her finger along the shadowed edge of his unshaven jaw. 'You know, I'll never hurt you, Salvatore.'

He dipped his head to capture her fingertip and nipped at it with his teeth. 'You can't say that.'

'Yes,' she contradicted, more certain now. 'I can. Oh, sometimes we might fight, or disagree—because that is the way of the world. But my heart is so full of love for you, that there's no room for anything else and there never will be.'

His eyes grew hard, and bright. She saw in them understanding, and fear. But the fear would fade in time. Love would make sure of that. It would soothe and smooth everything in its path. It would comfort and reassure. And it would also provoke—in ways which were emotional as well as physical.

She shivered as he stroked his thumb over one peaking nipple.

'I think it's time for bed,' he said, a little unsteadily. 'Don't you?'

EPILOGUE

'READY?' QUESTIONED SALVATORE.

Lina looked up into the glitter of her husband's beloved blue eyes and nodded. 'Ready,' she said.

The limousine was waiting outside to take them to the airfield. Soon they would be high over the skies of California, en route to Caltarina—their first trip since they'd married there, last year.

It had been the most gorgeous wedding Lina could have imagined—an unfussy ceremony, the tiny church bursting to the rafters with a mix of villagers and many of Salvatore's jet-setting friends. Siena had been there, eying up some Greek tycoon, and Lina had insisted on Henry, Shirley and Salvatore's chef, Ric, being present. There had been huge excitement when Sheikh Kadir Al Marara had flown in for the reception, and Lina's mother had been in her element, boasting to anyone who would listen that her beloved daughter was marrying one of the richest and best connected men in the world. But Lina didn't let that bother her—to be honest, she was so happy that nothing could bother her.

Reconciled soon after the announcement of her engagement, and determined to forget the harsh words of the past, Lina had asked her mother to make her wedding dress, and throughout those fittings they had talked in a way they'd never done before. Each stitch sewed into the delicate organza seemed to have helped heal their fractured relationship. She had learnt of her mother's desperate loneliness after the death of her husband and her realisation that she had transferred all that pain onto her daughter. Yet Lina's departure for the United States had forced her mother to re-evaluate her life, and to forge a new way of living, which was bringing her an unexpected kind of contentment.

The wedding dress had turned out to be a triumph of simplicity and Lina had worn her hair loose—of course. A single photograph of the happy couple had been sold to news outlets around the world, with all the profits going into Salvatore's charitable foundation.

A foundation for which Lina now worked, alongside her husband, because she'd decided that dispossessed children were closer to her heart than accessories for the rich and privileged. But she hadn't given up completely on her unique designs. Her handbags were now made by a dedicated team of out-workers and there was huge competition for these jobs, because the rates of pay were so favourable. There had already been talk of diversification. Of shawls and evening shoes, with the looping Lina signature embroidered on every product. There was also a simple Lina scent—an evocative lemon fragrance meant to evoke images of sunny Sicilian days.

She was happy about her success and the fact that

all profits went into the foundation. But most of all Lina was happy because Salvatore loved her with all his heart. He told her so every day, and every day she echoed that sentiment.

But...

She looked up to find him watching her, his eyes narrowed with interest. He was so intuitive, she thought happily.

But...

Her heart was beating very fast and she knew she couldn't put it off any longer. 'How...how would you feel about us having children?'

Salvatore didn't answer straight away, but then, he was pretty sure she didn't expect him to, because this was way too important not to give it his full consideration. But he didn't have to think about it for very long.

'I want to have a baby with you,' he answered simply.

Tears sprang to her eyes. 'You're sure?'

He nodded. 'As sure as when I knew I wanted to spend the rest of my life with you. But this isn't an academic discussion we're having here, is it, Lina?'

'I don't know how it happened!' she burst out.

He was smiling. 'You don't?'

'That's not what I mean. I don't want you to think that I—'

'Shh.' He pulled her into his arms and he could feel the pounding of her heart against the race of his own as he buried his lips in her hair. 'Contraception hasn't been my number one focus lately. It just seemed less important. I've probably been careless.' He smiled against her thick black curls. 'Or just too damned relaxed.'

She drew back and searched his face, dazzled by the blaze of his blue, blue eyes. 'You're saying...?'

'I'm saying that it feels right,' he said huskily. 'Just like you feel right. You always did.'

'And you think... You think we'll be okay parents? You're not scared?'

'Of course I'm scared,' he admitted slowly, in a way he would never have done to anyone else. But Lina had made him realise that it was okay to express your doubts and fears, and that being strong didn't mean you couldn't also be vulnerable. He cleared his throat. 'But we know what we do want for our baby,' he husked. 'And, more importantly, what we don't want. And we've got each other, Lina. We can help each other along the way.'

'I love you, Salvatore di Luca. Do you know that? I love you so very much.'

Her face was wet as they kissed and when he drew back and wiped her tears away, he shot a calculating glance at his watch. 'I think we could allow the car to wait a little longer.' His hands on her shoulders, he looked deep into her eyes. 'Don't you?'

'That depends,' she said, a little breathlessly. 'On what you had in mind.'

'You know exactly what I have in mind. I want you. And I want you right now.' The words came out ragged. Emotional and deliberate. It was a statement he'd made many times before but with Lina it meant something different. It meant way more than sex.

It was all about love.

* * * * *

PROOF OF THEIR FORBIDDEN NIGHT

CHANTELLE SHAW

CHAPTER ONE

'WHAT DO YOU think of the news that Papa is engaged to the Ice Queen? Isla has hooked her claws into him, make no mistake.'

Andreas Karelis came to an abrupt halt a few feet away from the helicopter which had brought him to his family's privately owned island, Louloudi, and stared at his sister, who had run across the garden to meet him. Nefeli's shrilly furious voice had risen above the *whomp-whomp* of the slowing rotor blades.

From the air the island, partially covered with a cedar forest and olive groves, resembled an emerald set amid the azure Aegean Sea. Andreas's happiest boyhood memories were of running free on Louloudi, away from his parents' expectations of the Karelis heir. He owned houses in California and the French Riviera and a penthouse apartment in Athens, but Louloudi was the only place he thought of as home.

'I have heard nothing from Stelios,' he said curtly and his sister's eyes widened. Usually Andreas kept a tight control over his feelings and no one, not even Nefeli, who was the only person he was at all close to, knew what he was thinking. But he disliked surprises, good or bad, and this was definitely the latter.

'I thought Papa might have phoned you. He dropped

the bombshell when I arrived.' Nefeli tossed her dark curls over her shoulders. She was petite with a volatile temperament—the opposite of Andreas, who owed his tall, athletic build to his Californian maternal grandmother and had learned early in his childhood to suppress his emotions. It was a lesson he had mastered with astonishing success.

'A press statement will be released tomorrow to formally announce Papa's engagement to Isla, but he wanted to share the news with his family first. God!' Nefeli's voice went up another octave. 'She's his housekeeper, and young enough to be his daughter. What is Papa *thinking*?'

Andreas gave a careless shrug to hide his violent dislike of his father's matrimonial plans. The strength of his reaction surprised him, and he reminded himself that Stelios was free to do as he pleased. There was no fool like an old fool, especially a widowed, elderly billionaire in thrall to a beautiful young woman, he thought sardonically.

A restlessness gripped him as he visualised the woman who was now apparently Stelios's fiancée. Isla Stanford was undeniably beautiful. An English rose with her spun-gold hair and creamy skin. But she had an untouchable air that Andreas would usually find off-putting. He preferred women who were sexually confident, which was why he had found his intense awareness of Isla on the few occasions that he had met her so puzzling.

'Papa has brought her to Louloudi and she is to attend my birthday party at the weekend,' Nefeli said sulkily. She slipped her hand through her brother's arm as they walked towards the villa. 'You will have to do something, Andreas.'

'What do you suggest?' His trademark lazy drawl with its blend of cynical amusement disguised his thoughts but his restless feeling intensified when Nefeli spoke again.

'Why don't you seduce her? I'm sure you could quite easily. Women always fall at your feet, and when Papa realises that the Ice Queen had only pretended to be interested in him for his money, he'll get rid of her and everything will return to normal.'

By *normal* Nefeli presumably meant that Stelios would revert to behaving like a man in his late sixties who should be preparing for his retirement instead of lusting after a blonde bimbo who saw cash signs when she looked at him. Except that Isla was not your average bimbo. It would make life a lot easier if she was, Andreas brooded.

'I don't want to risk getting frostbite,' he quipped. He swore silently. It wasn't that he had any objection to his father taking another wife. Just not *her*. Not Isla. Why couldn't the old man marry a woman of a similar age to him? A comfortably plump widow who would share Stelios's twilight years, rather than an ice-cool blonde with intelligent grey eyes and a Mona Lisa smile that drove Andreas to distraction.

His thoughts flew back to eighteen months ago when he had been summoned to the house in Kensington which his father had purchased shortly after his wife's death, some six months earlier. Stelios's decision to move to London had been a surprise, and after Andreas had handed his rain-spattered jacket to the butler and been shown into the drawing room, he'd intended to ask why his father had chosen to live in a country with such an infernal climate.

But his mind went blank and his gaze was riveted

on the woman sitting close to Stelios on the sofa. Too damned close, had been Andreas's first thought, followed by a strong urge to snatch her away from his father's side. She rose to her feet, as graceful and supple as a ballerina, and slipped her hand beneath Stelios's arm when he stood up. Her solicitousness as she hovered protectively next to his father had irked Andreas.

'Andreas, finally you have found the time to pay me a visit.'

Stelios's greeting held a note of criticism which Andreas had come to expect, and he gritted his teeth as he stepped forwards to kiss his father's cheek. 'It is good to see you looking well, Papa.'

In fact his father looked tired, but Andreas barely noticed and his attention was on the woman. Who was she? Stelios's personal assistant perhaps? Her appearance gave no clue to her role in Stelios's life. She was wearing a white dress with three-quarter-length sleeves and a softly flared skirt that fell to just below her knees. A narrow black belt around her slender waist and black patent stiletto-heeled shoes were elegant accessories. Her hair was the colour of pale honey, drawn back from her face and tied in a ponytail that reached halfway down her back. She looked as demure as a nun, but the curve of her full lips and her high, firm breasts suggested an understated sensuality.

Andreas couldn't take his eyes off her and he gave a jolt when his father said drily, 'Allow me to introduce my housekeeper, Miss Stanford. Isla, this is my son, Andreas.'

'I'm pleased to meet you,' she murmured.

Her voice made Andreas think of a cool mountain stream and at that precise moment he would have gladly jumped into an ice bath to put out the fire raging inside him.

'The pleasure is mine, Miss Stanford.' He had intended to sound sardonic, but the word *pleasure* hovered in the air, infusing his greeting with sensual heat and something that sounded to his own ears like a challenge. He noticed the faint flush of rose pink that stained her cheeks like the sweep of an artist's brush over a white canvas. Her eyes widened a fraction and Andreas glimpsed his confusion mirrored in those grey depths.

There was another emotion too. He recognised a flash of awareness, before her long eyelashes that were a few shades darker than her hair swept down and shut him out. Time juddered to a standstill. In the silence Andreas heard the harsh rasp of his breath and the unevenness of hers, but when she met his gaze again her expression was unreadable.

She turned to Stelios. 'I'll go and make tea.'

'Thank you, my dear.' A look passed between the old man and his housekeeper that Andreas could not decipher. Irritation swept through him. When the hell had his father, a lifelong coffee addict, started drinking tea?

'I prefer coffee,' he said abruptly, earning a frown from Stelios.

'Of course.' Isla Stanford gave a perfunctory smile that made Andreas long to ruffle her composure. He wanted, badly, to discover if there was heat beneath her ice and if her lips would fit the shape of his as perfectly as he imagined.

She stepped past him and her elusive perfume teased his senses. He watched the sway of her hips as she walked across the room and heard himself blurt out, 'Would you like some help?'

'I can manage, thank you.' She sounded amused.

Pausing in the doorway, she glanced back at him and her brows arched as she gave him a speculative look that made him feel like a wet-behind-the-ears schoolboy. 'Or don't you trust that I can make Greek coffee, Andreas?'

The way she spoke his name in her soft English accent had made him want to growl like a predatory beast. Andreas hadn't trusted *her,* and every time he had met Isla on subsequent visits to his father in London his instincts warned him that she was trouble. Now the news of Stelios's engagement to the woman his sister had christened the Ice Queen proved that those instincts had been right.

He followed Nefeli into the house, where the marble-lined entrance hall was blessedly cool after the heat outside. Andreas had left California sixteen hours ago. Admittedly, travelling by private jet was not arduous but he was looking forward to a leisurely shower and a drink. He was about to ask the butler Dinos to bring a whisky and soda to his room when his sister turned to him.

'You had better hurry up and get changed. You're later than expected. Papa has arranged a formal dinner party this evening to celebrate his engagement to Isla.' She grimaced. 'I can't believe he is planning to marry her. He's making a fool of himself. Can't you think of *anything* that might make Papa see sense?'

Nefeli's plea stayed in Andreas's mind when he entered his private suite of rooms and quickly showered, before he donned black suit trousers, a snowy white shirt and a black dinner jacket. He would have preferred to pull on a pair of old denim shorts and a T-shirt and stroll down to the beach, but instead he had to sit through a dinner party to mark his father's betrothal. *Theos!* He glowered at his reflection in the mirror and raked his fingers through his unruly dark hair that moments ago he'd attempted to tame with a comb.

He could in fact think of something that might make his father question his relationship with his erstwhile housekeeper who was now his fiancée. What if he were to reveal how Isla had come apart in his arms when he'd kissed her in London a month ago? Would Stelios be so keen to marry her?

Andreas's jaw clenched at the memory of Isla's wild response to him—the way she had opened her mouth beneath his and made a husky moan when he'd thrust his tongue between her lips. With a frown he acknowledged that he had kissed Isla to satisfy his curiosity, but she had tested his control in a way he hadn't expected. So much so that he had cut his trip to England short and flown back to California the next day.

Had Isla set her sights on a bigger prize? Stelios was the head of Karelis Corp—the family-owned business which operated the largest oil refinery in Europe. The company also ran the biggest chain of fuel stations in Greece and had interests in shipping and banking. Andreas was the heir to the Karelis business empire but he was in no rush to take over from his father. He had carved out a career as a champion rider in the World Superbike league until a serious accident had forced him to retire from motorbike racing.

Forcing his thoughts back to the present, Andreas muttered a curse and strode out of his suite. He paused in the corridor outside his father's private apartment and knocked on the door. If he could have a conversation with Stelios and his new fiancée before dinner, he might have a clearer understanding of the reason for their surprise engagement. There was no reply, and after waiting for a few seconds he opened the door and glanced around the sitting room. The door leading to the bedroom was closed and the idea that Stelios was in there with Isla evoked a corrosive feeling in the pit of Andreas's stomach.

The bedroom door opened and, before he had time to retreat, the butler walked through to the sitting room. 'I thought that my father and Miss Stanford might be here,' Andreas explained.

'Kyrios Stelios is downstairs in the salon. He asked me to fetch his glasses.' Dinos lifted his hand, in which he held a spectacles case. 'Miss Stanford's room is next door but she is down in the salon with your father.'

So Stelios and Isla were not sharing a bedroom at the villa, Andreas mused as he descended the marble staircase. It struck him as unusual behaviour for a couple who had announced their intention to marry. The whole situation of the sudden engagement was odd, especially as his father hadn't mentioned his marriage plans at their last meeting a month ago.

It was not his concern if Stelios made a fool of himself over his pretty young housekeeper, Andreas told himself. If he admitted that passion had flared between him and Isla, his father might not believe him, or might accuse him of trying to make trouble. Their relationship had never been close, especially after Stelios had been forced to choose between his wife and family, and his mistress.

Andreas had been twelve when his father had admitted that he'd been seeing another woman in England and intended to leave his marriage for her. Andreas's mother had been devastated, and Andreas had vowed that he would never speak to his father again unless he dumped his mistress and returned to his wife and children. He'd hoped that by taking his mother's side he would win her love, but she had continued to treat him with the same disinterest that she'd always shown him. His father had remained married but from then on he had been cool towards Andreas.

Helia Karelis had died two years ago from an overdose of her sleeping pills. A tragic accident, the coroner had recorded, but Andreas was sure his mother had known what she was doing when she'd swallowed a handful of pills, just as he was sure she had never got over her husband's affair, even though it had happened many years ago. Her unhappiness with her marriage had proved to Andreas the folly of falling in love. He avoided emotional dramas in the same way that any sane person would take precautionary measures against coming into contact with the Ebola virus.

As for Isla, Andreas shrugged his shoulders. He couldn't explain why he had come on to her like a teenager on a first date in London. It wasn't his style and he was confident that when he met her again he would see her for the gold-digger he suspected she was. The way she had responded to his kiss with a sweet ardency that had almost made him believe she was inexperienced must have been an act, he told himself.

He strode into the salon where pre-dinner cocktails were being served and stopped dead in his tracks. The room was full of guests—various relatives and, curiously, considering the dinner party was supposed to be a family gathering, several high-ranking representatives from the oil industry were present as well as members of Karelis Corp's board of directors. There was a low hum of chatter, the clink of glasses on silver trays carried by the serving staff. But Andreas only saw Isla and his blood thundered in his ears.

This was a different Isla to the decorous housekeeper

he had met on previous occasions at his father's house in Kensington. Tonight she was a lady in red—a sultry siren in clingy scarlet velvet, with sparkling jewels around her throat that drew his attention to the pale upper slopes of her breasts above the plunging neckline of her dress. Her blonde hair was swept up into a chignon to expose the delicate line of her neck. The scarlet gloss on her lips emphasised their fullness.

Lowering his gaze, he saw that the hem of her dress came to her mid-thigh and her long slim legs were enhanced by high-heeled strappy shoes. Isla Stanford was every hot-blooded male's fantasy and Andreas was burning up. She looked over at him, and as their eyes locked he saw a pink stain spread across her face. The convulsive movement of her throat when she swallowed told him that she was as aware as he was of the electrical current that arced between them. He stared at her mouth, so lush and red and infinitely inviting, and felt the urgent stirring of his desire swell beneath his trousers.

For a moment Andreas forgot that Isla was attending the party as Stelios's guest. Something primitively possessive swept through him and he strode across the room, driven to stake his claim on the woman who had been in his thoughts too often in the past months. He and Isla had unfinished business.

But just then his father finished talking to another guest and slipped his arm around Isla's waist. Andreas's eyes narrowed as he halted in front of the mismatched couple.

'Finally, you are here.' Stelios sounded irritable. 'I expected you to arrive several hours ago. We were about to start dinner without you.'

'Good evening, Papa,' Andreas greeted his father

drily. 'Miss Stanford.' He kept his expression bland as he glanced at Isla and back to Stelios. 'I apologise if I am late. I said I would arrive some time in the afternoon but I did not specify an exact time and I was unaware that you were giving a dinner party.'

Stelios sniffed. 'Well, you are here now. I hope you will offer your congratulations when I tell you that Isla has agreed to be my fiancée.'

Even though Andreas had been pre-warned by his sister of his father's engagement, the sight of a diamond the size of a rock on Isla's finger filled him with fury. It had to be a joke, surely? This grey-haired, wrinkled old man and an exquisite English rose who must be some forty years younger than her future husband.

He jerked his gaze to Isla's face and noted the faint quiver of her lower lip, the flash of sexual awareness in her wide grey eyes that she quickly concealed beneath the sweep of her lashes. She was *his*, goddammit. Yet it was his ageing father's arm around her slender waist and Stelios's obscenely gaudy ring glittering on her finger.

'Well, Andreas?' his father prompted. 'I can see you are surprised by my news, but I'm sure you will agree that I am a lucky man to have such a beautiful fiancée.'

At a rough guess, the diamond solitaire was worth a six-figure sum. Andreas gave a sardonic smile. 'Congratulations,' he drawled, directing his mocking gaze at Isla. 'You appear to have hit the jackpot.'

CHAPTER TWO

THE INSOLENCE OF the man! Isla's temper had simmered throughout the interminable five-course dinner as Andreas's loaded comment echoed in her ears. Thankfully, he had sat at the far end of the table from where she and Stelios were seated, but she'd felt his brilliant blue eyes watching her, and his speculative gaze added to her tension in a situation that was already uncomfortable.

From halfway down the table, she'd been aware of the poisonous looks that Stelios's daughter directed at her. At the end of the dinner, Stelios had stood up and asked the guests to raise their glasses in a toast to his new fiancée. It was taking the pretence too far and Isla's doubts about what she was doing on Louloudi had intensified.

Giving a soft sigh, she pushed open the French windows and stepped outside onto the terrace. It was dark now, and the stunning view across the gardens to the sea beyond was hidden. Although summer was coming to an end, the night was sultry and the air was thick with the scents of rosemary and lavender which grew in big terracotta pots.

Isla's hand strayed to the ruby and diamond necklace around her throat and once again she checked that the clasp was securely fastened.

'I'm terrified I might lose it,' she'd whispered to Stelios earlier in the day while they had posed for photographers in the boardroom of Karelis Corp in Athens. 'The necklace must be worth a fortune. I'd feel happier wearing something less ostentatious.'

Stelios had dismissed her concerns and taken hold of her hand, lifting it up to brush his lips across the enormous diamond ring that he'd slipped onto her finger just before they had faced the cameras. 'Try to relax and smile,' he murmured. 'The eyes of the world will be on you when the news of our betrothal is announced in the media tomorrow. I am a billionaire and people will expect my fiancée to wear fabulous jewellery and dress in haute couture.'

After the press conference recording they had boarded a helicopter for the short flight to Stelios's island. When they were seated in the helicopter's luxurious cabin he gave her a wry smile. 'I'm sure I don't need to remind you of the importance of making our engagement appear convincing in front of the press. It is vital at this time of financial turbulence that Karelis Corp's competitors believe I am a strong leader of the company. Just as importantly, I want to hide my illness from my family until after my daughter's twenty-first birthday.'

'I know you are trying to protect Nefeli. But I urge you to tell her and Andreas the truth. Your children won't be pleased about our engagement. They already dislike me.'

Stelios's daughter had barely hidden her hostility towards Isla whenever she had visited her father at his home in Kensington. And Andreas had nothing but disdain for her. Isla was quite certain of that, even though she had only met him a handful of times. Oh, on the surface he was polite enough. Quite charming, in fact. But she wasn't fooled by his laid-back air and the careless smile that curved his lips but did not match the coldly cynical expression in his eyes.

She didn't know why Andreas had disapproved of her when she'd been employed as his father's housekeeper, or why he'd kissed her the last time he had come to London. The kiss had been unexpected, which was why she had responded to him, she assured herself.

'You are mistaken. I am sure my children find you delightful.' Stelios had sought to reassure her. 'I need you to be the focus of attention. Everyone will be fascinated by my beautiful fiancée and they won't notice that I have lost weight. I will explain about my illness when the time is right to do so. But I want Nefeli to enjoy her twenty-first birthday party, spared from the knowledge that I will not be around to celebrate future birthdays with her.'

Isla couldn't argue with Stelios's reasoning or his desire to protect his daughter when she understood the devastation of losing a parent. It had taken her a long time to come to terms with her mum's death in a horrific accident. Tragically, Stelios had arrived in England in search of Marion six months too late.

The muted sounds of the party drifted across the terrace and Isla was glad to be outside, away from the spotlight for a few minutes. The ruby necklace felt heavy around her neck and she wished she hadn't allowed Stelios to persuade her to wear it. But he had insisted that the necklace and matching drop earrings were perfect accessories for the red dress he'd suggested she should wear to the press conference and dinner party. The tight-fitting dress clung to her body and the scooped neckline revealed more of her cleavage than Isla was comfortable with. She did not normally wear attention-grabbing clothes. But the point of her overtly sexy outfit and the reason for the announcement of their engagement was to draw attention away from Stelios's ill-health.

The sound of footsteps on the terrace behind her caused the hairs on the back of her neck to stand on end, a sixth sense warning her of imminent danger. She froze when a mocking voice drawled, 'Ah, the blushing bride-to-be! You *have* been a clever girl, Isla.'

Her heart gave an annoying flip, as it always did when Stelios's son was in the vicinity, and it took every ounce of her willpower to turn towards him when her instincts urged her to flee. Somehow she managed to say calmly, 'Whatever do you mean, Andreas?'

The simple act of uttering his name evoked a wild heat inside her, and she prayed he would think her cheeks were flushed because the temperature in Greece was much warmer than the chilly, grey England she had left two days ago. Isla hated that Andreas Karelis made her feel like a gauche teenager but she suspected he had the same effect on most women.

Handsome did not come near to describing his sculpted features, with those razor-edge cheekbones, square jaw and outrageously sensual mouth that looked as if it had been shaped entirely for the purpose of kissing. His hair was the same shade of dark brown as the rich Greek coffee she had served him when he had visited his father at the house in Kensington.

It was not just his height—she estimated that he was three or four inches over six foot—or his attractive features, dominated by his startling blue eyes, that set him apart from other men. Andreas possessed a smouldering sensuality that Isla could not ignore, however much she wished she could.

Although he had retired from motorbike racing he was still regarded as a sporting legend by an army of adoring groupies. His reputation as a playboy was reinforced by stories of his love-life played out in the pages of tabloid newspapers and celebrity gossip magazines. Not that Isla took the slightest interest in the scandalous headlines about Andreas, but she knew they upset his father and she had resolved to protect Stelios from stress and worry as much as she possibly could for the time he had left.

It was inexplicable the way her pulse quickened and her breasts rose and fell jerkily when she was anywhere near Andreas. Worse was the realisation that he knew the effect he had on her. He smiled, baring his teeth and reminding her of a wolf that had cornered its prey. Isla considered walking as quickly as her skyscraper stiletto heels would permit, back inside the villa where Stelios was chatting with some of his dinner guests. But before she could move Andreas stepped towards her and she found herself edging up against the stone balustrade.

In the moonlight he seemed even bigger and distinctly menacing as his muscular, whipcord body loomed over her. There was nothing she could do but brazen it out and she forced herself to tilt her head and meet his hard stare.

'I have a feeling that you were not paying me a compliment when you called me clever,' she remarked, pleased that she sounded composed when she felt anything but.

His eyes narrowed, but not before she'd glimpsed a flash of surprise at her challenging tone. 'There are words to describe women like you and none of them are complimentary.'

Isla blinked, taken aback by the ferocity in Andreas's

low voice. The contemptuous curl of his lips caused a stab of hurt beneath her breastbone. Her treacherous heart hammered when he lifted his hand and ran his forefinger over the rubies at her throat.

'Very pretty,' he said, still in that harsh tone that seemed to come from deep within him. But although he touched the blood-red stones strung alternately between sparkling diamonds, his eyes were on her face and his expression made her shiver and burn simultaneously. She held her breath when he moved his hand up to one of her ears and flicked his finger against the huge ruby surrounded by diamonds dangling from her earlobe. 'Was this jewellery, and the shiny bauble on your finger, your price for agreeing to marry my father?'

'I don't have a price.'

He gave a disbelieving snort. 'Tell me, Isla, why would a beautiful young woman choose to become engaged to an elderly billionaire if not for financial gain?'

Her temper flared at his implication that she was a fortune hunter. 'Do you think I'm a gold-digger?'

'Well done. I said you were clever,' he mocked.

The condemnation in Andreas's eyes was unjust. For a moment Isla was tempted to defend herself by explaining the truth about her relationship with his father. But she'd given her word to Stelios that she would keep his secret. A secret which was going to have huge implications for his family and possibly for his oil refining business. As yet Andreas was unaware that Karelis Corp was threatened by a hostile takeover bid from another company. Soon he would learn that her engagement to his father was intended to make Stelios appear strong and in control of the company, and Andreas might even thank her.

'Your father and I have an understanding...'

He swore, his voice low but no less savage. 'Does Stelios know about us?'

'Us?' Isla's brows lifted and she injected cool disdain into her tone. 'There has never been *us*.'

'We shared a scorching kiss at my father's house in London. *Theos!* The chemistry between us was explosive,' Andreas reminded her.

Heat spread across Isla's face. She needed no reminding of her uncharacteristically wanton behaviour. She had declined Stelios's invitation to join him and Andreas when she'd served coffee in the drawing room. Making the excuse that she was doing some baking, she had carefully not met Andreas's speculative gaze. But later he had returned the tea tray to the kitchen.

'Thanks. You can leave the cups in the sink,' she told him in a dismissive voice, hoping he would take the hint and return to his father. Her heart-rate quickened when he lounged against the kitchen counter.

'So you weren't lying,' he murmured, watching her take a tray of madeleines out of the oven. 'I assumed you'd said you were busy in the kitchen because you wanted to avoid me.'

'I never tell lies,' she said crisply, focusing her attention on lifting the delicate little cakes onto a cooling rack rather than look at Andreas. But she was fiercely aware of him, casually dressed in jeans that hugged his lean hips and a black T-shirt moulded to his muscular torso. His rampant masculinity disturbed her and the sensual musk of his aftershave in the warm kitchen assailed her senses.

'I'm glad to hear it. Perhaps you can explain why my father has fallen asleep in his armchair in the middle of the day. I know he is not getting any younger, but he has always had the energy of a man half his age.'

Weeks of gruelling chemotherapy had drained Stelios's strength, but Isla couldn't reveal to Andreas that his father was undergoing treatment for cancer. So much for her boast that she did not tell lies, she thought ruefully. 'Your father has been working hard recently,' she murmured. 'Why on earth would I want to avoid you?'

She had asked the question to distract attention away from Stelios's health—and her ploy worked. Andreas moved closer and there was a wicked gleam in his eyes as he slid his hand beneath her chin and tilted her face up to his.

'You tell me, *omorfia mou*. Do you think I haven't noticed the hungry looks you send me every time I pay my father a visit?'

'I don't...' she began, her face flaming with embarrassment that Andreas had guessed her fascination with him. It was so unlike her. She was always guarded with men, determined to protect her heart against the pain of rejection that she'd felt so deeply in the past. Andreas's sexy laugh sent a tremor through her and, fool that she was, Isla ignored her common sense which told her to step away from him.

'Yes, you do,' he drawled. 'What's more, you want me to kiss you.'

Her heart leapt into her throat. 'I do not...' she whispered, but her denial died away as he lowered his head until his lips were centimetres above hers and his warm breath grazed her skin.

'Liar.'

He had kissed her then. Although kiss was not an apt description of the way he had claimed her mouth with an arrogant possession that should have appalled her. Instead she had capitulated to his mastery, unable to resist his fiery passion and the bold sweep of his tongue between her lips.

The kiss was unlike anything Isla had ever experienced before. She had been kissed by other men—a few, although she could count on one hand the number of dates she'd been on that had got as far as a fumbling kiss at the end of the evening, she thought ruefully. When Andreas kissed her, she discovered a deeply sensual side to her nature that shocked her. But, before she had a chance to explore how he made her feel, he snatched his mouth from hers and stepped away from her so abruptly that she grabbed hold of the kitchen counter to support her legs that had turned to jelly. Andreas's hard-boned face gave no clue to his thoughts and he walked out of the kitchen without a word.

Isla felt humiliated by his rejection, which brought back painful memories of when she'd been a teenager and had introduced herself to her father. With hindsight, perhaps she had been naïve to hope that David Stanford would be delighted to meet the daughter he'd abandoned when she was a few months old. But his insistence that there was no place for her in his life had been a brutal end to her hopes of having a relationship with her father. Isla had vowed then never to allow herself to be hurt by any man ever again.

She was jolted back to the present when she felt the pressure of Andreas's hard thigh against hers. She hadn't been aware that he'd moved, but now she found herself trapped against the balustrade. Her breath hitched in her throat when he ran his finger lightly down her hot cheek. She realised that she had been staring at his sensual mouth while she'd relived the kiss they had shared in London. The gleam in his eyes told her he had read her thoughts.

'Tell me about your romance with my father,' he demanded in a cynical voice. 'It seems very sudden. A few weeks ago you were employed as his housekeeper and you were quite happy to kiss me.'

'The kiss was a mistake that I immediately regretted.' She flushed at his look of arrogant disbelief. 'It's true. You're a playboy who uses women for your pleasure and discards them like trash when you are bored of them. You asked why I accepted your father's proposal and I'll tell you. Stelios is a gentleman. He is kind and sweet...'

Isla's voice thickened with emotion. Stelios was the only person, apart from her mother, who had ever cared about her, but soon he would be gone from this world, just as her mother had gone, and she would be alone again. The one tiny comfort was that Stelios and Marion would finally be together.

'You expect me to believe that my father's wealth has no bearing on your decision to accept his marriage proposal?' Andreas gritted.

'I don't care what you believe. The truth is that I love your father.'

Andreas jerked as if she'd slapped him. His blue eyes burned into Isla like lasers, seeking out every last secret in her soul as his dark head came closer, blotting out the light from the room behind him so that there was just the darkness of the night and the harsh sound of his breaths echoing the erratic beat of her heart.

'Love?' he mocked. He captured her wrist between his strong fingers. 'I could kiss you right now and you wouldn't stop me, even though my father, who you profess to love, and the guests he invited to celebrate his engagement to you are only feet away from us.'

He dropped his gaze to the exposed upper slopes

of her breasts that were rising and falling jerkily. Isla knew she should demand that he release her. But she couldn't speak, could barely think. The spicy scent of his aftershave, mixed with something elusive and *male,* swamped her senses. His mouth, so close to hers but not close enough, was an unbearable torment. Heat swept through her and she felt an ache low in her pelvis. Her breasts felt heavy and she wanted... Oh, God, she wanted his mouth everywhere on her body.

Her tongue darted out to moisten her lips and Andreas swore. 'This is crazy,' he said hoarsely. He sounded as if he was waging an internal battle with himself and his voice jolted Isla to her senses.

She must be out of her mind to allow Andreas to undermine her defences. Even if she hadn't agreed to the pretend engagement with Stelios, it would be foolish to succumb to her desire for Andreas, which made her feel hot and shivery at the same time.

No other man had ever excited her the way Andreas did, and she longed to press herself against his whipcord body and burn in his fire. But the kiss they had shared in London had clearly meant nothing to him, she reminded herself, still smarting from the memory of how he had walked away from her without a backward glance. She would not be Andreas's plaything and she put her hand on his chest to push him away, not sure whether to be relieved or disappointed when he dropped his arms to his sides and stepped away from her.

Light spilled across the terrace from the drawing room as the door swung open and Stelios's slightly stooped figure was silhouetted in the doorframe. 'Isla?'

'I'm here,' she called out. She was still looking at Andreas and flushed at the contemptuous expression in his eyes when he stared back at her. Thank goodness she had come to her senses and stopped him from kissing her.

'What are you doing out here in the dark?' Stelios asked.

'I was pointing out the lights of some of the notable buildings on the mainland to Isla,' Andreas told his father, falling into step beside her when she walked back across the terrace. 'I explained that the villa stands on a hill, hence the excellent view.'

Stelios was silent as his eyes moved between Isla and his son. 'Yes, I see,' he said softly at last. Isla prayed he didn't. It was ridiculous to feel guilty, she told herself. Stelios had promised that he would explain to his family the reason for their fake engagement after Nefeli's birthday party. But the affection she felt for the elderly man was genuine and she smiled at him as she slipped her arm through his.

'I'm sorry you were looking for me. I should have told you that I was stepping outside for some fresh air.'

'Your advice is needed,' Stelios told her. 'My friend Georgios is planning to visit the British Museum in London and he is especially interested in seeing the collection of ancient Greek antiquities housed there. I explained that you will be able to advise him which galleries and exhibits he would enjoy.'

'Do you spend a lot of time in a museum, Isla?' Andreas's tone was sceptical.

'I work as an assistant curator in the Greek and Roman department at the British Museum. The position is part-time, allowing me to fit the hours around my job as your father's housekeeper in London, as well as studying for my PhD in classical civilisations.'

That wiped the smirk off Andreas's face, Isla thought with satisfaction as she allowed Stelios to escort her back into the salon to join the other guests. Andreas had accused her of being a gold-digger and she'd enjoyed his obvious surprise that she had a career. But she was annoyed with herself for caring about his opinion of her. Common sense told her that he was the last man on the planet she should be drawn to.

She glanced over her shoulder and saw that he had followed them into the salon and taken a drink from the butler. Andreas must have sensed her eyes on him and he turned his head to look directly at her, lifting his glass in mocking salute before he drained the amber liquid in one gulp. Isla watched the movement of his Adam's apple as he swallowed.

He was unashamedly masculine and she remembered how his body had felt as hard as steel when he'd trapped her up against the balustrade on the terrace with a muscular thigh. His olive-toned skin gleamed like bronze in the brightly lit room, and when he raked his hand carelessly through his dark hair her fingers itched to do the same.

Isla had never been this fascinated by a member of the opposite sex before. She had dated a few guys at university but was wary of being hurt and she'd never felt a desire for any of those relationships to progress as far as the bedroom, which was why she couldn't understand her response to Andreas. She did not like him and certainly didn't trust him, so why did he make her senses sing and bring her body to urgent life?

She had the unenviable title of the world's oldest virgin, Isla thought wryly. Although she doubted that Andreas would believe it. His cynical expression when he'd seen the sparkling diamond ring on her finger indicated that he was convinced she had used her feminine wiles to captivate his billionaire father.

CHAPTER THREE

ANDREAS'S FEET POUNDED on the sand where the waves rippled against the shore. The sun was climbing high in the sky and the temperature was already soaring. Usually he went for a run at the break of dawn when the day was fresh and full of possibilities. But he had woken late after a restless night. Sleep had eluded him for hours as he'd struggled to understand his behaviour the previous evening when he'd followed Isla out onto the terrace and been tempted to kiss her.

Theos, she had made him shake like a teenager at the mercy of his hormones. The chemistry between them had been almost tangible and if she hadn't pushed him away he doubted he would have been able to resist her. But the realisation that he could have been caught in a compromising situation with his father's fiancée had filled him with self-loathing. Even more incomprehensible was the fact that Isla had threatened his self-control with her mix of sensuality and innocence, which *couldn't* be real, he told himself.

He was convinced that Isla was a gold-digger. Andreas had learned from bitter personal experience that some women had no scruples and would do anything to get their hands on the Karelis fortune. His mouth thinned as he remembered the lies that an ex-girlfriend,

Sadie, had told the media about him after he'd seen through her attempt to deceive him. He should have realised sooner that Sadie had been more interested in his bank balance than him. He would bet his entire fortune that Isla was attracted to his elderly father's wealth. Her air of vulnerability, which evoked a protective instinct in Andreas he hadn't known he possessed, was no doubt part of her clever act, he thought grimly.

He ran faster, pushing himself until his lungs burned. But when he reached the end of the bay—after passing the old fisherman's cottage that he'd turned into his private bolthole—and climbed the headland of volcanic rock, he barely noticed the stunning view of the crystalline turquoise sea. Instead he visualised Isla in her sexy red dress and remembered how soft her body had felt against his when she'd brushed past him on the terrace.

She had insisted that she loved Stelios. Of course she was bound to say that, Andreas brooded. But, for all his cynicism, he could not deny that there had been genuine emotion in her voice. Another thing which had thrown him was learning that she was highly educated and worked in a goddamn museum. If she had been an airhead it would be easier to dismiss her relationship with his father. Isla Stanford was an enigma. Andreas did not know what to make of her and it irritated the hell out of him.

On his way back to the villa his phone rang. 'You are sure about this?' he questioned the security officer who he'd asked to look into Isla's background. 'I see. That's very interesting. Keep digging, Theo.'

His father and Isla were sitting at the breakfast table on the terrace which overlooked the infinity pool. Andreas hoped to slip unnoticed into the house, but Stelios waved to him and with a faint sigh he walked towards the table.

'*Kalimera*, Papa, Isla,' he murmured in greeting. The thought briefly crossed his mind that his father looked thinner than when he'd seen him in London a month ago. But his gaze was drawn to Isla and he forgot everything else.

In contrast to the sex-bomb image she'd projected last night, this morning she looked as pure as the driven snow in a pale lemon sundress with narrow straps that revealed her delicate shoulders. It was the first time Andreas had seen her hair loose and he wished he could run his fingers through the mass of honey-gold silk that tumbled in soft waves down her back.

Frustration darkened his mood. His fascination with Isla was something he'd never experienced before. Women came and went in his life without making any impact on him. He enjoyed their company as long as it was on his terms and he liked sex uncomplicated by commitment. Perhaps he wanted Isla so badly because she was off limits, he derided himself. For a man who had discovered while he was still a teenager that he could have any woman he wanted with the minimum of effort on his part, the fact that she was unobtainable made her exciting.

But maybe the reason why his heart jolted against his ribs when he met her cool grey gaze was simply that Isla was breathtakingly lovely. Tearing his gaze from her, Andreas glanced at the pile of newspapers on the table. Most of the European tabloids carried a photo on the front page of Stelios looking into the eyes of his new fiancée while he pressed his lips against the enormous diamond on her finger.

Andreas had woken to the storm on social media created by his father's marriage plans. The announcement had resulted in a spike in Karelis Corp's share price on the stock market. Investors liked strong company leaders, and presumably the news that Stelios was planning to marry a woman decades younger than him proved that the old man was still a force to be reckoned with, Andreas thought sardonically.

'I am surprised that you decided to make a public statement about your engagement, Papa. You have previously been critical whenever my name has made the headlines.'

Stelios's lips thinned. 'A kiss-and-tell story by one of your disgruntled ex-lovers in a downmarket rag is not the same thing as an announcement about my future plans to the media.'

Andreas was genuinely curious. 'You have always kept your personal life separate from business but I understand that you invited journalists into the boardroom of Karelis Corp to make your announcement. I am merely pointing out that it is not like you to court the paparazzi.'

Was it his imagination or did Stelios seem relieved when the conversation was curtailed by the arrival of the butler bearing a jug of coffee? Moments later, Dinos's wife Toula, who had worked as the family's cook at the villa for as long as Andreas could remember, bustled across the terrace carrying a plate with his favourite breakfast of spinach and feta wrapped in filo pastry. He was fond of the couple, who had taken care of him when he was a boy and had been sent to stay on Louloudi in the school holidays because his mother had preferred him to be out of the way.

'I am happy that you no longer race your big motorbike,' Toula told him after they had exchanged greetings. She glanced heavenwards. 'Always I used to pray that you would be safe. When you had your accident I was so worried about you.'

'As you can see, I am fully recovered,' Andreas reassured her, automatically rubbing his hand over the long scar on his chest that was hidden beneath his running vest. The loss of his racing career was still painful and the scar was an ugly reminder of the accident during a race two years ago in which he'd suffered a ruptured aorta that had almost proved fatal.

'We are all glad that Andreas has finally seen sense and given up fooling around on motorbikes and riding them at ridiculous speeds,' Stelios said in a gruff tone.

Andreas's mouth tightened. He hadn't expected sympathy from his father, who had disapproved of his racing career. But the lecture he'd received while he had been recovering from his injuries had driven a wedge further between him and Stelios. It had been the same old rhetoric: Karelis Corp was his destiny and his duty.

'I was the Superbike World Champion for four consecutive years,' he reminded his father. 'The racing team which I own and manage is regarded as a world leader in the development of analytics used to modernise engine configuration testing, and Aeolus Racing has sponsorship worth millions of dollars. I would not call that *fooling around*.'

Stelios frowned. 'Your place is here in Greece, not in California. You know that I would like to retire and you should be preparing to take my place as head of the company.'

'You have spent much of your time in England for the past eighteen months,' Andreas pointed out. 'Every time I visited you in London I tried to talk about Karelis Corp, and in particular some worrying rumours I have heard about the company, but you refused to discuss things with me.'

A dark flush appeared on Stelios's face. 'I need to be sure of your commitment to Karelis Corp. If you spent less time womanising, and there were fewer stories about your personal life in the gutter press I would feel more confident about handing the most powerful role in the company over to you.'

Andreas gritted his teeth. 'You know full well that the woman who sold her story to the papers was lying.'

But the damage to his reputation had been done, Andreas thought bitterly. When lingerie model Sadie Barnes had told him she was pregnant with his child he'd asked for a paternity test. She had tearfully accused him of not trusting her, but he'd insisted on a test. Instead, Sadie had sold a story to the tabloids saying that Andreas had abandoned her and his unborn baby.

The media storm had broken on the day he was due to compete in a motorbike race which, had he won, would have given him the title of World Superbike Champion for a record fifth time. But an hour before the race Stelios had phoned Andreas and accused him of bringing shame to the name Karelis and damaging the company. The furious exchange of words with his father had, Andreas was sure, contributed to his lapse of concentration that had resulted in the high-speed crash.

'I accept that that particular story turned out to be untrue, but your playboy image is not good for Karelis Corp,' Stelios muttered. 'You should be thinking about marrying a suitable wife and settling down.' Andreas gave a snort of derision and Stelios rose to his feet and shook his head when Isla immediately stood up. 'Sit down and finish your breakfast, my dear.' He spoke to her in a softer voice than he had used to his son. 'I need to phone my lawyer and I'll go to my study to make the call.'

Isla looked as though she wanted to argue as she watched Stelios walk slowly towards the house. After a few moments she sat back down and glared at Andreas. Clearly she blamed him for the argument with Stelios. The truth was that he and his father were both strong-willed, but Stelios wanted an heir he could mould into his likeness, not a maverick son who was determined to make his own mark on the world.

Andreas scowled at the plate of food in front of him, his appetite suddenly non-existent. He felt taut and strung out and his mood turned blacker with the realisation that for once he had no control over his feelings. For the first time in his life he wished he was far away from Louloudi, far away from the woman who had such an unsettling effect on him.

The floral fragrance of Isla's perfume assailed him and his skin felt too tight for his body. He wondered what she would do if he walked around the table, leaned over and claimed her mouth with his. Would she respond to him as she had done in London? She had wanted him to kiss her on the terrace last night. Her eyes had flashed silver-bright with desire and he'd sensed the effort it had taken her to resist the attraction that blazed between them. He forced his mind back to the present when Isla spoke.

'Your father loves you, you know,' she said softly. 'He told me that he wishes the two of you were closer.'

Andreas was outraged that Stelios had discussed him with Isla. It felt like a betrayal. 'With respect,' he said grittily, 'my relationship with my father is none of your damn business.'

'I was simply trying to help. I care about Stelios...'

He snorted. 'You sound convincing, but unlike my father I am not the least bit taken in by the role of ingénue that you play so well. Let's face it, Stelios is not the first wealthy old man to be susceptible to your charms. A few years ago you inherited a substantial sum of money from a Major Charles Walters who you had befriended.'

'It's true that I was friends with Charles and his wife Enid. I was shocked when I learned that they had left me a bequest but there was nothing grubby or underhand about it.' Hectic colour flared on Isla's cheeks. 'They were an elderly, childless couple who owned the manor house in the village where I grew up, and they were patrons of the local school. When I was a teenager I had a part-time cleaning job at the manor, and Charles and Enid encouraged my hope of going to university. They died within a few months of each other and left legacies to several young people in the village with the stipulation that the money was to go towards paying university fees. Without their generosity, I would have graduated with a huge debt and struggled to continue with my studies.' She frowned. 'How did you know I had been left some money?'

'You were investigated,' he told her smoothly, watching her grey eyes flash with anger. It gave him a sense of satisfaction knowing he'd rattled her. 'My family are one of the wealthiest in Greece and, although security here on Louloudi is discreet, I asked the protection team to run some checks on you. My father especially is at risk of being kidnapped and held to ransom by criminal gangs.'

'I'm not a *criminal*.' Isla's finely arched brows drew together in a frown. 'Does Stelios know that you had me investigated?'

'Does he know that you inherited money from another wealthy old man?' Andreas countered to avoid
answering her question.

'Your father knows everything about me.'

She met Andreas's gaze across the table and he found
himself looking away first, shaken by the honesty in
her expression. There was something else, an inexplicable sadness. The shimmer of tears made her grey
eyes glisten like wet slate. She was a damn good ac-
tress, he thought grimly, but he refused to fall for her
little-girl-lost look.

Isla stood up and Andreas was aware of the hard thud
of his pulse as the breeze flattened her dress against her
body, revealing the swell of her breasts and the gentle
curve of her hips. 'I wish you would believe that I mean
your father no harm.'

'Stelios doesn't seem to be himself.' Andreas also got
to his feet, frowning as he remembered how exhausted
his father had been at the end of the dinner party.

Isla hesitated. 'He has been working hard.'

The gentle affection in her voice for Stelios evoked
a feeling in Andreas that he refused to acknowledge
was envy. His mother had not shown him tenderness or
affection when he was a child, and since he'd reached
adulthood he'd avoided emotional relationships, assur-
ing himself that he neither wanted nor needed love. He
swore silently, irritated that Isla made him question the
status quo of his life that he'd been perfectly content
with until now.

'Perhaps Stelios is tired for another reason,' he
growled. Isla looked puzzled and he elaborated. 'You
are a lot younger than my father and he might be wearing
himself out trying to keep you happy in the bedroom.'

'Your father and I are not lovers,' she said stiffly.

'Why not?' Andreas's eyes narrowed when she did not answer. 'I'm curious about your relationship with Stelios. I watched the two of you at dinner last night and I'd swear you do not feel any sexual attraction for my father.'

'Not everything is about sex,' she snapped. 'Relationships—meaningful relationships, not the love-'em-and-leave-'em kind that you only seem capable of—are about mutual respect, friendship and trust.'

Andreas frowned, unsettled by her fervent words. In an ideal relationship those were the qualities he would want. But he did not believe in happy ever after. Isla certainly sounded convincing, but he was sure she had an ulterior motive for wanting to marry his father. His conscience pricked that he *wanted* to believe the worst of her. If he believed that she was untrustworthy, it might end his annoying fascination with her. His jaw hardened.

'My guess is that you are determined to make Stelios wait until after he has married you before you will allow him to take you to bed. As his wife you will have access to his fortune.'

Isla drew an audible breath and swung her hand up to his face, but Andreas's reactions were quicker and he captured her wrist before she could strike him. 'I wouldn't,' he advised softly.

'You have a vile mind.' She was breathing hard and her breasts rose and fell jerkily. Her grey eyes darkened with temper but Andreas could feel the pulse in her wrist beating erratically beneath his thumb. The air between them prickled with sexual awareness and he was certain that Isla felt it as intensely as he did. Her voice cracked when she spoke. 'I'm not surprised that Stelios doesn't—' She broke off and dropped her gaze from his.

'My father doesn't approve of me. Is that what you were going to say?' he drawled. It shouldn't hurt as much as it did. He and Stelios hadn't seen eye to eye for years.

'He doesn't feel able to confide in you,' Isla muttered. 'I wish you would talk to Stelios and resolve the differences between you, before...'

'Before...what?' Andreas's brows rose. But whatever Isla had been about to say she clearly thought better of it. She pulled her wrist out of his grasp and turned and walked away. He watched her go and cursed beneath his breath.

The differences between him and his father were not easily resolvable. Stelios had been a largely absent parent when Andreas was young, spending the majority of his time running Karelis Corp, and later with his English mistress. But Andreas was no longer a teenager who saw everything as black or white. He understood how his mother's poor health—she'd often reminded him that she had suffered a stroke due to complications during his birth—must have put a strain on his parents' relationship. He had never felt loved by either of them. He was the Karelis heir, born and raised to take over the company which had been started by his great-grandfather. His father had not forgiven him for putting his motorbike racing career ahead of his duty—especially as Stelios had put duty to his family before his personal happiness.

Nefeli's birthday party could not come round soon enough, Andreas brooded as he resumed his seat at the table and forced himself to eat the *spanakopita* that Toula had made for him. In a few days he would return to California and concentrate on managing Aeolus Racing. Maybe he'd look up the redhead who had flirted with him in a bar before he'd left for Greece. It was weeks since he'd had sex, and celibacy was not a natural state for him. Frustration was no doubt the reason for his inconvenient attraction to his father's fiancée.

CHAPTER FOUR

FROM HER BEDROOM window in the villa Isla could see a dozen luxury tents which had been erected on the lawn in the garden below. They would provide sleeping accommodation for Nefeli's many friends who would be staying on Louloudi for the weekend. It was glamping rather than camping, Isla thought wryly, remembering the few holidays that she and her mum had spent in a tent in very wet Wales. Not that the weather or a tight budget had spoiled their fun. Marion had made everything an adventure, and they had been so close. Her mum had been her best friend and Isla still missed her. Swallowing hard, she forced her thoughts away from the past.

Every bedroom in the villa was occupied by members of the extended Karelis family. For the past two days extensive preparations had been underway for Nefeli's twenty-first birthday party and an air of general chaos pervaded the house. No expense had been spared, and Isla had been amazed by the number of crates of champagne unloaded from the boat which had also brought an army of caterers and other staff to the island.

Stelios was determined that his daughter's birthday party would be perfect. But when Isla knocked on the door of his private suite before she walked in, she found him slumped in an armchair with his eyes closed. The past few days had taken their toll on his strength but he was adamant that no one must know about his illness until he was ready to break the news to his family.

'Is that the dress you are planning to wear tonight?'

'I thought you were asleep.' She smiled at the man who had come to mean so much to her. Stelios was like the father she'd never had. 'Yes.' She ran her hand down the skirt of her oyster-coloured evening gown. The dress had a high neck and long sleeves. Memories of the attraction that had flared between her and Andreas when she'd worn the low-cut red dress two nights ago had been behind her decision to cover up.

She had hardly seen him since he had accused her of being a gold-digger, and she sensed that for the past few days he had deliberately avoided her. But the previous day she had gone to the pool and slipped off her robe in preparation to climb down the steps into the water. She'd hesitated when she'd heard a familiar sexy voice say her name, and silently cursed herself for not noticing that Andreas was down at the other end of the pool.

He swam up to the shallow end with powerful strokes. When he stood up, she noticed a long red scar on his chest that sliced all the way down his abdomen. Water droplets glistened in the whorls of dark hairs that covered his chest and arrowed over his flat stomach. Of their own accord Isla's eyes lowered to his black swim shorts that sat low on his hips, and her mouth went dry.

'Come on in. The pool is heated—and you look cold,' he drawled.

'I'm not cold.' Following his gaze, she looked down and was mortified to see the hard points of her nipples jutting beneath her bikini top. The air around the pool suddenly felt stiflingly hot, and her awareness of Andreas was so intense that Isla's skin prickled. 'Actually, I've changed my mind about having a swim,' she muttered, quickly pulling her robe back on.

'Coward,' he called after her mockingly as she hurried away.

'Isla?' Stelios's voice jolted Isla back to the present, and she hoped he would not query why her face that she could see reflected in the mirror was suffused with colour. 'You look charming, my dear,' Stelios told her. 'But it will be better if you wear a more eye-catching outfit.'

'I don't want to look as though I am in competition with Nefeli at her party,' Isla murmured. The young Greek girl's unfriendly attitude had made it clear how much Nefeli resented her presence on Louloudi.

Stelios closed his eyes once more and Isla bit her lip as she studied him. His skin was grey and his cheekbones were prominent where he had lost weight, but he was desperate to hide the signs of his illness from his family for a little longer.

She sighed. 'I'll choose a different dress.'

'Wear the blue Oscar de la Renta.'

Ten minutes later, Isla returned to Stelios's suite wearing the dress he had suggested. 'You wanted eye-catching and this certainly fits the bill,' she said ruefully. The midnight blue dress was blatantly sexy with a plunging neckline and off-the-shoulder straps. It was made from satin overlaid with chiffon which had a sparkle of silver thread running through the material so that the dress shimmered. The side split in the skirt revealed her leg all the way up to her thigh when she walked. Silver high-heeled shoes gave her an extra four inches of height.

'No one will take any notice of me, and all eyes will be on you,' Stelios said with satisfaction. He handed her a velvet box and Isla gasped as she lifted out a diamond choker.

'I'm only borrowing it for tonight,' she insisted as she fastened the exquisite piece of jewellery around her neck.

'I need you to sparkle this evening,' Stelios told her. 'Nefeli and Andreas must not guess that the party is the last event I will be here to celebrate with them.'

'You don't know that,' Isla whispered. 'The specialist said you could have months left.'

Stelios levered himself slowly out of the armchair. 'You remind me of your mother in so many ways. Not only in your looks. You have Marion's gentleness and compassion. I am so glad that I met you again, Isla. The last time you were just a little girl and now you are a beautiful young woman. One day I hope you will fall in love with a man who will treasure you.'

Fat chance, Isla thought to herself as she followed Stelios out of his suite and they descended the marble staircase. Love was a fool's game, and she must be the biggest fool of all because she could not control the frantic thud of her heart when she walked into the ballroom and the first person she saw—the only person she saw in the crowded room—was Andreas.

He wore 'formal' with the easy air of a man who had been born into wealth and privilege. The Karelis heir in all his spectacularly handsome glory. His tuxedo drew the eye to his broad shoulders and narrow black trousers emphasised his lean, athletic build. Beneath the fine white silk of his shirt, Isla saw the shadow of his black chest hairs. His sophisticated clothes could not hide his raw masculinity and she felt an ache in her womb, a longing for something she could not explain to herself.

The woman hanging onto his arm was exotically beautiful. She had long dark hair cascading over one shoulder and looked as though she had been poured into her sequined green dress. Isla refused to acknowledge a stab of jealousy as she watched Andreas dip his head towards his companion and murmur something in her ear. The intimacy between them suggested that they were lovers. Not that she cared in the slightest who Andreas slept with, she told herself firmly.

Perhaps he sensed her scrutiny for he looked in her direction. Heat blazed in his eyes as he skimmed them over her, moving from her hair, piled in an elaborate chignon on top of her head, down to the daring neckline of her dress and lower to her bared thigh, exposed by the split in the skirt. Finally his gaze rested on the diamond choker around her neck and his lips twisted in a sardonic expression, before he turned his attention back to his glamorous companion.

Isla felt a hollow sensation in her stomach. Why was she allowing a notorious playboy like Andreas to get to her? she wondered. She had promised herself when she was sixteen and her father had dismissed her as if she was a nonentity that she would never again put herself in a position where a man made her feel vulnerable.

Resolutely, she pinned a smile on her lips and slipped her hand through Stelios's arm so that he could lean on her without it being obvious to the other guests. She had a role to play, Isla reminded herself. Stelios wanted her to sparkle and distract attention away from him, and she set about doing just that.

Much later in the evening when she noticed the lines of strain on Stelios's face, Isla ignored his protest and steered him across the ballroom to a sofa in a quiet corner of the room. 'Rest for a while,' she urged, her heart contracting when he gave a low groan of relief as he sank down onto the cushions. 'The party is a great success and Nefeli looks like she is having a wonderful time.'

She moved her eyes from Stelios's daughter, who was dancing with a group of her friends, and felt a stab of pain when she saw Andreas wrapped around a lissom brunette wearing a figure-hugging silver dress. 'Andreas also seems to be enjoying himself,' she said flatly as she became aware that Stelios had followed her gaze.

'I have a feeling that you disapprove of my son,' he murmured. 'Why is that?'

'I… I hardly know him.' Isla felt her cheeks grow warm. She was flustered by Stelios's question, afraid that she had unwittingly revealed her fascination with Andreas. 'I'm sure he's very nice,' she said lamely.

Stelios chuckled. 'I have never heard Andreas described as "nice" before.' He gave her an odd look. 'My son is a complicated man, but his heart is in the right place.'

'Can I get you another drink, or some canapés?' Isla said quickly, keen to move the conversation away from Andreas's heart, which she seriously doubted existed.

Stelios shook his head. 'I'll just sit here. I am feeling a little breathless. But you should go and dance.'

'I'd rather keep you company.' She had stayed at his side all evening and chatted to the other guests. Most people spoke at least a little English, and she had learned to speak modern Greek at the same time as she had been studying ancient Greek history. But Isla was not a natural social butterfly and she felt uncomfortable being the centre of attention. She was surprised that no

one had commented on how frail Stelios looked, but he
had been a powerful figure for so long and she guessed
that he was seen as invincible by his family and business associates.

Her eyes moved back to the dance floor and she
saw that Nefeli was dancing with Andreas. Isla's heart
missed a beat when the tune finished and brother and
sister walked over to where she and Stelios were sitting.

'Papa, will you come and dance with me?' Nefeli
ignored Isla and held out her hand imperiously to her
father.

'Why don't you take my place?' Isla said quickly,
standing up and indicating the empty space she had va-
cated on the sofa. 'Your father was just saying that he
would like to spend some time with you on your birthday.' There was no harm in a white lie if it meant that
Stelios could remain sitting, she told herself.

'An excellent idea,' Andreas murmured. 'We'll leave
these two alone while you dance with me, Isla.'

The gleam in his eyes sent her heart slamming
against her ribcage but she couldn't think of an excuse
to refuse him. Determined that he would not guess the
effect he had on her, she held herself stiffly when he
placed his hand between her shoulder blades and pro-
pelled her towards the dance floor. To make matters
worse, the DJ changed the tempo of the music from
disco to a slow number that prompted the couples
around them to move into each other's arms.

'Relax, I don't bite,' Andreas said drily as he captured her hand in his and splayed the fingers of his other
hand over her naked back, drawing her closer so that
her body brushed against his. The split in her skirt had
fallen open and she could feel his hard thigh muscle
against her stocking-clad thigh. 'You look incredible in

that dress.' His warm breath tickled her ear. 'Are you enjoying the party?'

Isla could not tell him that she longed for the party to be over because she knew it was an ordeal for Stelios. And she was certainly not going to admit that watching Andreas dance with a constant stream of beautiful women had evoked a sensation like sharp knives stabbing her in her stomach. She shrugged. 'Yes, of course. Your father is pleased that it has gone well.'

'You really care about him, don't you?'

Her eyes flew to his face and she expected to see his usual cynical expression, but he was looking at her intently as if he was trying to read her thoughts. Isla hoped that he couldn't because her thoughts were decidedly X-rated.

Andreas danced with a natural grace and rhythm. He moved his hand down and rested it at the base of her spine, drawing her subtly closer so that they were hip to hip. She was shocked to feel the rigid evidence of his arousal and knew he felt the tremor that ran through her when he swore softly and clamped her hard against him. Even though she was wearing four-inch heels she was much shorter than him, and her gaze was focused on his jaw, shaded with black stubble, that she remembered had felt abrasive on her skin that time he'd kissed her in London.

'Of course I care about Stelios,' she said, forcing her mind away from the dangerous path it seemed intent on following.

'But you are not in love with my father and he is not in love with you.' Andreas tightened his hold around her waist when she attempted to pull herself out of his arms. She discovered that while they had been dancing he had steered them towards the door of the ballroom.

Without giving her a chance to protest, he whisked her out to the entrance hall and across to the library.

'Well?' he demanded after he closed the library door and leaned his back against it, crossing his arms over his chest. 'What is the truth about your relationship with my father?'

'Why don't you ask him?' Isla prevaricated.

'I'm asking you.'

She stayed silent and Andreas shrugged. 'I'm prepared to stand here all night until you give me a believable answer. If you are not interested in Stelios's money, and I am convinced from my observations of the two of you that you do not have a physical relationship with my father, why did you agree to marry him?'

It would be wrong for her to betray Stelios's trust and reveal that he was dying. But Isla felt guilty that she could not be honest with Andreas. She chewed her bottom lip and then gave a heavy sigh. 'I met Stelios many years ago when I was a child.'

Andreas looked puzzled. 'Where did you meet him?'

'He was friendly with my mother. Mum worked for a company in England which had been bought by Karelis Corp. She was Stelios's secretary but their relationship developed and they became…close.' Her voice faltered when Andreas frowned. 'I was very young but I remember that Stelios used to come and stay with us.'

'Are you saying that your mother was my father's mistress?'

'You make it sound tawdry but Mum was in love with Stelios and he loved her,' Isla said defensively. 'I can only have been four or five, but I remember it was a happy time. My mum even asked me if I would like Stelios to be my father.'

Andreas swore. 'He was already a father to me and

my sister. Nefeli was a baby when he went off to play happy families with you and your mother in England.'

She bit her lip. 'I was too young to have understood that Stelios had a family in Greece.'

'Your mother must have been aware that Stelios was being unfaithful to his wife. Where was your father?'

'I have no idea. He left when I was a few months old.'

'So your mother became a rich man's mistress.'

Isla's grey eyes flashed. 'Mum loved your father. She never met anyone else after he stopped coming to visit. She didn't talk about him, and I had more or less forgotten him, but when she died I found letters that Stelios had written to her. In one letter he explained that he couldn't bear to be separated from his son and daughter and had decided to remain in Greece with his family. It was a tragic love story.'

She glared at Andreas when he gave a snort of derision. 'Stelios fell in love with my mother but there was no happy ending. After your mother died he came to England to look for Mum, but she had been killed six months earlier. I was struggling to cope with my grief. I had to move out of the house where we'd lived together because I couldn't afford to pay the rent on my income alone, and Stelios offered me a job as his housekeeper. He helped me when I was at my lowest, and when he was…' Just in time she stopped herself from revealing that Stelios had been diagnosed with cancer. 'Your father was lonely and he asked me to marry him.'

Andreas frowned. 'Why did you accept his proposal?'

She was digging herself deeper into a hole, Isla thought ruefully. 'Stelios is very charming and, as I said, he had been kind to me when I was a child. He promised to look after me.'

'So you regard him as a sort of father figure?'

'Something like that,' she mumbled.

Andreas's eyes narrowed. 'What about passion? You are a beautiful woman in the prime of your life and you must have a woman's needs.'

Isla felt herself blush. 'Sex isn't a big deal for me.'

'I don't believe that.' He uncrossed his arms and walked towards her. The evocative scent of his after-shave sent a shiver of awareness through her. 'You say that sex is not important to you but your response to me suggests you are lying. Maybe it's simply that you haven't met a man who can unlock your desires?'

'And you think you are that man?' She tried to sound scornful but her voice was high-pitched and fraught with emotions she was desperate to hide.

'Perhaps,' Andreas murmured. 'Your body betrays you so beautifully.' He lifted his hand and placed his thumb pad over the pulse beating unevenly at the base of her throat.

Isla caught her breath when he lowered his gaze to the outline of her nipples that had hardened betrayingly beneath her dress. His blue eyes glittered. 'I know you want me. You will be making a mistake if you marry my father.'

She felt something sharp and intense coil inside her, a longing that she must deny. 'Do you find it so hard to accept that not every woman on the planet wants to sleep with you?'

His hands dropped to his sides. 'You can deny it as much as you like.' His voice was harsher, scraping across her skin so that she felt raw. 'But this is real and you feel it as much as I do.'

She did not need him to explain what he meant. *This* was the intangible alchemy that shimmered between them and threatened to burst into flame with a shared look. She had never felt anything like it before. Every cell in her body thrummed with awareness of Andreas, but her reaction to him terrified her.

She sensed that he could strip away everything she thought she knew about herself if she allowed him to get too close. But from now on she would be on her guard against him, Isla assured herself as she pushed past him and hurried out of the library.

CHAPTER FIVE

STELIOS WAS ASLEEP when Isla popped into his suite to check if he needed anything. She made sure that a glass of water and his tablets were within his reach on the bedside table. The evening had drained him but he had insisted on remaining at the party until after the fireworks display at midnight. Only then had she persuaded him to leave Nefeli and her friends to continue celebrating.

The young people's voices and laughter drifted up from the tents in the garden and Isla crossed the room and closed the window. Her gaze was drawn to the sea in the distance, dappled by the silver moonlight. It was almost one a.m. but she felt too restless to sleep. She hadn't seen Andreas again after she'd left him in the library and she'd felt annoyed with herself for scanning the ballroom for him. The truth was that he made her feel alive and without his presence the party had seemed flat.

She returned to stand by the bed, listening to Stelios's regular breathing. In the next day or so he would tell his family that he had terminal cancer, and the reason for their fake engagement would no longer be necessary, in private at least. But she had agreed to maintain the pretence of being his fiancée in public until after he'd announced that he was handing over the leadership of Karelis Corp to his son. It was important, Stelios had reiterated, that news of his illness was not made public and he continued to be seen as a powerful leader of the company. Once Andreas became CEO, Isla would be free to return to London and her job at the museum, leaving Stelios to spend his precious final weeks with his family.

Reassured that he was unlikely to stir for many hours, she left him and went to her own room. It was a relief to kick off her high heels and exchange her ball-gown for comfortable jersey shorts and a cotton strap top. She pulled the pins out of her chignon and shook her hair loose, and then slid her feet into leather flip-flops and stepped out into the corridor.

The staff had finished clearing away after the party and the house was quiet. She paused outside Andreas's door, wondering if he was asleep or if one of the gorgeous women who had flocked round him at the party was sharing his bed. Jerking her mind away from images of him and a lover naked and entwined in each other's arms, she went downstairs and out of the house.

Avoiding the garden, she followed a path that led directly to the beach, kicked off her flip-flops and walked across the soft sand. The night was warm and still, the air filled with the scent of the white sand lilies which grew in the dunes and a faint salt tang from the sea. Lost in her thoughts, Isla strolled along the shoreline until the lights from the garden were distant and the stars in the inky sky sparkled as brightly as the diamond choker she had returned to Stelios after the party.

He had tried to persuade her to keep the necklace and the other jewellery she'd worn in her role as his fiancée, but she'd refused. 'You will keep the ring though, won't you?' he'd said when she removed the huge diamond from her finger and placed it in the safe with the choker. 'You have helped me greatly and I want to give you something to remember me by.'

'I'll always remember you,' she had told him softly. Now tears blurred her vision as she stood on the beach, alone beneath the vast heavens.

'I know a cure for insomnia.' The familiar cynical voice came from behind her. Isla spun round and felt her heart collide painfully with her ribs when she made out Andreas sprawled on a slab of rock further up the beach. Behind him was the cottage she'd noticed when she'd walked this way along the beach once before. In the moonlight she saw that the front door was ajar.

Andreas sat upright and proffered the bottle he was holding. 'Bourbon is a cure for most ills, I find.'

'I don't drink spirits. In fact I rarely drink alcohol at all.' She bit her lip when she realised how strait-laced she sounded.

Andreas lifted the bottle to his lips and took a swig. He had discarded his jacket and his bow tie hung loose around his neck. The top few buttons of his shirt were undone and his dark hair fell across his brow, adding to his rakishly sexy appearance. 'You should try it. Who knows, it might help you to loosen up a bit.'

'The man who killed my mother was found to be four times above the legal alcohol limit for driving.'

He swore softly. Isla turned her back on him and stared at the mysterious sea. She had no idea why she had told Andreas about her mum. The bereavement counsellor she'd seen a few times had suggested that talking about the accident might help her come to terms with the tragedy, but mostly she buried her feelings deep inside her and put on a brave face to the world.

'What happened?' Andreas's voice was suddenly close, and Isla gave a start when she discovered that he had moved silently and was standing beside her.

She shrugged. 'Mum was driving home from the call centre where she worked. She'd finished a late shift and the pubs had just closed. The other car hit her head-on. Miraculously, the driver escaped with minor injuries but Mum was killed instantly. In court the driver gave the excuse that he'd got drunk after breaking up with his girlfriend. The judge banned him from driving but didn't send him to prison because it was a first offence and it was felt that he deserved another chance. I wish Mum had been given a second chance.' She could not keep the bitterness out of her voice. 'She was forty-seven when she died.'

'I'm sorry.' The sympathy in Andreas's husky tone tugged on Isla's heart. She felt brittle, as if she might shatter. He moved to stand in front of her and slid his hand beneath her chin to tip her face up to his. She closed her eyes, not wanting him to see her emotions, which were still too raw. A tear slipped from beneath her lashes and she felt him gently brush it away with his thumb. 'When?'

'Two and a half years ago.'

'We have something in common. My mother died two years ago.'

'I know.' She opened her eyes and saw compassion in his gaze. The gleam of the moon made his face all angles and shadows. 'Stelios told me that your mother died a few weeks before you nearly lost your own life in a motorbike race. Were you close to her?'

It was odd how natural it felt when Andreas draped his arm across her shoulders and drew her towards him. Isla knew that she should pull away, and she would in a moment, she told herself. But her aching heart was comforted by this brief connection to another human being.

'No. I was sent away to boarding school at a young age. My grandmother was an American heiress who had married my Greek grandfather, and I spent most school holidays with my relatives in California or I was sent here to Louloudi.'

Andreas shrugged. 'I wasn't close to either of my parents. My father was busy running Karelis Corp and spent a lot of time away from home. When my mother discovered that he had a mistress in England, Stelios told her he wanted to end their marriage.'

Isla felt uncomfortable even though she knew there was no reason for her to feel guilty about her mum's relationship with Stelios. 'Was your mother upset when she found out about the affair?'

'My parents' marriage had been arranged. It was a business merger rather than a love match. Such things were not uncommon in Greek families years ago,' he added, catching Isla's shocked expression. 'They got on well enough until my mother learned of his infidelity and she was devastated.'

'You said that your parents hadn't been in love.'

'Stelios did not love my mother but she loved him.' Andreas exhaled heavily. 'My father wanted a divorce. I was a headstrong twelve-year-old and when I saw my mother crying I told Stelios that if he left the family I would never speak to him again. I forced him to choose between his English mistress and his heir.'

'He chose you,' Isla said quietly. 'Surely it shows that Stelios loved you?'

'He chose me because it was his duty to prepare me for power and leadership of Karelis Corp. But he resented me, especially when I was determined to pursue my own career and lead a different life to the one he had mapped out for me.'

Isla did not know what to say. She had been so young when Stelios had briefly been a father figure in her life, and of course she'd had no idea that he had a family in another country. It was a little less than two years ago, when Stelios had turned up at the house where she had lived with her mum and said that he was searching for Marion Christie, that Isla had learned the truth.

A low rumble of thunder pulled her from her thoughts. While she and Andreas had been talking a breeze had whipped up and raindrops the size of pennies stung her bare arms.

He captured her hand in his and pulled her up the beach. 'We'll shelter in the cottage.'

Within seconds the rain turned to a deluge and by the time they reached the cottage Isla was drenched. She followed Andreas through the front door. 'Wait here,' he ordered.

Moments later a flickering light filled the room as he lit a paraffin lamp and hung it on a hook on the wall. 'There's no electricity here,' he explained. 'The house is an original cottage from when the island was inhabited by a small community of fishermen and their families. The last family moved to the mainland many years ago and my grandfather bought Louloudi and commissioned the villa to be built. I renovated this place myself.'

Isla looked around the small sitting room, which had white-painted walls and bleached wooden ceiling beams. The room was simply furnished with a sofa and armchair covered with brightly coloured throws. A tiny kitchen led off the sitting room, and she thought how lovely it would be to prepare a meal on the rustic table with the sound of the waves breaking on the shore.

She imagined if she and Andreas were lovers relaxing over a leisurely breakfast after a night of passionate lovemaking. She hadn't lied when she'd told him that sex wasn't a big deal to her. She'd even wondered if she was frigid. But when she looked at his handsome face and imagined his sensual mouth claiming hers, the ache low in her pelvis became a throb of need that she had never experienced before.

It was as if she had been in a deep sleep until he had awoken her desire with his kiss. But Andreas was no Prince Charming, she reminded herself. Being trapped in the cottage with him was dangerous, but he was not the danger. It was the way he made her feel that both terrified and excited her.

She had prided herself on being cautious and sensible while the other girls she'd shared digs with at university had thrown themselves into love affairs that too often ended badly. Isla had allowed men to think she was unapproachable as a defence mechanism. The legacy of her father's rejection had made her a coward, she realised with sudden insight. She was twenty-five but she'd never been naked with a man, let alone had a physical relationship.

Telling Andreas about the accident that had claimed her mum's life, and seeing Stelios's health decline, were painful reminders that life was short and she had spent too long mired in hurts of the past. Andreas tempted her to lower her defensive barriers, especially when the fierce gleam in his eyes told her that he found her desirable.

'Storms are fairly common on the coast at this time of year but they tend to blow through quickly.' His voice pulled Isla from her thoughts and she watched him light a second paraffin lamp. He passed the lamp to her. 'Feel free to take a look around. There is a gas hob in the kitchen and I can make coffee if you would like some.'

'No, thanks.' Caffeine at this time of the night—it was actually morning, Isla amended—would not help her to fall asleep when she returned to the villa.

Holding the lamp aloft, she inspected the pretty blue-and-white-tiled kitchen and the shower room next door. A narrow hallway led to the only bedroom, and here the walls were unpainted, leaving the sand-coloured bricks exposed. The one big window had wooden shutters which were closed. In the centre of the room was a four-poster bed with white voile drapes. She stopped just inside the doorway, her gaze drawn to the bed. The sound of the rain drumming on the roof of the single-storey cottage made the bedroom, lit by the warm glow from the lamp, feel like a safe haven from the elements.

Footsteps on the stone floor behind her caused the tiny hairs of her body to stand on end. 'In daylight you must have a wonderful view from the bed,' she murmured.

'The view from where I'm standing right now is pretty good.' Andreas's deep voice rolled through her, and her heart missed a beat when she slowly turned around and found him close to her. She caught her breath when he dropped his gaze and stared at her vest top clinging damply to her breasts. Her nipples stood to attention and the husky groan he made caused Isla's stomach muscles to clench.

He took the lamp from her nerveless fingers and hung it on the wall. The sound of the storm raging outside became distant and she was aware of the unevenness of her breathing, *his*.

'I should go.' Common sense dictated that she should leave but her feet refused to move. She should have run back to the villa the moment she'd spotted Andreas on the beach, Isla thought ruefully. Instead she had walked towards him, forgetting her loyalty to Stelios, compelled by a force, a *need* that was beyond her control.

She had been surprised when Andreas revealed that his relationship with both his parents had been difficult. Isla sensed that his public image as a charismatic playboy hid a far more complex man—a man she wanted to know better. The truth was she was fascinated by him and she swallowed audibly when he lifted his hand and smoothed a few damp strands of her hair off her face.

'Stay until the storm has passed.' His voice was a low growl.

Isla wasn't sure if he meant the storm outside or the one that had simmered between them since they had been on the island. When he slowly lowered his head towards her she couldn't move, could hardly breathe. She wanted him to kiss her. There was no point pretending otherwise. She'd dreamed of his mouth on hers since he'd kissed her in London a month ago, and tonight, when her emotions were all over the place, he was something solid and safe to cling to in the storm—although the idea that this man represented safety would be laughable if she were able to think straight.

She felt the whisper of Andreas's warm breath on her cheek. He curled his hands over her shoulders, drawing her closer to his big, hard body. And then he brought his mouth down on hers and there was nothing but the intoxicating pleasure of his kiss. It was no gentle seduction but a ravishment of her senses as he increased the pressure of his lips and forced hers apart, allowing his tongue access to the moist heat of her mouth.

Isla sensed that Andreas had been fighting his attraction as much as she had, but tonight the barriers had come crashing down and their desire for each other was an unstoppable force. She succumbed utterly to his mastery, tipping her head back so that he could plunder her lips with a bone-shaking sensuality while she wrapped her arms around his neck and anchored herself to his strength.

He threaded one hand into her hair and ran his other hand down her body, cupping a breast and stroking his thumb over the nipple jutting beneath her damp top. The sensation was exquisite and a shudder ran through her as desire obliterated every sane thought and left only a greedy, aching need. She pressed herself closer to him when he shoved his hand under her top and spread his fingers possessively over her breast.

'Lift your arms up,' he said in a voice roughened by desire. The realisation that he was as powerless to resist the chemistry between them as she was dismissed the last of Isla's doubts. She lifted her arms and her heart thudded when he pulled the strap top over her head and then rocked back on his heels, his eyes glittering like blue flames as he stared at her bare breasts. 'You're so beautiful.' Dull colour winged along his high cheekbones. 'I sound like a bloody schoolboy.' He swore softly. *'Se thelo.'*

Isla knew the Greek words meant *I want you*. Desire hardened his features so that he looked feral with a hunger in his gaze that should have terrified her. But when he swept her up into his arms and carried her over to the bed she trembled, not with fear but a stark longing to feel his mouth on hers once again. To feel his mouth everywhere.

In a moment she would stop him, she assured herself. And she did not doubt that he would stop if she asked him to. Instinctively, she knew that Andreas would respect her wishes. But, like a drug addict desperate for her next fix, she was impatient for him to kiss her again. He laid her on the bed and she curled her arms around his neck, urging his mouth down onto hers.

Just one more kiss and then she would leave. Just one more. Her breath snagged in her throat when he trailed his lips down her neck and across the slope of one breast. He closed his mouth around her taut nipple and the effect of him sucking her felt like an explosion ripping through her, sensation building on sensation and sending a flood of heat right there between her legs where she ached so badly. Her body was unprepared for such an intensity of pleasure and when he captured her other nipple between his lean fingers and teased the turgid peak Isla lost all sense of who she was, of where she was.

Andreas had loosened the cord that held back the voile drapes and the filmy material surrounded the bed, separating them from the world outside, it seemed. Cocooning Isla from reality. Because this could not be real. She had fallen into a wonderful dream and she didn't want it to end. Her stomach muscles clenched involuntarily beneath the weight of his hand trailing over her abdomen and lower, to slip beneath the elastic waistband of her shorts.

The husky laugh he gave when he discovered that her knickers were drenched with her arousal reverberated through her, and the drumbeat of desire in her blood beat insistently. She lifted her hips towards his seeking fingers, her whole being focused on her need for him to touch her intimately. And when he did, when he parted her and eased his finger a few centimetres into her slick heat, she gave a low cry.

'*Theos*, you are incredible,' he said thickly. 'I knew

that beneath your cool refinement there was fire and passion.' In a deft movement he tugged her shorts and panties down her legs. Her shyness disappeared beneath the fierce glitter in Andreas's eyes as he stared at the cluster of neatly trimmed golden curls at the junction of her thighs.

She almost stopped breathing when he put his hand between her legs and skimmed his fingertips over her sensitive inner thigh, heightening her sense of anticipation as he moved inexorably higher. Finally he rubbed his thumb over her moist opening before pushing a finger into her, deeper than he'd done moments earlier. Her internal muscles immediately clenched and he gave a low laugh as he withdrew his finger a little way and then slid deep once more, in and out, again and again. All the time he kept his eyes locked on her face.

Nothing had prepared her for the swift, shattering orgasm that tensed her muscles as he held her there at the edge for frantic seconds, before he rubbed his thumb over her clitoris and she shuddered and pressed herself harder against his hand.

It had to be a dream, Isla thought when she opened her eyes and saw the filmy white drapes around the bed and the golden lamplight shining through them. It had to be a dream, because in her dreams Andreas had looked at her as he was doing now, with a hunger in his gaze that made her heart leap into her throat.

'You'll stay?' he asked thickly.

Her tongue cleaved to the roof of her mouth as she understood the real question he was asking. Her heart was thudding so hard she was surprised he couldn't hear it. She knew she was ready for her first sexual experience but it was a step too far to articulate her need. She nodded, and Andreas leaned over her and claimed her mouth in a slow, drugging kiss that made Isla tremble as anticipation coiled in her belly.

She watched him strip off his clothes, and the sight of his powerful erection sent a flicker of doubt through her. She was stunned by Andreas's rampant masculinity and it belatedly occurred to her that she should tell him how inexperienced she was. But if she did, he might stop. Even worse, he might be amused to learn that she was still a virgin at her age. Perhaps he would demand to know why she'd chosen him to be her first lover, and Isla had no answer to that, at least not a logical one. Her sense that she and Andreas were destined to be together would likely horrify him as much as it confused her.

He opened the bedside drawer, took a condom out of the packet and rolled it down his thick length.

'I…' Her words died away when he moved over her and claimed her lips in a blatantly erotic kiss that scattered her thoughts. Maybe he sensed her doubts and he lifted his mouth from hers and rested his forehead against her brow.

'If you want to change your mind you have thirty seconds to say so,' he growled.

Her brain urged caution but her body clamoured for his possession. The pleasure he'd induced with his fingers had left her wanting more. After years of suppressing her sensuality she had opened Pandora's Box and released her hungry desire that demanded appeasement. She could feel the swollen tip of Andreas's manhood press against her opening and her instincts took over and she spread her legs wide. 'I haven't changed my mind,' she whispered. 'But I need…'

'I know, *moro mou*. I need this too,' Andreas muttered. And then it was too late for her to explain what she needed to tell him. He lowered himself onto her and his erection was big and hard, stretching her as he pushed forwards and thrust his way into her.

Isla had been prepared for pain, but the pinching sensation between her legs was sharper than she'd expected and she drew an audible breath. Almost instantly the pain faded and there was simply a wonderful sense of him filling her—filling her until she could not say where she ended and he began. A complete union— their two bodies joined as one, she thought dazedly as she opened her eyes and met Andreas's furious gaze.

CHAPTER SIX

'WHY DIDN'T YOU tell me?' Andreas's jaw tensed as he stared at Isla's flushed face. She blinked and the dreamy expression in her eyes was replaced with a wariness that added to his sense of guilt. But damn it, she was a beautiful, sensual woman and he would never have guessed that she was a virgin.

He'd accepted her explanation that she and Stelios were not lovers. Isla had been grieving for her mother and had sought comfort with Stelios, who she had remembered from when he'd briefly been a father figure to her during her childhood. Nevertheless, Andreas hadn't intended for things to go as far as having sex with Isla tonight. He grimaced. Who was he kidding? he asked himself derisively. He'd wanted her since the day they'd met.

That kiss in London had blown his mind and he'd been unable to forget her. Even more unsettling was the realisation that his reaction to her was not only on a physical level. He had no idea why he'd told her personal stuff about his difficult relationship with his parents, which he'd never spoken about to anyone before. It was inexplicable that he felt a deeper connection to Isla. The startling discovery that he was her first lover should have appalled him and he did not understand why he felt a possessiveness that was alien to him.

After his conversation with her in the library he had left the party and headed down to the cottage so that he wouldn't be tempted to go to her bedroom at the villa. When he'd seen her walking towards him on the beach he'd decided that fate was helping him out.

'I thought you might stop if I admitted it was my first time.' She shifted beneath him as if she was seeking a more comfortable position. Andreas began to withdraw but hesitated when she stared at him with emotion-filled eyes that set alarm bells ringing in his mind. 'Are you going to stop?'

The rippling effect of her internal muscles around his shaft tested his self-control. 'Do you want me to?' he growled. *Theos*, she was so tight and hot. Sweat beaded his brow as he tried to think about anything other than the fact that he was buried deep inside Isla. But he could smell the erotic scent of her arousal, and when she moved again, arching her hips experimentally, he felt as though he would explode.

'No.'

'No?' For a moment he thought she didn't want him to continue and he forced himself to start to pull back, but she wrapped her legs around his hips.

'Don't stop.' The faintly pleading note in her voice made him forget that having sex with her was a bad idea. There were rules he would expect her to abide by, and having no expectations of him was at the top of the list.

'Fine, but you need to understand…' He wondered why he'd ever thought her grey eyes were cool. They gleamed like silver rings surrounding the mysterious black pools of her dilated pupils. He was distracted by her lush mouth and his urgency to crush her lips beneath his.

Andreas tried to marshal his thoughts. Isla needed to understand that sex was all he was offering. If he'd known she was a virgin he would have sent her back to the villa, but now it was too late for regrets or recriminations. They would come later. But his biggest regret was that he'd hurt her and the least he could do now was show her just how pleasurable sex could be and make her first experience one that she would never forget.

Isla released her breath when Andreas sank between her thighs so that his erection pushed deeper inside her. She had steeled herself for his rejection when he'd discovered she was a virgin. Her conscience pricked that she should have been honest with him. He had been shocked and angry, but his body was still joined with hers and now he began to move carefully, pulling back a little way and pushing forwards in a rocking motion that made her gasp as the ache inside her grew more intense.

He bent his head to her breast and drew her nipple into his mouth, sending starbursts of sensation shooting through her as he sucked the stiff peak. By the time he transferred his attention to her other nipple she was breathless and trembling. Molten heat swept through her and burned fiercest at her feminine core as Andreas maintained a steady pace, every thrust of his powerful body claiming her at a primitive level, reinforcing the message that she was his and his alone.

'Touch me,' he muttered. 'I want to feel your hands on me.' The rasp of his voice set her nerve endings alight and his intent expression, as if he was only just hanging onto his control, made her wonder what it would be like if that iron control of his cracked.

She explored his body with her hands, delighting in the feel of his satiny skin beneath her fingertips.

She traced a path down his long back to the cleft at the base of his spine while he moved rhythmically up and down, each thrust of his shaft inside her taking her higher. When she dug her nails into his buttocks he swore softly. 'Keep doing that, *omorfia mou,* and this will be over embarrassingly quickly.'

Could she really do that to him? She felt a thrill of feminine power as she pressed her face into his neck and nipped him with her teeth. His skin tasted of salt and sweat. He said something in Greek and bent his head to kiss her hard on her mouth.

'Witch.' He slid his hands beneath her bottom and angled her so that when he drove into her it felt deeper and more intense. At the same time he increased his pace, each stroke faster and harder than the one before. Isla stared at his face, at his clenched jaw and the fierce glitter beneath his heavy lids. There was something savage and untamed about him, no tenderness in the way he gripped her hips and plunged into her with devastating authority.

She felt a frisson of unease as the reality of what she was doing hit her. Andreas was all but a stranger, yet she was lying beneath him and allowing him to take astonishing liberties with her body. Not *allowing* but *relishing*, Isla amended with stark honesty. She loved what he was doing to her. The friction he was creating with every bold thrust was building to a crescendo, and now there was a new urgency in his relentless strokes that made her cling to his sweat-damp shoulders while he drove her towards some unknown place that hovered frustratingly out of reach.

And then, with shocking suddenness, she reached the peak, her body quivering as he held her there for timeless seconds before he drove into her a final time.

'Now,' he said harshly. His body was tense and his jaw clenched as if he was fighting an unstoppable force that overwhelmed him. The primitive groan he made as he climaxed increased Isla's excitement.

She cried out as her orgasm tore through her, causing her internal muscles to spasm, to clench and release over and over again. The pleasure was indescribable and utterly addictive. The tiny part of her brain that was still functioning warned her that Andreas had spoilt her for any other man. Her body had been fashioned for this, for *him,* and as the ripples slowly faded, leaving her limp and spent, she buried her face in his neck and felt the thunder of his heart echo the frantic thud of her own.

Her eyes drifted closed and her muscles relaxed. In a minute she would move away from him, she told herself. But it was beguiling to lie here in his arms and feel safe from the storm.

Andreas woke to find that he was lying on his stomach with his arms tucked beneath his head. His body ached pleasurably and he had never felt such a sense of completeness. Sex with Isla had been off the scale, but he'd known it would be. He hadn't expected her to be a virgin, but her sensuality had blown his mind.

He rolled onto his back and watched thin strips of sunlight slant through the slats of the shutters and make shadow stripes on the rumpled sheet. His sense of well-being faded a little when he discovered that Isla was no longer lying beside him. Last night she had fallen asleep in his arms and she hadn't stirred when he'd untangled himself from her with a reluctance that made him frown as he remembered it. He'd intended to wake her and escort her back to the villa, but the feel of her warm body curled up against him had been dangerously addictive and he must have fallen asleep.

He listened for sounds in the cottage to indicate her whereabouts but all he could hear was the mewing of the gulls outside. She was probably on the beach. Perhaps she'd woken first and hadn't wanted to disturb him, unaware that he would be more than happy to have early morning sex. His erection throbbed as he visualised her gorgeous body.

Before he'd fallen asleep, Andreas had acknowledged that his desire for Isla would not be satisfied by spending one night with her. He wanted her as his mistress. Obviously, she would break off her engagement to his father. Stelios must have believed that he was acting chivalrously when he'd met the daughter of his English mistress and wanted to take care of Isla by offering her a home with him.

Andreas swung his legs over the side of the bed and pulled on his boxer shorts before crossing the room to open the shutters. His mind moved ahead and he considered taking Isla to California and setting her up in an apartment. But he wouldn't want to live with her, or risk her thinking that their affair might lead to a meaningful relationship. He did not do commitment. It might be better to buy her a flat in London where he could visit her regularly so that he retained control of the situation, he mused.

He opened the window and scanned the beach, feeling irritated when there was no sign of her. He knew without conceit that he was a good lover and women were not usually in a rush to leave his bed. Shading his eyes from the bright sun with his hand, he spotted a figure in the distance and recognised Dinos running along the beach towards the cottage.

'*Andreas,* come quickly. Your father...'

Andreas glanced at his watch and cursed as he remembered that he had agreed to meet Stelios in his study at nine a.m. It was ten past. Yesterday his father had said that he had something important to tell him, but hadn't given any clues to what it might be.

The butler reached the cottage and bent over, gasping for breath. Andreas guessed that Isla had gone back to the villa and he felt an inexplicable tug beneath his breastbone that she had gone without saying a word. Before his meeting with Stelios he needed a shower and a gallon of coffee, he decided.

'Will you explain to my father that I overslept, and I'll meet him in fifteen minutes?' he told Dinos.

The butler made a choked sound. 'Kyrios Stelios is...*dead.* I discovered him when I delivered his coffee and newspaper to his room this morning. I knew immediately that something was wrong and I went to wake Miss Stanford.'

Andreas could have sworn that his heart stopped beating for several seconds. He felt as if he had been winded and he snatched a breath to drag oxygen into his lungs. Dinos's words did not make sense. Stelios wasn't dead. It had to be a mistake.

He stared at the butler, shocked to see tears in the older man's eyes. Dinos had worked for the Karelis family for decades. But it couldn't be true. His brain refused to believe it. 'Was Isla in her room?' In the midst of his confusion Andreas wondered when she had returned to the villa.

Dinos gave him an odd look. 'Yes, of course. Miss Stanford was asleep and I woke her and told her that Stelios was unconscious. She remembered that one of your sister's friends who attended the party is a junior doctor. I hurried to find the medic, and he...' Dinos's voice cracked '...he came and pronounced your father dead. The junior doctor is of the opinion that he suffered a heart attack. Stelios's own physician has been summoned from Athens.' Dinos wrung his hands. 'I am so sorry to have to break this terrible news to you, Andreas.'

A heart attack. Andreas's blood froze in his veins. 'My father did not suffer from a heart condition.' He stared at the butler. 'Did he?' The truth was that Dinos was more likely to have known about any health issues Stelios might have had than he was, he thought, feeling a stab of guilt. His father had never confided in him.

'I do not think so.' Dinos hesitated. 'Miss Stanford mentioned to the junior doctor that your father was suffering from cancer. It would be better to talk to her.'

Andreas was unable to process this latest shock. 'I intend to,' he said grimly. He strode back inside the cottage and pulled on the rest of his clothes, feeling numb. Dinos had started to walk back to the villa when Andreas sprinted past the older man. But it made no difference how fast he ran. He was too late to say to his father all the things that he wished he'd said.

It was early evening when Andreas strode out of his father's study and noticed a suitcase in the entrance hall. All the guests who had attended Nefeli's birthday party had left the island hours ago, and he had spent much of the day trying to comfort his distraught sister. A press statement had been released announcing Stelios Karelis's unexpected death. But it had not been unexpected by his father, Andreas brooded. Stelios had chosen to keep the news that he had terminal cancer a secret from his family, and only his doctors and one other person had been in his confidence.

He walked into the lounge and silently cursed the clench of his heart when he saw Isla standing by the window. The navy blue dress she was wearing was starkly plain and her hair fell in a long plait down her back, but a lack of adornments only accentuated her classical beauty. She appeared to be absorbed in the view of the garden but he sensed she was lost in her thoughts. That idea was strengthened when she visibly jumped as he halted beside her.

'Andreas, I didn't hear you.' She was pale but composed, always, he thought darkly, shoving away memories of how she had looked in the throes of her orgasm, her face flushed and her eyes wide with surprise and pleasure. She reached out and touched his arm in a brief show of sympathy, he supposed, but the light brush of her hand across his skin felt as if she'd branded him. 'I'm so sorry,' she whispered.

'Why didn't you tell me that my father was dying?' he demanded. He'd felt a hollow sensation inside him as he'd stared at Stelios's body and seen the signs of illness that he'd missed when the old man was alive because his attention had been distracted by Isla.

'He asked me not to. He intended to tell you and Nefeli after her party.' She sighed. 'Your father learned a few months ago that his cancer was incurable and he chose to stop having treatment which could only delay the inevitable for a short time. But he was determined that nothing would spoil Nefeli's twenty-first birthday.'

Isla twisted her hands together and Andreas noted that she was no longer wearing her diamond engagement ring. 'Stelios asked me to pretend to be his fiancée to divert attention away from him,' she said. 'He had lost weight and was often tired, but he thought no one would notice the signs of his illness if he announced his intention to marry a much younger woman.'

She was silent for a moment and tears shimmered in her eyes. 'I don't know if he was aware that chemotherapy had weakened his heart. He never mentioned anything to me. But during the party he said he felt breathless.' Her voice dropped to a whisper. 'If I had done something then, persuaded him to call a doctor...'

Emotions that Andreas had held back all day while he'd taken care of his sister and dealt with the numerous arrangements that needed to be made clogged his throat. 'It's doubtful that you or anyone else could have prevented what happened,' he said gruffly. 'I have received word from the hospital in Athens where my father's body was taken. A post-mortem confirmed that he suffered a massive heart attack and death would have been instantaneous.'

He glanced over at the drinks cabinet but resisted the urge to pour himself a stiff Scotch. Nothing could anaesthetise the dull ache in his chest which was made worse by the knowledge that his father had confided in Isla but not in *him*. It apparently counted for nothing that he was Stelios's son and heir. At least he presumed he would succeed his father as head of Karelis Corp. The family's lawyer, John Sabanis, was on his way to Louloudi to reveal the terms of Stelios's will.

'You *should* have told me,' he said curtly. '*Theos,* you let me believe that you were my father's fiancée.'

'You accused me of being a gold-digger.' The sting in her voice was unexpected and, even though he deserved her scorn, Andreas frowned.

'What was I supposed to think? My father brought you here to Louloudi and introduced you as the woman he intended to marry, despite the fact that you are young enough to have been his daughter.'

'And you were jealous because you wanted me,' she said flatly, coming too close to a truth he did not want to admit to. Isla had insisted that her loyalty to Stelios had prevented her from explaining the truth about her relationship with him. But had her actions been entirely altruistic, as she claimed? Andreas wondered cynically.

'Why did you agree to a fake engagement with my father? Did he offer to pay you?'

'Of course not,' she said angrily. 'I've told you I was very fond of Stelios after he had been kind to me when I was a child. When he was diagnosed with cancer I took care of him.'

From outside the window came the sound of the helicopter. 'That will be my lift to the mainland,' she muttered. 'Dinos has arranged for me to be flown to Athens. I've booked a hotel room for tonight and a flight to London in the morning.'

'You don't have to leave right away.' Andreas could not explain why the hollow feeling inside him expanded at the idea of Isla leaving. He was still in shock at Stelios's death. His throat felt tight as he sought to suppress emotions that he'd denied he was capable of feeling for most of his life. He had cultivated an image of a carefree playboy so successfully that he'd almost believed it was who he was, all he was capable of being. Right now he felt raw and out of control when he thought about his failings as a son and his complicated relationship with his father.

Isla was looking at him with concern in her grey eyes, as if she understood what he was going through, as if she cared. He told himself that he did not want her compassion. What he wanted was much more basic.

The only human interaction he really understood was sex, and he wanted to be inside her, to trace his hands over her satiny skin and sink between her pale thighs, allow pleasure to blot out for a few moments the pain that had lodged like a bur in his chest.

He watched her eyes darken, the pupils enlarging until the irises were thin rims of silver. Her tongue darted over her bottom lip and the emptiness inside Andreas became a huge, all-encompassing ache that he assured himself was nothing more than desire. He lifted his hand and ran his finger lightly down her cheek. Her skin had the texture of a velvety peach. He felt the tremor that ran through her and the idea that he affected her as much as she affected him made him feel slightly better. They were both prisoners of this crazy passion—crazy was the only word that came anywhere close to describing the thunder of his heart when Isla swayed towards him.

'Stay,' he said thickly. When she shook her head he clasped her shoulders and pulled her towards him. 'We could start over, without any misunderstandings this time.'

Her expression was unguarded and faintly wistful. 'Do you want to?'

He wanted *her*, which wasn't quite the same thing. Andreas ignored his conscience and moved his hand down to cup her bottom, his heart kicking in his chest as she gave a low moan when he hauled her against him.

'Does this give you an idea of what I want, *omorfia mou*?' he murmured before he angled his mouth over hers.

CHAPTER SEVEN

'ANDREAS—KYRIOS SABANIS has arrived...' Dinos halted in the doorway of the lounge and looked uncomfortable when Isla jerked out of Andreas's arms. He swore silently as he stared at her expressive features and watched her barriers go up. The butler's timing was terrible, but his own wasn't great, he conceded. His father had been dead for less than twenty-four hours and he was the only person who knew that Stelios's engagement to Isla had been fake.

'I should go. You will be busy with arrangements and things...' Isla avoided his gaze and walked quickly across the room. Dinos stepped aside as Andreas followed her into the hallway.

'At least tell me the name of your hotel in Athens...' He broke off abruptly and hid his frustration when his father's lawyer heaved himself up from a chair.

'Andreas, this is a dreadful day,' John Sabanis said, extending his hand. 'Isla, you have my deepest sympathy.'

'Thank you, John.' Catching Andreas's puzzled look, she explained, 'John and I met on several occasions when he visited your father's house in London.'

The portly lawyer nodded. 'Stelios's death will be a shock to many people. Despite his age, he was in the prime of his life, which was demonstrated when he announced his engagement to you, Isla. I could not help but overhear that you intend to leave Louloudi.'

She did not look at Andreas. 'Yes, Andreas and Nefeli need privacy.'

'It would be better if you delay your departure until after I have explained the terms of Stelios's will,' the lawyer said.

'Is that really necessary? You are aware that I witnessed the will you drew up for Stelios last year, which means that I cannot be a beneficiary.'

'Stelios recently made a new will.' John Sabanis looked at Andreas. 'You asked me here because you want to know who your father chose to succeed him as Chairman of Karelis Corp. I suggest that we discuss your father's last will and testament without further delay.'

'We'll go into the study.' Andreas opened the door and ushered the lawyer into the room.

Isla glanced towards the stairs and, following her gaze, Andreas saw his sister run across the hall.

'I'm surprised you are still here, Isla,' Nefeli said sharply. 'I thought you would already be looking for your next wealthy old man to sink your talons into.'

'There is no need for rudeness,' Andreas murmured. His sister was headstrong but she had been much closer to their father and her eyes were red-rimmed from crying. As yet he hadn't found the right moment to explain that Stelios's engagement to Isla had been an elaborate pretence.

'Why are you defending her? What's going on?' Nefeli demanded.

'John Sabanis is here to read Papa's will and he has asked Isla to be present.'

Nefeli glowered at Isla before she marched into the study and threw herself down onto the sofa. With obvious reluctance Isla walked into the room and perched on a chair close to the door. Andreas's phone pinged for what seemed like the millionth time and he frowned when he saw numerous messages from the COO of Karelis Corp, saying that they needed to talk urgently. Not now, he thought grimly as he switched his phone setting to silent.

The lawyer sat down at the desk and took a sheaf of documents from his briefcase. 'I will hand out copies of Stelios's will which he signed three days ago, on the fourteenth of September, so that you can read it at your own leisure. But to summarise—it was Stelios's wish that his son Andreas should succeed him in the joint roles of Chairman and CEO of Karelis Corporation, with the full backing of the board.'

It was what Andreas had expected. The sole reason for his existence as far as his parents had been concerned was so that he could step into his father's shoes and run the company with the same single-minded devotion to business that Stelios had shown. In due course he would make an advantageous marriage with the aim of producing the next Karelis heir. These things he would do, Andreas vowed to himself. He had not been the son Stelios had hoped for when he was alive, but he would honour his father in death by accepting his duty and doing his best to fulfil the old man's expectations.

The responsibility of his position was sinking in and it felt as if a heavy weight had settled on his shoulders. He had assumed that his father would live for many more years and the handover of power would have been a gradual process. He listened as the lawyer ran through various bequests Stelios had made to members of the extended Karelis family and some of the staff.

Dinos and Toula were to receive the deeds of the staff cottage attached to the villa which had been their home for many years. The bulk of Stelios's personal fortune, including the family home in Athens and the house in London, was split between Andreas and a trust fund for Nefeli which she could access on her twenty-fifth birthday.

'Why can't I have my money now?' Nefeli said sulkily.

'Your father was concerned that you would be the target of fortune hunters,' John Sabanis explained. 'You are one of the richest women in Europe but for the next few years Andreas will be in charge of your trust fund for your own protection.'

The lawyer cleared his throat. 'Finally, we come to the matter of Louloudi. It was Stelios's wish that ownership of the island, including the villa, will be shared equally between his son Andreas and Miss Isla Stanford.'

Andreas's jaw clenched. It was a trait he had perfected, allowing him to disguise his true feelings, which right now were a mix of incomprehension and fury. There were few things he cared deeply about but Louloudi had been his boyhood playground and it was the only place where he had spent any quality time with his father. Stelios's decision to bequeath fifty per cent ownership of Louloudi to Isla felt like the ultimate betrayal.

Nefeli leapt up. 'Papa *can't* have intended to give away Louloudi, which has been owned by the Karelis family for three generations, to his English tart. He must have been coerced into writing a new will.' She threw Isla a poisonous look. 'It was Papa who needed protection from a fortune hunter.'

Andreas exhaled heavily. 'The situation between Papa and Isla was not as it seemed. Stelios asked Isla to pretend to be his fiancée because he knew he was terminally ill and he wanted to keep the news from you until after your party.'

'Did Papa tell you that?'

'No, Isla explained everything.'

'And you believe her frankly suspicious story? What does Isla have that makes sane men lose their minds?' Nefeli said scathingly. 'I saw how you pawed her when you danced with her at my party. Men are such idiots.'

Guilt churned in the pit of Andreas's stomach. He should have paid more attention to his father, who had looked tired and old. But he'd barely registered Stelios's physical decline because he'd been obsessed with Isla. Something hard and cold congealed inside him when he remembered his mother's obsessive feelings for Stelios and her bitter unhappiness when she'd realised that he did not love her.

It was the reason why Andreas deliberately avoided relationships that required an emotional response from him. He had no intention of ever falling in love. Isla had overstepped the boundaries when she'd failed to tell him she was a virgin. He hoped she did not think there had been anything romantic about the night they had spent together because he certainly didn't.

She stood up and gave him a faintly pleading look. 'I did not coerce your father to include me in his will. The opposite, in fact. I made it clear to him that I didn't want him to leave me a bequest. I had no idea that he planned to make me a joint owner of the island.'

Andreas glanced at John Sabanis. 'When did my father decide to make a new will?'

'He phoned me a few days ago and requested that I meet him here on Louloudi,' the lawyer said. 'Following the news of Stelios's engagement to Isla, I was not surprised that he wanted to make provision for her in the event of his death, although I was not aware that he was suffering from incurable cancer.'

'My father chose to only confide in Isla,' Andreas said tersely.

'I refuse to accept the bequest Stelios left me.' Isla turned to John Sabanis. 'Louloudi should remain in the ownership of the Karelis family.'

'Actually, you cannot refuse it.' The lawyer shrugged. 'Like it or not, a fifty per cent share of the island will be held in trust for you for one year. After that you can sell your share but you must offer it to Andreas first, and it cannot be sold for less than its market value. The current value of Louloudi is one hundred million euros.'

Isla gasped and John Sabanis gave her a wry look before he continued. 'But you and Andreas must both return to the island on the first anniversary of Stelios's death and live here for one month. If either of you fails to carry out the terms of the will, then ownership of Louloudi will pass entirely to the other person.'

'Clearly my father thought it would be amusing to play games from beyond the grave,' Andreas growled. 'He can't have been of sound mind when he set out those ridiculous terms. There must be grounds to challenge the will.'

John shook his head. 'Stelios was completely sane and it was his right to dispose of his assets as he wished.'

Nefeli ran across the study and opened the door.

She spun round and glared at Isla. 'You poisoned my father's mind.'

'I promise you that I didn't.' Isla hurried out of the room after the young Greek woman.

'Leave her,' Andreas advised when he followed Isla into the entrance hall. 'My sister is still in shock.'

'I wish this hadn't happened,' she said in a low voice. 'I'm as stunned as you are by the terms of your father's will.'

He raked a hand through his hair. 'You can't lose, can you, Isla? You know I'll do anything to regain complete ownership of Louloudi and in a year from now I will have to buy your share.'

'If I don't return next year and live here for a month, then I will forfeit my share of the island.'

'But you will come back.' He gave a weary smile when she shook her head. 'Of course you will. You stand to inherit a fortune.'

Andreas wondered if Stelios had written his will as revenge because many years ago he'd forced his father to choose between his family in Greece and his English mistress. Isla was certain that Stelios had been in love with her mother. When Stelios had learned that his cancer was incurable, he'd made sure that the daughter of the woman he had loved would be provided for.

Love made fools of people, Andreas thought darkly. His mother had been so desperate to win Stelios's affection that she'd had no time or love for her son. What he felt for Isla was lust, nothing more, he assured himself. Yet he could not bring himself to step away from her.

'I'm sorry I couldn't tell you about your father's illness.'

'Couldn't?' He gave an angry laugh. 'You slept with me but still you said nothing.'

'My loyalty was to Stelios.'

Her words felt as if she'd shoved a knife between his ribs. 'And yet you gave your virginity to me. Why did you leave the cottage without waking me this morning?'

'I thought it would be less awkward for both of us.' She bit her lower lip and Andreas could not tear his eyes from her lush mouth. 'I can't stay here,' she whispered. 'Your sister is upset.'

'I'm hardly thrilled that Stelios left you a chunk of my birthright,' he said sardonically.

'Do you think I persuaded him to write that will?'

'I don't know what to think.' Andreas looked away from the hurt expression in Isla's eyes. His gut told him that she had spoken the truth, but for the sake of his sanity he needed to distance himself from her. He tensed when she stepped closer and he breathed in her evocative perfume.

'Your father loved you,' she said gently. Rising up on her toes, she brushed her mouth over his cheek and Andreas's breath became trapped in his lungs. He knew that if he turned his head a fraction, Isla's lips would meet his. But if he allowed her to kiss his mouth he did not trust himself to resist kissing her back. He wanted so much more than a kiss from this woman, who fascinated him more than any woman had ever done. And so he forced himself to remain rigid, his mouth a firm line of defence against her sweetly sensual onslaught.

After a few seconds that felt to Andreas like a lifetime, Isla lifted her lips from his cheek and gave a soft sigh before she turned away and walked across the hall. Her suitcase was no longer by the front door and he guessed that the pilot had taken it to the helicopter.

She opened the door and stepped outside. He wanted to call her back, go after her. Instead he clenched his hands by his sides when she closed the door behind her with a quiet click that was somehow more dramatic, more final than if she'd slammed it shut. Minutes later came the sound of the helicopter taking off.

'Andreas—' John Sabanis spoke from the study doorway '—you need to see this.'

The phone in Andreas's pocket vibrated constantly as new messages came in. Cursing beneath his breath, he strode into the study and stared at a live newsfeed on the computer screen.

> *Greece's largest petroleum company Karelis Corp is facing a hostile takeover bid from the French firm Moulet Energie, which has announced that it is near to acquiring a majority interest in Karelis Corp's stock.*

'What the hell?' As soon as he switched his phone setting from silent it started to ring, and the nightmare began.

It *couldn't* be true! Isla's legs gave way and she sank down onto the edge of the bath, staring at the pregnancy test in her hand. *Positive.* But how? Andreas had used protection the one and only time they'd had sex.

She choked back a sob as she remembered how she had hoped day after day that he would contact her when she'd left Louloudi. He had been busy dealing with major problems at Karelis Corp, she'd reminded herself. But as weeks passed and she did not hear from him, her sense of hurt had deepened. She had given Andreas her virginity but his silence made it clear that he had only wanted a one-night stand—and now she was expecting his baby.

Her stomach lurched at the thought that she did not even have anywhere to live. She had returned to Stelios's house in Kensington in the vain hope that Andreas would come to her. But she'd received a letter from his lawyer informing her that the house was being sold and she must vacate the property.

Isla tried to curb her sense of panic. Her period was late—very late—and she'd been feeling under the weather for weeks, but she'd bought a pregnancy test not really believing that her suspicion could be true. The blue line on the test stared back at her. She was ten weeks into her pregnancy but the risk of miscarriage was higher in the first trimester. Maybe there wouldn't be a baby.

Her hand moved involuntarily to her stomach as if she could protect the tiny life she carried within her. In that moment she knew without a shadow of doubt that she wanted her baby. Her pregnancy was not planned but the baby would be loved unconditionally by his or her mother at least. But what about Andreas? How would he react to the news that he was going to be a father?

'Isla, are you going to be long in there? I need to leave for work soon,' Beth called out from the other side of the bathroom door. Isla jumped up and shoved the pregnancy test in the bin. Her best friend from university had allowed her to sleep on the sofa in her tiny flat for the past few weeks while she'd been flat-hunting. Rents in the capital were high and she was struggling to find somewhere she could afford. How was she going to manage when she had a baby? She couldn't do this alone, she realised. But maybe, hopefully, she would have Andreas's support.

She opened the door and forced a smile for her friend. 'Sorry.'

'I heard you being sick again this morning,' Beth said, grabbing her toothbrush and standing over the sink.

'I must have picked up a stomach bug.' Isla followed Beth's gaze to the box that the pregnancy test had been in, which she'd forgotten to throw away.

'Oh, God, Isla.' Toothpaste squirted from the tube in Beth's hand and landed on the floor. 'What are you going to do?'

Tears blurred her vision. 'I don't know,' she admitted shakily. She wondered if her mum had felt the same sense of dread when she'd faced having to break the news to Isla's father that she was pregnant. What if Andreas did not want his child, just as David Stanford hadn't wanted his daughter? There was only one way to find out.

'There is a Miss Isla Stanford in Reception asking to see you. I've explained that your diary is full but she says she won't leave.' Andreas's PA sounded irritated. 'Do you want me to call Security?'

Holding the phone to his ear, he drummed the fingers of his other hand on the desk. He was seriously tempted to send Isla away but he could not deny he was curious about why she had come to Athens. It was two months since he'd last seen her on Louloudi, and lately he'd stopped thinking about her quite so much. But that was only because his workload was so crazy that he didn't have time to think about anything other than trying to save Karelis Corp, Andreas acknowledged grimly. At night it was a different matter and Isla invaded his dreams with annoying regularity.

Was she hoping for a repeat performance of the night they had spent together? He pictured her naked, supple body—her breasts that fitted into his palms as if they had been made for that purpose, and her long slender legs that she'd wrapped around his hips when he'd possessed her. His body clenched hard and he cursed beneath his breath.

'Show Miss Stanford to my office,' he told Daphne.

'Your meeting with the Dutch client, Mr Vanek, is in fifteen minutes,' his PA reminded him.

'This won't take long.' He'd made the decision when Isla had left Louloudi that he would not get involved with her. He would discover the purpose of her visit and then send her away, he assured himself. He walked over to the window that overlooked the Karelis refinery, one of the largest and most modern oil refineries in Europe. Although how long it would continue to be owned by Karelis Corp was the subject of much speculation in the business world and the media, Andreas thought with a grimace. Beyond the tangle of metal pipes and towers the Aegean Sea sparkled beneath the pale winter sun.

He was aware of his heart thumping in his chest and his inexplicable reaction to the prospect of meeting Isla again infuriated him. He heard his office door open, followed by the soft click of it closing again. But he did not immediately turn around until he was confident that he had himself under control.

'Hello, Andreas.'

Isla's cool voice did nothing to put out the fire raging inside him when he swung round and stared at her. She was even more beautiful than he remembered. A little thinner perhaps, and her face was paler now that the golden tan she'd had in Greece two months ago had faded. But there was something about her—a glow as if she was lit from within—that Andreas could not explain. She looked mouth-watering in tight-fitting jeans and a smoky grey jumper that matched the colour of her eyes.

He clenched his hands by his sides, fighting an urge to stride across the room, pull her into his arms and kiss her until they were both senseless. Somehow he managed to sound politely uninterested. 'Isla, this is a surprise,' he drawled.

'Is it?' Colour flared on her cheeks and he did not miss the bite in her tone. 'We were lovers. Does that mean nothing to you?'

He dismissed the erotic memories that barged unasked for into his mind, and shoved his hands into his trouser pockets to disguise the evidence of his desire. With another woman he might have instigated an affair, but not with Isla. She was the only woman who had threatened his self-control and he would not allow it to happen again. 'We had sex once. Take my advice and don't look for romance where none exists,' he told her.

She gave an odd laugh. 'Once is all it takes.'

His eyes narrowed. 'What do you mean?' He frowned when she did not reply and strode over to stand in front of her. Instantly he knew it had been a bad move as he breathed in her perfume and felt a throb in his groin. *Theos*, this woman made him feel like a teenager with an overload of hormones. He made a show of checking his watch. 'I have a business meeting scheduled and I'd allocated you five minutes of my time. You've used three of them.'

Her eyes flashed but there was a vulnerability about the way her tongue darted nervously over her lips. 'I'm pregnant.'

Andreas rocked back on his heels. He was totally unprepared for the bombshell she'd dropped, and his first thought was, *Not again*. He had been in this situation once before when Sadie had told him she was expecting his child. His response to Isla was the same as it had been to his lying ex-girlfriend. 'I suppose you expect me to believe it's my baby?' he said coldly.

She blinked. 'Of course it's your baby. You know quite well that I was a virgin when I slept with you.'

He nodded. 'Yes, that was convenient. But you could have had other sexual partners in the last two months.'

Twin spots of colour flared on her cheeks. 'Because, having lost my virginity to you, I was filled with uncontrollable lust and had sex with numerous men?' she suggested sarcastically. 'You are the only man I have ever slept with.'

Andreas could not explain the possessiveness that swept through him at the idea that she was exclusively his. 'Why me?' His brows rose. 'You are what, twenty-four or five? Surely you've had boyfriends. Why did you choose me to be your first lover?'

'God knows,' she muttered. 'It must be your charming personality.'

'Or perhaps you were attracted to my wealth,' he said drily. 'How can you possibly be pregnant by me when I used protection?'

'I don't know how it happened. No forms of contraception are foolproof and I guess we were just unlucky...or lucky—depending on your point of view...'

'Enough.' With an effort Andreas brought his temper under control. 'I don't believe the baby is mine but I am willing to accept there is a minuscule chance. The only way I can be certain if you are telling the truth is with a DNA test.'

The glimmer of tears turned Isla's eyes to the colour of wet slate. 'Do you really think I would lie about something this important? I *am* telling you the truth. I'm expecting your child.'

Sadie had used almost exactly the same words and she had cried prettily too, Andreas thought savagely. He would be a fool to believe Isla. He should tell her to contact his lawyer so that a paternity test could be arranged, before calling Security to escort her from the building. So why was he hesitating? What kind of witchery had she cast on him that tempted him to pull her into his arms and reassure her he would take care of her and the child?

His phone pinged and he read a message informing him that the Dutch client was waiting in the boardroom. Coming to a decision, he spoke to his PA and instructed her to organise some refreshments to be delivered to the hospitality suite. 'English tea, and some sandwiches,' he said, his eyes on Isla's slender figure. She did not look pregnant. Was she eating enough? *Theos*, why did he care?

Jaw clenching, he looked away from the wounded look in her eyes. It was highly unlikely that he'd made her pregnant, but he wasn't going to risk her selling a pack of lies to the tabloids like Sadie had done. He would insist that Isla remained in Athens until she'd had a blood test which would prove whether or not he was the father of her child.

'My secretary will take you to the hospitality room,' he told her. 'Wait for me there and we will continue this discussion later.'

It was unfair that Andreas was so handsome, Isla thought bitterly as she watched him stride out of his office. His arrogance infuriated her, but her pulse had raced when he'd stood close to her. She'd stared at his mouth, remembering the beauty of his kiss. The evocative scent of his aftershave lingered in the room after he had gone, evoking images in her mind of his sweat-beaded shoulders, his hair slicked back from his brow and his face contorted with pleasure when he'd climaxed inside her.

She gave an angry sigh. Andreas's reaction to the news of her pregnancy had been even worse than she'd feared. Now he expected her to wait patiently while he was in a meeting. His attitude showed that he thought she was a nuisance who he would have to slot into his busy schedule. She ground her teeth as she remembered how he had accused her of sleeping around. His contemptuous expression when she'd told him that he was her baby's father was something she would never forget.

It reminded her of when she was sixteen and her father, who she had met for the first and only time, had told her that, in his eyes, she did not exist. She'd slunk out of the art gallery where David Stanford had been exhibiting his work. But she'd hesitated in the doorway and looked over her shoulder, hoping even then that her father would call her back and apologise for abandoning her. But he hadn't looked in her direction and she knew he had already forgotten her. The memory still haunted her and she could not bear the idea of her child one day feeling rejected and humiliated by Andreas.

He had made it plain that he did not want his baby. There was no reason for him to demand a paternity test when he knew she had been a virgin. She was damned if she would be forced to prove that she had told him the truth, and Andreas could go to hell.

CHAPTER EIGHT

THE HELICOPTER DIPPED low over an olive grove and the villa came into view. Andreas remembered the excitement he'd felt as a boy coming to Louloudi every summer when his boarding school in England broke up for the holidays. His mother hadn't wanted him at the family home in Athens and he'd been glad to escape from her constant disapproval. Occasionally Stelios had spent a weekend on the island and Andreas had treasured those times that he'd had his father's exclusive attention. But mostly Stelios had been preoccupied with work.

He rubbed his hand over the stubble on his chin. In three days' time it would be the first anniversary of his father's death. For the past year Andreas had fought to save Karelis Corp from being bought out by a rival company. It had been a hellish time and he was mentally exhausted, but at least the company was safe. Now he was determined to save Louloudi from falling into the hands of the most unscrupulous woman he'd ever had the misfortune to meet.

His jaw clenched. Ten months ago Isla had turned up at his office in Athens and announced that she was pregnant. Not unreasonably, he'd demanded proof of paternity before he would accept responsibility for the child she alleged was his. But her tears had stirred his conscience and he had asked himself why she would lie. It couldn't be because she needed financial support for her child. Stelios had made provision for her in his will and she was due to inherit a fortune. Andreas had needed time to think, but when his meeting with a client had finished and he'd gone to find Isla, his PA informed him that she had already left.

He'd felt responsible for her, despite his suspicion that the child wasn't his, and he had instructed his security team to search for her, to no avail. She had seemingly disappeared into thin air. The fact that she had not contacted him again seemed further proof that if she had been pregnant it wasn't his child, Andreas brooded as he climbed out of the helicopter and walked across the lawn towards the house.

But he did not doubt that she would turn up on Louloudi to claim her inheritance. She wasn't going to miss the chance to become a multi-millionaire and he would have to bite the bullet and buy her share of the island. He was confident that the powerful attraction he'd felt for her would have died. He had dated a few women, although he hadn't had sex for a year. But he'd assumed that his lack of libido was down to his excessive workload. It was not because he subconsciously compared every woman he met to Isla, he assured himself.

He strode into the house and his vision was momentarily obscured while the lenses in his sunglasses transitioned from the bright light outside to the darker interior. He blinked—but the pram parked in the hallway was still there. Shock ricocheted through him until he remembered that Toula and Dinos's daughter had been pregnant. Maria must have brought her new baby to visit its grandparents.

Andreas stepped closer to the pram and saw an in-

fant, he had no idea how old, sleeping peacefully. The
blue blanket tucked around the baby suggested it was a
boy. He had an olive-gold complexion, a mass of dark
hair and impossibly long eyelashes that made crescents
on his cheeks. Andreas's heart missed a beat when the
baby's lashes lifted to reveal bright blue eyes. The exact
shade of blue as his own eyes.

Hadn't he read somewhere that all babies were born
with blue eyes? He tried to quell the panic that surged
through him. Of course this child could not be his. But
he felt strangely reluctant to move away from the pram.
The baby was so vulnerable. Perhaps the fierce protectiveness he felt was a normal response to seeing something so small and helpless, he thought. He'd never been
this close to a baby before. Some of his friends had children, but he'd pretended to admire the usually squall-
ing infant from a safe distance.

Behind him he heard a door open, followed by a
swiftly indrawn breath. 'Andreas! I wasn't expecting
you to arrive for a couple of days.'

Even then he did not take his gaze from the baby.
He was crazy to believe he could see a resemblance between himself and the infant, and crazier still to feel a
connection to the tiny scrap of humanity in the pram.
He finally turned his head towards the familiar voice
that had stirred something within him which was too
complicated to define.

Andreas's breath hissed between his teeth as he
stared at Isla. The white cotton shirt she wore tied
in a knot at her waist revealed her flat stomach, and
skimpy denim shorts showed off her long slender legs.
Her honey-gold hair was drawn back from her face in
a ponytail and a few tendrils clung to her pink cheeks.
Despite the villa's air conditioning, the atmosphere in

the entrance hall was sultry and prickled with an electricity that was almost tangible.

'I thought you were in New York.' Her tone was faintly accusing. 'A photo of you and one of your girlfriends who was almost wearing a dress was on the front page of several of the tabloids.'

'You sound jealous, Isla.'

Her flush deepened. 'Yeah, right,' she muttered. 'Your trouble, Andreas, is that you think you're God's gift to womankind.'

'Is that your opinion?' He didn't know why he enjoyed teasing her so that her eyes flashed silver with temper. Andreas refused to question why seeing Isla again made him feel more alive than he'd felt for months.

'You don't want to know what I think of you.'

'Your body is sending out clues,' he murmured, dropping his gaze to the hard points of her nipples jutting beneath her shirt. He laughed softly as she quickly crossed her arms over her breasts.

'It's chilly in here,' she snapped, her tongue darting out to lick a bead of sweat above her top lip.

Andreas was aware of his body's damning reaction. His blood pounded in his ears and his erection pressed uncomfortably against his trousers. So much for his assumption that he would no longer be attracted to Isla. Desire swept like molten lava through his veins and he was desperate to take her to bed. He stepped closer to her and breathed in the delicate floral fragrance of her perfume mixed with another scent that he could not name but reminded him of vanilla.

She did not back away from him and he felt the tremor that shook her slender frame. Her soft pink mouth was a delectable temptation but, as he lowered his head, his body tensing with anticipation of claiming her lips with his, a cry came from the pram, shattering the spell that Isla had cast on him. He jerked back from her and raked a hand through his hair.

'Where is Dinos and Toula's daughter?' Isla looked puzzled, and he growled, 'I assume the baby is Maria's.'

'No. He is mine.' She scooped the infant into her arms and her expression softened. 'It's all right, sweetheart. Mama's here,' she murmured. The look of love in her eyes for her child made her even more beautiful.

'So you weren't lying about being pregnant,' Andreas said curtly.

'I've never lied to you.' She took her gaze from the baby and her eyes glittered. 'Loukas is your son.'

'Like hell he is.' Even as he refuted her claim Andreas recalled the sense of recognition he'd felt when he'd looked into the baby's blue eyes. But it couldn't be true, his brain insisted. 'Why did you disappear from my office after claiming that I was responsible for your pregnancy? And why did you refuse a DNA test?'

'I felt humiliated that you expected me to prove I was telling the truth,' Isla said fiercely. 'You *are* Loukas's father.'

He stared at her, wondering if her cheeks were flushed with anger at his refusal to believe her, or did she feel guilty because she was lying? 'It's not unheard of for women to accuse rich men of fathering their child,' he said sardonically. 'I barely know you, yet you expect me to take your word without any degree of certainty that this is my baby.'

'You can be certain that I was a virgin when I slept with you.' Pride replaced the anger in her voice. She tilted her chin and held his gaze. 'Have you any idea how insulting you are to accuse me of pretending that

Loukas is yours for financial reasons? I don't want your money. Stelios made me a beneficiary in his will and I'm not after a maintenance payout from you.'

She played *outraged* very convincingly, but Andreas wanted hard facts before he would be convinced. 'Why would you object to a paternity test unless you are worried that the result will show you are a fantasist?'

Her eyes flashed silver. 'You are unbelievable. Loukas is your son, but I am prepared to raise him on my own. Are you prepared to walk away from your flesh and blood? Think hard before you give me your answer because your decision is final and you can't change your mind in the future if the idea of fatherhood suddenly becomes more appealing.'

The baby started crying in earnest, his little face turning red. It was a heartrending sound that evoked an unexpected emotional response in Andreas. He wanted to reach out and take the baby in his arms to comfort him but Isla turned away and walked across the hall, holding the baby against her shoulder. She paused in the doorway to the lounge and glanced back at Andreas.

'If you refuse to accept that Loukas is your son I will tell him when he is old enough to understand that his father is dead. It will spare him the heartbreak of wondering why you rejected him.'

The bitterness in her voice startled Andreas as much as her ultimatum. He was reeling with shock that quickly turned to anger.

'If you *are* telling the truth why didn't you contact me when you gave birth?' he demanded as he followed her into the room. He found her sitting on the sofa, crooning softly to the baby while she unbuttoned her shirt. The tender expression on her face as she held the baby to her breast evoked an ache in his chest. He wondered if his mother had ever looked at him with such loving affection when he was born. He certainly had no recollection of her doing so when he was older.

The sun streaming through the window picked out the golden strands in Isla's hair as she sat feeding her baby. She seemed to Andreas like the biblical Eve, the first woman and mother but also a temptress who he was determined to resist.

'Can you pass me a muslin? The square of material in the change bag,' she said when he frowned.

Andreas spotted a large colourful bag, opened it and handed Isla a piece of white cloth. 'You need all this equipment for one small baby?' he said in astonishment. The bag contained disposable nappies, feeding bottles, a dummy and various other items that he had no idea what they were for. He put the bag on the coffee table and a red booklet slipped onto the floor.

'It's Loukas's record book for when I have him weighed,' Isla explained as he bent down to retrieve it.

Andreas flicked through the pages and read the baby's date of birth. 'It says here that Loukas was born on the eighteenth of May, which makes him four months old.' His jaw hardened. 'We had sex in mid-September a year ago. If you had conceived my baby then, as you say you did, you should have given birth three months ago, in June.' He gave a cold laugh. 'You appear to have slipped up on rudimentary mathematics, Isla.'

'He was born three weeks early.'

'How convenient,' he drawled. '*Theos*, what kind of a fool do you take me for?'

Hectic colour stained her cheeks. '*You are such a jerk!* You're so high and mighty, but you are wrong about me. Loukas had to be delivered at thirty-seven weeks because I developed a serious complication with my pregnancy which threatened his life and mine.'

Through her tears Isla saw Andreas's shocked expression and her conscience pricked that she could have been gentler when she'd revealed that their baby had nearly died at birth. But maybe he didn't care, she thought bleakly. She was still traumatised by memories of the routine antenatal appointment when it had been discovered that her blood pressure was sky-high and the baby was showing signs of distress. She had read about pre-eclampsia, but she'd been fit and healthy throughout her pregnancy and hadn't expected to develop a potentially life-threatening complication.

'You have no idea how terrified I was when I was rushed into hospital in an ambulance and immediately prepared for theatre,' she said rawly. 'Loukas's heartbeat was dropping and they had to get him out quickly by caesarean section. He spent the first week of his life in the neonatal intensive care unit and it was touch-and-go if he would survive.'

She brushed her hand across her eyes. 'The worst thing of all was knowing that Loukas was alone while he fought for his life. I was too unwell for a few days after the birth to visit him. Where were you then, Andreas?' she demanded bitterly. 'You failed Loukas when he needed you. I don't know why I thought that there might be a shred of decency in you when I brought him to Louloudi so that you could meet your son.'

Andreas's hard-boned features gave no clue to his thoughts and he did not say another word as he strode out of the room. It was becoming a regular occurrence for Andreas to walk away from her, Isla thought bitterly. She remembered how he had snatched his mouth from hers when he'd kissed her at Stelios's house in London more than a year ago. His abrupt departure had left her wondering what she had done wrong.

Loukas gave a loud wail. 'Don't cry, baba,' she whispered, blinking away her own tears. Usually he was a contented baby but he had been restless during his feed and his yells broke her heart even more than Andreas had done. How idiotic she had been to hope that when he saw Loukas he would realise that the baby was his son. They looked so alike, but perhaps all babies looked the same and only their mothers saw every unique detail of their child's features, she thought. Loukas had even inherited his father's piercing blue eyes, but the cold rejection in Andreas's eyes would stay with Isla for ever.

Was this how her mother had felt when David Stanford had abandoned her and left her with a three-month-old baby? Isla refused to think of David as her father. He'd stuck around long enough to put his name on her birth certificate, but Andreas had not even done that for Loukas.

There was no point in feeling sorry for herself. She wiped her eyes with the edge of the baby's shawl and stood up to rock him in her arms. 'Don't cry,' she told Loukas again, her voice resolute this time. 'We'll be fine, you and me. We don't need anyone else.' A sob rose in her throat and she forced it back. She had grown up wishing that she knew her father and now her own child would have to do the same.

It had been a mistake to come here, Andreas brooded as he looked around the old fisherman's cottage. The cottage was his private retreat, but when he walked into the bedroom he was assailed by memories of the night a year ago when Isla had responded to him with a sensuality that had blown his mind.

It hadn't been his intention to make love to her when they had sheltered from the rain, but the chemistry between them had been as powerful as the electrical storm which had raged outside. He felt himself harden as he pictured her gorgeous naked body spread out on the sheets, the shy smile she'd given him when he'd positioned himself above her.

There was no question that she had been a virgin. He felt guilty even now, remembering the gasp of pain she'd made when he had thrust his shaft into her and met the fragile barrier of her innocence. But it had been too late to pull back and he had claimed her with a hunger he'd never felt so intensely with any other woman.

Andreas raked his hand through his hair until it stood on end. He was not a saint and he hadn't kept a tally of the number of women he'd had sex with in the past, but he always used protection and there had never been a problem. Sadie had said that the condom must have failed, but after she had publicly accused him of being her baby's father he had been given permission by a judge for a DNA test which had proved she was a liar.

Apart from Isla, the only other woman he had brought to the cottage was the wife of a Greek government minister, who had appreciated the privacy of the island. But his brief affair with Katerina had happened several years ago. Frowning, Andreas opened the bedside cabinet and picked up a box of condoms. He had been glad to find them in the drawer when he'd had sex with Isla. But now, as he checked the use-by date and saw it had expired two years ago, he realised that it *was* possible he was the baby's father. More than possible;

it was highly likely. His gut instinct told him that Isla had spoken the truth when she'd insisted he was the only man she had been with.

Andreas swore. His life was spinning out of control and he did not know what to think or feel. He'd assumed that one day in the future he would make a suitable marriage and produce the next Karelis heir. But the idea that baby Loukas was his son, his flesh and blood, unleashed emotions that he'd buried deep within him for most of his life. Not least was the realisation that having a child with Isla meant that his life would be linked with hers for ever.

Like it or not, she was the mother of his heir. To say that he found the situation unsettling would be a laughable understatement, he thought grimly. Isla undermined everything he thought he knew about himself. The truth was that he hadn't wanted to accept that he could be her baby's father.

On his way back to the villa he passed the jetty and saw Dinos loading luggage onto the boat. The butler had a fear of flying in the helicopter. A brightly coloured bag caught Andreas's attention. 'I thought you and Toula were going to Athens for a few days, but you have enough cases for a month,' he joked.

Dinos grimaced. 'You know what women are like about clothes. Toula has packed four outfits for our son's wedding because she can't decide which one to wear. But the green suitcase and the striped bag belong to Miss Stanford. She asked if she and her baby could come on the boat with us over to the mainland.'

Andreas gave a nonchalant shrug to disguise his anger. 'You know how women change their minds. Miss Stanford has decided to stay on Louloudi. I'll carry her bags back to the house.' He glanced up at the grey clouds scudding across the sky. 'I suggest that you and Toula leave before the storm breaks.'

The baby was lying in the pram when Andreas strode into the villa. He did not know where Isla was, and he was too furious to care. If he hadn't returned from the cottage before Dinos and Toula had left on the boat, he would not have known until it was too late that Isla had gone, and taken his son with her.

His son. Andreas stood over the pram and felt a tightness in his chest when the baby fixed unblinking blue eyes on him. Eyes that were the same colour as his own. Everything inside him told him that Loukas was his baby. He closed his eyes and took a deep breath that hurt his chest. When he opened them again the baby's rosebud mouth curved into a smile and Andreas felt as though an arrow had pierced his heart.

Emotions ran riot inside him and the fiercest, overriding emotion was something he had thought he was incapable of feeling with any depth. Love. Instant and all-consuming. His knees felt weak and a lump formed in his throat.

Something powerfully possessive swept through Andreas, compelling him to slide his hands beneath the baby's small body and lift him out of the pram. He held him against his shoulder, marvelling at how tiny he was, how fragile and vulnerable. 'My son,' he said gruffly. '*Geia sou.* It means hello in Greek.'

His jaw hardened as he acknowledged the reality of the situation. He had a son who did not bear his name and who lived in England with his mother. But Loukas was half-Greek and he should grow up knowing how to speak the language of his father. More importantly, he would know that his father loved him.

Andreas's parents had not been demonstrative and

when he was a boy he had longed for their affection, but his mother had seemed to dislike him and his father had been too busy to give him attention. By the time he was an adult he had dismissed the concept of love as an irrelevance and assured himself he had no need of such an unreliable emotion.

He touched the baby's hand and Loukas curled his tiny fingers around his forefinger. Andreas felt his heart swell until it seemed to fill his chest. 'That's right. Hold on tight,' he whispered to his son. 'I will never let you go.'

He glanced across the hall when he heard footsteps running down the stairs. Isla had changed into jeans and a pink T-shirt and her blonde hair was caught up in a loose knot on top of her head. Desire ran swift and hot through Andreas's veins as he noticed how the faded denim jeans clung to her pert derrière.

'What are you doing?' Her face was flushed and she hurried forwards, hands outstretched to take the baby from him. 'Was Loukas crying? I didn't hear him.'

'He wasn't crying. I picked him up so that I could introduce him to his father. It should have happened when he was born but, thanks to you, I have missed the first four months of his life,' Andreas bit out.

Isla's startled expression turned to puzzlement when she noticed her suitcase and the baby's bag that he'd brought back to the house. 'I thought Dinos had taken my bags to the boat. Your attack of conscience is too late, Andreas.' Her eyes glinted like polished steel. 'I've decided to leave with Dinos and Toula and take Loukas back to England.'

His gaze narrowed. 'You have to live on Louloudi for a month in order to claim your half-share, but if you fail to fulfil the terms of my father's will, the island will belong solely to me.' He made a derisive sound. 'Do you seriously expect me to believe you will walk away from a multi-million-pound fortune? What game are you playing now?'

'I'm not playing any game. I came back because Louloudi is Loukas's heritage and I had the idea that I could bring him here sometimes. But I won't risk him finding out when he is old enough to understand that you refused to accept him as your son. Of course the money would have been amazing. But I can work to support Loukas. Besides, wealth means nothing compared to love.'

'I agree,' Andreas said tautly. 'Our son deserves to grow up knowing that he is loved by, ideally, both his parents.'

'*Our* son? You have changed your tune,' Isla snapped.

Her anger surprised Andreas. He had expected her to be more conciliatory. *Theos*, she had stolen his son from him and he would never regain the first precious months of Loukas's life, he thought savagely. 'If you were certain Loukas was mine, why didn't you contact me when he was born? You had no right to keep him secret from me.'

'*No right?*' She glared at him. 'You forfeited any right to be involved with him when you wouldn't believe you were his father. You made the humiliating accusation that I'd slept with other men. Do you really think I'd have called you to announce his birth after the way you treated me?'

Loukas had fallen asleep and Andreas carefully laid him back in the pram. He pointed to the study. 'We'll go in there so that our voices don't wake the baby,' he told Isla.

After a moment she followed him into the room. He

leaned his hip against the desk and ran his eyes over her, irritated to have to admit that it was not only anger simmering inside him.

Her slim figure belied the fact that she'd given birth a few months ago, and her T-shirt moulded the sweet curves of her breasts. He moved his gaze up to her face and glimpsed awareness in her eyes before her lashes swept down. It did not help his determination to resist her to know that she still wanted him.

'I was shocked when you told me you were pregnant,' he growled. 'It didn't seem possible that I could be responsible.'

She shook her head. 'I didn't want you to feel *responsible* for Loukas. All I hoped was that you would love him. Nothing else matters and material things aren't important,' she said fiercely. 'Loukas deserves a daddy who will read him a bedtime story, who will comfort him when he's scared and play football with him. More than anything, I hoped he would have a father who was better than my father—although it would be hard to be a worse one,' she muttered.

'You told me that your father wasn't around when you were growing up.'

'I know the name of the man whose genes I carry. His name is on my birth certificate and when I was a teenager I found him and told him that I was his daughter. But he didn't want to know me. In fact he threatened to take out a court injunction to stop me pestering him.'

It was difficult not to feel sympathy for Isla, Andreas conceded. Her story gave him a better understanding of why she had behaved the way she had. But nothing altered the fact that she had deliberately denied him the first four months of his son's life.

'When a pregnancy scan revealed that I was expecting a boy, I decided to change my name by deed poll from Stanford to my mother's name, Christie,' she said flatly. 'I didn't want my son to bear the name of his grandfather who he would never know, and he is Loukas Christie.'

'The fact that you'd changed your name would explain why you couldn't be found. My security team did everything to try to locate you.' He frowned. 'Why didn't you give Loukas my surname?'

'You were not present when I registered his birth and so your details are not on his birth certificate.'

'His birth certificate can be amended to include me as his father, and his surname will be changed to Karelis.'

'No.' Isla walked across the room and stood in front of him, her eyes stormy. 'I don't want to have to explain to him that he has his father's name but there was no place for him in your life.'

'You won't have to do that because it's not going to happen,' Andreas said coolly. 'My son will have my family's name and he will grow up in Greece.'

Her eyes widened with shock. 'Loukas's life is in England with me. If you've decided that you want to have a relationship with him, then you can visit him. Maybe he could spend occasional weekends with you, or come to Greece for part of the school holidays when he is older. But while he is a baby he needs to be with his mother and I am taking him home.' She stepped away from Andreas and headed for the door. 'I must to go now. Dinos and Toula will be waiting for me.'

'They have already left Louloudi.'

She stopped dead and swung back round to face him. 'How do you know?'

'I told them that you had decided to remain on the

island. A storm is forecast and Dinos agreed with me that they should go before the bad weather made the crossing to the mainland uncomfortable.'

Temper flashed in her eyes. 'I can't believe you lied to Dinos and Toula. I refuse to stay here. You will have to call your helicopter pilot and tell him to come and collect me.'

He shouldn't be enjoying this, but hell, Isla deserved to suffer a little after what she had done, Andreas thought grimly. 'I'll arrange for the helicopter to take you to Athens by all means,' he drawled. 'But Loukas stays here with me.'

Her jaw dropped and he pressed home his point. 'My son is a Karelis and he will want for nothing. You say that material things don't matter, but you know that is not entirely true. I can give him the kind of lifestyle that few people are fortunate enough to have. Security, luxury, the best education—and love.' He pre-empted the word forming on her lips. 'Make no mistake, I will love my son and I will be a good father to him.'

'This is ridiculous.' She marched back across the room and halted in front of him. 'You can't separate a four-month-old baby from his mother.'

'You're the one who wants to leave. I didn't say that you have to go.'

'I know what this is. It's about power, isn't it?' Isla jabbed her finger into his chest. 'You don't really want Loukas. You didn't even know he existed until an hour ago.'

'And whose fault is that?' Andreas gritted. 'You changed your name so that I couldn't find you.'

'I didn't...'

'If you had contacted me when my son was born, I would have been there instantly. You told me that Loukas almost died at birth, but even then you didn't give me the chance to be with him. But I have him now and I won't allow you to disappear with him again.'

'You can't keep me a prisoner here,' she yelled, and poked him in the chest again. Hard. The cool, composed Isla who Andreas had first met at his father's house in London had turned into the fiercely passionate woman who had given herself to him in the cottage. Now it was anger instead of desire blazing in her eyes, but when he captured her hand before she could jab her finger into his ribs for a third time he watched her pupils dilate and knew she was fighting her awareness of him.

He tugged on her hand, jerking her closer so that their bodies were almost touching and he could feel the heat between them. Their chemistry was a potent force, and a complication he could do without, Andreas thought darkly. It tested his willpower to resist the temptation to lower his head and claim her mouth with his. Her eyes widened and her tongue darted across her bottom lip. It did not make it easier to know that she wanted him with the same urgency that pulsed hard and hot in his blood.

With a choked sound she wrenched her hand out of his grasp. 'I hate you.' She flung the words at him before she marched out of the study. A few moments later, Andreas glanced out of the window and saw her pushing the pram down the path that led to the jetty. He let her go. She could not escape from the island, and when she returned to the villa he was going to tell her how things were going to play out from now on. It was time he took back control.

CHAPTER NINE

THE BOAT WAS no longer tied up next to the jetty. Isla hadn't really expected it to be, but she had clung to the faint hope that Andreas had lied when he'd said that Dinos and Toula had gone to the mainland without her.

It was Andreas's fault that she was stranded on Louloudi. How dare he make her his prisoner? But he wasn't as clever as he thought. She had travelled to the island by water taxi and had stored the boatman's number on her phone. All she had to do was call him and ask him to come and pick her and Loukas up and take them to Athens.

Isla looked up at the sullen clouds scudding across the sky. The sea was choppy and she didn't like the thought of taking the baby in a boat, but she couldn't stay on Louloudi when Andreas was threatening to keep Loukas in Greece. She was furious at his accusation that she had deprived him of his son.

It had occurred to her a few weeks after Loukas was born and they had both recovered from the traumatic birth that she should phone Andreas at his office—the only way she had of contacting him—to let him know he had a son. But the memory of his refusal to believe she had fallen pregnant by him, and his scornful suggestion that she'd had other lovers, had stopped her.

She'd had enough rejection to last a lifetime and she was stunned that Andreas now appeared to accept Loukas was his son.

Her conscience reminded her that he had said he would love his child and he wanted to be a good father. If that was true, would it be better for Loukas's sake if his parents could set aside their hostility and negotiate how they could both be involved with their son? She gave a bitter laugh. Andreas hadn't sounded like he would negotiate when he'd insisted that Loukas would grow up in Greece. But if he thought she would hand over her baby to him, he was wrong. Her little son was all she had and she adored him. No one was going to take Loukas away from her.

Before she'd left the house she had hung her handbag on the handle of the pram, and now she searched through it and discovered that her phone and Loukas's passport were missing. Andreas must have taken them, and she was trapped on Louloudi. Trembling with rage, she pushed the pram along the track that wound around the island, not trusting herself to return to the villa while she felt like murdering him. She had reached the furthest point on Louloudi when a helicopter buzzed overhead.

Maybe Andreas had changed his mind and was going to allow her to take Loukas to England, Isla thought hopefully. But another possibility made her go cold inside as she wondered if he intended to put her on the helicopter and send her away from her baby. She would fight him with every last breath in her body, she vowed.

To her surprise the helicopter rose into the sky and disappeared into the low clouds. A storm had threatened to break all afternoon and now raindrops stung her bare arms. She pulled up the pram's hood over Loukas and began to walk quickly in the direction of the villa. Her feet slipped on the loose stones and she stumbled and gave a cry as pain shot through her ankle.

Where were they? Andreas pushed a hand through his wet hair as he strode along the beach. Isla and the baby had been gone for hours and dusk was falling. Panic made his heart thud painfully hard in his chest. The wind drove the rain into his face, and the waves crashing onto the shore threw up sprays of white foam.

He retraced his steps and reached the path leading from the beach to the villa. Ahead of him he spotted Isla and he felt a combination of anger and relief. She was walking slowly and leaning heavily on the pram.

'Where the hell did you go?' he demanded when he caught up with her. She was soaked to the skin and her face was ashen. 'Why are you limping?'

She spoke with an effort. 'I tripped and I think I've sprained my ankle.'

They reached the house and Andreas manoeuvred the pram up the steps and through the front door. Isla followed slowly and sank down onto a chair in the hall. She closed her eyes and her face was screwed up with pain. He looked at her feet and swore when he saw that her right ankle was twice the size of her left one.

'You need to take your shoe off before your foot and ankle swell even more,' he told her as he knelt down and untied the lace of her trainer.

'I can manage,' she muttered. He ignored her and gently eased the shoe off her foot, grimacing when she gasped and turned even whiter.

'I'll get some ice and you will have to keep your foot elevated until the swelling goes down. You might have broken a bone.'

'I'm sure it isn't broken.' She levered herself out of the chair and gave a sharp cry before sinking back down. 'Oh, *hell*. Loukas will wake up soon for a feed.' She ran a hand over her eyes. 'I wish I had never brought him to Louloudi. And I wish even more that I hadn't slept with you a year ago.'

'Are you saying that you wish you did not have Loukas?' An icy hand gripped Andreas's heart. He realised that he had only been concerned about how he felt to have a child, and he'd never considered that Isla might have resented her unplanned pregnancy. She seemed devoted to Loukas, but what if she stopped loving him? Andreas had spent his childhood desperate to win his mother's affection. He wanted his son to know that he was loved by both of his parents, but if Isla regretted sleeping with him, she might also regret the child who had been conceived as a result of their passion.

'Of course I don't regret having him,' Isla said fiercely. 'My baby is the best thing that has ever happened to me.' A shiver ran through her and Andreas forced his gaze away from the outline of her nipples jutting through her sodden T-shirt.

'I'm going to carry you upstairs so that you can change into dry clothes,' he explained when she made a violent sound of protest as he lifted her up into his arms. Her breath hissed between her teeth and he guessed she was in too much pain to argue. 'Loukas will be safe in the pram until I come back for him.'

She weighed next to nothing, he thought as he held her against his chest while he mounted the stairs. 'Why are you so slim? Have you been dieting? Wouldn't it be sensible to eat well so that you can feed the baby?'

Her eyes flashed silver with temper. 'Suddenly you are an expert on childcare? Have you ever tried to prepare and eat proper meals with one hand at the same time as holding a baby who cries whenever you lay him in his cot? Being a new parent is hard work, and being a single parent is even harder. But you wouldn't know about that because you weren't around to help when Loukas had colic and didn't sleep for more than an hour at a time.'

'You should have called me after he was born,' Andreas said tersely. His conscience pricked uncomfortably that Isla had struggled to cope on her own. But dammit, he *had* tried to find her after she'd told him she was pregnant.

'Why would I have called you so that you could insult me again?' She gave a bitter laugh that sounded more like a sob. 'I was too tired and sick to fight with you then. My friend Jess from the village in Suffolk where I used to live came and took me and Loukas back to stay with her on her farm. I don't know what I would have done without her kindness.'

Andreas's body clenched when Isla shifted in his arms and her breasts brushed against his chest. He felt the hard points of her nipples through his shirt and when he glanced at her face he saw a telltale pink stain run along her cheekbones. Damn this woman and the effect that her sensuality had on him, he thought grimly as he strode into her bedroom and through to the en suite bathroom. He placed her on a stool and opened the door of the shower cubicle.

'The quickest way to warm up is to have a hot shower. If you stand on your good leg and hold onto the towel rail, I'll help you take your jeans off.'

'I can manage. I'd rather die than let you undress me.'

He rested his gaze on her flushed face, and said sardonically, 'We both know that's a lie.' He hoped she did not notice that his fingers were unsteady as he fumbled with the button on her jeans.

'I'll do it.' She slapped his hands away and ran the zip down. But when she gingerly stood up she gave a gasp of pain and didn't stop him when he eased her jeans over her hips and pulled them down her legs.

The sight of her tiny black knickers evoked a throb of desire in Andreas's groin, and it tested his willpower to resist the urge to press his mouth against the lace panel between her legs. If there was a hell, he was surely destined to burn in its eternal fires, he thought grimly. Isla sat back down on the stool and he carefully tugged her jeans over her swollen ankle.

'Now your T-shirt.'

She shook her head. 'If you help me into the shower, I'll finish getting undressed in there. Will you go and get Loukas? He's probably awake by now.'

The baby had kicked off his blanket and he waved his chubby arms and legs in the air when he saw Andreas. He had heard other people speak of their hearts melting and now he discovered that it could really happen.

'Hello,' he said softly as he picked Loukas up and the baby snuggled into his neck. Andreas remembered the list Isla had recited of things that a father should do for his child. 'I am your Papa and I will read you bedtime stories and teach you to play football and take care of you when you are scared,' he told Loukas. He breathed in his evocative baby scent, as sweet as vanilla. When he held him against his shoulder, he felt the softness of the baby's downy dark hair against his chin. His son—but was he?

Doubt crept into Andreas's mind. Sadie's lies when she'd accused him of being her baby's father had driven a wedge deeper between him and his own father. 'You have brought shame on the Karelis family,' Stelios had told him. 'You were a fool not to get a paternity test done before your girlfriend sold a damaging story to the newspapers.'

He would not be a fool for a second time. A short while ago a helicopter had delivered a DNA testing kit to the island. Andreas laid Loukas back in the pram and pushed him into the study where he'd left the test kit. It was a simple, painless procedure to take a mouth swab from the baby and from himself. The samples would be collected and analysed and the result would confirm the truth of Loukas's parentage. Andreas felt a flash of guilt for doing the test without Isla's knowledge, but he had to know for certain that this baby who was making inroads on his heart was his son and heir.

Isla was sitting on the edge of the bed when he carried Loukas into her room. She had wrapped a towel around her and the idea that she was naked beneath it had a predictable effect on Andreas's libido. 'I don't have anything to wear because I packed all my clothes thinking I was leaving Louloudi with Dinos and Toula. My suitcase is still downstairs in the hall.'

'Wait a minute.' Andreas walked down the corridor to his own room and took a shirt from the wardrobe. 'You can wear this for now and I'll bring your case up later,' he said, handing her the shirt.

'Thank you.' She glared at him when he stood in front of her. 'Turn around while I put it on.'

Obediently, Andreas turned his back on her and was confronted with the view in the mirror of her naked, slender body as she unwrapped the towel. His mouth ran dry and he ignored the voice of his conscience that said he should close his eyes. He'd never professed to be a saint! Isla's hair fell damply around her shoulders and

beads of moisture glistened on her breasts. He wanted
to put his mouth there and taste her peachy perfection
before trailing his lips lower to the cluster of gold curls
between her legs. He gave a silent groan of disappointment when Isla slipped the shirt on and fastened the
buttons. Andreas had almost forgotten the baby in his
arms until Loukas gave a whimper.

'He's hungry,' Isla said. 'He usually has a bottle at
this time but I haven't made up his formula milk. Give
him to me and I'll feed him myself.'

He carefully placed the baby in Isla's arms and could
not assimilate the feelings that poured through him as
he watched his son feeding from his mother's breast.
The two of them had had four months in which to form
a bond, but Andreas had known his son for a few hours
and he felt as though he was intruding on the special relationship that existed between a mother and her child.
Every mother but his own, he thought, his mouth twisting. His mother had made it clear that she didn't love
him and he'd assumed it was his fault, some failing on
his part that made him unlovable.

He walked over to the window and moodily watched
the rain lash the glass. For the first time in his life he
did not know how to proceed. He was determined to
keep his son with him but it was patently obvious that
Loukas needed to be with his mother. Somehow he was
going to have to persuade Isla that from now on her life
would be in Greece, Andreas brooded.

'Why were you so adamant that I couldn't be expecting your child when I told you I was pregnant?'

He exhaled heavily. 'It seemed so improbable.' He
considered telling Isla what had happened with Sadie.
But he'd felt such an idiot when details of his private
life had been headline news and the rumour mill had

gone mad on social media. The fact that the story was untrue hadn't seemed to matter to the tabloid editors who fed like voracious sharks on the scandal.

'I didn't really believe I was having a baby until my first scan when I saw a tiny heartbeat. I have some pictures of Loukas on my phone, taken when he was a few days old in the neonatal unit.' Isla glared at Andreas when he turned away from the window. 'You stole my phone and Loukas's passport out of my bag. Can I have them back?'

'I have locked his passport in the safe,' he told her unapologetically. He took her phone out of his pocket and walked over to the bed to return it to her.

Isla touched the keypad and handed the phone to him. 'Because Loukas was preterm he was placed in an incubator at first, but when I was well enough, a nurse took me to see him and I was able to hold him.'

Scrolling through the pictures, Andreas felt a tightness in his throat when he saw how tiny Loukas had been, lying in a plastic incubator and wearing only a nappy, with wires attached to his skinny little body. There was a picture of Isla cradling him in her arms. She looked pale and scared, and guilt clawed in Andreas's gut as he remembered her accusation that he'd failed Loukas. The truth was that he had failed both of them.

'You said that you have been staying with a friend in England since Loukas was born. Don't you think it would be better for him if you had a home where he could grow up?'

'Of course it would. I have been looking for a place, but my job is in London and properties in the city are so expensive.'

He frowned. 'Who looks after him when you are at work?'

'I'm on maternity leave and not due to go back to the museum until Loukas is six months old.'

'What will you do with him then?'

She looked down at the baby and sighed. 'I suppose he will go to a nursery. I was able to finish my PhD while I was pregnant and I've been offered a full-time position at the British Museum as an assistant curator.'

'Is that what you want, to leave Loukas all day long while you go to work?'

'It's not ideal. I wish I could spend his first year with him, but I'll have to work full-time hours and earn a decent salary so that I can give Loukas a good standard of living.' Isla bit her lip. 'I meant it when I said I don't want the half-share of Louloudi which was left to me in Stelios's will. The island belongs to you and your family.'

'Loukas is my family.' Andreas's eyes narrowed. 'I have told you that my son will grow up in Greece. My apartment in Athens is not an ideal place for a child but I inherited the house where I lived as a boy. It is undergoing refurbishments and will be Loukas's home.'

Isla's face had turned almost as white as the pillows. 'Are you threatening to take my baby away from me? You denied he was yours, but now you are demanding that he will live in Greece with you.'

His jaw clenched. She looked so damned vulnerable and he hated that he was responsible for the fear in her eyes. 'I meant that you and Loukas will both move to Greece and we will all live together as a family. It will allow you to be a full-time mother to him for as long as you like, and there will be no need for you to get a job unless you want to return to your career in the future.'

The baby had finished his feed. Andreas watched Isla expertly hold Loukas against her shoulder while she pulled the shirt over her breast. She was so beautiful. Motherhood had made her softer somehow and even more desirable. He wanted his son, he reminded himself. That was the only reason why he was prepared to sacrifice his freedom. Isla had disappeared once, and he would not risk her taking Loukas away from him again.

She looked puzzled. 'Let me get this straight. You're asking me to live with you?'

'I'm asking you to marry me,' Andreas told her coolly. He ignored her shocked gasp. 'And I will take care of both of you.'

CHAPTER TEN

'You don't want to marry me,' Isla said flatly. She had no illusions that Andreas's proposal had been in any way romantic. But she was quickly discovering that his acceptance of his son had changed things irrevocably. She was glad that he wanted to play a part in Loukas's life but a loveless marriage was her idea of hell.

He did not deny it. 'I am determined to be fully involved with Loukas and it makes sense for us to marry so that we can provide him with the stability of growing up with both his parents.'

'We don't have to marry to do that. We can live independent lives and still be good parents.'

'How would that work, exactly? I have to live in Greece to run Karelis Corp. Would Loukas live in England with you one week and with me in Greece the next? It seems to me that he would spend much of his life on an aeroplane, being passed between us like a parcel. Does it sound ideal to you?'

'No, of course not.' She chewed her bottom lip. 'I suppose I could move to Athens and look for a job, and you could see him whenever you wanted.'

Andreas shook his head. 'I am not going to be a remote figure like my father was when I was growing up. I'm already planning to cut down my working hours, and I *will* be there for Loukas every night to read to him and kiss him goodnight.'

Isla felt a lump in her throat. Hearing Andreas state his intention to be a hands-on father to Loukas touched her deeply. More than anything in the world she wanted her baby to have what she had never had—a daddy. Andreas had promised to love his son, to protect him and care for him. To her shame she even felt the tiniest bit jealous that Andreas would give those things freely to the baby but not to her. If she married him, he would tolerate her because she was the mother of his child, but he wouldn't love her. It was a shock to realise how much that hurt.

'It's a crazy idea,' she muttered. 'We don't even like one another.'

'We don't actually know each other very well.' For some reason Andreas was staring at her hair, which had dried in loose curls after her shower. 'Sexual chemistry drew us together,' he said bluntly. For the next month we both have to stay on Louloudi, and I suggest we call a truce. For our son's sake we should try to establish a cordial relationship. I don't want Loukas to grow up thinking that his parents hate each other, and I'm sure you don't want that either.'

She bit her lip. 'I don't hate you, but I won't marry you.'

'I am a very wealthy man. Think of the life I can give him, and you.'

'I don't care about money,' she said fiercely, remembering how Andreas had once accused her of being a gold-digger.

He nodded. 'I believe you. But this isn't about you or me. We need to do what is best for Loukas.'

Isla leaned her head against the pillows. Her ankle

was throbbing and she felt mentally and physically exhausted. The storm was still raging outside and it was almost dark. Andreas switched on the lamps and crossed to the window to close the blinds. While she had showered he'd changed out of his wet clothes and he looked powerfully masculine in black jeans and a polo shirt. A little voice inside her head asked her why she didn't simply accept his marriage proposal and allow him to take away all her worries about how she would manage to be a working single mother.

Her eyes felt heavy and she forced them open. Loukas needed his nappy changed and a clean sleepsuit before she put him in his cot for the night. She gave a start when Andreas lifted the baby out of her arms.

'Does he sleep in there at night?' he asked, glancing at the travel cot.

'Yes, Toula uses the cot when her baby granddaughter comes to stay and she lent it to me for Loukas.'

'Tomorrow I will order nursery furniture and everything else he needs. But for tonight I'll put the cot in my dressing room and you can spend the night in my room with me.'

Her heart lurched. 'I will not.'

'You can't walk while your ankle is painful,' he reminded her patiently, 'and you certainly can't risk carrying Loukas. The obvious solution is for you and him to move into my suite so that I can help take care of him.'

'I appreciate that I'll need help until my stupid ankle is better,' Isla muttered, 'but we don't have to share a bed.'

'Are you worried that I will be unable to control my sexual urges if we are in the same bed?' Andreas's blue eyes darkened with anger. 'You have been trying to hide how much pain you're in but you are as white as a ghost. I am not so crass as to try to take advantage of you when you are at your most vulnerable.'

Now she felt guilty! Isla sighed heavily. 'All right, I suppose it makes sense,' she muttered. 'But only for to-night.' She looked at Andreas. He was cradling Loukas in his arms and the tender expression on his face as he stared at the baby tugged on her heartstrings. For the first time she really believed that Andreas intended to be a devoted father to his son, and in her opinion that was worth more than all the money in the world. He had said that they must do the best for Loukas. But how could a marriage between two people who mistrusted each other possibly work?

He turned his head towards her and their eyes met and held. If only Andreas wasn't the most beautiful man she had ever seen, Isla thought with a sigh. But the sense of connection she felt with him was in her imagination, she told herself. When he had made love to her a year ago she'd felt that they belonged together, but he had discarded her and made her feel that she was just another blonde who had briefly shared his bed.

With a sigh she concentrated on practical matters. 'Loukas needs a nappy change. Can you manage to do it?' She fully expected him to refuse to volunteer for such a mundane task, but he nodded.

'I'm sure I'll learn. I meant it when I said I want to be fully involved with him, and that includes changing his nappy.' Andreas smiled at her obvious surprise. 'Once Loukas has settled, I'll go and make dinner.'

Her brows lifted. 'I hadn't got you down as the do-mesticated type.'

'Careful, *moro mou*,' he said softly, 'or I will de-mand you return my shirt immediately.' The glitter in his eyes sent a frisson of sexual hunger through Isla.

Her breasts felt heavy and when she glanced down she was embarrassed to see her nipples jutting beneath the shirt he had lent her.

'I'm curious,' she mumbled. 'Did your mother teach you to cook?'

'*Theos*, no!' His smile faded. 'My mother had an army of servants to run around her and I doubt she ever set foot inside a kitchen. She wasn't interested in anything except her ill-health and her unhappiness, for which she blamed me.'

'Why did she blame you?'

'She suffered a stroke after I was born, brought on by a long and difficult labour. My mother never fully recovered, physically or mentally, from the trauma. When I was a small boy I had no idea why she seemed to detest me, but when I was older she never missed an opportunity to tell me that all her problems were my fault.'

'It sounds as though you had an unhappy childhood.' Isla imagined Andreas as a little boy, wondering why his mother seemed not to care for him. Loukas would never doubt how much she loved him, she promised herself.

'I was away at school a lot and I spent most of the holidays here on Louloudi with Toula and Dinos.' He shrugged. 'I learned to be independent and self-sufficient from an early age and those qualities helped me when I was starting out in my racing career. My father did not approve of me racing motorbikes and refused to give me financial backing, but it only made me more determined to succeed.'

It was not difficult to understand why Andreas seemed so emotionally guarded, Isla thought later that night. He had grown up feeling unloved by his mother.

And his father's affair with her mother had meant that Stelios was often not around for his family.

With a sigh she checked Loukas on the baby monitor before she switched off the bedside lamp. Andreas had shut himself in his study, saying he needed to do a couple of hours' work on his laptop. Her ankle was turning an interesting shade of purple but the pain had settled to a dull throb and she hoped she would be more mobile tomorrow.

But first there was the night to get through. Andreas's bed was enormous but she wriggled over to the edge of the mattress so that when he came to bed he would know that she was only sharing it with him with extreme reluctance.

Who was she kidding? Isla asked herself ruefully. She only had to be in the same room with Andreas and her body went haywire, every cell, every nerve fiercely aware of him. Earlier he had carried her into the sitting room of his suite and sat her at the table before he served dinner.

'I'm impressed that you made moussaka,' she'd told him, thinking that her own culinary skills didn't extend much further than omelettes.

His grin had done strange things to her heart. 'I am not very domesticated. Toula prepared meals and left them in the fridge. I simply heated the food up.'

She had found herself smiling back at him and, although she only had half a glass of wine topped up with soda water, she felt relaxed yet at the same time more alive than she'd ever felt.

'Loukas looks like you when you both smile,' Andreas murmured.

'I think he looks more like you. He has your colouring and his eyes are the same deep blue as yours.'

'He has a mixture of our genes and he's bound to have a physical resemblance to both of us.'

'I suppose so.' Emotion had suddenly clogged her throat. Loukas wasn't just a baby; he was a link between her and Andreas that would last for their lifetimes. 'When you asked me to marry you, what kind of marriage were you suggesting?' She blushed and felt herself floundering. 'What I mean is, would you want a proper marriage?'

Andreas had given her a speculative look. 'By *proper* I assume you mean would we have a sexual relationship? Why not? We have already proved that we are sexually compatible.'

She was glad he hadn't pretended that he was in love with her, Isla assured herself. There was nothing romantic about Andreas's proposal and marriage was simply a way for them to bring up their son together—with added benefits.

Thinking about their sexual compatibility made her feel hot all over. For the past year she'd frequently had dreams of Andreas making love to her, but tonight, lying in his bed, those memories were sharper than ever before. Her nipples tingled as she remembered how he had caressed her breasts with his hands and mouth, and how he'd moved down her body, pressing hungry kisses over the sensitive skin of her inner thighs. Isla's breathing slowed and her eyelashes brushed her cheeks as sleep claimed her and she slipped into a delicious dream.

She woke with a start and opened her eyes. It was pitch-black and she could not see anything, but her other senses took over and she realised that the wind had died down and the only sound she could hear was Andreas's regular, deep breaths. She hadn't been aware that he had come to bed, or that at some point during the night she had moved across the mattress towards him. He was so close she could feel his warm breath on her cheek, and his male scent—an elusive mix of his sandalwood aftershave and something muskier and uniquely him—stirred a fierce longing low in her pelvis.

He was fast asleep. Now that her eyes were accustomed to the dark, she was able to study his face. His sculpted features were softened slightly and she glimpsed the boy he had once been, and imagined how Loukas would look when he grew up. Emotion tugged on her heart. She and Andreas had made a beautiful child together but they were separated by a chasm of mistrust. Except that right now the only thing separating them was the shirt he had lent her.

Her mind was still full of the dream she'd had about him. She could not resist touching him and felt the heat of his silken skin and the slight abrasion of his chest hairs beneath her palm. Closing her eyes, she imagined if they were a proper couple instead of almost strangers linked by a baby they had not planned to have. If they were lovers she could trace her fingertips over the hard ridges of his abdominal muscles and discover the indent of his navel, before following the arrowing of hairs across his flat stomach and down to where they disappeared beneath the waistband of his boxer shorts.

She froze when he stirred. But his chest rose and fell evenly and she released her breath and pressed her face against his shoulder. She couldn't resist kissing his satin-smooth skin. He tasted of salt on her tongue. If they were lovers she could slip her hand beneath the elastic waist of his boxers and trail her fingertips over a hair-roughened thigh. Her heart skipped a beat when she came up against his impressively hard, thick arousal.

Before she could snatch her fingers away, he clamped his big hand over hers.

'Just so that there are no misunderstandings, *omorfia mou*, you were the one to take advantage of me,' he growled.

Isla stared at his face, so hard and angular with the skin pulled tight over his sharp cheekbones. His eyes gleamed with a predatory hunger that sent a quiver of response through her. 'I advise you not to start something unless you are prepared for me to finish it.'

Embarrassed heat scorched a path from Isla's face right down to her toes. 'I was having a dream,' she choked.

'I thought I must be dreaming when I felt you touching me but the reality is even better.' The lazy satisfaction in Andreas's voice and the gleam of triumph in his eyes made her feel sick with mortification.

What had she done? She had shown him that she was still desperate for him, despite the fact that he had never bothered to get in contact with her after the night she had spent with him. Sure, he had been busy trying to save Karelis Corp but he could have phoned her after she'd left Louloudi. He had told her he'd looked for her after she'd visited him in Athens to tell him she was pregnant, but she only had his word, Isla thought bleakly. The truth was that Andreas had viewed her as a sexual diversion. The chemistry between them was a bonus in a marriage that he had only suggested because he wanted his heir.

She sat up and pulled the sheet up to her chin. 'I don't want to have sex with you.'

'You could have fooled me,' he drawled. But his dry comment did not disguise the bite of frustration in his voice. 'I know you want me. Your body has been sending

out signals from the moment we met each other again.'
He ran his finger lightly down her cheek and then lower,
skimming over her throat before slipping beneath the
sheet and finding the hollow between her breasts.

She wondered if he could feel the frantic thud of
her heart. In the darkness his eyes glittered like blue
flames as he lowered his head until his mouth almost
grazed hers. Almost, but not quite. Part of her wanted
him to take control and kiss her. If he did, she would not
be able to resist him. The hunger inside her craved his
touch—his lips, his hands, his body driving into hers.

'Let me make love to you, *moro mou.*'

Temptation clawed in her stomach. It would be so
easy to let him ease her loneliness. When she was in his
arms she could pretend that he was offering more than
sex. But afterwards he might walk away from her as he
had done in the past, leaving her self-respect in tatters.

'No.' She shifted across the mattress away from him.
'Just because I had a dream doesn't mean that I want to
get involved with you again. You are the father of my
child, but we are practically strangers and the little bit
I know of you I don't like very much. I'm won't be your
convenient wife and provide sex on demand.'

'*Theos*, I would not make any demands on you,' Andreas ground out. 'When we have sex it will be because
you are as willing and eager as you were when you gave
your virginity to me. And note that I said *when*, not *if.*
You will come to me, and I can wait.' He cursed when
she swung her legs over the side of the bed and yelped
as she tried to put weight on her injured foot. 'What
are you doing?'

'I can't stay in your bed. I'll sleep on the sofa in
your dressing room. At least I'll be nearer to Loukas
if he wakes up.'

'Get back into bed,' Andreas said tersely. 'I'll take the sofa. Do not argue with me, Isla. You have already tested my control to its limits,' he told her as he strode into the adjoining room and closed the door with a thud that spoke volumes.

The next few days were difficult. Isla had felt thoroughly ashamed of her behaviour when she woke the next morning, alone in Andreas's huge bed, and recalled how she had touched his body while he slept. If she had woken in the night and found him caressing her, she would have accused him of taking advantage of her, she acknowledged on a fresh wave of embarrassment. She was aware that she was sending out mixed signals, and she felt silly and childish. She was a grown woman and a mother, but once again she was letting her past and her fear of rejection prevent her from satisfying her sexual needs with Andreas.

To her relief he did not mention what had happened—or not happened—she thought ruefully. She had expected him to make a mocking comment when he'd carried her downstairs and she'd stiffened in his arms and avoided his gaze. But he seemed to understand that her emotions were all over the place, and he kept their conversations to neutral topics, mainly about Loukas, so that Isla gradually began to relax.

By the third day the swelling on her ankle had reduced enough for her to be able to wear her shoes and she could hobble about, although Andreas always carried Loukas in case her ankle gave way. He continued to sleep in his dressing room, and in the morning when Loukas woke he brought the baby to her so that she could feed him. Those moments when they were all to-

gether and their son was at his most winsome made Isla
wonder if she had been too hasty when she'd refused to
marry Andreas. But he did not mention marriage again
and her fear of rejection stopped her from asking him
if his proposal had been serious.

Dinos and Toula arrived back on Louloudi, and a
couple of days later Andreas said he had business meetings in Athens and left on the helicopter early in the
morning. Isla missed him and she wondered how much
longer they could continue to remain in limbo, with
their desire for one another unfulfilled.

The day had dragged and her heart leapt when she
heard the helicopter return. Toula had said that Andreas
had asked for them to have dinner on the terrace, and
the Greek woman was going to babysit.

'Loukas can spend the night at my house. I am used
having my grandchildren to stay, and it will do you
good to have an evening off,' Toula told Isla firmly.
'The baby will be fine with me, so stop worrying and
enjoy some time with Andreas.' Her eyes twinkled and
Isla didn't have the heart to explain that her relationship with Andreas was not the great romance that Toula
clearly believed.

Nevertheless she felt a sense of anticipation when
she took a silk wrap-around dress in soft green out of
the wardrobe and slipped it on. The material felt sensual against her skin and the dress flattered her slim
figure that she'd been lucky enough to regain quickly
after giving birth to Loukas. She teamed the dress with
strappy silver sandals and slid a chunky silver bracelet onto her wrist. Her hair had grown like crazy while
she was pregnant and reached almost to her waist. She
clipped the front sections back from her face, added a

slick of rose-pink gloss to her lips and sprayed perfume to her pulse points.

Andreas was already outside on the terrace and Isla hesitated in the doorway and roamed her eyes over him. He looked incredibly sexy in black trousers and a black silk shirt, open at the throat to reveal a vee of olive skin and a sprinkling of his chest hairs.

He looked over at her, and as their eyes locked Isla glimpsed a predatory hunger in his gaze that made the weakness in her limbs so much worse. For a moment she allowed herself to imagine if this scene played out differently—if they had been a loving couple and devoted parents to their son. Andreas would ask if Loukas had settled, before he drew her into his arms and kissed her mouth—slow and sensual with a promise of the passion that would explode between them after dinner, when he would lead her up to their bedroom and make long, sweet love to her.

Longing for all that she could not have pierced like an arrow through her heart but she forced herself to smile. 'Are we celebrating something?' she murmured, eyeing the bottle of champagne in an ice bucket. There was a huge bouquet of flowers on the table and a few packages gift-wrapped in silver paper.

Andreas popped the cork on the champagne, filled two glasses and offered her one. 'Happy birthday.'

She swallowed hard. 'How did you know that today is my birthday?'

'I saw your date of birth in your passport. By the way, I have put Loukas's passport in your bedside drawer.'

Isla buried her face in the mixed bouquet of pink roses, white lilies and blue freesias. Their perfume was heavenly. 'I haven't celebrated my birthday since Mum died,' she said in a choked voice.

* * *

'No tears on your birthday.' Andreas brushed his thumb over Isla's damp cheeks. He felt a tug in his chest when she blinked and gave him a wobbly smile.

'I can't believe you bought me presents.'

'They're nothing much,' he said, feeling awkward. He'd spent hours when he should have been at work, walking around the shopping district in Athens and wondering what to buy her. He'd never actually chosen a gift for a woman before. That was something he left to his PA to organise, and he had an account with an exclusive jeweller who provided something suitably sparkly and expensive when he ended an affair with a mistress.

But Isla was different from any other woman he'd known, and she seemed genuinely delighted when she unwrapped a book on Greek mythology, a framed photo of Loukas smiling and showing his first tooth, and lastly a sky-blue topaz pendant suspended on a filigree silver chain. The necklace hadn't been expensive but Isla gave a gasp of delight as if it was the most valuable piece of jewellery in the world.

'I chose it because the pendant is the colour of Loukas's eyes,' Andreas explained as she lifted the necklace out of its box.

'And your eyes,' she murmured. She turned around and held her hair up so that he could fasten the chain around her neck. Andreas breathed in the floral fragrance of her perfume and his stomach clenched. He wanted to press his lips against her slender neck. Sexual tension had simmered between them since the night he'd been woken by her hands caressing him. How he hadn't lost it then, he did not know, but he had promised himself and Isla that he would wait until she was ready to make love with him.

It was not surprising that she was wary of him, he'd acknowledged as he'd tried to get comfortable on the sofa, which had not been designed for a man of his height. He had done nothing to earn her trust, but that needed to change because she was the mother of his son and he would do whatever it took to convince Isla that Loukas deserved the happy family life which neither of them had had when they were children.

'Thank you for the necklace and the other gifts. I love them.' Her smile stole his breath and Andreas felt a frisson of unease. He would not fall in love with her, he assured himself. He'd witnessed the damage and devastation wrought by love and its associated hopes and expectations. But he liked Isla and it was important to win her trust so that Loukas would grow up with two parents who were friends.

'Let's eat,' he said, holding out her chair for her to sit down. The starter was a *meze* platter with a selection of olives, cubes of feta cheese, wedges of pitta bread, hummus dip and stuffed grape leaves. Andreas wasn't hungry, at least not for food. Isla looked divine in her sexy, clingy dress and his body stirred as he imagined unwrapping the green silk to reveal her soft curves and those perfect breasts of hers. He took a gulp of champagne and said gruffly, 'Tell me what Loukas has done today.'

CHAPTER ELEVEN

THE SUNSET WAS spectacular. A kaleidoscope of pink, orange and gold that stained the sky and set the sea aflame. Dusk announced the first stars, pinpricks of silver against a purple backcloth, and, high above, a crescent moon dominated the heavens.

Isla glanced at her watch and was shocked to realise that she and Andreas had been talking for hours. Dinner had been followed by a decadent dessert of honey and rosewater *baklava,* accompanied by rich, dark coffee.

'Why did you study ancient Greek history?' he asked, sipping a glass of ouzo, which Isla had declined.

'So much of modern culture is influenced by ancient civilisations, and Greek literature, philosophy, astronomy and medicine still have a profound impact on our lives today. When I was sixteen I went on a school trip to Mycenae as part of a history project about the Bronze Age and I was hooked.'

'With your qualifications, I have no doubt that you will be able to continue your career in Greece.'

Isla could argue that she wanted to take Loukas to live in England. But she knew she would be wasting her breath. Andreas was determined that his son would grow up in his homeland and more than anything she wanted Loukas to see his daddy every day.

'I would like to work when Loukas is older. But he is growing so fast and I don't want to miss a day of his development.' She bit her lip, feeling guilty that Andreas had missed his son's first few months. 'I was upset when you refused to accept that I was pregnant with your baby,' she said huskily. 'I thought you didn't want Loukas, like my father didn't want me.'

Andreas leaned across the table and his eyes held her gaze. 'Have I convinced you that I would give my life for Loukas? I am absolutely committed to being the best father that I can be.' Emotion deepened his voice as he said, 'I love my son and I will make sure he knows how precious he is.'

Andreas's promise was everything she had hoped for, Isla thought. Well, not quite everything, she amended when he stood up and held out his hand to draw her to her feet. He wrapped his fingers around hers and she was intoxicated by the warmth of his skin. The spicy scent of his aftershave filled her senses and she was so aware of him it *hurt*.

'We'll go inside if you're cold,' he said when a shiver ran though her.

'I don't want to go in yet. It's such a beautiful night.' She walked over to stand by the balustrade and stared across the garden to the sea glimmering in the moonlight. Not so long ago she would have hurried away from him, too afraid of the feelings he aroused in her to stay when he roamed his hungry gaze over her. But she was tired of being a coward. She knew he desired her and she ached to be in his arms and in his bed. 'I don't want this evening to end,' she whispered.

'Well, it doesn't have to end yet.' His smile made her heart beat so hard she could feel it slamming against her ribs. 'What would you like to do? Can I get you another drink?'

'I want you,' she said breathlessly before she lost her nerve.

His jaw clenched but he did not move towards her. 'If this is out of gratitude because I gave you a birthday present…'

'It's not.' She didn't know how to make him understand her need that made ache so terribly. With a moan of frustration she flung her arms around his neck and pulled his mouth down so that it was a whisper away from hers. 'Kiss me, *please*. I think I might die if you don't.'

'In that case,' he growled, before he angled his mouth over hers and kissed her with a devastating passion that rocked her to her soul. The heat inside her burst into flame and she pressed her body closer to his, trembling with excitement when she felt the hard proof of his arousal nudge her thigh.

Andreas roamed his hands over her and cupped one breast, rubbing his thumb pad across her swollen nipple so that it hardened even more and she gave a whimper of pleasure. It was a whole year since he had shown her what her body was capable of and a white-hot flame shot from her breasts down to the molten core of her femininity. 'You drive me insane,' he muttered against her mouth. The evidence of his desire was a potent force and when he claimed her lips again with a barely restrained savagery she felt exultant.

She had missed him. It was crazy because they had scarcely spent any time together a year ago. But he had lodged like a bur beneath her skin, a constant torment to her. When he lifted his mouth from hers, he was breathing hard and a nerve flickered in his cheek. His blue eyes had darkened and were almost black, gleaming with an unconcealed hunger that drove everything from Isla's mind but her desperation to throw herself into his fire and burn in the fierce passion promised by his kiss.

Driven by an age-old instinct that pulsed hot and heavy between her thighs, she put her hands on his shirt front and felt the scorching heat of his body through the silk. It wasn't enough and she tugged open the buttons and smoothed her palms over his naked chest, glorying in the satiny feel of his skin and the slight abrasion of his chest hairs.

The long scar running down his chest did not detract from his male beauty. His powerfully muscular body made her aware of her softer feminine curves. She shivered when he spread his fingers over her breast, a possessiveness in his touch that made her heart-rate quicken. The ache deep down in her pelvis became an insistent throb as he skimmed his other hand over her silk dress, burning a path across her skin as he moved down her stomach and thighs until he came to the mound of her sex and pressed his palm against her. The effect was explosive and she gasped and arched her hips towards his hand, desire pounding a heavy drumbeat through her veins.

He kissed her again, without tenderness. But she did not care. His mouth was everything and her lips fitted the shape of his so perfectly that she could convince herself they had been designed for each other. She answered his demands with demands of her own and felt a surge of triumph when he groaned.

It had been so long since he'd made love to her and she was desperate to feel his hard length inside her once more. He drew the strap of her dress over her shoulder and peeled the material away to bare her breast. Her nipples were ultra-sensitive and she moaned softly when he rolled the swollen peak between his fingers, sending starbursts of pleasure down to her feminine core where she was so wet and ready. For him. Only for him. The world tilted as he lifted her into his arms and carried her into the house.

Mine. The word pounded inside Andreas's head and a possessiveness that he hadn't known he was capable of feeling ran like wildfire through his veins. He'd been startled when Isla had unexpectedly launched herself at him. Her rather clumsy attempt to seduce him had been endearing. She might not have the sophistication of his previous lovers but her sensuality blew his mind. It was just desire, he assured himself. The hunger that clawed in his gut was a kind of madness after a year in which he hadn't done more than disinterestedly take another woman to dinner.

He carried her up the stairs and into his bedroom. 'Are you sure this is what you want?' he muttered when he set her down on her feet next to the bed. He captured her hand and held it against his chest where his heart was doing its best to escape. 'Feel what you do to me, *omorfia mou*. If I kiss you again there is a danger that I won't be able to stop.'

Her eyes shone as bright as the stars. 'I want to go to bed with you, Andreas,' she said softly.

Theos, he was shaking like a schoolboy on a first date. His usual panache had deserted him and he cursed beneath his breath as he fumbled with the tie on her dress. Finally he was able to unwrap the green silk from her body and he released his breath on a ragged sigh.

'You are so beautiful,' he said hoarsely. Her black

bra was semi-transparent and her darker nipples were clearly visible. Moving his eyes lower, he felt his erection strain beneath his trousers as his greedy gaze settled on her sexy black thong. 'Did you choose your underwear for me?'

'Yes.' She gave him a shy smile and he felt a tightness in his chest. It was just sexual attraction that made him ache in a way he never had before, he told himself. How could it be anything else? Emotions played no part in what he wanted from Isla and all he felt for her was lust. Satisfied that he was in control of the situation, he removed her bra and could not stifle a groan of raw desire when he cupped her bare breasts in his palms.

A saint would find her irresistible, and Andreas knew that he had been damned a long time ago. He stripped off his clothes and his heart gave a kick when her eyes widened as she stared at his powerful erection. He needed to slow things down, but when he pulled her down with him onto the bed the silken glide of her skin against his made him catch his breath. Supporting his weight on his elbows, he looked into her eyes, which were smoky with passion.

'Do you have any idea how many nights I've dreamed of doing this?' he muttered, not caring that his admission might betray the urgency of his need for her. He kissed her mouth, teasing her lips apart with the tip of his tongue.

She tasted of honey and the sweet ardency of her response tugged a little on his heart and made him wish for something he could not begin to explain. He liked the low moans she made when he cradled her breast in his palm and rubbed his thumb pad across her nipple until it was stiff and hard, before he transferred his attention to her other breast. Her skin felt like satin as he trailed his lips over her flat stomach and down to the neat triangle of gold curls between her thighs.

'Andreas!' Her shocked gasp made him smile. 'I'm not sure…'

'Let me show you,' he said thickly, moving down the bed so that he was kneeling over her and gently pushed her legs apart. He took a moment to study her as she lay there, all flushed and pink with sexual warmth. When he had first met Isla at his father's house in London, a lifetime ago it seemed, he had wanted to shatter her cool composure, and the knowledge that he was about to do just that made his heart pound with anticipation.

With a low growl Andreas lowered his head and ran his tongue over her moist opening. She gave a whimper and threaded her fingers into his hair but did not try to pull him away. He slid his hands beneath her bottom and lifted her towards his mouth. The scent of her arousal was the sweetest perfume and he felt the throb of his painfully hard erection. But he ignored his urgency. This was about Isla and he was compelled to satisfy her needs before his own.

And so he pressed his mouth against her feminine core and licked his way inside her. He explored her with his tongue and heard her cries grow louder as she arched her hips and dug her nails into his shoulders. Finally he found the tight little nub of her clitoris and sucked it. The effect was explosive.

Isla shattered around him and the keening noise she made was the most erotic sound Andreas had ever heard. It evoked a wholly primitive response in him, a need to claim his woman. He took a condom from the bedside drawer and quickly sheathed himself. Isla's eyes were closed and her breaths came in fast pants. She lifted her lashes and stared at him, her passion-stunned gaze mixed with a vulnerability which mocked Andreas's belief that nothing existed in his chest but a hollow void.

He shoved the disturbing thought away and positioned himself over her. 'Tell me what you want,' he demanded.

Her lips curved into a sweet smile that made the hollowness inside him expand. 'You, Andreas. I want to feel you inside me.'

He closed his eyes to block out the image of her golden beauty, her slender, lithe body so ripe and ready for him. *Theos*, he was going to come before he'd even touched her. It had *never* happened to him before. Breathing hard, he somehow regained control of his libido and pressed the tip of his erection against her opening. She was slick and hot and he groaned as he slid deeper, forcing himself to take it slow as her internal muscles stretched to accommodate him.

It felt good. So, so good. He let out a ragged breath and thrust deep, heard her give a soft gasp as he withdrew a little way and then drove into her again. She matched his rhythm, lifting her hips to meet each hard stroke, while she clung to his shoulders and tipped her head back, giving him perfect access to her lips. He kissed her hungrily, the taste of her sweet breath filling his mouth and the delicate floral scent of her perfume assailing his senses until he could not say where he ended and she began. They moved together as one, their bodies in total accord in a timeless dance that quickly built to a crescendo.

It couldn't last. It was too intense and he knew he was losing control. Gritting his teeth, he increased his pace, each thrust faster and harder than the last, driving them both to the edge. He slipped his hand between them and rubbed his thumb over the sweet, tight heart of her. She bucked against him and sobbed his name, shuddering with the force of her orgasm. And only then did Andreas's control crack and he pressed his face into her neck and groaned as wave after wave of pleasure engulfed him.

A long time afterwards he rolled off her and lay on his back, shocked by how much he hated being separated from her. Alarm bells rang inside his head. It was just sex, he reminded himself. Amazing sex, it was true, but it did not mean anything to him. It never had and it never would. Did Isla understand that?

He wondered if she would cuddle up to him and he would have to tactfully extricate himself from the inherent danger of post-sex emotions—hers not his. He wasn't into the whole cuddling thing. But when he turned his head towards her, he discovered that she had moved across to her side of the mattress and was fast asleep.

Of course he was relieved that she wasn't the clingy, needy type, he told himself. But the thought that she was unmoved by their tumultuous passion which had blown his mind was unsettling. Cursing beneath his breath, he rolled onto his side, fighting his awareness of her, so close to him and yet a million miles away. The pale glimmer of dawn slipped through the slats in the blinds before he finally fell asleep.

Isla stretched luxuriantly as she woke from a deep sleep. Her body ached in unexpected places but it was not an unpleasant feeling. She opened her eyes and stared at the clock. Eight thirty! Loukas usually woke for a feed at around seven a.m. Her panic subsided when she remembered that the baby had stayed with Toula the previous night—so that she and Andreas could spend some time together!

She turned her head on the pillow and stared into his bright blue eyes. Her hand moved to her throat and she traced her finger over the topaz pendant he had given her on her birthday because the stone was the colour of their baby son's eyes. It had been such a thoughtful gesture but she must not read too much into the present or Andreas's devastating tenderness when he had made love to her so exquisitely, she told herself.

'You look serious this morning. Is that because you regret spending the night with me?'

Did he? Isla wondered. Andreas's expression was unreadable, and old habits meant that for a moment she was tempted to say that last night had been a mistake. If she rejected him first she wouldn't feel so bad if he said he regretted making love with her. But she hadn't been the only one to have come apart utterly. Passion had overwhelmed both of them and the groan Andreas had made as he'd climaxed inside her had sounded as though it had been ripped from his soul.

'I don't regret anything about last night,' she said honestly. She wondered if she'd imagined a look of relief that flashed in his eyes. He smiled and her heart skipped a beat.

'Good.' He kissed her mouth, slow and sweet but with the promise of more. 'Last night was incredible. You are incredible, *glykia mou*.' He knelt over her and caught her chin in his fingers to that she couldn't look away from him. 'Why did you have sex with me?'

Was he worried that she had fallen in love with him? The truth slammed into Isla like a speeding bullet aimed at her heart. Right back when she had been Stelios's housekeeper in London and Andreas had visited his father, she *had* felt an inexplicable connection with him. Love at first sight was something she'd thought only happened in romance films and novels. She *couldn't* be in love with Andreas, she told herself desperately. Her heart contracted as she was forced to accept the truth she had tried to deny. A harsher truth was that Andreas did not love her. But he desired her and he wanted them to bring up their son together.

She searched his hard-boned face for a hint of softness that might indicate he felt something for her other than desire, but there was none. 'I decided that you were right,' she said lightly, although it cost her to keep her wild emotions out of her voice. Andreas's brows lifted in silent query and she explained. 'We are sexually compatible and there seemed no point in denying that you turn me on.'

His eyes narrowed. 'That's the only reason?'

'What other reason could there be?' she countered. 'We both want to be full-time parents to Loukas, and we're good in bed. The sensible solution is for us to be together.'

Something flickered on his face that she could not define and, although he gave her one of his heart-melting smiles, his eyes were cool and guarded. 'It's good that you are so sensible,' he said drily.

He lowered his head so that his mouth was a whisper away from hers, but Isla held him off with her hands flat against his chest. She was afraid to make love with him when her emotions were on a knife-edge, scared of what she might reveal while they were as close physically as they could be.

The warmth of his body seeped into her, melting her resistance, and with a sigh she wound her arms around his neck and urged his mouth down on hers. She told herself she was imagining a tenderness in his kiss. At first his lips were warmly persuasive, teasing hers apart and encouraging her response, which she could not deny him. As always, passion exploded between them and the kiss became a ravishment of her senses. He trailed his mouth down her throat and along her collarbone, while she ran her fingers through the dark silk of his hair and arched her trembling body towards his in mute supplication.

Andreas muttered something in Greek as he knelt up and shaped her breasts, tested their weight and rubbed his thumb pads across her nipples until they were stiff and tingling.

'Touch me,' he said thickly, and she was happy to obey, running her hands over his powerful chest. But then he captured her hands in one of his and held them above her head while he kissed his way down her body. He pushed her legs apart, his warm breath stirring the cluster of curls at the junction of her thighs before he put his mouth on her and took her to the edge of insanity with his wickedly inventive tongue.

By the time he drove his bold erection deep inside her, Isla was still trying to catch her breath after he'd given her two shattering orgasms with his mouth and fingers. She loved the feel of him inside her, filling her, and she lifted her hips to welcome each hard thrust as he took her to the edge of the precipice yet again.

He paused and stared down at her, and she could not define the almost haunted expression that darkened his blue eyes. The air between them trembled with something fragile and ephemeral, and then Andreas pulled back and drove into her one last time, his harsh groan mingling with her cries of pleasure as they tumbled over the edge together.

CHAPTER TWELVE

THE HELICOPTER LANDED on Louloudi and Andreas climbed out and scanned the garden, hoping to see Isla walking across the lawn to meet him. There was no sign of her and his jaw clenched with disappointment. He had only been away for a few hours but he'd missed her.

The thought made him frown. Missing her suggested that he'd formed some sort of emotional bond with her, but that was a ridiculous idea. He separated the people in his life into distinct categories: family, friends, work associates and lovers. Isla fell somewhere between the first and the last. She was the mother of his child, although neither she nor his son bore his name. Yet to describe her as his mistress simply did not cover his fascination with her.

They had been living together on the island for almost three weeks and Andreas felt a contentment he'd never felt before. Karelis Corp was safe and its share price had continued to climb since the problems it had faced a year ago. He had the full support of his board and had proved he was a worthy successor to Stelios. But he was determined not to allow work to dominate his life like his father had done and, although he went to his office in Athens most days, he returned to Louloudi every afternoon so that he could spend time with Loukas.

He thought about Isla all the time. He was addicted to her as if she were a narcotic in his blood, and he was fairly certain that she was as swept away by their passion as him. But, apart from her cries of pleasure every time he gave her an orgasm, she was otherwise coolly composed so that he had no idea what she was thinking, and it frustrated the hell out of him.

Holding the box which he had brought with him from Athens under his arm, he walked into the villa and checked the ground floor rooms before he went upstairs in search of Isla. Concern for her had been the reason why he had left work early. He strode across the sitting room of his private suite, halting in the doorway that led into the nursery.

Isla was rocking Loukas in her arms. Her eyes widened in surprise when she glanced over and saw Andreas but there was no welcoming smile on her lips. She placed the baby in the cot and walked towards him. His stomach clenched when he saw tears on her lashes.

'I suppose you've seen the awful things that are being said about me on social media?' She closed the nursery door and picked up her phone from the coffee table. 'Many of the tabloids printed a photo of us kissing. The picture must have been taken without our knowledge when you took me shopping in Athens last week. It was such a lovely day, but now this—' She thrust her phone at him.

Andreas did not need to look at the screen. He'd already seen the damning photograph, and he silently cursed the impulse that had come over him while they had been strolling through a park to pull her into his arms and kiss her. He never made a public spectacle of himself, but Isla had said something which had made him laugh, and when he'd looked at her lovely face he'd felt as though they were the only two people in the world.

He had given in to his urgent need to kiss her, forgetting that as the head of one of Greece's most prominent companies he was easily recognisable by the paparazzi. Evidently a journalist had also recognised that Isla had been Stelios Karelis's fiancée.

'The most popular story trending on social media platforms is that I am a gold-digger who had previously hooked up with your ageing father, and now I've turned my feminine wiles on you,' she said in a choked voice. 'I'm just glad that we left Loukas on Louloudi with Toula, and the media haven't found out that we have a baby.'

'But we can't keep him hidden for ever,' Andreas said quietly. Their privacy was protected while they remained on the island but it couldn't last. 'I haven't even told my sister that we have a baby. But I don't want a nosey journalist to find out about Loukas and write an exposé about our—' he made speech marks with his fingers '—"secret love child". We need to take control of the situation and issue a press statement to announce that we have a son. And...'

He hesitated and caught hold of her hands. As he stared at her, he was aware of an indefinable tugging sensation in his chest when he saw that her eyes were the colour of wet slate, glistening with tears.

There was only one option open to them that made sense. It was Loukas's right to grow up a Karelis and have the support and love of both his parents. Determination swept through Andreas. Over the past weeks he knew that he and Isla had become friends as well as lovers.

In truth, it had surprised him. He'd never before had

a friendship with a woman. He got on well with female work colleagues and he usually parted on good terms with his mistresses. But essentially he was a man's man, and during the years that he'd raced motorbikes his friends had been mainly other bikers and engineers. The high testosterone atmosphere of the racing circuit hadn't given any opportunity for soul-searching conversations, he thought wryly.

Isla was intelligent with a dry sense of humour, and her passion for Greek history was something Andreas shared. He was proud of his homeland and glad that his son would learn about his heritage from both his parents. He and Isla could make a good life together, he brooded.

'And?' she prompted him.

He tightened his hold on her fingers. 'And at the press conference we will also announce our forthcoming marriage.'

A host of complicated emotions swept through Isla but above all she felt a sense of relief. Since Andreas had accepted that he was Loukas's father, and he'd proposed to her, he hadn't mentioned marriage again. She had wondered if he'd changed his mind, or if he had actually been relieved that she'd turned him down. The facts had not changed however, she reminded herself. They were only discussing marriage because Andreas felt duty-bound to marry her. Yet she could not help but feel pleased that he wanted the world to know Loukas was his son.

'Do you think a marriage without love would work?' she said slowly.

'I believe it has a better chance than a so-called lovematch with all the expectations and often false promises people make when they mistake lust for love. But there will be love,' Andreas murmured, and Isla's heart skittered in her chest. 'We both love our son and want what is best for him. You grew up without your father and neither of my parents had much time for me. Surely the most important thing is for us to give Loukas the family life that we both longed for when we were children?' Andreas lifted her hands up to his mouth and brushed his lips over her knuckles. The feral gleam in his eyes set Isla's pulse racing. He never tried to hide his desire for her, and he only had to look at her to evoke an ache of longing in the pit of her stomach. But was it enough? Could a marriage based on white-hot sex and a desire to create a family for their son really succeed? If she didn't marry him the alternatives—custody arrangements for Loukas, alternate birthdays and Christmases, perhaps sharing him with a stepmother if Andreas married someone else—made her go cold.

'I have something for you.' He released her hands and picked up a large, flat box that he'd placed on the sofa.

Isla looked at him uncertainly. 'What is it?'

'Why don't you open it and see?' he said drily.

She recognised the logo of a well-known fashion designer on the lid of the box and remembered that on the recent shopping trip to Athens she had visited a boutique in Kolonaki, the famous fashion district in the city. Andreas had persuaded her to try on a few dresses but she had refused to allow him to buy her anything and insisted on paying for a gorgeous blue silk dress with her own credit card.

Isla opened the box and her heart gave a jolt when she glimpsed white lace beneath the froth of tissue paper. She was stunned into silence as she lifted the dress out of the box and held it up. It was the most exquisite wedding gown imaginable—pure white silk overlaid with delicate lace and embellished with tiny sparkling crystals. The bodice had a scooped neckline and the dress was fitted at the waist and hips before flaring dramatically in a fishtail style with a long train at the back.

'While you were trying on dresses the other day, I wandered into the designer's studio and saw this wedding dress which she had just finished creating. It is elegant and breathtakingly beautiful and I thought it would be the perfect dress for you,' Andreas said softly.

Isla swallowed. The dress was like something out of a fairy tale, the kind of dress that little girls dreamed they would wear when they married a prince. But little girls grew up and discovered that even handsome princes had flaws. She wouldn't let herself get carried away by an unashamedly romantic dress, she told herself firmly.

'I don't know what to say,' she murmured.

Andreas's eyes glittered as he took the dress from her and laid it over the back of the sofa. 'Say yes, *omorfia mou.*' He captured her chin between his fingers and tilted her face up to his. 'I won't take no for an answer. Why are you hesitating when you know in your heart that it is the right thing to do? The passion we share is unlike anything I have ever experienced.'

She had only ever experienced passion with Andreas and he was the only man she wanted or would ever want, but she had more sense than to tell him. 'What will happen if it burns out?' Isla asked the question that ate away at her soul. 'Will you take other lovers? Oh, I'm sure your affairs would be discreet, but would you expect me to turn a blind eye, or take lovers of my own?'

A nerve flickered in Andreas's cheek and a savage

expression turned his eyes almost black. 'I don't suggest you try it, *moro mou*. I don't share what is mine.'

She should have been horrified by his outrageously possessive statement but Isla felt a deep sense of relief. Their relationship might be based on sex but she was secretly thrilled that Andreas had staked his claim on her. She reminded herself that she was a modern, independent woman. 'I'm not yours,' she whispered.

He snaked his arm around her waist and hauled her against him. 'Tell me that when you are lying beneath me, and I am inside you,' he growled. 'Tell me you are not mine when you scream my name and rake your nails down my back every time I make you come.'

His head swooped and he covered her lips with his and kissed her without mercy, without tenderness or gentleness. It felt as if he was branding her and she did not resist him. Instead she succumbed willingly to his mastery because the only place she wanted to be was in his arms, in his bed and in his life.

When at last he lifted his mouth from hers, they were both breathing hard. 'I am prepared to commit totally to our marriage,' he told her. 'I will expect you to do the same.'

It was a far cry from a declaration of love, but strangely she was reassured by his blunt words more than if he'd pretended to have feelings for her. She stared at his harshly handsome face and her heart turned over when he said intently, 'So what is your answer, Isla? You are the mother of my son. Will you also be my wife?'

She took a deep breath and prepared to leap from the mountaintop. 'Yes.'

'Have I told you how incredibly beautiful you look tonight?' Andreas's deep voice wrapped around Isla like a velvet cloak and helped to calm the butterflies that were leaping in her stomach.

She looked out of the car window and grimaced when she saw dozens of press photographers armed with cameras waiting on the pavement outside the Karelis Corp building in Athens. The party to celebrate the company's return to the top of the rankings of Greece's most successful businesses was *the* social event of the year and the paparazzi were out in force.

'The media have labelled me a scarlet woman so I thought I might as well dress the part,' she said wryly.

Her ballgown had come from the same fashion design house as her wedding dress and it was also made of silk overlaid with lace. But there the similarity between the two gowns ended. The red dress was overtly sexy. It was a halter-neck style and the chiffon top was semi-transparent at the front and left her back and shoulders bare. The long skirt had a side split that reached her mid-thigh. She was wearing more make-up than usual and her scarlet lipstick gave the illusion of self-confidence that she was far from feeling. But evidently she did not fool Andreas.

'Try to relax, *moro mou*,' he murmured as he picked up her hand and pressed his lips to the exquisite engagement ring—a rare and stunning round-cut blue diamond surrounded by white diamonds—that he had slipped onto her finger two days ago. 'I have already given a press statement explaining that our relationship began after my father's death, and I have told family members and close friends the truth—that your engagement to Stelios was a pretence so that he could hide the fact that he was terminally ill. At the party I will announce that we are engaged and soon to be married, and that we have a son.'

She bit her lip. 'But if the press find out Loukas's date of birth it will be obvious that we must have slept together while I was pretending to be Stelios's fiancée.'

Andreas shrugged. 'I won't give specific details. And I doubt anyone will care, certainly not the share-holders. They will be pleased that I have thrown off my playboy image and settled down to family life and produced an heir.'

The car stopped and the chauffeur jumped out and came to open the rear door. Andreas's words were a timely reminder to Isla of why he was marrying her. He had been so attentive since she had agreed to marry him that she'd almost started to believe he saw their marriage as more than a convenient arrangement which would give him his son.

She followed him out of the car, half blinded by the flashbulbs that went off around her. The photographers pressed forwards but Andreas's security guards kept them back. He put his arm around her waist, holding her close to him in a protective manner that made her foolish heart leap.

The opulent hospitality suite on the top floor of the building was packed with guests, all eager to glimpse the woman who had apparently captured the heart of Karelis Corp's notoriously commitment-phobic CEO. There were murmurs of surprise when Andreas intro-duced Isla as his soon-to-be wife and the mother of his baby son. But the news was well-received by every-one—with one exception.

Halfway through the evening, Andreas's sister fol-lowed Isla into the cloakroom, which happened to be empty. Nefeli launched straight into a verbal attack. 'I suppose you think you're clever to have trapped An-dreas with a baby. God, it's the oldest trick in the book.

But I've got news for you. The only reason he is prepared to marry you is so that he can regain control of
Louloudi. You persuaded my father to leave you a half
share of the island, but when my brother divorces you
he will make sure you get nothing.'

Isla told herself that there was no truth in Nefeli's
spiteful words. Andreas had mentioned that his sister
was still struggling to accept Stelios's death and Isla
knew from when she had lost her mum that grief was
a dark place. She pinned a smile on her face when she
returned to the party, but a few times during the evening she looked round to find Andreas's speculative
gaze resting on her.

'Are you going to tell me what's wrong?' he said
later when they walked into his penthouse apartment
in the city. They had left Loukas behind on Louloudi in
Toula's care. The Greek grandmother adored the baby
and Isla was grateful for her advice and experience that
she missed from her mum. Andreas crossed the sitting
room and slid open the glass doors which led onto the
balcony. It was a warm night, and a huge, bright moon
hung like a silver disc above the Acropolis.

Isla followed him outside and stared at Greece's most
iconic landmark, widely regarded as the most important
ancient site in the Western world. She had been excited
by the thought of living in Athens and perhaps working at the Acropolis museum when Loukas was older.
But now she was full of doubts and stood twisting her
engagement ring on her finger.

'If you don't like the ring you can choose a different one.'

Her eyes flew to Andreas. 'Oh, no, I love this one.
I didn't even know there was such a thing as a blue
diamond.'

'The clarity and intensity of colour is superior to a sapphire. I like how the stones reflect the light, like the sun sparkling on the Aegean Sea.'

She chewed her bottom lip. 'It's not the ring.'

'We could spend all night playing guessing games, but I have something much more enjoyable in mind,' he murmured.

'If we didn't have Loukas you wouldn't have asked me to marry you…would you?'

He made an impatient sound. 'But we do have our son, and he is a very good reason for us to marry. What do you want me to say?' He raked his hair off his brow and stared at her, his eyes glittering with an emotion she could not define. And she was probably imagining it, Isla thought. Andreas did not do emotions.

Why did she give her heart to men who did not want her love? she asked herself bitterly. She had idolised her father when she was growing up, despite the fact that she'd never met him. He had been a heroic figure in her mind, but she had discovered that he was selfish and not worthy of the tears she'd cried when he had told her to stay out of his life.

'Your sister said that you are only marrying me as a way of regaining full ownership of Louloudi and then you intend to divorce me.'

Andreas swore. 'Nefeli is still upset but it does not excuse her lies. I will speak to her.' He moved to stand in front of Isla and ran his finger lightly down her cheek. 'It's true that I suggested marriage as a sensible solution to our situation.'

Hearing him say it, even though he had never pretended to have feelings for her, felt like a knife through her heart. Fortunately her pride kicked in and she lifted her chin. 'With the added advantage of hot sex,' she suggested drily.

'It's more than just good sex,' he said thoughtfully. 'I have enough experience to know that the chemistry between us, the passion, is different than with other women. It's...special.'

Special! The word wrapped around Isla's heart like a security blanket. She had learned enough about Andreas to know that he did not say things he didn't mean. If he thought that making love with her was special it gave her hope that over time his feelings for her might grow.

'And there will be no divorce.' His voice was resolute. 'There has never been a divorce in the Karelis family.'

'Perhaps it would have been better if your parents had divorced as the marriage made your mother unhappy.'

'She made herself unhappy because she loved my father and it became an unhealthy obsession.' Andreas's jaw tightened. 'But that won't happen with us,' he said in a hard voice that sounded as though he was warning her not to fall in love with him. He was too late, she thought heavily. But if she told him how she felt, it would put her in a vulnerable position. He might even decide not to marry her and instead seek custody of Loukas. She shivered and Andreas frowned.

'You are getting cold out here. Let's go inside and I'll warm you.' His eyes gleamed with sensual promise as he swept her up into his arms and carried her inside the penthouse. The master bedroom had floor to ceiling windows on three walls and the views over the city were spectacular, but Isla only had eyes for Andreas as he stripped off his shirt.

Heat radiated from his skin and he smelled divine.

The only place she wanted to be was in his strong arms. She traced her finger over the long scar that ran down his chest, a legacy of the motorbike accident that had almost killed him. Life was precarious and uncertain but he was offering her a future with him and their baby son, who they both adored.

When he bent his head and claimed her mouth with his, she wrapped her arms around his neck and pressed herself closer to him so that she felt the erratic thud of his heart beating in time with her own. There was tenderness in his kiss tonight and something close to reverence in the way he undressed her slowly, trailing his lips over every inch of her skin that he exposed and paying homage to her breasts before he knelt between her thighs and pressed his mouth to the molten heart of her femininity.

By the time he tumbled them onto the bed and lifted her on top of him she was shaking with need, and even more shaken by the realisation that his hands were unsteady when he guided her down onto his hard length. She rocked her hips, taking him deeper inside her so that he filled her, completed her.

He cupped her bottom cheeks in his big hands as she arched above him. 'You will never find passion as intense as this with anyone else,' Andreas gritted. '*Esai dikos mou.*'

His words thundered through Isla's blood.

You are mine.

CHAPTER THIRTEEN

'ISLA, WAKE UP, *agapimenos*.' The deep voice, as rich and dark as bittersweet chocolate, roused Isla from a peaceful sleep. She stretched luxuriantly and opened her eyes to find Andreas leaning over her.

'You remind me of a sleepy kitten and I have the marks made by your sharp little claws on my back,' he teased softly.

She blushed and sat up, tugging the sheet over her breasts, although heaven knew it was too late for modesty, she thought as memories of their wild lovemaking the previous night surfaced in her mind. Her disappointment that Andreas was dressed must have shown on her face. He looked breathtaking in a dark grey suit and a silk shirt the exact shade of blue as his eyes, but she preferred him naked.

'If you carry on looking at me like that I will definitely be late for my flight to New York,' he drawled. At her faint frown, he murmured, 'I told you about my business trip last night but I don't think you were concentrating on what I was saying.' His sudden grin made him seem almost boyish and even more gorgeous.

No, she had been focused on what he was doing with his long fingers and wicked tongue. 'How long will you be away for?'

'Three days.' A gleam lit his eyes when she gave a faint sigh. 'Come with me? Toula won't mind looking after Loukas.'

Isla was startled by his invitation. 'But you will be working.'

'Only during the days, but we would have the evenings and nights to ourselves.'

She was tempted, especially when he dipped his head and covered her mouth with his in an achingly sensual kiss. When she parted her lips he groaned and tangled his tongue with hers.

'I don't want to leave Loukas for that long,' she muttered when a need for oxygen made them break apart. Did she imagine a look of regret in his eyes as he stood up?

'I'll cram three days of meetings into two days so that I can return home early,' Andreas said thickly. He glanced at his watch and cursed. On his way out of the bedroom he halted in the doorway and looked back at her. 'Will you miss me?'

She wanted to deny it but she was a hopeless liar. 'Maybe a bit,' she whispered.

He held her gaze for what seemed like eternity. 'I'll miss you too.'

It was just a figure of speech, Isla told herself after Andreas had gone. She doubted he would really miss her, but she was already counting the minutes until she saw him again. The penthouse felt empty without him. She showered and dressed and was about to walk outside to the helipad, where the pilot was waiting to fly her back to Louloudi, when her phone rang.

Andreas sounded tense. 'I'm at the airport, but I left in a hurry this morning and forgot my passport. You should find it on my desk, and I've sent a motorcycle courier to collect it.'

Isla went into his study. 'I can't see your passport on the desk.'

He swore. 'The maid has probably tidied up. Can you check in the drawers for it?'

She opened a drawer and sifted through some paperwork in case the passport had slipped between the pages. She was amused that Andreas was so untidy. It was an endearingly human trait in a man who she still found enigmatic. The headed notepaper on one document caught her attention: *DNA Assured.*

Her curiosity got the better of her and even though she felt guilty to read his private correspondence she quickly skimmed her eyes down the letter. Her heart slammed into her ribs and her confusion turned to shock when she realised that the letter was from a DNA testing clinic where Andreas had requested a paternity test. The letter was dated almost a month ago, when he had met his son for the first time. But clearly Andreas had suspected that Loukas wasn't his child.

'Isla, have you found it?' Andreas's voice jolted her out of her state of numb shock. She pulled open another drawer and saw his passport.

'Yes, it's here.' Heaven knew how she managed to keep her voice steady.

'Good. The courier will be there soon. I have another call that I need to take.' Andreas's brisk voice turned husky. 'Think of me while I'm away, *moro mou.*'

Oh, you bet I will, Isla thought grimly as her phone slipped out of her trembling fingers and she stared at the damning letter. I'll think what an absolute bastard you are, Andreas Karelis. The last paragraph of the letter from the DNA clinic explained that the result of the paternity test would be sent to Andreas in a sealed envelope, but because a sample from the child's mother had not been sent for testing the result might take longer than usual.

A wave of nausea swept over her and she collapsed onto the chair as the extent of his betrayal sank into her stunned brain. All the time that she and Andreas had spent together on Louloudi—becoming friends as well as lovers—he hadn't trusted her. That meant he either didn't believe she had been a virgin when she had slept with him at the fisherman's cottage, or that she'd had sex with another man, or men, after him.

Isla crumpled the letter in her fist and pressed her other hand against her mouth to hold back a sob. She was beyond hurt, but she was angry too. Fury bubbled up inside her. How dare Andreas go behind her back and have Loukas tested? She tried to think rationally. He seemed to genuinely adore the baby, which suggested that he *did* believe Loukas was his. And if he really had doubts, why had he asked her to marry him?

She remembered Nefeli's claim that Andreas was prepared to marry her because when she was his wife her assets would become his and he would regain full ownership of the island. And then there was the highly publicised photo of him kissing her. He needed to convince Karelis Corp's board and shareholders that he was a reformed playboy and so he had announced their engagement. Presumably he'd intended to call off their marriage if the paternity test showed he wasn't Loukas's father. But of course he was, and she would have married him unaware of his deceit.

What a fool she was. Isla covered her face with her hands as tears seeped from beneath her lashes. She had thought that they had grown closer in the past weeks but now she had proof that Andreas did not have any faith in her. She had accepted that he didn't love her, but she'd thought she had earned his trust. She deserved his trust, *dammit*. And she deserved his love. But he wasn't worthy of her love.

Her backbone stiffened and she choked back another sob, angrily brushing away her tears. It struck her that she had spent far too much of her life longing to be loved, first by her father and then by Andreas. But she was wasting her time. Andreas was cynical to his core. He had even gifted her an exquisite wedding dress, knowing that their future hung on the result of the paternity test he'd had done behind her back.

God, she *hated* him. But she loved him too, and she despised herself for her weakness. She couldn't marry him now, and she dared not risk seeing him again for fear that he would undermine her fragile defences with his charm and charisma, which she knew were fake.

An hour later the helicopter landed on Louloudi. Isla asked the pilot to wait while she collected Loukas and then they were to immediately return to Athens. She had booked tickets for her and the baby on a flight to London.

Loukas was asleep in the pram when she entered the villa, and she ran upstairs and quickly packed the clothes she had brought to Greece almost a month ago. In three days' time she was due to inherit the half-share of Louloudi left to her by Stelios, but only if she remained on the island. It was Loukas's birthright but it was a poisoned chalice and she was determined to sever all links with the name Karelis.

Her heart clenched at the thought of her little boy growing up without his father. Was she allowing her hurt pride to influence her decision to take Loukas away from Andreas? The thought pricked her conscience. For her son's sake perhaps she should stay and confront Andreas, and they would have to find another way to be parents to Loukas that didn't involve a farce of a marriage.

She opened the wardrobe and her throat ached with tears as she stared at her wedding dress that she would never wear. Andreas had chosen a white dress that symbolised purity but he suspected that she'd had other lovers besides him. Isla felt heartsick. It was the only way to describe the tearing pain in her chest at the loss of a dream that she had wanted so desperately. She squeezed her eyes shut but hot tears escaped and slid down her cheeks. It had been cruel of him to give her the beautiful dress and let her hope that fairy tales could come true. Why was she so weak that she loved a man who treated her feelings in such a cavalier way?

Anger and frustration with herself as much as with Andreas swirled black and rancid inside her. She opened the drawer in the dressing table and picked up a pair of scissors. Driven beyond reason, she slashed the dress with them. The scissors were small but sharp and the blades cut through the delicate lace easily. Isla made another cut and another, destroying the dress just like her hopes had been destroyed. Above the sound of the ripping material and her uneven breaths she heard Loukas crying. Sanity returned and she dropped the scissors, utterly horrified by what she had done. The destruction of the lovely dress that a seamstress had painstakingly sewn filled Isla with shame. Loving Andreas had turned her into someone she did not recognise, and she did not want to be the person she had become.

When she ran downstairs she found that Toula had

picked Loukas up from the pram. The Greek woman looked troubled when she saw Isla's bags.

'I have to go back to England urgently,' Isla mumbled as she took the baby into her arms. Loukas stared at her with his big blue eyes that were so like his father's and gave an angelic smile that squeezed her heart.

'When will you come back?'

'I… I don't know,' she lied, aware that she would never return to Louloudi. Tears filled her eyes as she hugged Toula. When she and Loukas were on the helicopter and it took off, she watched the island grow smaller and smaller and felt her heart shatter into a thousand pieces.

In his hotel room in New York, Andreas sloshed bourbon into a glass and paced restlessly around the room, halting by the window which overlooked Times Square. Neon lights flashed and yellow taxis were bumper to bumper on the road below, but he wasn't interested in the view. Why the hell wasn't Isla answering her phone? He'd been in meetings all day and hadn't had a chance to call her until now. The time difference meant that it would be late at night in Greece, and maybe she was asleep. But something didn't feel right.

She had sounded strange when he'd phoned her from the airport to ask her to look for his passport. And after the party, when she'd asked if the only reason he wanted to marry her was because of Loukas and he'd agreed, Isla had looked hurt and, more than that, she'd looked disappointed, as if he had failed her.

He swirled the amber liquid around in the glass. The truth was that he had failed her consistently. He knew she had doubts about marrying him but he'd steamrollered her into agreeing, telling her and himself that it was only because he wanted his son. Isla had seemed to accept the limitations he had put on their relationship, but he wondered if she wanted something other than the emotion-free zone that he had decreed their marriage would be.

His jaw clenched. Whatever it was that she wanted he was incapable of giving to her. He simply wasn't wired that way. And he didn't want to be, he reminded himself. He had decided when he was a boy that he would never be a hostage to his emotions like his mother had been for most of her wretchedly miserable life.

He lifted the glass to his lips and swallowed its contents, feeling the whisky's fire at the back of his throat. Isla would be all right, he assured himself. She would marry him because she wanted Loukas to have a better father than hers had been. And he would give her a good life, financial security and the opportunity to pursue her career. He wanted her to be happy but he wanted their relationship to be on his terms, he acknowledged.

His phone rang and his heart leapt, mocking his belief that he was emotionally detached. It must be Isla returning his calls. 'Toula?' Andreas's disappointment turned to foreboding when the Greek woman spoke. 'What do you mean, they've gone?' Dread settled like a heavy weight in the pit of his stomach. 'Where are Isla and Loukas?'

Toula sounded tearful. 'Isla said she was taking the baby to England. Andreas, you need to come back to Louloudi. There is something you must see.'

CHAPTER FOURTEEN

THE SUFFOLK FENS on a dank day towards the end of October were bleakly beautiful. Isla took a chance when the rain stopped for a while to take Loukas out in the pushchair that her friend Jess had lent her. The cottage where she had been staying since she'd left Greece ten days ago was a converted barn on Jess and her husband Tom's farm.

'Stay as long as you like,' Jess had told her. But Isla knew she needed to make plans for the future, find a job and a nursery for Loukas and start living again, instead of existing in the fog of despair that had settled over her. It didn't help that Loukas was unsettled. According to the baby book, he might be teething, but she sensed that he was missing Andreas as much as she was and guilt made her feel worse than ever.

As she walked up the lane leading to the cottage her heart gave a jolt when she saw an expensive-looking saloon car parked outside the house. Andreas had no idea of her whereabouts, she reminded herself. She watched the driver's door open and panic surged through her when he got out.

Despite everything he had done, despite hating his guts, her eyes swept over him greedily, taking in his big, dark figure dressed in black jeans and a black wool coat.

Taking a deep breath, she forced her feet to move forwards. When she drew nearer to him she was shocked by how haggard he looked. He could never be anything other than beautiful but there were deep grooves on either side of his mouth and several days' growth of black stubble on his jaw. He looked like she felt—defeated. But Isla reminded herself that Andreas was far too arrogant to know the meaning of defeat.

She reached the front gate and curled her fingers around the key in her pocket, wondering what her chances were of pushing the buggy up the path, unlocking the door and getting herself and Loukas inside the cottage before Andreas stopped her. Unlikely, she decided, her panic escalating. She did not fear him but she didn't trust herself to be anywhere near him. Already she could feel the betraying tightening of her nipples when she breathed in the spicy tang of his aftershave as he walked towards her.

'What do you want?'

His eyes glittered with some of their old fire. 'You, *moro mou*. Always you.'

He was too much. 'Go away,' she said thickly.

'You would deny me my son?' His voice tugged on her emotions and she swallowed hard.

'Do you know for certain that Loukas is your son? I assume then that you have received the result of the DNA test. If you were any other man I might have thought that you had come to apologise, but no doubt you're here to issue demands or threats.' She could not hide her bitterness. 'That's more your style, isn't it, Andreas? How did you find me, anyway?'

'You mentioned that you had stayed at a friend's farm in Suffolk after Loukas was born. I would have been here sooner but it took my security team ten days to locate you.'

'Why did you bother?' She pushed the buggy up the garden path. Loukas had fallen asleep on the walk but he would wake soon and want his milk. She grimaced when she discovered Andreas was close behind her.

'I want to talk to you.' A nerve jumped in his cheek. 'Please,' he added gruffly.

He had the benefit of superior height and strength and could overpower her easily if he chose to. She affected a careless shrug. 'Fine, you can say what you have to and then leave.'

She parked the buggy in the hallway and left Loukas to finish his nap. Shrugging off her coat, she walked into the sitting room and threw another log into the wood-burning stove. The cottage was tiny and Andreas had to stoop to avoid hitting his head on the low ceiling beams. He had also removed his coat and his grey cashmere jumper was the colour of the stormy sky.

Pain tore through Isla. Andreas's autocratic features gave no clue to his thoughts. He was a remote stranger and she wanted to weep for the closeness that she was sure she hadn't imagined between them on Louloudi.

'How dare you arrange a paternity test behind my back?' she said in a choked voice. 'I have never slept with any other man but you.'

His mouth gave an odd twist and he pulled an envelope out of his back pocket. 'This contains the result of the paternity test. As you can see, it is unopened. The laboratory's seal is unbroken.'

She stared at him as he walked over to the woodburner and wrapped the cloth around his hand before he opened the metal door. The crackle and hiss of the fire sounded loud in the silent room.

'Wait! What are you doing?' she cried as he threw the envelope into the flames. 'Don't you want to know if Loukas is your son?'

Maybe he didn't care. She could cope, just, with the knowledge that he did not want her, but it was agony to realise that he was rejecting his baby. She leapt forwards and tried to reach the letter but it was already blackened and curling at the edges as it caught light.

'Careful, you'll get burned.' Andreas grabbed her hand and pulled her away from the fire. 'I received the test result a couple of weeks ago but I didn't bother to open the letter and I shoved it in a drawer in my desk.' He turned her to face him and clasped her shoulders. 'I *know* Loukas is mine, just as I know that you have never given yourself to anyone but me.'

She shook her head, stunned by the urgency in his voice and the fierce intensity of his gaze. His eyes were almost black but the terrible devastation in his expression couldn't be real.

'If you believed me, why did you arrange the test? It can only be because you don't trust me. But why would you?' Her voice cracked. 'I mean nothing to you.'

'That's not true.' His jaw tensed at her look of disbelief. He released her and raked his hand through his hair. 'I forgot about the damned DNA test.'

'You *forgot* about it?'

'I knew Loukas was mine the instant I saw him. But three years ago an ex-lover told me she was pregnant with my baby. I knew she hadn't only slept with me, and I asked for a paternity test. Instead Sadie sold a story to the tabloids saying that I was the father of her child but I had refused to support her and the baby. You can imagine the headlines,' he said harshly. '*Bil-*

lionaire refuses to pay for his baby's nappies was just one example.'

Andreas exhaled heavily. 'By the time a legal ruling gave me permission to insist on a DNA test—which proved that Sadie had lied and her baby wasn't mine—the damage had been done. My father was furious that the scandal reflected badly on Karelis Corp. Soon after the story broke I nearly lost my life in a motorbike race. If I hadn't spent the next few months in Intensive Care I would have sued Sadie for defamation of my character.'

'But why did she lie to the newspapers?' Isla's mind was reeling from Andreas's revelation.

'Money, of course,' Andreas said grimly. 'She knew the baby wasn't mine but she sold the story for hundreds of thousands of pounds.'

'If you had told me about Sadie, I would have understood why you wanted proof that Loukas is yours.' She bit her lip. 'Your lack of trust was hurtful. I thought we were friends but when I read the letter from the DNA clinic it made me realise that our relationship was hopeless.'

Andreas spun away from her and walked over to stare out of the window, as if he wanted to avoid her gaze, Isla thought. Looking past his big, powerful frame, she saw the skeleton of the apple tree in the garden, its branches stripped of their last few leaves by the autumn gale. Despite the cheery fire in the sitting room, she shivered.

'I wanted you the second I saw you at my father's house in Kensington,' he said harshly. 'If I'm honest, I assumed the chemistry between us would fizzle out fairly quickly. No other woman has ever held my interest for long. And I reminded myself why I didn't want to get involved with you.'

He turned to face her, his eyes narrowing when she made a muffled sound that betrayed how badly he'd hurt her. 'As a boy I had watched my mother sink into depression and a crazy obsession that ultimately destroyed her because she was unable to win my father's love. I was determined not to repeat the mistakes of my parents' marriage in our relationship.'

Isla had thought he couldn't hurt her more than he already had, but she discovered she was wrong. 'You were worried that I might be unhappy like your mother was—because I loved you but you didn't feel the same way about me? God, Andreas,' she choked, 'do you enjoy humiliating me?'

He crossed the room in two strides and grabbed her by her shoulders, his fingers biting into her skin through her jumper. His eyes blazed in his tense face and his beautiful mouth twisted. 'No, *omorfia mou*. I was terrified that if I admitted to myself that I love you—knowing that you don't, that you can't possibly love me, just as no one else ever has—then I would face a lifetime of pain, yearning for something that would never be mine. Yearning for your heart,' he said thickly, in a voice so raw that Isla trembled.

'You sent me away,' she whispered. It still hurt to remember how cold he had been when she'd met him at his office in Athens and told him of her pregnancy.

He nodded. 'In the year that we were apart I convinced myself I'd dealt with my inexplicable fascination with you. But when I walked into the villa and saw a baby with blue eyes like mine, I lost it. You were the mother of my child and even more beautiful than my memories of you. Loukas gave me an excuse to force you back into my life.'

Isla swallowed. 'You didn't force me,' she said with

stark honesty, and watched a nerve flicker in Andreas's cheek. 'How many other women did you take to bed as a way of dealing with your alleged fascination with me?' she asked in a low voice.

'None.' He stared into her eyes, his own unguarded, and the fierce emotion she saw in his brilliant gaze made her heart miss a beat. 'You are the only woman I have ever made love to rather than have sex with, and I haven't been with anyone since you gave me your virginity. I told myself it was nothing more than amazing chemistry, but desire is only a tiny fraction of what I feel for you.'

Isla took a swift breath, afraid to believe what Andreas seemed to be saying. 'And what do you feel?' she whispered.

Silence stretched between them and disappointment crushed her. Fool, she told herself. 'If this is about Loukas, I won't stop you seeing him. He needs you and we can work out a way for you to be part of his life.'

Andreas closed his eyes and when he opened them again Isla was stunned to see that his lashes were wet. 'Your generosity after everything I have done wrong shames me. It's not Loukas. He is my son and of course I love him and want to be with him. But I was wrong to insist that you marry me when I could see that it wasn't what you wanted.'

'I didn't want a loveless marriage,' Isla agreed.

'What about a marriage filled with more love than you can imagine?' He dropped his hands from her shoulders and wrapped his fingers around hers. 'I found your engagement ring in the bedroom at the villa.'

She bit her lip, knowing he must have seen the ruined wedding dress. 'The ring and the dress made a mockery of all I had hoped for. I couldn't marry you after I found that you didn't trust me.'

'I'd trust you with my life.' He lifted her hands to his mouth and pressed his lips against her fingers. '*Theos*, when I discovered your ring and the damaged dress, I thought I had lost you for ever, and I knew it was no more than I deserved. I realised then that my life meant nothing without you. I had tried so hard not to love you because I am a coward,' he said with savage self-derision. 'What I should have done was try to win your love, and that is what I intend to spend the rest of my life doing, if you will let me.'

Isla's heart was pounding with a mixture of fear that she had misunderstood what Andreas seemed to be saying, and burgeoning hope. 'Why do you want to win me?' she asked shakily.

'Because I love you more than I believed it is possible to love. Because I can't bear the thought of living without you in my life.' He swallowed convulsively. 'I want to see your face on the pillow beside me when I wake every morning and hold you in my arms every night. You have my heart and my soul, *agapi mou*. And if you will give me a chance, I will spend the rest of my life proving that I am worthy of you. If you will love me just a little.'

Tears slipped down her cheeks and he kissed them away with such heartbreaking gentleness that she felt as though she would burst with happiness. 'I can't love you a little.' The sheer agony in Andreas's eyes made her continue quickly. 'My love for you is so huge that my heart overflows with it.'

She cradled his beloved face in her hands and reached up on her tiptoes to kiss his mouth. He allowed her to be in control of the kiss for a few moments before he groaned and wrapped his arms around her, hauling her up against his hard body and kissing her with a mastery and bone-shaking tenderness that convinced her his love would last for eternity, as her love for him would last to the end of days.

Their son's cries made them reluctantly break off the kiss. 'Loukas has bad timing,' Isla murmured ruefully as Andreas dropped his hand from her breast and she tugged her jumper down.

'There will be plenty of time for us, *kardia mou*. We have our whole lives to fill with love, laughter, family.' The baby stopped crying and they heard him gurgling happily. Andreas smiled at Isla, his love for her there to see on his handsome face and in his eyes as blue as the diamond ring that he pulled from his pocket and slid onto her finger. 'Will you marry me for no other reason than I love you more than anything in the world?'

She blinked away her tears of joy and smiled back at him. 'I will.'

EPILOGUE

THEY WERE MARRIED in the little white church on Louloudi. The December sky was a vivid blue and the sun
was surprisingly warm, gleaming on Andreas's beloved
Aegean Sea. Isla wore her wedding dress, which had
been remade, and she carried a bouquet of white orchids
and tiny blue freesias.

Loukas looked adorable in his navy blue outfit and
smiled contentedly during the wedding ceremony, held
in his Aunt Nefeli's arms and watched over by his hon-
orary grandmother, Toula. Andreas's sister had quickly
come round to the idea of her brother marrying Isla
when she saw how happy he was, and she adored her
little nephew.

Nefeli had been waiting outside the church when Isla
arrived, escorted by a proud-looking Dinos. 'I want to
apologise for the awful things I said to you,' the young
Greek girl said ruefully.

'Why don't we start again, as friends as well as sis-
ters-in-law?' Isla murmured.

'I've never seen my brother looking nervous,' Nefeli
told her. 'If he paces up and down the church much
more he'll wear a hole in the floor. He loves you, you
know.'

'I do know.' Isla was smiling as she walked down

the aisle towards the man she loved with all her heart. Andreas looked breathtakingly handsome in a black tuxedo. No longer austere and remote, his expression softened as he waited for his bride to join him in front of the altar, and pride blazed in his blue eyes when they made their vows and the priest pronounced them husband and wife.

'Well, Kyria Karelis, you're stuck with me now,' he whispered in Isla's ear as they posed on the church steps for the photographer.

'For ever, my darling love,' she replied softly, lifting her face for his kiss.

The family's lawyer, John Sabanis, strolled over and handed them an envelope. 'Stelios asked me to give you this on your wedding day,' he said.

'But how on earth could he have known that we would get married?' Isla was puzzled as she looked at the wedding card Andreas had opened. He read out what Stelios had written.

To my dearest son Andreas and his beautiful wife Isla.

I knew the first time you met each other that you would fall in love, and on this day, the joyous occasion of your wedding, I wish you all the happiness that you both deserve.

'I wonder how your father guessed that we would fall for each other,' Isla mused later that night when she and Andreas were lying naked in each other's arms. He propped himself up on his elbow and bent his head to claim her mouth in a lingering kiss.

'Stelios was watching my expression when he introduced us in London and he saw what I couldn't hide.'

She tenderly stroked a lock of dark hair off her new husband's brow. 'What did he see?'

'The look of love,' Andreas told her softly. 'Always and for ever.'

* * * * *

COMING SOON!

We really hope you enjoyed reading this book. If you're looking for more romance, be sure to head to the shops when new books are available on

Thursday 6th March

MILLS & BOON

Coming next month

A SCANDAL MADE IN LONDON
Lucy King

'Miss Cassidy?' said the concierge a moment later, his voice bouncing off the walls and making her jump. 'Mr Knox will see you now.'

Finally.

'The lift on the right will take you directly to the penthouse.'

'Thank you,' she said, mustering up a quick smile as she got to her feet and headed for said lift on legs that felt like jelly.

The doors closed behind her and she used the smooth ten-second ascent to try and calm her fluttering stomach and slow her heart-rate. It would be fine. She and Theo were both civilised adults. They might be chalk and cheese, but they could handle this. What was the worst that could happen? It wasn't as if she was expecting anything from him. She just had a message to deliver. It would be fine.

But when the lift doors opened and she stepped out, all thoughts of civility and messages shot from her head because all she could focus on was Theo.

He was standing at the far end of the wide hall, with his back to a huge floor to ceiling window, feet apart, arms crossed over his chest. The interminable rain of the morning had stopped and sunshine had broken through the thick cloud. It flooded in through the window, making a silhouette of him, emphasising his imposing height and the powerful breadth of the shoulders. Although clothed in jeans and a white shirt, he looked like some sort of god, in total control, master of all he surveyed, and she couldn't help thinking that if he'd been going for maximum impact, maximum intimidation, he'd nailed it.

Swallowing down the nerves tangling in her throat, Kate started walking towards him, her hand tightening on the strap of her cross-body bag that she wore like a shield. His gaze was on her as she approached, his expression unreadable. He didn't move a muscle. His jaw was set and he exuded chilly distance, which didn't bode well for what was to come, but then nor did the heat suddenly shooting along her veins and the desire surging through her body. That kind of head-scrambling reaction she could do without. She didn't need to remember how he'd made her feel when he'd held her, kissed her, been inside her. She needed to focus.

'Hi,' she said as she drew closer, his irresistible magnetism tugging her forwards even as she wanted to flee.

'What are you doing here?'

The ice cold tone of his voice stopped her in her tracks a couple of feet away, obliterating the heat, and she inwardly flinched. So that was the way this was going to go. No 'how are you, let me take your jacket, would you like a drink'. He wasn't pleased to see her. He wasn't pleased at all.

Okay.

'We need to talk,' she said, beginning to regret her decision to deliver this information in person. With hindsight, maybe an email would have sufficed.

'There's nothing to talk about.'

'I'm afraid there is.'

His dark brows snapped together. 'Your sister?'

'She's fine,' she said. 'Thank you for what you did for her.'

'You're welcome.'

'Did you get my note?' Shortly after he'd fixed her finances she'd sent him a letter of thanks. It had seemed the least she could do. She hadn't had a response.

He gave a brief nod. 'Yes.'

'She loves the flowers.'

'Good.'

'It was thoughtful.'

'It was nothing.'

Right. Beneath the force of his unwavering gaze and impenetrable demeanour Kate quailed for a moment and was summoning up the courage to continue when he spoke.

'Are you in trouble?' he asked sharply.

'That's one way of putting it.'

'What?'

'Sorry, bad joke,' she said with a weak laugh although there was nothing remotely funny about any of this.

'Get to the point, Kate,' he snapped. 'I'm busy.'

Right. Yes. Good plan. She pulled her shoulders back and lifted her chin. 'There's no easy way to say this, Theo,' she said, sounding far calmer than she felt, 'so here goes. There's been a...*consequence*... to our...afternoon together.'

A muscle ticked in his jaw. 'What kind of consequence?'

'The nine-month kind.'

There was a moment of thundering silence, during which Kate's heart hammered while Theo seemed to freeze and pale. 'What exactly are you saying?' he said, his voice tight and low and utterly devoid of expression.

'I'm pregnant.'

Continue reading
A SCANDAL MADE IN LONDON
Lucy King

Available next month
www.millsandboon.co.uk

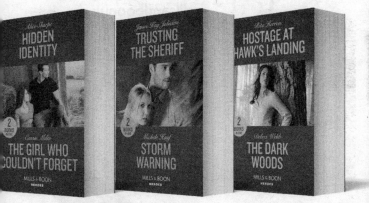

MILLS & BOON

THE HEART OF ROMANCE

A ROMANCE FOR EVERY KIND OF READER

MODERN

Prepare to be swept off your feet by sophisticated, sexy and seductive heroes, in some of the world's most glamourous and romantic locations, where power and passion collide.
8 stories per month.

HISTORICAL

Escape with historical heroes from time gone by. Whether your passion is for wicked Regency Rakes, muscled Vikings or rugged Highlanders, awaken the romance of the past.
6 stories per month.

MEDICAL

Set your pulse racing with dedicated, delectable doctors in the high-pressure world of medicine, where emotions run high and passion, comfort and love are the best medicine.
6 stories per month.

True Love

Celebrate true love with tender stories of heartfelt romance, from the rush of falling in love to the joy a new baby can bring, and a focus on the emotional heart of a relationship.
8 stories per month.

Desire

Indulge in secrets and scandal, intense drama and plenty of sizzli hot action with powerful and passionate heroes who have it all: wealth, status, good looks…everything but the right woman.
6 stories per month.

HEROES

Experience all the excitement of a gripping thriller, with an inten romance at its heart. Resourceful, true-to-life women and strong, fearless men face danger and desire - a killer combination!
8 stories per month.

DARE

Sensual love stories featuring smart, sassy heroines you'd want as best friend, and compelling intense heroes who are worthy of the
4 stories per month.

To see which titles are coming soon, please visit

millsandboon.co.uk/nextmonth